D1040643

ALSO BY DAVID BRUNS AND J. R. OLSON

NOVELS

Weapons of Mass Deception

Jihadi Apprentice

Rules of Engagement

SHORT FICTION

"Death of a Pawn"

"Battle Djinni"

"The Athens Job"

THE

PANDORA
DECEPTION

DAVID BRUNS

AND

J. R. OLSON

St. Martin's Paperbacks

This is a work of fiction. All of the characters, organizations, and events portrayed in this novel are either products of the authors' imagination or are used fictitiously.

Published in the United States by St. Martin's Paperbacks, an imprint of St. Martin's Publishing Group.

THE PANDORA DECEPTION

For information, address St. Martin's Publishing Group, 120 Broadway, New York, NY 10271.

www.stmartins.com

ISBN: 978-1-250-78355-4

Our books may be purchased in bulk for promotional, educational, or business use. Please contact your local bookseller or the Macmillan Corporate and Premium Sales Department at 1-800-221-7945, ext. 5442, or by email at MacmillanSpecialMarkets@macmillan.com.

Printed in the United States of America

St. Martin's Press hardcover edition published 2020
St. Martin's Paperbacks edition published 2021

10 9 8 7 6 5 4 3 2 1

CAST OF CHARACTERS

THE AMERICANS

Donald Riley, Deputy Director of Operations, Emerging Threats group at CIA

Judith Hellman, Director of National Intelligence

Roger Trask, Director, Central Intelligence Agency

Lieutenant (j.g.) Janet Everett, Submarine Officer; Analyst, Emerging Threats group at CIA

Ensign Michael Goodwin, US Navy Cyberoperations Officer; Analyst, Emerging Threats group at CIA

Lieutenant (j.g.) Andrea Ramirez, USS *Michael Murphy* (DDG-112) Comms Officer; Analyst, Emerging Threats group at CIA

Lieutenant Commander Minto, Executive Officer of USS *Michael Murphy* (DDG-112)

Elizabeth Soroush, Special Agent in Charge, Minneapolis Field Division

THE ISRAELIS

Rachel Jaeger, Mossad operative

Noam Glantz, Mossad Kidon team leader; Rachel Jaeger's operations chief

Benyamin Albedano, Mossad Director of Operations

Shira Fishbein, Mossad Head of Cyber Operations

THE MONEY MEN

Alyan Sultan al-Qahtamni, Saudi business tycoon

Saleh bin Ghannam, Saudi business tycoon and former head of the Saudi Secret Service

Haim Zarecki, Israeli business tycoon

Itzak Lehrmann, Israeli business tycoon

PROJECT DELIVERANCE TEAM

Jean-Pierre Manzul, CEO, Recodna Genetics; boyfriend of Talia Tahir

Dr. Talia Tahir, doctor with the World Health Organization; girlfriend of Jean-Pierre Manzul

Dr. Lakshmi Chandrasekaran, research scientist for Recodna Genetics; Indian microbiologist

Dr. Katie McDonough, research scientist for Recodna Genetics; Australian synthetic biologist

Dr. Greta Berger, research scientist for Recodna Genetics; Swedish CRISPR expert

Dr. Lu Xianshan, research scientist for Recodna Genetics; Chinese expert in aerosolized transmission of viruses

Dr. Faraj al-Harbi, research scientist for Recodna Genetics; Saudi national

MINOR CHARACTERS

Kasim, head of security at the Recodna Genetics laboratory

Sven Gunderson, Director, World Health Organization, Eastern Mediterranean Office, Cairo, Egypt

Jason Winslow, archaeologist; specialist in Arctic field research

Dylan Mattias, Directorate of Operations, CIA

CHAPTER 1

USS Donald Cook *(DDG-75)*
On patrol in the Gulf of Oman

Commander Alan Renner, commanding officer of the *Cook,* dragged a handkerchief across his brow, then stowed the damp material in the hip pocket of his blue coveralls.

He would have expected that after twenty-seven days on station in the Gulf his body would have adjusted to the heat and humidity, but every day felt like a new assault on his person. He positioned himself directly under a blast of air-conditioning raining down from the overhead vent. The sweat on his forehead turned clammy.

An officer dressed in green camouflage appeared in the open doorway of the port bridge wing.

"You wanted to see me, Captain?" With an open, freckled face and blond crew cut, Lieutenant (j.g.) Zack McCoy looked substantially younger than his twenty-three years. Renner was comforted to see the tall, muscled figure of Chief Ramone behind the young man. Ramone was a veteran of countless boarding operations. He would keep the rookie lieutenant out of trouble.

Renner addressed the quartermaster of the watch, a trim woman with her dark hair pulled back into a bun. "The XO and the Commodore are in Combat, Quartermaster. Ask them to join us for the briefing, please."

"Aye, sir."

Executive Officer Seth Gooden held the door for the Commodore as the two men entered the bridge. Gooden was a solid officer on his third tour in the Gulf, and Renner trusted his judgment. Renner sensed a tension in the XO as he led the senior officer to the chart table.

The source of Gooden's tension wasn't a secret. Captain Jack Tasker, newly appointed Commodore of Destroyer Squadron 60, was conducting a tour of his new command. His first stop on the tour was the *Cook*.

Tasker was a tall man with a rangy frame and long arms that hung loosely by his side. Since the Commodore had only been on board the *Cook* for less than a day, Renner hadn't made a determination about his new boss, but he could already tell one thing.

Tasker was aggressive. He planned to make his mark on his new command quickly, as in today.

"XO, conduct the briefing, please," Renner said.

Gooden's trim fingernail tapped the Iranian port city of Chabahar. "Contact departed the port at 1030 local, crossed into international waters one hour later." He dragged his finger diagonally across the blue of the Gulf of Oman. "Probable small cargo vessel, making a steady nine knots. Course and speed indicate she may be headed toward Yemen. In accordance with the latest Fifth Fleet guidance, Captain, I recommend we intercept the contact and launch a VBSS team."

The new orders the XO referred to had arrived with the Commodore. Intel had picked up new weapons among the Iranian-backed Houthi rebels in the Yemen civil war. All ships on patrol in the region had orders to stop and search all Iranian and unflagged ships headed in the direction of Yemen. If weapons were found, the ship was to be seized and sailed to the nearest friendly port.

Armed and specially trained US Navy action teams, known as Visit, Board, Search, and Seizure teams, were comprised of ship's crew volunteers. Most stops turned up dirt-poor sailors trying to eke out a living in cross-Gulf trade, but every boarding operation was a risk to the safety of Renner's crew.

"Mr. McCoy, you will lead the VBSS team," Renner said. "Let's keep it safe, professional, and thorough. Understood?" Renner clocked a look at Chief Ramone as he gave the order to McCoy.

"Aye, sir," McCoy replied. "Permission to issue small arms?"

"Permission granted," Renner said. He turned to his boss, the Commodore. "Anything to add, sir?"

Tasker shook his head, but his gaze raked over the youthful face of McCoy.

Decision made, action flowed swiftly. Renner set an intercept course for the contact and increased speed to twenty-two knots. In the background, the XO passed word for the VBSS team to muster at the small arms locker.

Renner strode to the open doorway of the bridge wing and into the hot sun. In addition to their numerous electronic sensors, the ship maintained a visual lookout watch on each side of the bridge and on the fantail. He nodded to the sailor. "Let me know as soon as you have a visual, lookout."

The young man's eyes remained glued to the binoculars. "Aye, Captain. I've got smoke, but no ship yet, sir."

Renner scanned the horizon with his own glasses. A smudge of thick black smoke marred the hazy blue line between water and sky.

As they drew closer, the contact was revealed to be an ancient dhow with a single smokestack. It was a big ship, over a hundred feet long, with a beam of at least thirty feet and a high square aft deck. The vessel still had two masts from its days as a sail-powered ship, but Renner saw no evidence of sails. Or a flag to indicate where the vessel was registered.

Unflagged, shallow-draft ships like this one were usually family owned and were commonly used for shipping commodities—food, lumber, livestock—across the Gulf. They were also a favorite of arms smugglers.

"All ahead one-third," Renner ordered. As the ship slowed, the howl of the wind on the bridge wings lessened and a fresh wave of sticky heat rolled in the door.

"XO," Renner said. "Would you invite our friends to stop, please?"

Gooden grinned. "Aye, Captain." He gripped the handset of the VHF radio. "Unflagged vessel, this is

USS *Donald Cook*. You are directed to stop and prepare to be boarded. In accordance with UN Security Council directives, we have authority to search your vessel for illegal arms shipments."

He repeated the directive, then passed the handset to a sailor, who repeated the message in Farsi and Arabic. Petty Officer Jahandar was a thin young woman with sharp features and skin the color of walnut. She was dressed out in black body armor, and a dark green ballistics helmet covered her bobbed hair. An M9 service pistol was strapped to her right thigh.

The *Cook* had matched the course and speed of the dhow. Through the binocs, Renner watched a group of men gather on the foredeck of the smaller ship.

Jahandar's radioed warning received an angry response from the dhow. Renner raised an eyebrow in question.

"They say they don't have to stop for us, sir," she said.

"Combat, this is the captain. Ready the five-inch gun to put a warning shot across their bow."

"Ready the five-inch for a warning shot, aye, sir." Even as the order was repeated, Renner saw the Mk 45 turret slew into position.

The men assembled on the deck of the dhow noticed it, too. Still, the ship did not slow down.

"Five-inch gun ready in all respects, sir."

"Fire," Renner said.

The report of the 62-caliber gun reverberated off the windows of the bridge. Renner watched the ejected shell from the turret bounce onto the deck.

The firing of the gun had the desired effect. The

dhow slowed immediately, and a thick cloud of oily black smoke settled over the open water between the two ships.

"All stop," Renner said. "XO, launch the VBSS teams."

Renner made his way to the bridge wing, binoculars in hand, to find the Commodore already there.

Together, they watched the rigid-hulled inflatable boat containing Lieutenant (j.g.) McCoy and his eight-man boarding team lower to the water. The pilot gunned the engine, and the small craft shot away from the ship.

A second RHIB, containing a second team, had been launched from the opposite side of the *Cook,* and it roared into view. Renner nodded in approval as one craft took a cover position on the stern of the dhow and the other circled the boarding target.

"*Cook,* Boarding Team," McCoy's voice said over the open circuit. "Commencing boarding now."

"McCoy, *Cook,* copy." The XO's voice filtered out from the open doorway to the bridge.

Renner watched the boarding RHIB come alongside the dhow and two team members use telescoping poles to raise a boarding ladder. One armed sailor scrambled up the ten feet from the boat to the deck and took a cover position, his M4 at the ready.

Chief Ramone was next, followed by McCoy, then Petty Officer Jahandar, the Farsi translator. In less than two minutes, the team was on board and the helmsman of the RHIB gunned away from the side of the dhow.

The wind had died and Renner could hear voices

across the flat water. The sharp tones of Jahandar rang out as she and another sailor herded the crew of the dhow to the high aft deck. Renner counted fifteen crew members, all men, most in dirty T-shirts, shorts, and sandals.

She peppered the crew with questions and fed a steady stream of information back to McCoy. The ship was en route to Mirbat, Oman, carrying wheat and a hold full of sheep.

Ramone's deep voice carried over the water as he broke up the remaining team members into pairs to search the ship.

Ten minutes ticked by, then fifteen.

Renner heard one of the boarding team groan. "Chief, I can confirm there are sheep and they have shit all over the—"

"Stow it, Vasquez," Ramone's voice thundered over the circuit.

Five more minutes, then Vasquez again: "Mr. McCoy, you need to see this."

Renner and the Commodore exchanged a glance. "XO, status report," Renner called.

Before he could respond, McCoy's voice came over the open circuit. "Bridge, boarding team, we've got weapons on board. At least a hundred antitank guided missiles and two more crates with missile components."

"Captain!" the XO interrupted. "We've got company, sir."

On the bridge, Gooden was hunched over the radar repeater. "Combat, identify this incoming target. Now."

"Bridge, Combat, probable high-speed patrol boats. Looks like a swarm, sir. A dozen at least."

"Boghammars, Captain." The XO's voice was grim. "Recommend we go to general quarters."

"Do it," Renner said. As the XO took charge of getting the ship to action stations, Renner moved to protect his crew members still on the boarded vessel.

"All ahead full," Renner ordered.

"Answers all ahead full, sir."

Renner felt the reassuring surge of one-hundred-thousand-shaft horsepower propel the *Cook* through the water. One of the bridge crew handed him a flash hood and he pulled it over his head.

"Ship is at general quarters, Captain," the XO reported.

"Very well, XO. Left ten degrees rudder"—Renner eyeballed a heading that would put the *Cook* between the incoming patrol craft and the dhow—"come to new course two-eight-zero."

"Bridge, Combat, we estimate twenty incoming fast attack craft."

Iranian patrol boats were essentially armed cigarette boats. Extremely fast and maneuverable, they could carry about a thousand pounds of light arms such as .50-caliber machine guns, rocket-propelled grenades, and 107-millimeter rockets. While devastating to unarmed tankers, they were no match for a US Navy warship.

"Combat, Captain. I'm treating this as a show of force. We will respond if fired on."

"Bridge, Combat, aye. Five-inch gun is standing by, sir."

Renner raised the binocs. The incoming craft were visible now, arrayed in a line of sharp-pointed hulls. Churned white water rooster-tailed behind them.

This was just a show of force by the Iranians. The pack would break off in a few minutes.

"Bridge, Combat, we have incoming aircraft! Two fast-movers bearing two-niner-zero, range three-zero miles, four hundred knots."

Renner felt his stomach clench, but kept his glasses trained on the incoming patrol boats. Under magnification, he could make out the sailors on board the ships.

Aircraft and patrol boats? A multi-layered attack?

"Get me an ID on the bogeys, Combat," Renner replied.

"Probable ID is Iranian Kowsar fighters, sir. Time to intercept—" The weapons officer's voice broke. "Incoming fire from the patrol craft!"

Renner saw repeating flashes as one of the patrol craft released a volley of rocket fire. He responded by instinct:

"Helm, right full rudder, all ahead full. Combat, return fire with the five-inch gun."

The steady *blam* of the *Cook*'s heavy gun was like a metronome as every three seconds a new round was released.

One of the incoming Iranian patrol craft evaporated in a geyser of water. Then a second, and a third.

The incoming rockets sped toward the *Cook*. Renner heard the Phalanx CIWS engage, adding a blaring drone to the din as the six-barreled Gatling cannons spat out fifty twenty-millimeter rounds every second. In the background, he heard the roar of the ship-mounted .50-calibers opening up.

It was over in less than ninety seconds. The united front of patrol ships scattered, leaving a crazy quilt of crisscrossing white wakes in their hasty retreat.

"Cease fire!" Renner roared.

The five-inch gun went silent.

"Combat, light up those Iranian fighters with fire-control radar. Stand by to launch VLS on my command."

A second that felt like an hour dragged by, then another.

"Bogeys are breaking off and bugging out, Captain."

Renner walked to his captain's chair and hoisted his body into the leather seat. He gripped the armrests until his knuckles turned white.

Any second now, the adrenaline rush would fade and he'd start shaking like a leaf. He took a deep breath, held it, then released it slowly.

"XO?"

"Yes, sir."

"Secure from general quarters. Let's get a prize crew on the dhow and pilot that illegal cargo to Oman."

"Aye, aye, sir." Normal bridge activity resumed around him, the comforting noises of the familiar.

Renner stripped the flash hood off his head and dug into his pocket for his handkerchief.

"Congratulations, Alan."

Renner paused in wiping his face. He'd completely forgotten the Commodore was on board.

"For what, sir?"

"For not starting World War Three."

CHAPTER 2

Don took the stairs to the executive level of the Liberty Crossing complex. He showed his ID at the final security checkpoint and entered the outer office for the Director of National Intelligence. A young woman wearing a sleek headset manned a multiscreen computer behind a desk.

Her eyes broke away from the screens. "May I help you, sir?"

Don smiled nervously. "Yes, three o'clock appointment with the director." His tone made it sound like a question, even though he had checked the time and location three times. In the drive over from Fort Meade, he had debated with himself about what the DNI wanted.

The Iranian attack on the USS *Donald Cook* two days ago had spiked tensions in the Gulf, but Iran was only a small part of his current job as deputy J2 at Cyber Command.

The receptionist gave him a bright smile. "Oh yes, Mr. Riley, the director will see you immediately. Go right in."

The director's office was large enough to fit at least ten Cyber Command cubicles, without including the separate sitting area with a leather couch and two armchairs arranged around a low coffee table. Out the window, Don glimpsed treetops and the blue skies of springtime in Virginia.

When Judith Hellman glanced up from her desk, her normally stern face took on a warm look. "Don, come in." She strode across the room with her hand extended.

Don shook the director's hand with a firm grip. Hellman was a tall, handsome woman with fiery red hair and a personality that could flip on a dime. Any other time Don had met her she'd been all business, but today she seemed relaxed, borderline friendly.

"It'll just be a few minutes before Roger joins us." She waved her arm at the sitting area. "Join me for a coffee while we wait?"

In this setting, "Roger" could only mean Roger Trask, the director of the CIA. The thought of sitting with two of the most powerful people in the US intelligence community for coffee on a Friday afternoon did nothing to stem his curiosity or ease his nervous stomach.

He followed Hellman to the sitting area, where she had a thermos of coffee waiting. "I swear if you took a blood sample right now, I'd be fifty percent coffee," she said with a laugh. Don's nervous chuckle sounded like a noise from a squeaky toy. Still, his hand was surprisingly steady when he took the proffered cup.

Hellman sat on the couch and crossed her legs. Her hazel eyes studied him. "How's the leg?" Don's index finger unconsciously probed at the scar tissue through the material of his pant leg. The bullet wound from Rafiq Roshed's handgun had long healed, but he still thought about it every day.

"Fine, ma'am. PT is complete and I have a clean bill of health."

"And Captain McHugh's family?" Hellman said. "Do you keep in touch?"

Don focused on his coffee. Brendan McHugh, his best friend, hadn't made it back from North Korea.

"I do," Don said finally. "Liz is still at the Bureau. She's the strongest woman I know. And a great mother. Brendan—Captain McHugh—can't be replaced, but his family is doing okay."

Hellman nodded, her mood suddenly subdued. As she attempted to restart the conversation, the door opened and the CIA director strode in.

Roger Trask was an energetic man in his midsixties with a full mane of thick gray hair. "Don! Good to see you." His handshake was warm, his meaty palm enveloping Don's clammy grip.

Hellman and Trask chatted for a few moments, trying to include Don in the conversation, without much success. Don's anxiety multiplied as the minutes ticked by. He plucked at the collar of his shirt.

"So, you're feeling healthy, Don? Up to snuff?" Trask's genial exterior faded and he had a sharp look in his eyes.

"Absolutely, sir." It was the truth. He did feel good.

Don had committed himself to a brand-new healthy regimen in his life. Between daily exercise, a healthy diet, and no snacking in between meals, he had already lost twenty pounds and he was up to running a 5K in under thirty minutes, a personal best.

The CIA director set his coffee cup on the table. "We may have a new assignment for you," he said. "Something new we've been cooking up."

Hellman let out a snort of derision. "Something *you've* been cooking up, Roger. I'm happy to keep Mr. Riley right where he is at CYBERCOM."

Don watched the verbal jousting, but inside he was bursting with curiosity.

Trask knew how to build anticipation. He steepled his fingers. "Your team's actions in the North Korea situation were exemplary, Don." He shot a look at Hellman. "The DNI has given me permission to replicate that kind of operation into a new directorate."

Don leaned forward in his seat as Trask paused for a sip of coffee.

"It's no secret the Iranians are our biggest headache right now. It's sucking up all the energy at the White House and Congress, but the shattering of ISIS has created chaos out there. They haven't gone away, they've just gone underground—and online. We'll see them again, re-formed into a new threat in a new place."

Since the defeat of ISIS inside Syria and Iraq, the level of online activity had spiked. More and more Salafist jihadi groups were flooding the Web with propaganda, inciting more young people to join the cause.

"In my view, the strength of the North Korean op was

how your team identified the real threat amidst all the noise. You were willing to look past the obvious answers, think outside the box. And when it came time to go after that threat, you were able to put together cyber assets, analysts, and field operations assets into the kind of team that got the job done."

Don kept the thoughtful look on his face. "What do you have in mind, sir?"

Trask sat back in his chair and let Hellman take over. "I've authorized the formation of a new group inside the Operations Directorate at CIA. Cutting-edge stuff. We're calling it Emerging Threats. We want you to lead it as DDO."

DDO: Deputy Director of Operations. Don sat back in his seat. A new task group was a huge responsibility.

"This is rocket fuel, Don," Trask said. "North Korea made us wake up to the fact that we need a team that looks in the darkest corners for the next big threat. Cyber is a contact sport. We need to have embedded cyber operators who can take action in real time."

"I can choose my own team?" he asked.

Trask nodded. "You'll also have the ability to draw on NCS assets as needed. Analysts, too."

National Clandestine Service assets. CIA-trained case officers. Covert action operators from CIA's Special Activities Division. Military operators from the Joint Special Ops Command. Access to those kinds of assets meant the DNI was serious.

If he chose the right people around him, he could make this work. The key would be his core team.

"You're thinking about the midshipmen," Hellman said with a chuckle.

Don nodded. "They're commissioned officers now, ma'am. Well, two of them are. Goodwin graduates in a few weeks. Everett and Ramirez are in the fleet. That makes them fair game for recruitment, right?"

"They've proven themselves," Hellman said, "but remember: They need to agree to the transfer." She toyed with her coffee cup. "If I've learned anything after thirty years, it's that this life . . . it's not for everyone. After North Korea, they may not want that kind of responsibility."

Her comment made Don pause. Because of his guest lecturer status at the Naval Academy, he saw Goodwin regularly, but his contact with the two women had been sporadic.

Trask stood. "I'm not sure about the rest of you, but the weekend is calling. I'm going to take my leave, Director."

Don stood also, but Hellman said, "Stay for a moment, Don."

As the door closed behind Trask, Hellman poured herself more coffee.

"This is a great opportunity for you, Don, but we should talk about a few things. As a DDO, you're playing in the big leagues. Politics, infighting, budgets." She sighed. "Do you hear what I'm saying? This will be much different than being the deputy J2 at CYBERCOM."

"Yes, ma'am."

She studied his face. "I'm sorry about your friend.

I only met Captain McHugh once, and as I recall, he wasn't a fan."

"Brendan spoke his mind, ma'am. That's why he was good at what he did."

"Protect your flank, Don. Not everyone is as nice as me." She offered him a wolfish smile. "I meant what I said before. This lifestyle takes a toll. Remember that."

CHAPTER 3

Gulf of Aqaba, near Haql, Saudi Arabia

From a distance, the massive yacht shone like a gleaming jewel on the dark ocean. Alyan Sultan al-Qahtamni leaned forward in the custom leather seat of the helicopter until his face nearly touched the glass.

Al-Buraq came into sharp detail as they drew closer. Sixty meters of the finest seagoing custom-built luxury money could buy. The ship was at anchor, but the clever illumination on her superstructure made her seem as if she were racing forward into the dark seas of the Gulf of Aqaba. In Arabic, her name meant "lightning," but the religious overtones were clear. Al-Buraq was the winged steed who carried the prophets of Islam to heaven.

Both the forward and aft helicopter landing pads were occupied and both of the side landings were down, a sure sign that the owner of the yacht, Saleh bin Ghannam, had put the yacht staff on shore leave for the evening. As was his custom for a meeting of the Arab-Israeli Benevolence Coalition, he kept only a skeleton crew of trusted security men on board.

Saleh was the kind of man who liked to control his environment—completely. As the former head of the Saudi secret service, Saleh made his money the old-fashioned way: by trading in secrets. Indiscretions of the royals, business deals with multinationals, even arrangements with the right kind of Israeli. All done in the service of his beloved country, of course. For Saleh, his life's mission would be complete only when the Saudi Kingdom was raised to the status of a true world power.

For that to come to pass, all other regional powers needed to come under the sway of the House of Saud.

The MD 902 Explorer helo slowed, then hovered, as the pilot waited for clearance to land from the security team on *Al-Buraq*.

Alyan watched as another helo lifted off from the yacht. He had been told the Israelis would be arriving by boat from the nearby port of Eilat, Israel, so that must be their visitor for the evening. For Saleh to invite a potential business partner to his yacht for a full meeting of the coalition spoke volumes about the strategic importance of that partner.

Perhaps Saleh was finally recognizing the need to increase the pace of their investments in the Nile River basin, just as Alyan had been advocating for the last year.

The pilot acknowledged a command over the radio

and pushed the cyclic forward. *Al-Buraq* came into sharp detail as they came in for a landing.

It was a beautiful ship, with long, clean lines, and technology integrated into every nook and cranny. Undoubtedly filled with electronic surveillance devices of every possible design. Alyan laughed to himself. One could take the man out of the secrets business, but never the secrets business out of the man.

The pilot executed a gentle touchdown and the side door opened immediately. The security man who greeted Alyan was armed with a submachine gun on a strap around his neck, a sidearm, a Taser, and a knife. And his hands. All of Saleh's men were ex-Saudi special forces and trained killers.

"This way, sir," he said in Arabic. With his free hand, he gestured toward the staircase aft of the landing pad.

"I know the way," Alyan said. The security man spoke into his throat mic and stepped back with a nod.

The meeting room of the Arab-Israeli Benevolence Coalition was in the heart of the big yacht, one level below the main deck. The richly carpeted hallway leading to the room was a tribute to the owner's long career. Pictures of Saleh with world leaders from the decades: Ronald Reagan, Anwar Sadat, Muammar Gaddafi, Abdullah II of Jordan, Erdogan of Turkey, Sheikh Khalifa of the United Arab Emirates, and finally, the current leader of the House of Saud.

Alyan noted that Saleh scrupulously avoided showing pictures of himself with famous female world leaders. In his less guarded moments, the old warrior railed against the recent efforts to allow more freedoms to women in the kingdom.

Alyan rapped on the door to the meeting room and entered. The sharp smell of burning tobacco nearly stopped him in his tracks.

"Finally," growled Haim Zarecki, as he crushed out a cigarette. "You're late—again." He slipped a fresh Noblesse from a silver case and lit it even as smoke from the last cigarette leaked out from between his lips. The arms dealer's skin was the color and consistency of water-spotted parchment, and he wheezed as he spoke.

From the clock on the wall above Zarecki, Alyan could see that it was two minutes past ten. He ignored the comment and dropped his mobile phone into the EM-shielded box by the door—another of Saleh's meeting requirements.

"*Salaam alaikum.*" Saleh's voice came from behind a cloud of cigar smoke. "Welcome to my humble home, my friend."

"*Alaikum salaam,*" Alyan replied. He sometimes thought that Saleh smoked at these meetings as a way to fight back against his Israeli compatriot's cigarettes.

In contrast to Zarecki's obvious illness, Saleh was the picture of health. The hair brushed back from his forehead was snow white, contrasting with the deep bronze of his skin. High cheekbones, a firm jaw, and a generous nose gave the retired intelligence chief a royal look. His sharp eyes took in the newcomer at a glance, leaving Alyan with the feeling that he'd been measured and found lacking.

Alyan suppressed a flash of annoyance at Saleh's demeanor as he took a seat next to the third man in the room, Itzak Lehrmann. Although he was a decade younger than Lehrmann, he liked to think of the man as a generational ally.

Lehrmann was impeccably dressed in his preferred garb: a dark blue, double-breasted jacket, white shirt, dark tie, and lapel pin. While technically a banker by trade, Lehrmann had made his real fortune in legal money laundering, mostly real estate deals. The über-wealthy Lehrmann family was the closest thing Israel had to business royalty.

Two Israelis, two Saudis—an unlikely grouping if there ever was one—bonded by the shared goals of financial and political power. As billows of cigarette smoke curled in the artful illumination, the silence in the room lengthened.

"Well, let's get started," Zarecki growled. Another cigarette butt joined its companions in a nearly full ash-tray.

Saleh set his cigar aside and jetted a fresh cloud of smoke across the table. As he touched the control panel on the glass-topped table, the surface came alive with graphics. Another touch and the image morphed into a map of the Nile River basin.

Across the table, Zarecki moved his ashtray so as not to cover up the Central African Republic.

Spanning 4,500 kilometers, the Nile River was popularly associated only with Egypt, but Alyan had foreseen decades ago that the real wealth of the Nile lay upstream. As if on cue, Saleh reoriented the map to zoom in on the countries of the upper Nile basin: Sudan, Eritrea, and Ethiopia.

Alyan's gaze traced the Nile south from Cairo, as it snaked across the desert to Khartoum, in Sudan. There, the mighty river broke into two branches: the White Nile ran from Lake Victoria, deep in the continent of Africa, and the Blue Nile drew its flow from the mountains of Ethiopia and Eritrea. A half dozen bright red bars transected each branch of the Nile River, denoting the location of dams being built.

The dams were the reason these four men were in the same room. The Arab-Israeli Benevolence Coalition, through an elaborate series of shell companies run by Alyan, had invested billions in each project. Each dam equaled potential untold wealth to the men at this table.

Like the Aswan High Dam, built in Egypt half a century ago, each new dam tamed the waters of the Nile, reducing uncontrolled flooding in the rainy season and making farming and development much more predictable. But the real wealth lay in the rapid industrial development in the nations bordering the mighty Nile and its tributaries.

Dams meant plenty of cheap electricity, predictable water supplies, and millions of customers hungry for a chance to live a modern lifestyle in the twenty-first century—all ingredients needed for massive business investment.

And the coalition won at every turn. Their initial investment in the dam construction paid them interest— heavily padded by Lehrmann's connections—as did their share of the energy-generation revenue. Now they were about to embark on the expansion phase of their plan: luring multinationals to invest in the region.

There was only one problem—the Egyptians. After the political instability of the Arab Spring, the Egyptian political elite never fully recovered. While the countries controlling the flow of the Nile River built dams and made plans for their future, Egypt was locked in political turmoil. Now the fate of Egypt was in the hands of its upstream neighbors, causing tensions to ratchet up on both sides of the growing conflict.

The members of the coalition spoke in English, the only language they shared.

"Have we made any headway with the damned Egyptians, Saleh?" Zarecki grumbled as he sucked another cigarette to the filter.

Water treaty negotiations between Egypt, Sudan, and the Ethiopians had been going on for the better part of a year now with little to show for it. The Egyptians wanted guarantees of water flow during all seasons. The upstream countries wanted the freedom to fill their massive reservoirs quickly, which would reduce downstream flows for as much as two years or more. Then there was the fact that Sudan and Ethiopia would control water flow indefinitely to Egypt, which was unsettling for a nation that only existed because of the Nile.

Negotiations were stalled. Alyan feared that the next step was armed conflict, and armed conflict was bad for business.

"We have not." Saleh discarded his cigar. "In fact, I

have new intelligence that suggests a much bigger problem than Egyptian saber rattling." His fingers tapped the keypad, and the map cleared. In its place was a photograph taken from a car window at night. The blown-up image was grainy, but the face unmistakable.

Zarecki smacked an age-spotted fist on the table and cursed. "Where was this taken?"

Alyan stared at the picture of Mahmoud Alavi, the head of the Iranian Ministry of Intelligence and Security. Unlike Zarecki, who was raised Jewish in Iran and fled during the revolution, and Saleh, who spent his career fighting the Shiite theocracy, Alyan had no special animosity toward Iran. His concern was strictly financial. Iran represented instability, and instability was bad for business.

"Cairo," Saleh said. "He was spotted going into the president's personal quarters. He stayed for nearly two hours."

"Do we have anyone on the inside?" Zarecki pressed.

Saleh grimaced. Intelligence for the coalition was his responsibility. "They met alone."

The men at the table digested the information and more secondhand smoke. Lehrmann broke the silence.

"They're baiting us," he said. "There's no way the Egyptians would ally themselves with a Shiite theocracy."

Zarecki cursed again. Saleh's expression remained sour. Alyan watched both men closely. When it came to matters of Iran, their judgment was colored by decades of regional violence. His own mind was pure business, uncluttered by the politics of the matter.

"We need to focus on the long-term here," Alyan said. "We will crush the Iranians by harnessing the power of the Nile River basin into the greatest business engine of the modern world. The untapped wealth from resource extraction alone is beyond imagination—as long as we can get the infrastructure in place. That is our only goal now."

Saleh nodded, clamping his now-dead cigar between his teeth. "I'll deal with the Iranians for now. Let's move on."

Zarecki pointed his cigarette at Saleh. "Bring him in."

The door opened to admit a man dressed in a conservative blue business suit.

"Gentlemen," Zarecki said in his wheezing voice. "I'd like to introduce you to Jean-Pierre Manzul, CEO of Recodna Genetics. He has expansion plans that will fit into our portfolio very nicely, I think."

Manzul was tall and lean, with just enough gray in his dark hair to look distinguished. His tanned face was relaxed, even though he knew he was talking to four of the wealthiest men in the world. His dark gray eyes scanned the room, his stance easy. He handed a thumb drive to Saleh, and the table screen shifted to a professional montage of vast fields of flowing wheat and other grains, herds of cattle, goats, sheep.

"The wave of the future is genetic science," Manzul began in a pleasant, but intense, baritone voice. "For decades, the developed world has had a monopoly on this technology. They have been able to do gene manipulation on crops and livestock to improve yields and disease resistance—and then they sell it to African nations at exorbitant prices." He nodded at Saleh, who changed the screen to show a model of a business park.

"That ends today, gentlemen. I am proposing a string of new Recodna campuses at every major dam in the Nile River basin. Using energy and water from these new installations, we will take back the technological leadership in genetic engineering and become the engine of growth for the region."

Manzul was a persuasive speaker, with just the right amount of intensity and detail for his audience. Alyan found himself nodding in agreement. The coalition's plans had always called for recruiting high-tech manufacturing to the region—industrializing the region in stages, with high tech being one of the later phases.

But Manzul's vision offered a shortcut. Today, the region was based mostly on subsistence farming. The new dams controlled the river flow, making farming more predictable and stable year over year. Instead of transitioning to industry, they could add true genetic innovations to the mix, transforming the Nile River basin into the breadbasket of the region—perhaps even the world.

He devoured Manzul's talk of secure bio research centers, recruitment of leading scientists, plans for world-class manufacturing facilities. The multibillion-dollar investment was steep, but the rewards . . .

By the time Manzul left the room, Alyan's imagination was on fire with the business potential.

"I thought you would appreciate his vision, Alyan," Zarecki declared as he fired up a celebratory cigarette.

"I move that we provide an initial investment as per the proposal."

There were no dissenting voices in the room.

Alyan and Lehrmann departed immediately for the flight deck. Outside, Alyan drew in a deep breath of sea air.

"It's like a fucking gas chamber in there," Lehrmann said, loosening his collar. "It's our own Arab-Israeli War, but with cigarettes and cigars as weapons."

"And us civilians are collateral damage," Alyan said. He patted his pocket for his phone, realizing he had left it in the conference room. "Be back in a moment."

The dimmed hallway lights left Saleh's wall of famous people in shadow. Alyan's feet made no sound on the rich plush carpet.

The door to the conference room was cracked open, casting a thin line of light into the hallway. He heard the voices of his older colleagues inside and thought nothing of it—until he heard a third voice.

Alyan eased closer.

"The facility is ready." Manzul's voice carried into the hallway. "Recruiting has already begun."

"How long?" Zarecki growled.

"My partner has access to the needed samples. With the team we're building, we can have a functional weapon within months, a year at the most."

A weapon? Alyan froze.

"And the genetic component?" Saleh's voice was intense. "You can guarantee that feature?"

Manzul took a long time to answer. "My partner is

the best and the team is second to none, but I need two things from you. I need your assurance that the test sites will be contained."

"One phone call." Saleh's voice. "A simple phone call and it will be like the place never existed. What else?"

"Money," Manzul said.

"I don't care what it costs," Zarecki said, the sound of his fist pounding on the table punctuating his reply. "I just want them"—he launched into a coughing fit—"wiped off the face of the . . ."

Alyan backed down the hall slowly. At the far end, he clattered his shoes against the uncarpeted steps and coughed as he made his way down the hall. He pushed open the door to the meeting room.

Manzul was gone.

Alyan smiled at Zarecki and Saleh. "Forgot my phone." He extracted the device from the EM-proof box and slipped it into his pocket.

He met their eyes—Zarecki's first, then his countryman Saleh's—giving each of them an opportunity to say something about Manzul's second visit and their mysterious conversation. Neither man's gaze wavered.

"Good night, then," Alyan said.

CHAPTER 4

Mocímboa da Praia, Mozambique

It was well past midnight before the young prostitute made her way down the alley toward Rachel Jaeger. Rachel waited in the dark, hearing the distant pounding of the surf and the occasional roar of a plane taking off from the nearby airport.

The night was dark and humid and overlaid with a heavy, sweet smell from the battered dumpster a few meters away. As the girl picked her way down the littered alley, a small furry creature scurried across her path. The young woman did not flinch or cry out. Rachel crossed her arms and waited.

The woman stopped a few paces from Rachel. Like most of the prostitutes in the area, she was from Tanzania, working in Mozambique to send money home. Looking all of sixteen years old, she was half a head shorter than Rachel, with a long, lean frame and a generous bosom. She was dressed in neon-yellow hot pants and a matching halter top that left little to the buyer's imagination. Her hair was braided, and when she turned to look behind her, Rachel saw a scar on her right cheek. She also noticed the young woman's fierce expression.

Rachel relaxed a tiny bit. Whatever this woman's motivations for being here, she was unafraid of the consequences.

"Neema?" she asked.

The woman's smile of acknowledgment made a slash of white in the dimness of the alley.

"I have the information you seek." She spoke in broken Portuguese, the official language of Mozambique. She pointed back toward the light at the end of the alley. Rachel took a step to the right so she could see the neon sign: ESTRELLA'S BAR AND RESTAURANT. "He's in there now, drinking, and alone. He likes this place. I sent all the other girls away for the rest of the night." She smiled again. "He's all yours."

Rachel nodded, feeling a thrill of excitement race up her spine. Neema was involved in the two oldest professions on earth: prostitution and spying. The Mata Hari network in this region of Africa had originally been put in place by al-Shabab, a radical Islamist group, as a way to spy on corrupt police officers.

Rachel, a Mossad agent, had been looking forward to this particular job for a very long time.

"Tell me about him," Rachel said. "Anything you know, even the smallest detail. His favorite drink, his preferences in bed. Anything."

Neema grimaced. "You can't miss Abdul. He takes the—" She mimicked a hypodermic being inserted into her biceps. "I don't know what you call them. Muscle drugs."

"Steroids?" Rachel asked.

The young woman shrugged and mimed big puffy muscles on her arms. "He has big strong muscles, but a very little prick." She held her thumb and forefinger a few centimeters apart.

Rachel shared her laughter. "What else?"

Neema made the local crude hand sign for anal sex. "He is a pig. He hits the girls, too. He likes that." She touched the scar on her cheek and her face twisted into a mask of fierce fury. "I'm glad you're going to kill him."

Rachel froze. Was that just an expression or did she understand what Rachel was here to do?

"Why do you say that?" she said as casually as she dared, wishing they had a better common language.

The young woman grinned again. "I know who you are." She pointed at Rachel's strapless black lace bustier, flaming red miniskirt, and four-inch high heels. "You are no prostitute. You not from here."

Rachel allowed herself to take a beat. That admission alone was enough to kill the operation. If Neema knew, then there had to be others, possibly including her mark. She was alone in a strange city with no backup.

On the other hand, she had tracked this asshole for months, carefully figuring out the best way to get close to him. Leaving now would mean starting over, letting a known murderer walk free for another day.

Abdul Wenje and his al-Sunna gang were nothing but common thugs hiding behind a thin veil of Islamic rhetoric to extort money from local businesses. The murder of ten Israeli tourists on the Quirimbas Islands had more to do with real estate than religion.

Rachel was assigned to end him—but quietly. The last thing Mossad wanted was international headlines about revenge killings, no matter how justified.

As a lone operator, she had leeway to interpret the local conditions. Rachel decided to trust Neema. "Who else knows?"

The young woman shrugged. "The girls, we talk, we see things." Her eyes flared. "But we do not *say* things."

Rachel's mind raced. The threads of intel that she had gathered to pull this op together were not reproducible. If Wenje slipped away tonight, it might be years before her agency had another chance at him. Years before those ten innocent tourists were avenged.

"Can I count on you to stay quiet?"

Neema's braids, silhouetted in the light of the bar, swayed as she nodded. "Like I said, he is a pig. You are doing us a favor."

Rachel reached into her tiny clutch purse for some money. Neema shook her head again. "This I do for free."

Rachel forced the money into her hand. "Take it," she said. "Divide it among the other girls, but stay quiet."

Neema stuffed the bills into her bra. "Wait," she said. "I fix." She hooked a finger into Rachel's bustier and tore the lace apart so the flesh of her breast squeezed out the side. Then, gripping the hem of her miniskirt, she ripped it open all the way to her hip. She stepped back to survey her modifications to Rachel's disguise. "Now you look like one of us."

Rachel watched Neema hurry away. If she was ever in a fight in a dark alley, she would want that one beside her.

The interior of Estrella's Bar was as tacky and run-down as it looked from the outside. The place seemed to be in the midst of an identity crisis. With the Mozambique airport less than a mile away, it had the feel of a bar for weary business travelers. But it was also near the beach and tried to play on that theme with a spray of neon palm trees on the wall. Lastly, Estrella's bordered a seedy neighborhood and gave off a dive-bar vibe.

Rachel paused in the doorway, peering through the thick clouds of cigarette smoke darkening the interior. Besides the neon palm trees, lighted signs for European beers penetrated the gloom as well as an advertisement for Tipo Tinto, the local rum.

She headed to the bar in a slow saunter, allowing her hips to roll suggestively underneath her now-ventilated miniskirt. She parked herself in the center of the bar between two men, a heavyset European who was sweating despite the air-conditioning and a large black man in a business suit.

She caught the bartender's eye. "Rum and Coke," she said as she extracted a pack of cigarettes from her clutch and put one between her painted lips. The bartender gave her a light and she sipped her drink.

She felt the two men on either side of her sizing her up, trying to decide if they wanted to make an offer. She smiled at the heavyset white man first.

"Good evening," she said in Portuguese.

"Beautiful night," the man responded in English. She shifted into his language.

"You are from Europe?" she said.

The man's jowly face creased into a smile. "Scotland," he said, as if his accent didn't make that fact abundantly clear to her. "My company is bidding on a construction project at the airport. You speak very good English."

Rachel nodded and let her eyes slide past him to a man sitting along the far wall. The man wore a short-sleeved, collared shirt, but he had rolled up the sleeves to his armpits to expose his biceps. Thick neck muscles sprouted from the shirt collar.

His eyes met hers for an instant and she took a pull of her cigarette before she looked away. He lifted a shot glass of brown liquid and drank it in one go. Wenje was a rum drinker, then.

Rachel turned back to the bar, flirting with the large black man on her right. He was a chemical engineer from South Africa in town to work on a water treatment project. He seemed in a hurry and made her an offer quickly. Rachel refused him and he departed.

She slid onto his vacated seat, leaving an open space between her and the Scot, who continued to chatter away. Another patron took the seat next to her and made an offer. She pretended to consider it, then countered with what she knew was a very high price.

The new john laughed in her face, calling her a whore in a loud voice as he left. Rachel flipped him off as he walked away, then ordered another drink.

It took nearly an hour for her mark to come off the back wall. He inserted himself into the space between her and the voluble Scot, who tried to lean forward to continue his conversation with Rachel.

Abdul Wenje glared at him. "Move on."

The Scot paid his tab and left.

Rachel sighed and ran a finger down Wenje's bulging biceps. "Impressive," she said. "How often do you work out?"

"Every day," he said. He twisted his arm so the triceps popped. "Sometimes twice a day."

Rachel slid closer so the flesh of her exposed breast brushed against his biceps. "I like a man who takes his work seriously. Buy me a drink?"

His eyes narrowed. "I saw you refuse two offers tonight."

Rachel took his newly poured shot of rum and drank it in one gulp. The liquid burned all the way to her stomach. "Tonight is my night off. I'm looking for something more than just money." She leaned over and let her tongue trail along his biceps. "I was planning to walk the beach later . . . maybe you'll join me."

Wenje snorted and tossed back a shot of rum, but Rachel noted the way his pupils dilated and his posture stiffened.

She had him hooked. Now to reel him in.

"Another rum for me," she said to the bartender. "He's buying."

Wenje looked at her sharply but said nothing. He gave a wolfish smile. "Why not?"

Rachel drank one more shot, then feigned drunkenness and spilled the next one. She laughed loudly at the mess, all the while sidling closer to Wenje. She rubbed her hand up his thigh. "I think I want to go to the beach now," she whispered, nipping his ear with her teeth. Rachel stood, pretending to sway.

Wenje dropped some bills on the bar and seized her hand, causing Rachel to nearly trip in her ridiculous heels.

The street outside was deserted and quiet. Besides the tap of her own shoes, the only sound was the surf a few blocks away. The night air was humid and still, settling on Rachel's bare shoulders like a thin damp blanket.

Wenje held her hand firmly and walked at a fast clip. They moved between pools of light from the few functioning streetlights. Rachel, still feigning drunkenness, clung to his meaty arm with her free hand.

At the corner, she leaned left, toward the beach, but Wenje pulled her to the right, deeper into the city.

Rachel balked. "I want to go to the beach," she cooed. "It's romantic."

Wenje crushed her hand, then reached across to grip her free arm. He pulled her close enough for Rachel to smell the sourness of his breath. "Is there a problem?"

Her heart beat quickly, but she let her head droop and her words slur together as she replied. "The beach . . ."

Wenje released her arm. He slid his hand into the ripped side of her miniskirt and dug his fingers deep into the cleft of her buttocks. Rachel kept her face impassive as her stomach recoiled at the violation. Instead, she nuzzled his chest and moaned.

He withdrew his hand and reversed his direction, now drawing Rachel toward the beach.

Rachel's instincts flared an alert. He was toying with her. Something was wrong.

"You're hurting me," Rachel said, trying to extract her arm from his grip. With her free hand, she fumbled with her clutch, trying to get at the tiny syringe inside. One quick stab of the needle and the bastard's heart would stop for good.

Wenje ignored her. Midway along the block, between streetlights, he paused at the opening to a dark alley and gave a low whistle. There was a dragging sound; then a man stepped out of the shadows. He threw something at Wenje's feet that made a wet, slapping sound as it hit the pavement.

It was a body. Rachel looked down, focusing on a yellow glow in the dark. With horror, she realized she was looking at Neema's neon-yellow halter top.

She sensed more than saw Wenje's fist swinging toward her. Rachel ducked and jammed the spike of her high heels into his instep, causing him to release her. With the second man, she wasn't so lucky. He tackled her, driving her body back into the brick wall.

Rachel felt all the air leave her lungs and saw stars as her head cracked into the wall. She dropped both elbows onto his back as hard as she could, then launched a knee up into his face. His grip weakened, and she hammered her knee up in another strike. He slid to the ground.

Frantically, she ripped open the clutch purse, her fingers seeking the two-inch syringe hidden inside a tampon.

But Wenje was back in action. The big man loomed before her, his shadowed face a mask of fury. He gripped her throat with both hands and pressed her back against the wall. The clutch purse slipped from her hands as she tried to free herself.

She felt the skin on her back scrape away as he pressed her flat against the bricks and slid her upward. Rachel kicked at his chest, but it seemed to make no difference. She tried to claw at his eyes, but the big man had a longer reach and all she did was scrape at the flesh of his upper arms.

She gasped for breath, feeling her vision starting to tunnel. She tried to kick at his chest with her heels, but she had no leverage . . .

Heels. High heels.

Rachel twisted her leg up, clawing at the clasp on her shoes. She felt the blood vessels in her eye start to rupture. The clasp came free and she tore off the shoe.

Her strength was draining away. With all her remaining might, Rachel drove the tip of the four-inch heel into Wenje's eye.

He screamed as he let her drop to the ground. The damp, foul air of Mozambique was the sweetest breath she had ever drawn. Rachel stripped off the other heel and clawed herself upright. A weeping Wenje staggered down the street. She stalked after him, feeling stronger with each step, the shoe still in her hand.

Wenje stopped, turning to face her, his fists up. "Who are you?" he yelled at her.

Rachel moved with a speed and fluidity born from years of training. She rushed him, seeing him telegraph his punch and ducking under it. She used the spiked heel to dig into his ribs, then stepped away.

Wenje lowered his hand to clutch the injury, and she struck again—this time delivering a roundhouse kick that dropped the big man to his knees. He jabbed out a fist. She let it slip past her, then kicked him in the teeth. He fell backwards and she leaped onto his chest.

"Who are you?" he said again. His right eye was a deep hole of welling blood, his left glassy with tears.

Rachel positioned the point of the heel under his chin.

"My name is Death," she said in Hebrew. She used her fist to jam the heel up into Abdul Wenje's skull.

Rachel rolled off the corpse, lying flat on her back in the dirty street. With a grunt, she got to her feet and went back to the alley.

Neema was dead, beaten to death. Wenje's accomplice was unconscious. She felt along the ground for her lost clutch purse. The syringe hidden in the tampon was still there, as was the infrared flashlight. She needed that to signal her extraction team, waiting for her offshore.

Rachel drove the tip of the needle into the unconscious man's neck and waited for his heart to stop.

Then Rachel got to her feet and walked toward the sound of the surf.

CHAPTER 5

Khartoum, Sudan

Just like every morning, the Muslim call to prayer woke Jean-Pierre Manzul before sunrise. He swung his feet to the tile floor.

"JP," said a sleepy voice beside him. A slender hand with red-painted fingernails snaked out from under the covers and snagged the waistband of his underwear. "Come back to bed."

JP chuckled. "I'm a good Muslim man. I need to get up for the call to prayer."

"Bullshit. You're going for a run."

JP removed the fingers and stood. He leaned over and rooted his face into the covers until he found soft flesh. He deposited a loud kiss. "I'll be back soon—and I'll make it worth your while."

The woman pushed his face away and rolled over. "You do this to make me feel bad about myself."

JP changed into the workout gear that he had laid out

the night before and quietly left the penthouse apartment.

The desert air was chill in the early morning. He could see the sky lightening behind the distant mountains as he stretched. He began at a walk, then a slow trot. These days, his body needed time to warm up.

He jogged two blocks east to the promenade overlooking the Nile River and turned south. The streets at this hour were mostly deserted except for a few stragglers making their way to the mosque. This was the way he liked the city. Quiet, empty, cool. In a few hours, the heat from the sun would bake the streets. The din of cars and crush of bodies on the sidewalk would choke the magic out of the setting.

He picked up the pace, letting the sound of his own breathing set a rhythm in his head. He felt a flush of heat in his face, and a sheen of sweat broke out on his forehead, evaporating in the dry air almost immediately. His breathing evened out and he settled into a solid pace.

JP squinted into the distance. The first rays of the new day touched the Victory Bridge, his turnaround point. He picked up the pace, passing a fruit seller and his donkey cart along the street.

Although born and raised in France, Jean-Pierre Manzul was a man of Africa, the land of his father's birth. His mother, a Parisian woman to her core, fell in love with JP's father when he came to the Sorbonne to study medicine at the Pierre and Marie Curie University. Their marriage didn't last, but young JP came away from the union with an everlasting love for his father's native land. At university, he studied languages and medicine like his father, but after undergrad, his life took a different turn.

JP was approached by the French Direction Générale de la Sécurité Extérieure, better known by the acronym DGSE, the French equivalent of the CIA. With his mixed heritage and facility with languages, JP was a cultural chameleon. His first posting was to central Africa, where he supported DGSE operations against the rebel Rwandan Patriotic Front.

In Rwanda, JP's field skills were noticed and he was recruited to the counterterrorism branch. There he immersed himself in the murky world of covert operations.

In the pre-9/11 era, JP trained agents to infiltrate al-Qaeda in Afghanistan. After the attacks on the World Trade Center and the resulting military actions, JP's operation was crushed in the American military onslaught. His men were lost—all of them.

After he was called back to France, his frustration only grew. He had been to the front lines, lived with the local operators risking their lives for their country. He knew the only way to get to the real masterminds behind the terrorist movements was to get men on the inside, operations requiring close coordination of small teams of highly skilled agents.

In contrast, the French government painted a picture of a terrorist bogeyman that could only be defeated through military might. He watched the destructive forces of radical Islam creep across his adopted homeland of Africa and filter back into Europe. Again and again, he witnessed careful operations crumble under the weight of political expediency . . . and he lost faith in the system.

Retiring from his specialty in the DGSE was never an option, so JP Manzul did the next best thing.

He disappeared.

Breathing hard now, he passed a bakery, plowing through the mouthwatering aroma of freshly baked croissants. The shopkeeper raised his hand in greeting, and JP waved back. For the last half kilometer, he picked up the pace to a sprint.

He paused at the bridge to savor the new morning and to stretch. Morning prayers were over and the streets were coming alive with men in business suits and women in robes and head scarves. A gaggle of children in school uniforms paraded by with book bags under their arms.

JP set a brisk pace for home.

For three years, JP wandered across the African continent. For six months, he volunteered at a Doctors Without Borders medical mission, using his language and first-aid skills as a triage specialist. There he met Talia Tahir.

JP paused at the coffee seller outside his apartment building and purchased two cups in to-go containers before taking the elevator up to the penthouse.

As he entered the apartment, JP called out, "Get up, my sweet, I have coffee for you."

To his surprise, Talia was in the living room curled up on the couch, coffee in hand already. His lover was still wearing her silk nightdress, and the shoulder strap had slipped down her arm, exposing the creamy warm brown of her upper breast. She was staring at the eight-by-ten pictures on the whiteboard they had set up in the living room. Strewn across the coffee table were piles of résumés and technical papers from each of the final five candidates.

Talia smiled absently at his good-morning wishes. Tucking her feet under her haunches, she gestured with her coffee at the board.

"That's the final cut," she said. "We need them all to make this work."

"And you shall have them all, my dear," JP replied. "Saleh has given me all the money we need. Every man—and woman—has a price. We just need to find it."

He sat down next to her and leaned over for a kiss, but she pushed him away. "You're all sweaty and you smell. Go take a shower."

"Only if you join me," he said with a wink.

"Go!" She rolled her eyes. "If you're a good boy, I might join you."

JP laughed as he entered the bedroom and stripped off his workout gear. Their shower was a large glass-and-tile affair with four showerheads. He turned on the water and inspected his naked body in the mirror as he waited for the water to heat up.

He pinched the loose skin around his waist. Not bad, but he could stand to drop a few pounds. JP sighed and stepped under the steaming jets of hot water. As he rinsed shampoo from his hair, he felt Talia's fingers snake around his waist and pull him close.

She planted a kiss on the nape of his neck. "You smell much better now." He turned to face her.

Even after years together, she still took his breath away.

Whereas JP's heritage left him with lighter skin, Talia's mixed Egyptian, Sudanese, and British parentage left her with tawny skin and eyes the shade of a brilliant blue sky. He first met her when Talia was only twenty-five, a graduate of the University of Khartoum with a doctorate in microbiology. She was a product of the region, orphaned at the age of twelve, her parents taken by violence.

Talia, an only child, returned home to Sudan to live with her aunt. She emerged from that emotional crucible with two guiding principles: the continent of Africa belonged to the African people and real power was not awarded for good behavior. It was seized by the bold.

Her education and her job with the World Health Organization addressed the first principle. Her partnership with JP would address the second.

Talia stepped under the shower jets and raised her face. JP slipped behind her and ran his hands over her slick body. She pressed back against him and JP responded.

———————

Dressed in matching white terry cloth bathrobes, JP and Talia reconvened in front of the whiteboard. Five pictures had been tacked to the board with magnets. A sixth photo stood apart from the others.

"Take me through them one at a time," JP said.

Talia began with the headshot of a dark-haired Indian woman. "I'll handle Lakshmi. We were roommates in undergrad and she's got a solid microbiology background."

JP frowned. "Are you sure we need her? You're a better scientist and—"

"I trust her."

JP shrugged. "As you wish. Next?"

Talia held up the photo of a young Scandinavian woman. "Greta Berger. We'll need her for the CRISPR work on the paleo samples."

"Assuming I can get paleo samples, my dear," JP said.

Talia ignored him, instead moving a picture of a bearded Saudi next to an attractive brunette woman. "Synthetic biologists are key to developing the combination. It would be best to have both Faraj and Katie McDonough, but in a pinch, we can do without one of them."

JP shook his head. "They will both join." He grinned and waggled his eyebrows. "I can be very persuasive."

Talia tapped the photo of an Asian man, mid-fifties, square eyeglasses. "The key to the genetic component of the weapon is Lu Xianshan. He's a must-have. No substitute."

"I'll get him," JP said. The Chinese researcher was studying a recent plague outbreak on Madagascar. His research on the epidemiological patterns of an outbreak would be essential to the later stages of their work.

Talia pointed to the sixth photo and made a sour face. "And that leaves the Nazi."

"Now, now, dear. I believe the socially acceptable term these days is 'white nationalist,'" JP said, as he plucked the photo of Jason Winslow off the board. As with all of their potential recruits, they had researched the backgrounds of their marks extensively.

The University of Washington researcher had an active alter ego on social media that sprayed a steady stream of bigoted invective. While that made him unsuitable for the research team, he was still their best resource to procure the delicate paleopathogenic samples.

Luckily for JP, Jason Winslow could be bought.

JP tossed Winslow's picture onto the coffee table and took a seat next to his lover. He slid his arm around Talia and drew her close. It was all falling into place: the money, the research facility, and now the personnel to bring their project to fruition.

It would take at least a year to build the most sophisticated targeted bioweapon in history, but once it was finished . . .

Talia took his hand and pressed it to her lips.

"This is how we change the world."

CHAPTER 6

Navy–Marine Corps Memorial Stadium,
Annapolis, Maryland

Lieutenant (j.g.) Janet Everett hurried across the stadium parking lot, already sweating into her summer white uniform. The cool breezes of her home port in Groton, Connecticut, had made her forget about the heat and humidity of Annapolis in June.

She popped a salute to an admiral and entered the welcome shade of the tunnel underneath the stadium. Janet had considered wearing civilian clothes to Michael's graduation ceremony, but pride had intervened. She glanced down at the brand-new gold dolphins insignia over the left pocket of her white uniform shirt. The qualification pin felt heavy and conspicuous, but she'd worked over two years to qualify as a US Navy submarine officer and she wanted the world to know it.

As she emerged from the tunnel into sunlight, the sight of the football field made her stop.

Arranged on the green of the field was a solid block

of empty chairs facing a stage with the trident seal of the United States Naval Academy. Strains of "Pomp and Circumstance" played in the background as the first graduates began to file in on each side.

She paused to drink in the familiar sight. The young men and women were outfitted in service dress whites, their most formal uniform, consisting of a long-sleeved white tunic with gold buttons down the front, white trousers, and white shoes. They all looked tanned and healthy, strong and vital. Mixed in the sea of white was the occasional dark blue of the US Marine Corps dress uniform jacket.

This was their last moment as a class. After today, they would disperse all over the world. Marching onto the field were future pilots, surface warfare officers, cybersecurity officers, Marines, and of course submariners. Janet sneaked another look at her warfare pin and swelled with pride.

Her ticket was for the upper deck. She spun around and began to climb the concrete steps, thankful that Michael had scored tickets in the shade.

The stadium around her was packed with celebrating family and friends. Women in bright summer dresses, men in suits and ball caps, grandmothers sporting parasols against the sun. Graduation from one of the service academies was an all-family affair. By the time the ceremony started, not a place in the thirty-five-thousand-seat-capacity stadium would be empty.

"Janet!" She heard her name shouted above the excited murmur of the crowd.

Don Riley waved at her with both arms. He was

wearing a blue blazer with a white shirt and a blue-and-gold bow tie. His pale skin was flushed in the heat, but he looked healthy and fit. She climbed the rest of the steps and sidestepped her way down the aisle, where Don crushed her in a bear hug.

"Janet, it's been too long." Don spied the submarine warfare pin. "And you completed your quals! Well done."

Janet checked her ticket and found a stately black woman with iron-gray hair in the seat between her and Don.

"I want you to meet someone very special to Michael," Don said. "Janet, this is Miss Eustace Jenkins, Michael's guardian."

The woman stood and extended her hand. She wore a conservative dark blue business suit with a high-necked white blouse, but she appeared cool despite the heat. Janet found the woman's palm dry and her grip firm.

"Ms. Janet Everett." The woman's voice was soft and modulated, but with a hint of steel in the tone. "I am so honored to meet you. My Michael speaks so highly of you, I half expected you to fly up here on angel's wings."

Janet blushed. "I think a lot of your son," she managed to say over Don's hearty laughter. "I'm so glad you could make it out here for the ceremony."

"I wouldn't miss this for the world. This place, and people like the two of you, have made young Michael into the man he is today."

The soon-to-be graduates had filled the block of

seats on the field, and they stood at attention. The last of the academic professors took their places on the stage, followed by the military chain of command. The commandant of midshipmen, the superintendent, and finally the secretary of defense took the stage, and the assembled graduates took their seats in unison.

Although Janet knew it was boiling hot down there on the field, she also knew the graduates didn't care a whit. Four years of hard work—academics, physical training, military training—was about to pay off for them. There wasn't a man or woman on that field who wouldn't crawl over broken glass to get their commission and their degree. Nothing could dampen their enthusiasm today.

"I'm afraid you're going to have to explain this all to me, Janet," Eustace said. "I've been to graduations before, but Michael tells me this is much more than a graduation. He's very emphatic on that point."

Janet laughed. "He's right about that, ma'am. This is an academic graduation, but the real point of today is when they take the oath of office. After that, they're commissioned officers. That's what it's all about."

Eustace nodded. "That's what he said. I don't think he had much trouble with the academic part, but the rest of it . . . well, I'm so glad he met you and Andrea when he did." She paused to press a tissue to her eyes. "His mother would just be so proud right now. And she would give you a big old hug if she was here."

Janet instinctively squeezed the older woman's hand.

"Michael didn't have a lot of friends growing up," Eustace said softly. "Didn't have any friends really. But you and Andrea. He looks up to you and thinks of you as his friends and that means all the difference to me." The older woman dabbed at her eyes again.

Janet swallowed. If she didn't change the subject soon, she would be crying herself. She leaned over to Don.

"Any word from Dre? I haven't heard from her in months."

Don shook his head. "I've been trying to reach her, but nothing back. I know she's busy with her surface warfare quals, but there's something I need to talk to her about."

The music ceased and the first speaker stepped up to the podium. "Ladies and gentlemen, please rise for the playing of the national anthem."

The crowd fell silent and stood as one. Janet put on her cover at the correct angle and saluted as the music started.

Déjà vu welled up around her. The packed stadium, the patriotic crowd peppered with saluting officers and proud parents, the block of brand-new graduates on the field.

A few years ago, she had been among the graduates, but it had been a very different experience for her. With her left arm in a sling, Janet's uniform on graduation day was not as sharp as she would have liked, but she had managed to salute with her classmates.

She remembered the slick feel of tears on her cheeks, just glad to be alive after the North Korea operation.

She owed her life to Michael Goodwin's quick first-aid actions. She couldn't tell Eustace Jenkins that part, but she felt the tears brimming again. When the national anthem finished, she felt Eustace press a tissue into her hand.

"Thank you, ma'am," she muttered, and swiped at her eyes.

The crowd around them buzzed with laughter as they bided their time for the big moment. No one was here to listen to a government official speak. Finally, the superintendent directed the graduates to stand.

Funny, Janet could barely remember walking across the stage for her diploma. She recalled that the guy in front of her had done a backflip after he received his, but everything after that was a blur.

Around them, blocks of friends and family perched on the edge of their seats waiting for that electric moment when their graduate's name was called. They leaped to their feet, cheering and ringing cowbells for the few seconds it took their graduate to cross the stage, then sat down again.

"Michael. Goodwin." Janet, Eustace, and Don stood and bellowed as loud as they could.

She hadn't seen Michael since her own graduation. He strode across the stage with a confidence she didn't remember and shook the secretary of defense's hand as he accepted his diploma. The superintendent paused, giving the young man a whispered word before he released his hand. The stage was very far away, but Janet saw Michael raise his head in acknowledgment of their shouts.

"He's changed a lot since you last saw him," Don said. "You'll be impressed."

Finally, all the graduates were back in their seats. She could see them chattering excitedly to one another as she searched the crowd for Michael. He was staring ahead, quiet, lost in the moment. She smiled to herself. That was the Michael she remembered.

"Graduates, please rise." The entire stadium drew a collective breath. "Raise your right hand."

Janet's heart pounded as she heard the words again.

". . . I will support and defend the Constitution of the United States against all enemies, foreign and domestic; that I will bear true faith and allegiance to the same; that I take this obligation freely, without any mental reservation or purpose of evasion; and that I will well and faithfully discharge the duties of the office on which I am about to enter. So help me God."

Eustace sobbed and Janet put her arm around the older woman. "Watch, Eustace, you don't want to miss this part."

"Hip, hip, hooray!" On the third repetition of the cheer, a thousand uniform caps launched into the air in the iconic moment of celebration captured by so many photographers. As caps came down, they were relaunched, creating a boiling effect in the center of the field.

All around them, parents, siblings, grandparents, friends, and lovers all wept and hugged each other.

The superintendent stepped to the microphone.

"Dismissed!"

———

Janet, Don, and Eustace waited in the shadow of the Tecumseh statue in front of Bancroft Hall, the US Naval

Academy dormitory for the entire brigade of 4,500 midshipmen. New graduates and their guests criss-crossed the white pavers of the open formation space known as T Court, named after the statue.

"I'm sure there's a reason why there is a statue of a Native American warrior in front of this building," Eustace said.

Janet recalled one of the many facts every plebe had to memorize during their first year at the Academy. "The statue is a bronze replica of the figurehead of the USS *Delaware*, placed here in the 1930s. The statue is actually of the peacemaker Tamanend, but midshipmen preferred to call it Tecumseh and the name stuck."

"And you just know that fact off the top of your head?" Eustace said.

Don and Janet laughed together. Janet said, "It's a re-quirement—"

"There he is," Don interrupted.

Janet followed Don's pointing finger to see a tall black man in dress white uniform, striding their way. That could not be Michael. The Michael she remembered was a reserved plebe, distant and barely able to make eye contact, not this smiling, waving man who walked toward them with purpose and drive. He looked taller than she remembered and had put on weight in his shoulders and arms.

He stopped a few paces away, looked Janet in the eye, and saluted. She drew herself up and returned the honor. To her surprise, he flipped a coin at her, which she caught in midair.

"What is this?" she asked. He surged forward to

engulf her in a hug. The embrace confirmed her obser-
vations of his height and weight. He set her back on the
ground, then hugged Don and Eustace.

"That silver dollar is Captain McHugh's," Michael
said. "Liz wanted you to have it."

Janet stared at the battered silver dollar. The tradi-
tion of a newly commissioned officer giving a silver dollar for their first salute was as old as the Navy.

She hadn't thought of Brendan McHugh in months,
but this coin—*his* coin—made him feel very near on this
special day. Captain McHugh gave his life on the North
Korea mission where she had been gravely injured. She
remembered the calm in his voice as he talked to her
on the helo ride onto the island. How he'd steadied her
nerves, made her feel ready for the trial to come. . . .

She closed her fingers around the coin, feeling the
edge bite into her palm. "I don't know what to say,
Michael."

"It was Liz's idea," Don said. Brendan McHugh had
been Don's best friend. Don blew out a long breath.

"All right, enough tears for one day. We'll drink to
absent friends later." He extracted a trifold packet of papers from his jacket pocket, which he handed to Michael. "As promised, sir, your new orders."

Janet perked up. "New orders? Michael's going to
work for you?"

Don cocked an eyebrow, then pretended to reach into
his pocket again. "I've got a second set in here for you,
if you're interested." He locked eyes with Janet. "I'm
serious."

Janet felt the weight of the gold dolphins on her uniform. She had been qualified only a few months. She loved her new life on a submarine and she was good at her job. But the chance to work with Michael and Don again . . .

"I'm listening, Don," she said.

Michael stuck out his elbow. "Miss Eustace, I suggest we go back to the hotel and let these two talk. We'll see them at dinner."

Eustace, obviously impressed with Michael's new-found confidence, took his arm and bussed his cheek with a kiss. "Your mother would be so proud of you right now, Michael. I just can't stop thinking that."

Michael returned the kiss, then led her away.

Janet and Don strolled down Stribling Walk, the wide, red-brick boulevard that ran the length of the Naval Academy grounds, known as the Yard. The excitement of the recent ceremony was still palpable in the groups of people they passed.

"How did you manage to recruit Michael right out of the Academy?" Janet asked.

"All things in good time, my impatient young friend," Don said.

The sleek lines of Hopper Hall, the cybersecurity studies building, loomed over them. As the first new academic building built on the Naval Academy grounds in over forty years, Hopper managed to look both natural to the Academy aesthetic and futuristic at the same time.

Janet knew that the façade and the academic setting

were deceptive. This was a secure building, with multiple SCIFs, or sensitive compartmented information facilities, inside and a state-of-the-art communications array on the roof. This site was as up-to-date as any intelligence facility in the greater Washington, DC, area.

Don had a visitor's badge waiting for her at the reception desk and led her to a first-floor conference room that he had reserved.

"You were that sure I'd say yes to this meeting?" she asked.

In reply, he drew a single sheet of paper from his inside pocket and slid it across the table toward her along with a pen.

Janet scanned the sheet. "Is there ever a time when we just have a conversation that does not involve a nondisclosure agreement?"

Don shrugged. "It's the life we lead."

Janet took the time to read the document carefully. Still, as her logical brain processed the text, her emotional brain ran wild.

The CIA? She had worked hard for her gold dolphins. Was she really willing to consider putting aside her new life as a submarine officer for a tour at the CIA?

She scribbled her signature and the date on the bottom of the sheet. "Let's hear your pitch, Riley."

Don's demeanor became serious. "I'm building a new directorate at the CIA. The North Korea situation woke up a lot of people. Top brass realized that when everyone is focused on the big threat and reacting to emergent events, no one is looking for the stuff bubbling just below the surface. Emerging Threats, that's what it's called."

"I'm listening," Janet said.

"This is not just another analyst job," Don said. "We get the stuff that falls between the cracks, the cases that don't fit neatly into anyone's portfolio. New terrorist groups, cyberattacks with no attribution, proliferation of WMDs, coups d'état, regional conflicts—if it's weird and new, we get first crack at it. And once we find the next threat, I'll have the authority to run field operations on that threat."

Janet glanced down at the gleaming gold dolphins on her uniform. Don noted the unconscious movement.

"I know what you're thinking," he said. "You have a job and you're good at it. I talked to your commanding officer and he raved about you—"

"You talked to my CO?"

Don drew a trifold sheaf of papers out of his inner pocket.

"I'm here to offer you a job, Janet. What you're doing as a submarine officer is honorable and you're a top-notch warrior. If the bubble goes up, I'll be glad you're out there, but this . . ." He tapped the papers. "With this, we will solve problems *before* they become major events on the world stage. We will stop wars. We will save lives. It's not glamorous and you won't see your name in the paper, but this is how we change the world, Janet."

He slid the papers across the table. "There's a set of orders for you. If you want the job, it's yours. If you want to stay in subs, I won't ask again." Don stood. "I'll see you at dinner."

Janet let the door close behind Don, let the silence of the room settle around her.

Then she unfolded the sheaf of papers and started reading.

CHAPTER 7

Tel Aviv, Israel

Rachel wondered if the fluorescent lights in these conference rooms were designed as a subtle torture device. The slight buzz, the harsh glare, the high-frequency flicker. That would be something the Israeli government would do, she thought.

The windowless room, located deep in the bowels of the Defense Ministry headquarters, was a beige, all-purpose meeting room with whiteboards along the front wall. The smudged shadows of past writing were barely visible on the dirty white expanse.

Today, the interior was mostly empty and the remaining furniture arranged courtroom-style, with a four-person panel at the front of the room and a small table at which she sat next to Noam Glantz, her boss. Their table was bare save for a clear pitcher of water flanked by two inverted glasses and a spidery black microphone for each of them.

Neither she nor Noam had notes, and their mobile phones had been deposited in an EM-shielded box in the hall.

Noam slumped in his chair, his heavy belly straining at his belt, the buttons on his shirt almost giving up the ghost in their effort to hold back his girth. He looked glum, like a bored toad, the corners of his lips turned down, his jowls overflowing his collar.

His expression was an act. This was his version of a look of contrition that might make the panel take pity on this poor case officer and his rogue field operative.

"This board of inquiry will come to order." The speaker was a young man, barely Rachel's age, but brimming with bureaucratic zeal. He had a reedy voice and trendy horn-rimmed glasses. He was flanked by two women, both dark-haired and middle-aged; one wore glasses. Their body language indicated to Rachel that they were perfectly willing to defer to their younger colleague.

Rachel glanced at Noam, but he just stared straight ahead. The lead investigator's manner gave her pause. She had scant experience with these inquiries, but she would have been more comfortable with a bureaucrat who didn't look so . . . *eager.* She wondered, had the more senior investigators fobbed off a sensitive case on the new guy so they didn't get any political blood spatter on their shoes?

She was sworn in and Noam was roused long enough for the same, then resumed his glum silence. The panel did not introduce themselves.

"This inquiry is into the lawful execution of Abdul

Wenje in Mozambique in May of this year by officer Rachel Jaeger," the young man with the reedy voice said.

Rachel straightened, acknowledging her name with a nod.

Reedy Voice continued, "You were ordered to infiltrate the local population in this section of Mozambique, locate the target, and eliminate him. Is that correct?"

Rachel nodded.

"The witness will please provide a verbal response to all questions," Reedy Voice said.

"Yes," Rachel said, leaning toward the microphone.

"Can you describe the nature of the execution method you were ordered to use?"

Rachel took a deep breath. "The subject was a habitual user of anabolic steroids, so I was given a small syringe to dose the target. The plan was to make his death seem like an accidental heart attack."

"And what was your operating status?"

"Deep cover," Rachel said. "No backup. This was a low-risk operation, easily handled by a single operator, but required the ability to fit into the local population and get close to the target."

Rachel wondered if she should speak more plainly. Her Ethiopian heritage and language skills made her one of the few Mossad agents suitable for the job. Noam stirred and rested his elbows on the table.

"Steady," he said in a low voice.

"Did you have something to add, sir?" Reedy Voice asked.

Noam shook his head.

Rachel continued, "The operation was designed to maintain a low profile. For political considerations."

The logic of these operations never worked out in her head. Terrorists killed Israeli citizens. The government of Israel wanted the terrorists dead. But no one wanted it to show up in the newspapers.

Reedy Voice interrupted her thoughts. "And was the operation successful?"

Rachel leaned toward the microphone. "Abdul Wenje is dead. The operation was successful."

Reedy Voice's brows bunched together. "Did you have information that suggested your cover may have been compromised prior to the assassination attempt?"

Noam finally stirred. "Sir, this was not an attempt. The job was completed. Satisfactorily."

Reedy Voice's tone went sharp. "Let me rephrase my question: Did you maintain a low profile, as instructed?"

In her report, Rachel had been open about Neema's warning that her cover might have been compromised. She could have left it out, but what was the point? They always found out. Always. Better to be honest about every detail up front and deal with the consequences than be called a liar later.

"I was working with a local prostitute who had provided valuable information in other contexts. I deemed her to be reliable."

One of the female panel members spoke up. "How does that work?" Her voice betrayed a hint of distaste that set Rachel's teeth on edge.

"The street girls in that region are mostly from neighboring Tanzania, there to make money to send home. We have observed how al-Shabab often used prostitutes as proxies to gather information about corruption within the local police department. They're called the Mata Hari network. We used the same infrastructure for our operation."

The woman pressed the point. "And you considered their information reliable?"

Rachel shrugged. "I was satisfied."

The woman did not seem to share Rachel's assessment, but Reedy interrupted her. "Back to the matter at hand, Ms. Jaeger. Were you compromised?"

For Noam's benefit, Rachel pretended to consider Reedy's question. Then she said, "I decided it was worth the risk."

Her answer was greeted with a scowl. "So, you proceeded to enter the bar and make contact with the target, is that correct?"

Rachel remembered every detail of Estrella's Bar like it was last night. The tacky beer signs, the Scotsman who tried to hit on her, and Abdul Wenje's sleeves rolled up to show off his magnificent biceps as he leaned his chair against the back wall.

But now she saw details she had missed. The way Wenje watched her as he checked his mobile phone every few moments and sent out text messages.

She'd broken the cardinal rule of her business, the thing that kept field officers alive: Patience. The willingness to walk away. If she had been less anxious to finish the job, she might have broken off contact and figured out another way to get Wenje.

Now she was dealing with the consequences of her decision.

"And what was the result of your contact with the target?" Reedy asked.

"It was a trap," Rachel said.

"Can you elaborate, please?" The smugness had returned.

"The plan was to make contact with Wenje as an undercover prostitute, lure him to the beach with the promise of sex, and inject him with the drug that I had hidden in my purse."

"And what happened?" Reedy's tone took on a slight note of triumph.

Rachel made eye contact with every member of the panel. Reedy leaned toward her, but the others pretended to find their paperwork intensely interesting.

"I made contact with the target," Rachel said. "I lured him out of the bar and convinced him to go to the beach with me. It was a setup. On the way to the beach, we were intercepted by a second man, one of Wenje's, who had the body of my informant with him."

"That's when you realized you had been betrayed by your informant?"

Rachel recalled the bloody pulp that had been Neema's face. She saw the flash of her neon-yellow halter top in the dim light of the alley.

"I was not betrayed," she said. "The informant was tortured. Beaten to death."

Reedy's bright demeanor dimmed a notch. "I see."

"Then I completed my mission," Rachel said.

"You just stated that a second man arrived, so you continued your mission?"

"I said I completed my mission," Rachel said. "I had two men who wanted to kill me. I killed them first."

Reedy exchanged glances with the rest of the panel. "You administered the poison to the target?"

Rachel shook her head. "I used the poison on the second man. I was forced to kill the primary target by other means."

"Other means? What other means?"

Rachel leaned toward the microphone. "I killed him with my shoe."

The two women on the panel gasped and Reedy looked uncomfortable. "You killed him with your shoe?"

Out of the corner of her eye, Rachel saw Noam lift his head. There was a tiny upward teasing of the corners of his mouth. He was enjoying this.

"I was wearing high heels." She held her fingers apart to show the height of the heel. "It was a weapon of opportunity. I used the pointy part and jammed it into his brain."

Reedy struggled to regain his composure.

"I see," he said. "And then you dispatched the second man using the poison which was originally intended for the target. Is that correct?"

"That is correct."

He cleared his throat. "Thank you for your testimony, Ms. Jaeger. If you could please wait in the hall while we consider this case."

Rachel paced up and down the deserted hall, her high

heels tapping on the shiny linoleum. She hugged her arms across her chest in the chill of the air-conditioning.

"What the hell was that all about, Noam?" she said. "Who was that guy?"

Noam shrugged, a gentle heave of his broad shoulders. "Some politician's kid probably. They give him a few cases and he feels special because he talked to field operatives like yourself. This was supposed to be a formality." He glared at Rachel. "Did you have to tell them about the high heels? Your report said 'weapon of opportunity,' right? You could have left it at that."

Rachel grinned. "Did you see the look on his face when I told him?"

Noam's angry exterior cracked and he laughed, a deep rumbling in his chest. "High-heeled shoe . . . that was a good one."

The door to the inquiry room opened and one of the female panel members beckoned them back into the room. When Rachel and Noam had reseated themselves, Reedy took charge of the proceedings again.

"In the judgment of this panel the actions of Officer Rachel Jaeger in the lawful execution of terrorist Abdul Wenje were justified." His eyes glared at her over the rim of his glasses. "However, the panel is concerned about Ms. Jaeger's attitude toward the sensitive nature of kill operations. Specifically, the low-profile nature of this mission was designated to minimize international tensions. Her actions led to potential compromise of the Israeli government and she should be administratively disciplined for her error in judgment."

As the panel vacated the room, Rachel leaned over

to Noam. "So, you're going to administratively discipline me?" She smiled wickedly.

Noam's massive head swiveled toward her. He did not appear to be sharing her sense of amusement. "You're ordered back to Scorpion's Ascent. Immediately."

CHAPTER 8

Seattle, Washington

Dusty's Bar was sandwiched between a sushi restaurant and an ice cream shop advertising something called the Volcano Sundae. The narrow entrance, framed in distressed wood and set back from the street, was a black glass door that offered no hint of the interior.

JP pushed inside and waited for his eyes to adjust to the dimness. This was his final stop of a whirlwind recruiting trip around the world. After Madagascar, he had gone to Egypt, then two stops in Europe and now the United States. His body was time-zone confused and all he wanted to do was go home to Talia.

But first, he had one more deal to strike.

Rustic wood tables and matching chairs dotted the room. Ancient iron stools lined a bar made to look like an old-style saloon with a mirrored back wall. The waitresses wore cowboy hats, short denim miniskirts, and tight gingham shirts tied up to bare their midriffs. The air smelled of stale beer and the mildewed sawdust that covered the floor.

A row of worn leather-cushioned booths lined the far wall. The only person in the place at 2:00 P.M. on a Wednesday afternoon occupied a booth far from the window. He hunched over his phone. In front of him, lined up precisely, were three long-neck beer bottles and three empty shot glasses.

JP had grown a salt-and-pepper goatee, and he wore round tortoiseshell eyeglasses. He approached the booth slowly, shuffling his feet as he moved. He allowed his shoulders to slump inside his worn tweed jacket.

"Jason Winslow? Dr. Jason Winslow?" Instead of his normal confident baritone he phrased everything with a questioning lilt on the end. Apologetically, as if he expected the answer to be no.

"Who's asking?" Winslow replied without looking up. He wasn't slurring his words yet, but he was well on his way to drunkenness.

"May I buy you a drink?" JP asked.

The question earned him a look away from the phone. JP quickly averted his gaze.

"Well?" Winslow let the question hang in the air.

JP extended his hand slowly, hesitantly. "My name is Harold Mortimer," he said. "I'm from . . ." He paused, lowering his voice. "I represent . . ." JP named a Fortune 500 genetics company based in the US.

Winslow slid out of the booth and stood to shake JP's hand. The shorter man came to JP's shoulder and his midsection sagged over his beltline. JP's top-down view of Winslow confirmed that the man had dyed his thinning hair and wore a toupee over his bald spot, neither of which did anything to make him look younger than his fifty-seven years. He wore contacts that left his eyes looking irritated and yellowed.

He was a repulsive human being, but necessary. JP smiled as they shook hands.

Winslow repeated the name of the company in a loud voice. "Why didn't you say so?"

JP lowered his voice again. "I am here . . . I'm here on a matter of some delicacy."

Winslow's eyes narrowed. "Delicacy? I don't understand."

He was fishing, JP knew. Trying to figure out whether JP knew about his suspension from the university. Better to let him dangle a bit.

"I was hoping we could talk a bit about your work?" JP said.

Winslow relaxed, revealing a gap between his two prominent front teeth. He raised his hand and snapped his fingers at the waitress deep in conversation with the bartender.

"Jenny, babe, bring us a couple of drinks, willya?" The girl at the bar rolled her eyes but nodded. Winslow pointed to the open side of the booth and reseated himself. He swept the empty shot glasses and beer bottles against the wall.

He grinned at JP. "I like to come here on Wednesday afternoons. I've got my eye on that little number over there at the bar." He jerked his chin toward Jenny, still at the bar.

The waitress overheard them. "In your dreams, Jason."

Winslow blew her a kiss, then turned back to JP. "You said you wanted to talk about my work?"

JP nodded, overdoing the gesture like he was nervous. "Yes, please, I'd like to hear the progress you've made at your dig site."

Winslow leaned back into the cushions of the booth and spread his hands across the table. "We've made magnificent progress. Our preliminary samples indicate we've discovered an ancient settlement. The permafrost up there is like one enormous freezer. Specimens are preserved in pristine condition. So far, we've found mastodon bones, stone tools, pottery shards—"

"Any human remains?" JP asked.

Winslow looked at him sharply. "Not yet, but we're close. When you've spent as much time above the Arctic Circle as I have, you get a feel for these things and I can feel it. This is my life's work. I know what the hell I'm talkin' about."

The laziness in his tone was gone, and his voice took on an intensity that reinforced to JP that he had found his man in Winslow.

"I thought the digging season in that part of the world was short. Isn't it going on right now?"

Winslow's face twisted into a grimace. "Politics," he spat.

Jenny arrived with the drinks, setting a long-neck

beer and a shot glass in front of each man. She side-stepped Winslow's grasping hand. "What do you say, Jenny?" he said. "You and me? After your shift?"

"Fuck off," Jenny said. "And leave a decent tip this time, will you?"

Winslow pretended to wince as if her insult had struck home. "Let me know if you change your mind," he called to her retreating back. She replied with a middle finger.

"It's sort of our thing," Winslow said to JP, exposing his teeth again. "The way Jenny and I josh back and forth. She digs me, I can tell, but she doesn't like people to know that she's dating an older guy, you know what I mean?"

JP kept his expression neutral. "You were saying? About the digging season?"

Winslow knocked back the shot in one gulp, then followed it with a long pull from the beer bottle. "Yeah, politics. That's what I was saying. Politics."

"I don't understand," JP prompted.

"My funding," Winslow said. "The fuckers at the university pulled my funding. This politically correct, liberal-elite bullshit board of regents didn't find my research 'compelling enough' to continue this season." He made mocking air quotes around the term "compelling enough."

JP knew that was a lie. The real reason Winslow lost his funding was because he had been accused of sexual harassment. From what he'd seen in the past five minutes, those accusations were probably all true. But he'd also read Winslow's grant proposal, and for all his vitriol, the man's professional work was sound.

"That's actually why I'm here today," JP said. "I may have a solution to your funding issue."

Winslow stopped in midswallow and set his beer bottle down on the table with a loud clack. "Who are you? I lose my funding and one week later you show up. That seems pretty fortuitous to me."

"My firm likes to keep abreast of these kinds of developments," JP said. "And take advantage of new opportunities."

"New opportunities?" Winslow eyed him, his eyes greedy. "Let me guess: You fund me and keep all the results to yourself. You put your name all over my research, right? That's what you're after. I get this close"—he held his thumb and forefinger an inch apart—"and then you rush in and steal the spotlight." He seized the beer bottle and drank the rest of the contents in one go. "No, sir."

JP waited for him to calm down. This was the most delicate part of the manipulation. Too eager and Winslow would be suspicious. Too slow and Winslow would think he was being strung along.

"We don't want to be named in your research at all," JP said. "We wish to remain anonymous. The only thing we want is first access to your samples for our own research."

"First access? What does that mean?"

"When you make a find—a human find—you let me harvest samples," JP said. "The rest is up to you. You never see me again. You publish whatever you want. We want nothing other than first access to biological samples."

JP could see Winslow calculating, looking for a loophole, trying to see how JP was going to screw him.

"How much?" Winslow asked.

JP took a sip of the beer, ignoring the shot. It was a bland American lager as tasteless as carbonated water. He set the beer back down.

"How much do you need to start right away?" JP replied.

Winslow's eyebrows hiked up. JP saw the wheels turning as the other man tried to figure out how much he could stick this guy for. He already knew Winslow's lost funding from the university had been a hundred thousand dollars for the season.

"To staff a team this late in the season and get them up there as quickly as possible is expensive. We've got eight weeks left . . ." Winslow began. He pretended to do some mental calculations. "I'd say we need two hundred and fifty thousand dollars." He watched JP's face carefully, ready to retract the number if he got a negative reaction.

"How about we make it an even three hundred?" JP replied. "For contingencies."

"That's . . ." Winslow's voice trailed off as he realized he could've asked for more. "That's perfect. How soon can I get it?"

JP slid an envelope across the table. "Fifty thousand dollars cash. Consider that a down payment."

He plucked a folded sheet of paper out of his inner pocket. "This is the banking information for the balance of the funds. The account is anonymous, and we wish to remain that way. Our agreement on first access to samples is between the two of us. Is that clear?"

Winslow fingered the fat envelope. "Absolutely."

JP reached into the other pocket of his jacket and pulled out a slim satellite phone and charger. He set them on the table between them. "When you find what we're looking for, Dr. Winslow, call me immediately. After I have what I need, then the rest is yours. Publish, sell the stuff, get rich. All up to you. Is that clear?"

Winslow nodded and licked his lips. "Perfectly."

"As an added incentive," JP said. "If you find something this season and I'm able to get the samples I need, there will be another envelope for you as a bonus. I hope cash is acceptable?"

Winslow licked his lips. "Cash is fine."

CHAPTER 9

Nadia Hirsi-Simpson sighed as she considered the queue of incoming intercepts on her computer screen. She imagined computers all over the world Hoovering up streams of data from computers, mobile phones, and every other digital device. The data was sifted by algorithms, and suspicious bits were sent to analysts like her for further investigation.

Her eyes slid to the clock in the lower right-hand corner of her monitor. Only one hour to go until the weekend. She had reservations with her husband at the new Indian restaurant on Dupont Circle, then maybe a movie . . . anything but listening in on the conversations of other people from the other side of the planet.

She'd only been to Yemen once, as a teenager, a trip that still stuck with her to this day. The country she remembered was young and vibrant, full of colors and rich smells and wonderful food. But the Yemen she

pictured in her mind as she translated selected intercepts might as well have been another planet. So much
destruction and death . . .

It broke her heart to watch the news here in the US.
The average American couldn't even find the country
of Yemen on a map, much less understand that Iran and
Saudi Arabia were fighting a proxy war on the backs of
the Yemeni people.

She sighed as she highlighted an audio file on her secure terminal. Nadia adjusted her headset and clicked
the little arrow to play the recording.

The file was a poor-quality audio recording of a
woman's voice on a mobile phone, strained across distance and partially unintelligible in places. It sounded
like she was weeping.

"Hamdi!" the voice sobbed. There was a long pause.
"Hamdi, can you hear me?"

"Yes, Zahra. I can hear you." The man was shouting.
"Go ahead. The connection is very bad."

"They're all dead! Everyone in the village is dead."
The digital signal faded and Nadia lost Hamdi's response.

". . . Mira is dead. The children are dead. Everyone
in Yousap." The woman was ranting, repeating herself.
The man tried to stop her, but she just kept going, bab-
bling about dead people and blood and bodies melting. It
made no sense.

Nadia paused the recording and listened to it again.
After tracing the call to the cell tower near the town of
Haydan and studying detailed maps from the National
Geospatial-Intelligence Agency, she finally found a

place called Yousap. It was a flyspeck on the screen, not even dignified with a population estimate.

One eye on the clock, Nadia studied the latest intel. These places were far from the front lines of the fighting. An attack in this remote village made no sense. Nothing added up.

Nadia flagged her supervisor. Mark Gallarita was a heavyset NSA analyst with a perpetual frown and dark hair that flopped into his eyes whenever he moved his head. The Yemen desk was not where Mark wanted to be in his career, and he made that point perfectly clear every day.

"What is it, Nadia?"

She colored slightly, embarrassed. Mark's demeanor was brusque, but she told herself he was just a guy trying to do his best on an assignment that he hated.

"I got a fragment of a cell-phone call," Nadia said. "It sounds like a bunch of civilians are dead."

Mark leaned over her terminal, where she had the maps pulled up.

"The caller made a reference to this village." Nadia pointed to a tiny dot fifteen kilometers past Haydan. "It looks like it's only accessible by footpath, not even a place to drive a car up there. Subsistence farmers, goat herders. Maybe fifty people at the most."

Mark stared at the screen, still silent.

"She was panicked." Nadia realized she was talking faster, trying to convince her supervisor she was right. She tried to calm her voice and slow down. "Said everyone was dead. She mentioned the bodies looked like they were melting."

That piqued Mark's interest. "Melting? Chemical weapons, maybe? But why in the middle of nowhere?"

Nadia tried to backpedal. "Well, I think she said melted. It's a terrible connection and the dialect was tough for me." There were dozens of Arabic dialects in the country of Yemen alone, especially when you went into the deep countryside. Her parents had insisted she learn Arabic when she was growing up, but her parents had both been raised in Sanaa, the capital city of Yemen, and were born to wealth. She could understand the gist of any conversation well enough, but the subtleties might be lost in translation. On reflection, Nadia was increasingly concerned that maybe she was misinterpreting some of the words from the intercepted phone call.

Mark straightened up. "Okay, here's what we're going to do. Send this intel on to the theater commander as unverified. Then get on the horn with Creech and see if we can get a Reaper to make a surveillance pass for us. Maybe they can pick something up from the air."

Nadia nodded, looking at the clock. If she hurried, she might just have enough time to do this before she got off shift. Overtime on Friday night was not in her plans.

She routed a secure call to Creech Air Force Base in Nevada into her headset and spoke to the duty officer. "This is Nadia from the NSA Yemen desk. Requesting a flyby on these coordinates." She read out the location of the tiny village in the mountains of Yemen.

A tired voice repeated the coordinates back. "Stand by, ma'am."

Nadia listened to the Muzak in her headphones until the duty officer came back on the line. "We have an MQ-9 UAV in the area, ma'am," he said, using the official designation of the Air Force Reaper drone. "I've emailed you a secure link to the drone feed and I'm patching you through to the operator now."

Her phone clicked and a new voice came on the line. "NSA, this is your pilot, Charlie," the voice drawled. "To whom do I have the pleasure of speaking on this fine day?"

"Hello, Charlie, this is Nadia from the Yemen desk in DC."

"Well, welcome aboard, Nadia. Please place your tray tables in an upright and locked position and fasten your seat belt. You will be seeing a live feed from my drone in three . . . two . . . one . . . mark."

Nadia's screen popped to life, showing an image of the mountainous Yemen countryside at night using a high-definition, low-light camera. A three-quarter moon cast the scene in silver.

"Looks like it's about one in the morning in lovely Yemen, Nadia. Our low-light cameras are pretty good, so I'll do a visual pass first, okay?"

"Acknowledged." She raised her hand to beckon Mark to her desk and handed him a spare set of headphones.

The mountain hamlet of Yousap came into view on her screen. To call it a village was an insult to villages. It consisted of ten structures bisected by a footpath barely large enough to accommodate a donkey cart. A few crude corrals surrounded the buildings and some gardens.

"I believe that is our target, Nadia. Looks like a lovely rustic—make that *very* rustic—hideaway. What are we looking for?"

Nadia quickly filled him in on the basic situation.

"Roger that. The fastest way to tell if we have any warm bodies is to use infrared. Stand by."

The screen updated to show a ghostly image of heat gradients. Nadia could make out at least a dozen person-shaped images with barely perceptible heat signatures. Inside one of the houses, she made out a warm body—probably the woman who made the phone call.

Charlie's voice was subdued when he spoke again. "Based on what I am seeing here, Nadia, I would say we have a whole lot of recently dead or dying people in this little burg."

Nadia leaned closer to the screen. "Concur, Charlie. I'd like to see if we can ascertain a cause of death. The eyewitness described the dead as looking like they had melted."

"Roger that. Let me see how much detail I can get for you. Stand by."

Nadia and Mark watched as the remote pilot increased magnification. Charlie's voice sharpened. "Nadia, we have a high-speed incoming bogey on an intercept vector."

"I don't understand, Charlie. What is—"

An aircraft entered the field of view. Charlie froze the image and Nadia was able to make out the desert camouflage painted on the top of the fuselage and the seal of the Royal Saudi Air Force.

"Jesus," Mark said, "that's an F-15E."

"Nadia," Charlie said, "we have been ordered by in-theater commander to vacate. Breaking off now."

"Charlie, wait!" Nadia said. "Give us a visual of the target for as long as you can."

There was no reply from the pilot, but the image stayed on her screen.

The F-15E released a weapon from under its wing. It streaked down toward the tiny hamlet of Yousap. Seconds later, the mountaintop erupted in a ball of flame.

"Laser-guided bomb," Mark whispered. "Two-thousand-pounder. Enough to vaporize a city block. What the fuck is going on over there?"

"Nadia, this is Charlie. It's been a pleasure, but I'm outta here."

Nadia's screen went dead.

"That woman was alive," Nadia said. "We saw her heat signature. She was the one who made the call."

Mark blew out a long breath and pushed his glasses up his nose. "We don't know that for sure, Nadia." He stripped off his headphones and handed them to her. "We don't know what happened. It's a war zone over there, and for all we know that heat signature might have been the next Osama bin Laden."

Nadia stared at him until Mark looked away.

"All right, I'll tell you what. There's a new group over at CIA called Emerging Threats. My new standing orders are if it smells funny and doesn't fit in our mission, we're supposed to send it over to the ET group."

"The ET group. Really?" Nadia looked askance at her supervisor.

"Hey, if this was chemical warfare, it certainly falls outside our normal mission."

Nadia looked at the clock on her screen. Quarter past five.

"Fine. Emerging Threats it is."

CHAPTER 10

Grand Ethiopian Renaissance Dam, Guba, Ethiopia

Over the course of his years working on the site of the Grand Ethiopian Renaissance Dam, Seifu had seen the project grow from an airstrip next to a river in the middle of the desert to a concrete-and-steel mountain that spanned that same river.

For the first year it seemed that the number of workers on the site doubled every day. In the early days, the site crawled with earthmoving equipment. Bulldozers, dump trucks, backhoes. The ground shook with blasting all through the day and night as the workers scraped away the desert down to bare rock.

They built a concrete plant and all day and night trucks carried wet concrete from the plant to the dam site, where even more workers had put together enormous spiderwebs of steel rebar. They poured the cement into molds, layer by layer replacing the earth they had scraped away.

In its place, they left a stepped mountain of man-made stone across the river. At night, after he was done with his driving for the day, Seifu would go to the highest point above the dam and look out over the upstream valley. Below him, men worked in the glare of lights, building yet another layer of the dam.

He tried to imagine what it would look like when the desert was covered with blue water as far as the eye could see. It was hard to picture, but the engineers said it would happen and he believed them.

When he first started at the work site, Seifu's plan was to earn enough money to go back to school. He wanted to be an engineer, or maybe an architect.

But that was years ago and he was still just a driver. His job would last as long as there was a single worker on the site. It didn't matter if his customers were engineers or truck drivers or janitors, they all had one thing in common.

They all had to eat. Seifu drove a food truck.

His menu was simple. In the mornings, he served *kinche,* a mix of boiled grains seasoned with a spiced butter. In the afternoons, he offered *wat,* a thick stew, and a side of *injera* flatbread.

His portions were large, his prices reasonable. Everyone knew Seifu's battered white Toyota pickup truck with the blue tarp canopy. Twice a day, he was waved through security checkpoints as he made his rounds.

Occasionally, he made some extra money by carrying a package past the guards into the work site. He knew they were probably drugs, but the extra cash was always welcome and he didn't see any harm in it.

When a man approached him late one afternoon with a request to carry something into the lower dam build site, Seifu didn't think anything of it. He quoted the man his normal rate.

"My package is large," the man said.

Seifu didn't recognize the man. He was tall, at least two meters, with broad shoulders and biceps that strained the elastic of his blue polo shirt. His hard hat was brand new, as was his yellow safety vest. He also had an accent, but that wasn't unusual. There were thousands of workers from all over Ethiopia and Sudan, and they changed all the time.

"How big?" Seifu asked.

The man spread his arms about a meter apart. He indicated a half meter of height and width.

Seifu shook his head. "Too big. Won't fit in my truck."

"I can pay," the man replied. "Name your price."

Seifu wasn't about to fall for that trick. He shook his head and started to get up.

"Wait." The man clamped his hand on Seifu's arm. With his free hand, he pulled a wad of cash—American dollars—from his pocket. "I told you I can pay."

The outer bill was a crisp one-hundred-dollar note.

"Two hundred," Seifu said. "And fifty."

The man released his arm and peeled the top one-hundred-dollar bill off. There was another one underneath.

"I'll meet you here in the morning," the man said. "You'll get the rest of the money after I load the crate."

All through the evening, Seifu's conscience nagged at him. Smuggling in a small package was one thing, but an entire crate? Yet every time he shifted position, the crisp bill crinkled in his pocket.

The next morning, a dusty black SUV was parked next to Seifu's food truck. The man he had met the day before got out of the passenger side. He raised the rear hatch. Inside was a black plastic Pelican case, like the kind the surveyors used to store their sensitive equipment.

It was also much bigger than Seifu had expected. Too big to fit into the back of his truck once all the food was loaded.

"I can't do this," Seifu said. "It's too big."

The driver's-side door opened and a second man got out. He was even bigger than his partner, dressed in blue jeans and an untucked shirt. "Is there a problem, Rocky?"

"No problem, Kasim," the first man replied. "We just need to make it fit."

The driver pointed to the cab of Seifu's food truck. "Put it up front."

===

"What's in the crate, Seifu?" the guard at the lower dam site asked through the open window. "Dessert?"

Seifu had fended off the question at every checkpoint on his route, so the answer was rote by now. "The engineers asked me to carry it for them."

"Your problem is that you're too nice, Seifu," the guard laughed. "Save some *kinche* for me, okay?"

Seifu wanted to wave back, but the enormous crate hindered his movement. It had taken all three of them to fit the heavy case into the cab, and it jammed

Seifu's frame up against the driver's-side door, but it was worth it. Three crisp hundred-dollar bills crinkled in his pocket.

As soon as he parked his truck, he would finally get rid of the thing. All he had to do was call the mobile number the man had given him and someone would come to pick it up. The man had warned him—three times—not to call the number until he reached the lower dam site.

He parked his pickup in the shade of a dump truck. Even at ten in the morning, the sun hammered down on the lower dam site, turning the shallow bowl into an oven.

All over the work area, men were dropping tools and heading his way. Seifu smiled to himself. Today, he'd made a month's salary before breakfast.

He opened the truck door and slipped his mobile from his pocket. He dialed the number the man had given him.

The phone on the other end rang once.

Behind him, Seifu heard a ringing exactly matched with his mobile.

He twisted around. His mobile rang again and he heard the response.

Seifu placed his ear against the black Pelican case. The ringing was coming from inside the case.

―――――――――――

On a hilltop overlooking the Grand Ethiopian Renaissance Dam site, two men sat inside a black SUV. The man in the passenger seat watched the lower dam site through a pair of field glasses.

Far below them, there was a bright flash, a mushroom of dirt and rock. A second later, the sound of the blast reached them, and their vehicle rocked gently.

The driver fist-bumped his passenger, then thumbed his mobile down to a saved number.

"Sir, it's done."

CHAPTER 11

Tysons Corner, Virginia

It was still dark outside when Michael Goodwin pulled into the parking lot of E-Tech Ltd., the new home of the Emerging Threats group.

The TechWorld business park on the outskirts of Washington, DC, looked like any other suburban collection of nondescript, three-and four-story office buildings surrounded by generous parking lots. The concrete-and-glass structures were not unattractive, but also not eye-catching. The gaze of any passerby would glide over them as just another boring business park.

But a close observer might notice government license plates sprinkled among the cars. Not that unusual for northern Virginia. Perhaps a defense contractor, one might guess.

The truly astute would begin to notice the sheer number of cameras in the area. They were located on the corner of every building and atop every one of the overhead lights in the parking areas; it was impossible to approach the TechWorld business park without being monitored. And finally, there was the cluster of antennas and other communications gear on top of some of these buildings.

Even at this early hour, there were a sizable number of vehicles parked around the E-Tech building. Michael parked his new BMW 330i well away from the other cars and stepped into the early-morning humidity.

When Michael pulled open the front door of E-Tech, he entered a hundred-square-foot enclosed box of bulletproof glass. This was one of two entrances to this secure building: the front door and an underground loading dock. Both were guarded by independent teams of two security professionals, armed, willing, and able to use deadly force should the need arise.

He faced the camera over the front door for a facial-recognition scan. ID cards were not used here. Your biometrics were your security card in this facility.

He heard the snap of a magnetic lock and the doors parted.

"Good morning," Michael called to the young woman dressed in a dark blue business suit sitting behind a reception desk. Her eyes followed him to the heavy door leading to the offices. She buzzed him in as soon as his hand touched the door handle. In addition to the Glock nine-millimeter in her holster, the receptionist had the ability to lock down the entire building with the touch of a button. If the desk agent was incapacitated, her two compatriots located in the security office behind the wall mural of the foyer would take over.

After a stop for coffee, Michael settled into his office chair with a sigh of satisfaction. He liked to get into the office early so he could plan his day before anyone else showed up.

The screen saver showed a detailed map of the Nile River basin. His latest project was an analysis of the water-security issues of the region. His eye traced the thin band of green that wound through brown deserts in Egypt, Sudan, Ethiopia, and Eritrea. For centuries, the Nile River had been the thread on which their lives had hung.

But all that was changing now, and swiftly.

The commissioning of the Merowe High Dam north of Khartoum, Sudan, brought much-needed flood control and energy to the host nation, but heightened tensions between Egypt and its southern neighbors.

Meanwhile, on the Blue Nile, Ethiopia and Eritrea, two of the poorest countries in the world, had finally resolved a decades-long territorial dispute. A 2018 peace treaty provided much-needed stability, and foreign investment flooded into the region. The Grand Ethiopian Renaissance Dam, or GERD, would be the largest hydroelectric power plant in Africa and a massive development boost for the region.

But water resource allocation was a zero-sum game. Gains by Ethiopia and Sudan were Egypt's loss. At least, that was what some politicians in the region were stating.

Don had been correct to target this region as a potential flash point. The region was a double threat. Terrorist groups looked for existing points of conflict to exploit for their own gain, and the Nile River basin was a tinderbox waiting for a match. It was just a matter of time before ISIS refugees set up shop in this volatile region.

Even more concerning were the Iranians. As they lost ground to the Saudis in the Yemen proxy war, there was growing concern that Iran might try to open up a new front on the opposite side of the Red Sea.

Either scenario was a perfect fit for Emerging Threats.

As he did every morning, Michael scanned the English-language news sources from the region looking for anything with the potential to escalate. The classified intel briefings would come out later in the morning. This was his way of staying in touch with how the news media outlets saw the ebbs and flows of the regional happenings.

A news alert from Al Jazeera flashed up on the screen: *Hundreds dead in car bomb attack.*

Michael clicked on the link. Under the blaring BREAKING NEWS banner, a dark-haired man in a navy-blue suit was speaking at the camera.

". . . a vehicle-based improvised explosive device claimed the lives of hundreds of workers at the Grand Ethiopian Renaissance Dam today in western Ethiopia . . ."

The picture over the anchor's shoulder showed the carnage of a massive car bomb—a blackened crater, an overturned dump truck, emergency-response vehicles, and working men in yellow safety vests carrying people.

In the background, an enormous concrete structure rose up in tiers. Michael clicked on the printed news story and scanned the contents with growing concern. A bomb hidden in a food truck had been detonated in the lower dam basin. Hundreds of workers were killed or injured. The bombers had chosen the spot carefully. The concave structure of the lower basin concentrated the blast to maximize the casualties.

Finally, at the bottom of the page, Michael saw what he was looking for: a claim of attribution.

The Mahdi. Michael had never heard of any terrorist group named the Mahdi. He performed an unclassified web search and got an immediate hit.

Michael stared at the screen. The website was a simple black homepage with a two-line message in the center of the screen:

The Day of Judgment is upon us.
The Mahdi has returned.

It took Michael a moment to realize that the website had recognized his originating ISP and translated the text on the screen to match his native language. That was high-level programming, not commonly found on a stand-up site for a terrorist group.

He clicked on the link, and a video came up. A prompt box popped onto his screen: Choose your language.

A terrorist website that asked for his language preference to view a video?

Intrigued now, he clicked on English.

His screen shifted to a high-definition video of a well-appointed room with colorful rugs on the floor, a low-slung Arab-style floor sofa with plush pillows, and a rich tapestry along the back wall.

A man stepped into the frame, his face and hands blurred to avoid identification. When the man spoke, although his voice had been run through a synthesizer, he spoke excellent English.

"For too long, the infidels have used their money and their power and their weapons to subjugate the children of Islam. No more. I am the Mahdi, the Redeemer, the Reborn, the Uniter.

"The Day of Judgment is nearly upon us. I call on all people of this region to reject all foreign investment in the Bahr al-Nīl, the Nile River basin. Anyone who accepts money from infidels or participates in building programs by infidels is subject to the wrath of the Mahdi.

"By now you have seen what I am capable of doing, but I do not condone violence. I honor life and faith. I am the Mahdi. Follow me."

When the video ended, Michael played it again. It was short, no more than a minute, but well produced, with excellent graphics and background music. He was willing to guess that the blurring tech on the man's face and hands and the voice synthesizer work were both top-notch.

Whoever this Mahdi was, he had skills. He was just about to watch the video again when Janet entered the office.

"We've got something," he said. Janet crowded close to his screen as he replayed the video for her.

"They want your language preference?" she asked.

Michael replayed the video a fourth time. "And that's not all. The quality of this production is all top-notch stuff. If these guys are ISIS castoffs, they have seriously upped their game."

"Have you told Don about this yet?"

When Michael shook his head, Janet picked up the phone. A few minutes later, Don was standing behind Michael's workstation.

He crossed his arms and listened with pursed lips as Michael demonstrated what he had found and gave them both the highlights on the tech used to produce the video.

"Have you tried to break into the website yet?" Don asked.

"I was just getting there," Michael replied. He shifted his screen to look at the website coding and immediately ran into a firewall.

"Hmmm." Michael opened a second screen and pulled up his tool kit.

After a few minutes, he sat back. "These guys are good," he said. "Really good. This might take some time. If Dre were here, she could knock it out much faster than me."

Don clapped Michael on the shoulder.

"You leave Dre Ramirez to me, Michael," he said. "Stay on this lead. This is what we've been waiting for."

CHAPTER 12

Mossad training facility, Negev Desert, Israel

Rachel fell in love with Scorpion's Ascent the first day Mossad sent her there.

She fell out of love with Scorpion's Ascent the very next day.

The Mossad special operations training center was deep in the Negev Desert in southern Israel. The landscape was stark. Long reaches of bare mountains and ancient wadis, carved by millennia of wind and water into fantastic shapes. A few kilometers to the west, tourists climbed the famed Scorpion's Ascent, unaware that some of the deadliest killers in the world trained within their sight.

The setting was beautiful, the trainers were top-notch, the facilities were outstanding, and it was unbelievably boring.

The routine of the facility was ironclad. Early mornings were spent with physical training, followed by breakfast. The rest of the morning hours were spent in the classroom on language training. In addition to Hebrew, Rachel already had decent Arabic, strong English and Portuguese, native fluency in Amharic from her Ethiopian heritage, and conversational Somali. Her new course of study had her learning a Sudanese dialect of Arabic as well as branching out into French.

After lunch, they trained with small arms, a different handgun or rifle each day, so they were familiar with whatever weapon was available on a mission. On alternate afternoons, they trained with knives or hand-to-hand combat techniques.

Rachel liked to take a long swim before dinner or get a massage. After-dinner hours were filled with intel briefings.

The days passed like carbon copies of one another. The schedule varied not at all. Even the intelligence briefings began to sound the same.

And that was the problem. All Rachel really wanted was another assignment, something far from this contained existence. Someplace where she knew no one. Someplace where she was forced to expend her entire intellectual and physical capacity to stay alive.

Rachel never intended to pursue a career as an Israeli agent. She had been studying for a doctorate in African languages and literature when Mossad first approached her. She was under no illusion why they had come to her and they did not do her the disservice of pretending otherwise. They were looking for officers of color, operatives who could blend into the population on the African continent.

She accepted their invitation for a weekend seminar on a lark, thinking it might make good fodder for a book one day. In the space of those two days, she met her future husband and found her vocation in life.

Her relationship with Levi lasted less than two years, ending when her husband's remains came home in a container the size of a shoebox. Her relationship with Mossad lasted for the rest of her life. The staff psychologists told Rachel she had an addiction to adrenaline, to action, to running away from her problems.

They were right, but she didn't care. She was good at her job. For her, that was reason enough to keep going.

One psychologist, after hearing about Levi's death, wrote in her consultation notes that Rachel was searching for her own shoebox. Rachel had a hard time disagreeing with the woman.

But until then, she lived for the next mission. The next opportunity to suspend her existence as Rachel Jaeger and become someone else.

On a mission, there was no past, no future, only the now. Constant movement, constant awareness. On a mission, no one had time for regrets.

After dinner, she often took a short hike into the desert just as the sun was setting. The brutal heat of the day waned in these moments and she loved the way the setting sun turned the barren landscape into a rich palette of deep reds, purples, and blues. This was her meditation, her one moment of the day when she stilled her mind and tried to be at peace.

After a few days at Scorpion's Ascent, there was no peace for Rachel.

At the end of each day, before she went to bed, Rachel sent a message to her *kidon* leader. A reminder that she was still waiting.

What do you have for me? she would text Noam.

Be patient, he would always text back.

But patience was the one quality Rachel Jaeger lacked.

CHAPTER 13

World Health Organization, Eastern Mediterranean Office, Cairo, Egypt

Sven Gunderson was a tired man. He ran his hands through his thinning white-blond hair and squinted at his computer screen again. The rumor in the ranks was that the organization was set to raise the retirement age from sixty to sixty-five. But they wouldn't make it effective until the end of next year, so if he made his decision now . . .

He moved to his window overlooking the streets of Nasr City, Cairo. This was a quiet suburb, with safe streets and walled gardens shaded by palm trees. Yet, only a kilometer away were teeming streets and squalor.

He was fifty-nine now, almost sixty. If he announced his retirement soon, he would be in compliance with current rules and could use the long transition period to train his replacement.

His replacement . . . another issue to solve. Headquarters would want one of their own, but this region needed someone with real field experience, not some bureaucrat from Geneva looking to bolster his résumé.

The Eastern Med had been rocked by the Arab Spring. And where there was political chaos, disease followed. Syria, Yemen, Somalia, Tunisia—he'd been on the ground in all of them . . . and he was tired.

Sven deserved retirement. Someplace warm. Someplace that was not Cairo.

When he was a young doctor, fresh out of medical school in Stockholm, he wanted to save the world. Now he wanted to save himself from the world.

He turned back to his desk, decided. He would draft his retirement letter this weekend and schedule a sit-down with the secretary-general at the next meeting in Geneva.

The intercom on his desk buzzed. "Sven, Dr. Tahir is here. She doesn't have an appointment. Should I set up something for later in the week?"

Sven hurried back to his desk. "No, I'll see her now."

Talia Tahir—she would be an interesting choice as his replacement, he mused. An unconventional choice, but with so many positive attributes. A woman, with deep experience in the region, and impeccable professional credentials. A magnificent young doctor, Madame Curie in the body of a supermodel, someone had once commented to Sven.

He pinched his lip. Yes, Talia Tahir could be a perfect choice as his replacement.

At the same time, Talia showing up for an unannounced visit with the head of the office was a flashing red warning sign. He'd seen this story play out many times in his career.

A young doctor joins the WHO wanting to save the world . . . until they get a taste of what the world can do. There was so much pain and suffering out there, and the WHO staff saw the worst of it. The Ebola outbreak of 2017, for example. He and Talia had been in Sierra Leone together, working side by side eighteen hours a day, seven days a week.

Most new recruits lasted no more than a few years before the world broke them. Talia had been here for eight years and most of it in the field. It was time she made a move into management, before the organization lost her to the private sector.

He punched the button on his phone again. "Shani, please bring in coffee, will you?"

The door to his office opened, and Talia Tahir stepped in. Tall and slim, with flowing auburn tresses and skin the color of molten caramel. An open white lab coat covered a sleeveless dark blue sheath dress that fit her figure like a glove and set off her brilliant blue eyes. She crossed the room with an easy, confident stride.

"Talia," he said, as he kissed her on both cheeks. "You're just back from Yemen, right?"

She smelled heavenly, a subtle mixture of jasmine and musk that evoked smoldering innocence. He ushered her to the sitting area in his office.

"I'm so glad you stopped by," he said. "Please, have a seat."

His heart sank at the sight of a manila folder in her

hand. Talia would be one of the prepared ones, the kind who would bring a signed resignation letter to a meeting like this.

Shani brought in the coffee service, a welcome chance to gather his wits. Talia took over from the secretary, pouring the thick, sweet liquid from the copper *cezve* into two brightly painted cups.

"There's something I'd like to discuss with you, Sven," Talia said, her voice low and professional.

Sven accepted the cup and saucer. She had managed to achieve the exact right amount of foam on the top of the liquid.

"Well, that makes two of us," he said. "I have something I'd like to discuss with you."

A tiny crease formed on Talia's brow when she thought hard about a problem. "You should probably hear what I have to say first."

Sven eyed the manila folder. He needed to take charge of this situation. He could not afford to lose this doctor from his team.

"If you don't mind, Talia, I insist on exercising my prerogative as your supervisor." He put his drink down and rested his folded hands on his crossed knees. "You know how much I appreciate the work you've done for this organization."

Talia started to protest, but he stopped her with a gesture.

"You are a gem," he said. "You've been to Yemen— what? Three times in the past six months? Before that, Syria, the Congo, Sierra Leone. There is no assignment too tough for you, no ask too big.

"I think it's time this organization showed its appreciation for your truly remarkable work. I'm leaving in the new year, and I want you to take over this office."

He returned to his coffee, enjoying the surprised expression on her face.

It was Talia's turn to set down her saucer. She picked up the manila folder, and Sven's heart dropped. He'd missed the warning signs. Big Pharma would snap up this experienced doctor in a split second. He'd been so wrapped up in his retirement planning, he'd blown it.

"Now I feel like a heel," she said. "I need a favor. For a friend."

Sven was so relieved he almost dropped his cup. He took a sip of the sweet dark liquid.

"The Brazzaville office is moving into a new facility," Talia began, "and my friend was in charge of the sample transfer." She gave him a pained smile and blushed. "There were problems and the samples were destroyed."

Sven knew about the new location for the WHO Africa office in the Republic of the Congo.

"Problems? I didn't hear anything," Sven replied, trying not to gush at the fact that she didn't want to resign.

"There was a power failure and . . . Oh, I'll just tell you the whole story. It's going to come out eventually." She threw up her hands.

"There was a malfunction in one of their freezers and they lost all their samples. It wasn't her fault, but she'll get blamed. A woman in that office . . . it's not like here, Sven, with you."

Suppressed tears made Talia's blue eyes sparkle. She took a deep breath and wiped her eyes. "I'm sorry to put you on the spot like this, Sven. She's like a sister to me and this could ruin her whole career."

Sven toyed with his coffee. Each regional office in the WHO was entrusted with a full slate of biological samples of the world's most deadly viruses to use for quick-response comparisons in regional outbreaks. Cryogenic storage was an imperfect solution in places with challenged infrastructure.

Field offices like his struggled to maintain a professional reputation beside better-funded establishments in Europe or the US, where things like stable utilities were taken for granted, or backup power generators were funded without a second thought.

Talia was right. A mistake like this would mean embarrassment and possible dismissal for the responsible employee.

"I can call down to Brazzaville and see what we can do to help," he said.

"I was hoping we could take care of this quietly," Talia said with a shy smile. She put her hand on his knee. Her touch was electric.

"We have extra samples here," she said. "I've prepared a list. If we could spare a few, that might be enough to get them on their feet." She held out the manila folder to him.

"I just need your signature," she said. "The samples are packed. I can take them myself, tonight."

"But the job?" he said. "What about the regional director position?"

Talia unleashed a dazzling smile. "Well, I suppose, if I was the regional director, I could just sign over the samples myself, right?" She laughed as she poured him another cup of coffee. "I'd be honored, Sven, really."

Sven opened the folder and scanned the contents. Ebola Zaire, Nipah, Lassa fever, smallpox, SARS, some of the worst epidemic diseases in the world.

Talia handed him his refilled coffee cup, her smile still brilliant.

Sven scribbled his name at the bottom of the paper and handed the folder back.

═══════════

When Sven got to the office the next morning, Shani was not at her desk.

But even that inconvenience was not enough to dampen his mood. In a burst of enthusiasm, he had written and sent his resignation letter last night, along with an email recommending Dr. Talia Tahir as his replacement.

He hummed to himself as he made his own coffee and walked back to his office. Shani was behind her desk, but instead of her normal sunny smile, her face was chalk white.

Sven stopped in the doorway. "What's the matter?"

Shani opened her mouth, then closed it again and began to cry. "Talia—" she began. Sobs took over.

Sven set his cup on her desk. "What about Dr. Tahir?"

Shani gathered herself.

"There was a plane crash. She's dead."

CHAPTER 14

USS Michael Murphy *(DDG-112), Pearl Harbor, Hawaii*

Andrea Ramirez held an ice-cold can of Diet Coke against her forehead and closed her eyes. She could feel her eyeballs quiver every time her heart beat.

The wardroom celebration at the Reef Bar had gone into the wee hours, and Dre had stayed for the duration. The XO was over the moon about capturing the squadron Battle E, and he showed his appreciation by buying round after round of drinks for his officers. She was happy for the XO and proud of her ship. Everyone had done their part and they all deserved the praise that was coming. A ribbon, a note in their service jackets, and the upcoming ceremony to unveil the "E" painted on the side of the bridge.

With a sigh, she removed the cold can from her forehead and cracked open the soda. She took a long drink and sat down at the SIPRnet terminal, the secret IP router network that handled all the ship's secret message traffic.

She let out a tremendous burp in the empty radio room. "Excuse me," she said to no one.

There were at least a hundred messages in the queue, quite a load for a Saturday morning, but Dre was an experienced hand. She scanned the messages, culling out the ones the CO, the XO, and Ops needed to see right away.

Dre chuckled to herself. The XO would be in no shape to spend much time in front of a screen this morning.

She polished off the rest of the soda and tossed the empty container into the nearby recycling bin, which rang with a loud clang in the empty room. Strangely enough, she wasn't even tired. She decided to do her morning walk-through of the ship before breakfast.

The *Murphy* was nearly deserted on a weekend in port. As usual, the weather in Hawaii was fabulous, a pleasant seventy degrees, with a soft breeze coming off the water. On the fantail, she raised her face to the sunshine. The gentle heat felt good after the chill of the air-conditioning in the radio room. When she had soaked up enough sun, Dre walked the interior spaces of the ship from the lowest levels of the engine room up to Combat and finally the bridge. She reviewed the quartermaster's logs and then made her way to the wardroom.

To her surprise, the XO was there, dressed in civilian clothes, a plate of bacon and eggs resting on the table next to the message boards.

"Ramirez, top of the morning to you, young lady," he said. Lieutenant Commander Minto flashed her a wide grin. "Pretty great time last night, huh?"

Dre laughed. How could this guy not have a raging hangover?

"Yes, sir. You do know how to celebrate, XO."

He attacked his breakfast. "Work hard, play hard, Ramirez. Of those from whom much is demanded, the beer shall be free."

"Which philosopher said that one, sir?"

Minto's face sobered. He put down his fork and hoisted his coffee cup. "I don't normally tell this story, Ramirez, but you caught me in a good mood, I guess. When I graduated from the Academy, I service-selected as a SEAL."

"I didn't know that, sir."

Minto grimaced. "Yeah, the captain knows because it's in my service record, but that's it. I was one week from finishing BUDS and blew out my knee big-time. I cried like a little baby when they told me I was medically disqualified. They sent me to the surface fleet. Didn't even have a choice, the orders just showed up."

He sipped his coffee. "The guys in my class gave me a huge send-off party. A year later, my best friend—Academy roommate since plebe year—was dead, killed in a raid in Afghanistan. Don't even know where exactly, but I know he went down swinging wherever it was."

Minto got up suddenly. He filled his cup and poured

one for Dre. "You know what the moral of the story is, Dre?"

He sat down and continued without waiting for an answer.

"We don't choose this life, it chooses us. Turns out I'm a pretty damned good ship driver. I thought I wanted to be a SEAL. I thought my life was over when that dream ended, but here I am." He smiled. "Driving ships, shaping young minds, and buying beer for those to whom I owe so much."

Dre sipped her coffee, welcoming the burn of the hot liquid on her lips. "You heard about my new orders."

The XO nodded, leaning back in his chair. "CIA. I knew there was something about you that didn't add up. When an ensign shows up to her new command and part of her service record is classified . . ."

He studied her as he sipped his coffee. "We can get the orders turned off, if that's what you want."

Dre didn't respond.

"What's the job?" the XO asked. "The part you can tell me, I mean."

"My old boss wants me back in DC. He's leading a new team. Wants me as his pet computer geek."

"Sounds perfect for you, Dre. What's the issue?"

Dre felt her face grow hot. "It's complicated, XO. I was in an op and . . ."

Her voice faltered. In her mind's eye, Janet Everett lay on the deck in the North Korean bunker, pale, bleeding, dying . . . and the overwhelming feeling of helplessness as Dre's body froze.

"I choked," Dre said finally. "My best friend almost died because I couldn't handle the pressure."

"So you're ashamed." Minto's eyes bored into hers. "You're afraid it might happen again. You're afraid next time your friend won't make it and it'll be your fault."

Dre felt hot pressure behind her eyeballs. She nodded, not trusting her voice.

The XO placed his hands flat on the table and leaned in, his gaze pinning her in place. "That might happen, but if they're requesting you by name, then your boss is willing to take that chance.

"You're a damned fine officer, Ramirez, and you can come work for me anytime, anyplace—no questions asked. But you're a Ferrari on a go-cart track out here, girl. And you know it." He drained his cup and pushed the message boards across the table.

"You think I should accept the orders," Dre said.

Minto shook his head. "Not what I said. I said we don't choose this life, this life chooses us. If you feel the work calling you to DC, then you should go. You're welcome here for as long as you want to stay." He plucked a ball cap off the rack. "If you'll excuse me, I have a tee time."

Dre ordered bacon and eggs for breakfast and ate in silence. Still full of nervous energy, she went down to her stateroom and reorganized her closet, then cracked open her laptop. When she opened her email, at the top of the queue was a message from Michael Goodwin. The subject line read: *Please look at this. If you have a chance.*

Intrigued, Dre opened the email. Her friend's message was short:

> *Dear Dre—*
> *I can't seem to crack this website. Let me know*
> *if you see anything I'm missing.*
> *Love—M*

Dre sat back in her chair, feeling the aftereffects of the night before catching up with her now.

She should take a nap, but maybe just a peek first. Her fingers stole to the keyboard and clicked on the link.

A black webpage opened up with two lines of white text in the center of her screen:

> The Day of Judgment is upon us.
> The Mahdi has returned.

She stared at the screen. Although this was clearly a site designed for Arabic speakers, the words were in English. That meant the site had to have a smart filter to adapt the site text based on the user's location. Not your typical jihadi website.

When she clicked on the link, it opened a video. A man, his identity blurred, spoke as soft music played in the background. The words rolled over her. *Subjugate the children of Islam . . . infidels . . . the wrath of the Mahdi.*

Dre slapped the lid of the laptop closed, feeling her heart beating faster.

She would not be drawn back into this. She drove ships. She read radio messages. She fixed fire-control systems. This was her life now.

Dre paced the room until her heart rate returned to normal.

But this was Michael asking, the closest thing she had to a sibling in this world. He wouldn't have asked unless he was stumped.

She went back to the desk. She watched the video all the way through and forced herself to watch it again. The man in the video was talking about an attack. She did a quick search on the internet and found a link to an attack in Ethiopia.

She scanned the news accounts of the attack at something called the Grand Ethiopian Renaissance Dam.

Dre went back to the Mahdi website and shifted screens to view the code for the website. She tried a simple hacking technique using HTML coding and got nowhere. She tried SQL injection, and that failed as well.

These were basic tricks that anyone could look up on the internet, but they worked for ninety-nine percent of the sites out there. Michael would have used some of the more advanced tools at his disposal.

Time raced by as she dug deeper. The more closely she observed the website behavior, the more intrigued Dre became. Not only was this unlike any security she'd seen on a terrorist website, this was unlike any security she'd ever seen on any website.

The call to colors over the 1MC startled her into

awareness. Dre looked at the clock over the door to her stateroom. 1955 . . . where had the day gone?

As she closed the lid of her laptop, her gaze caught the picture taped to the inside of her fold-up desk.

Michael, Janet, Liz Soroush, Don Riley, and Dre in the US Naval Academy cemetery. It had been taken at the funeral for Captain McHugh, not long after they returned from North Korea. Janet's arm was in a sling and Don Riley was walking on crutches. Everyone in the picture was doing their best to smile, but the shadow of the moment hung over them and no one looked convincing.

She studied Liz's face. Of all the people in the picture, Liz had lost the most, and yet she still made an attempt to smile.

Dre hurried to the fantail for the colors ceremony to take down the United States flag for the night. At the precise time of sunset, Dre saluted as the speakers on the naval base played "Retreat."

After the ceremony, the enlisted man who had lowered the flag grinned at her. "Heard it was quite a party last night, ma'am. Did you catch up on your sleep this afternoon?"

"Actually, I was working on a really cool computer program . . ." She let her voice trail off when she saw the young man's eyes glaze over in disinterest. "Never mind."

Dre stayed on deck for a long time, listening to the sounds of the naval base at night. Shouts of laughter in the distance, the gentle lapping of water against the hull, the slam of a steel hatch.

The *Murphy* represented a safe haven for her. Here she could hide. She would do her job and do it well, but she was still hiding.

Dre marched to the radio room and logged into the SIPRnet terminal. She opened a new email and addressed it to Don Riley.

Subject: *Count me in.*

CHAPTER 15

Undisclosed location, somewhere in the Sudan

From the outside, the two-story pole building looked like an agricultural warehouse. With a large roll-up garage door and a few tractors inside, the interior carried the appearance. On the second floor was a barracks built to house and feed thirty men.

But inside the warehouse, a squat concrete block structure sprouted from the ground, facing the roll-up door. It had two stainless-steel elevator doors and a single call button.

The elevator was the only access to the underground combination laboratory and living quarters for the newest—and secret—research lab for Recodna Genetics.

The ultramodern facilities were the best money could buy, and JP was confident everything was in perfect working order. Before he had moved a single spade of soil in Sudan, he'd built and tested every feature in a duplicate site in Switzerland.

JP liked to think of the site as a labor of love, his love for the woman who paced the carpeted floor of the bedroom they shared deep inside the underground bunker.

"Talia, calm down," he said from his perch on the edge of the bed.

"They should be here by now," she snapped. "Why haven't we heard from the pilot?"

"They're twenty minutes late," JP said. "A million things could have delayed the plane."

In truth, his internal early-warning system was alarming just as loudly as hers. Today was move-in day for the scientists at the research facility. After two weeks of isolation near Khartoum, the scientists were about to begin two years of self-imposed exile in a state-of-the-art research lab with the promise of a massive payoff at the end. All five of their marks had agreed to the terms of the contract, but had one of them had second thoughts?

The stress would be worse for Talia. She had faked her own death to be here. For her, there was no going back to her old life as a respected scientist. She had brought with her a full suite of hand-selected virus samples to supplement the few she had in storage at the bunker.

Kasim, their head of security, appeared in the doorway. He was a mountain of a man with muscles that rippled under his coal-black skin. He dressed in a dark-green paramilitary uniform and carried a MAC-10 machine pistol on a strap around his neck, a Beretta 92X on his hip, and a knife in his boot.

"They're ten minutes out," he said.

"Bring our guests to the common room, Kasim," JP said. "We'll join you there."

Kasim nodded and left.

JP hated having to rely on former Janjaweed militiamen, but it was a compromise he had to make. Every outside person who knew the details of this laboratory was an added security risk. There could be no leaks in this operation.

Kasim ruled his men with an iron hand, but these were men with bloody, brutal histories that represented the worst of African political violence.

In his time with the French DGSE, JP had worked with men like Kasim. There was no job too violent for men like him. In fact, the biggest issue was not getting them to do what was necessary, it was getting them to stop.

"There they are," Talia said, pointing to the tiny security monitor screen.

Five passengers disembarked from the jet into the blazing sunshine. Kasim's men directed them into two cargo vans with blacked-out windows. As JP had instructed the driver, the vehicles moved slowly on the dusty, rutted track to the warehouse, careful not to jostle the occupants behind the tinted windows.

"Are you ready to get started, my dear?" JP asked.

As she watched the tiny screen, Talia's eyes were full of emotion.

With the arrival of the scientists, the real work

began. The empty labs below his feet would finally be put to their ultimate purpose.

A targeted bioweapon, designed to attack only a specific genetic sequence. A weapon like that could erase political boundaries. If they were successful, war could truly become a precision event. Collateral damage would be a thing of the past.

These scientists would help Talia develop a weapon so potent and so precise that if it were released on an airplane, it could be programmed to kill only a single person.

And not just kill them. Destroy them. JP had seen firsthand the effects of deadly viruses like Marburg and Ebola, seen how the viruses turned their hosts into bags of bloody gelatin. . . .

Today was Talia's moment. He knew her well enough to realize the source of the fiery spark that drove her.

Revenge.

As a young girl, when her parents were killed in Lebanon by Iranian proxies, she could have shed the loss and gone on with her life.

But Talia Tahir was not one to forget. Through what remained of her childhood, her education, her career, she bided her time. When JP met Talia for the first time, it was as if a relay switch clicked to the closed position in his head, energizing a circuit that drove him.

He was a man looking for a purpose; she was a woman with a life's mission.

They fit together, like puzzle pieces. It was Talia who conceived the idea, Talia who selected the research team, Talia who suggested he start a business relationship with Haim Zarecki that led to the Arab-Israeli Benevolence Coalition.

And JP was her willing tool.

As she continued her career in the World Health Organization and JP built his biotech company, together they planned to change the world.

"Sir, it's time to go," Kasim said. His head of security held the door open for JP and Talia.

Kasim strutted ahead of JP down the gleaming hallway toward the common room. They passed another security monitor, and JP saw the van door opening and the scientists being escorted toward the elevator. Kasim spoke softly into his radio in Arabic, instructing the men in the garage to search the scientists' baggage for any electronics.

They waited in the common room, where the elevator doors opened. The space was set up as a family room, with a large dining table adjacent to a kitchen. Stainless-steel appliances gleamed next to modern white cabinets and a snow-white quartz countertop where a bottle of champagne on ice waited. Opposite the kitchen was a large lounge area with couches and armchairs, two massive flat-screen TVs, and a stocked library.

A stack of laptops and tablets waited for the staff. They were not allowed to bring any devices into the compound, and all the provided electronics worked only on the local area network. The sole internet access point was located in the bunker behind a secure door adjacent to Talia's bedroom.

Dr. Lakshmi Chandrasekaran exited the elevator first, the rest of the group trailing her, uncertainty evident in their posture. Lakshmi was Talia's age, but shorter and darker, with a round face and a high-pitched, tittering laugh. She rushed to embrace Talia.

Of all the recruits, Lakshmi was the only one with whom either JP or Talia had a prior connection. Talia had been adamant that her undergrad roommate be part of the team. While the young Indian woman's microbiology credentials were solid, she was not essential to the effort. Moreover, there was something about Lakshmi that bothered JP, and his long-ago DGSE training told him not to dismiss the feeling.

Without asking, Lakshmi assumed the role of hostess as Talia circulated among the new arrivals. She poured flutes of champagne and a fruit juice for Dr. al-Harbi, who was a strict practicing Muslim.

JP mingled, welcoming the scientists and assessing their states of mind after the trip. Katie McDonough, the Australian synthetic biologist, and Greta Berger, the Swedish CRISPR expert, seemed to have formed a friendship during their travels. They greeted JP warmly, then went back to their discussion of genetic tailoring without missing a beat.

Good, JP thought. Their collaboration would be essential if Winslow came through with the paleo samples.

Dr. Lu Xianshan, an expert in aerosol mechanisms in viruses, greeted JP in his perfunctory way and went back to his drink. His square face absorbed the surroundings and he seemed satisfied.

JP moved on to Dr. Faraj al-Harbi, a shy, bearded Saudi national. He had hooded dark eyes that avoided contact with JP's gaze and soft hands with long thin fingers, like a piano player. "Thank you for the fruit juice," he said in a soft voice.

JP nodded, trying to engage the younger man's gaze with a smile. "I honor your commitment to your faith, my friend. And to your work."

He was about to go on when Lakshmi appeared at his elbow with a glass of champagne. "I think this might be a good time to say a few words, Jean-Pierre."

JP tamped down a flash of anger. Nevertheless, he tapped his glass with a pen and waited for their attention.

He could feel their intrigue about the mysterious journey they had taken to get here. They had all met for the first time in Khartoum, where JP had people in place to rid them of excess baggage and anything that might possibly be used as a communications device to the outside world. They were signing up for an extended stay in a secure location, and he wanted to make sure the location stayed secure.

The plane trip from Khartoum to the nearby airstrip should have been less than thirty minutes, but he had the pilot take a roundabout route of nearly two hours to confuse anyone who was trying to track their final destination.

All they knew was that they were somewhere in Africa.

JP raised his glass, offering his best professional smile. "Welcome to Project Deliverance."

He saw glances shift between new acquaintances. Lakshmi moved among them, topping off their glasses.

"It has been one of the highlights of my professional

career getting to know each of you and bringing you into our endeavor. I appreciate your patience during the process of traveling here. I can assure you: It was all necessary." He offered a self-deprecating chuckle.

"You are about to embark on one of the most important scientific journeys of the twenty-first century. That sounds grand, I know, but I believe what we are about to undertake is no less significant than the space race was in the last century."

He rested his glass on the counter and clasped his hands behind his back. He needed to project sincerity.

"The space race of the last century was between two superpowers. The United States and the Soviet Union embarked on a technological battle that yielded untold benefits for the rest of mankind. Microprocessors, advances in food preservation, satellite TV—okay, maybe we shouldn't be thankful for that one." JP earned a laugh from the group.

Tensions were easing. Dr. al-Harbi leaned toward him.

"The twenty-first century offers a new race, a race where one does not need billions of dollars to be a player. A race where the arena is microscopic. Genetics is the future of humanity. We can use that knowledge for good—or for evil."

He went from face to face, slowly, searching for connection and finding it.

"We should not kid ourselves. The space race was about military superiority. The ICBMs that threaten our very existence today are a result of that time. But the threats of today are even more dangerous. Today, if you have a lab in your basement, and just a little expertise, you can make a virus that could kill millions of people."

JP stabbed at the air with his finger as he picked up the cadence of his speech. "We talk about this in ethics classes. We lament our fate at conferences. It's the curse of Pandora's box, we say. The genie is out of the bottle." JP paused for dramatic effect.

"Project Deliverance is more than just a research project. It is a plan to save the human race from itself. Together, we will stamp out the most vile diseases that can be created by the hand of man. But to slay a monster, you must know that monster. You"—he swept his finger across the semicircle of scientists—"are only half of Project Deliverance. Colleagues of equal brilliance are sequestered in a location not unlike this one waiting to slay whatever viral dragon you send to them."

Greta Berger raised her hand. "You mean we're going to create new viruses? Bioweapons?"

JP nodded. "Exactly. This is a Red Team–Blue Team exercise. You create the problem, they solve it. Over time, we will not only build up the vaccination defenses against any conceivable disease, but we will write the book on how to rapidly defend against anything new that might slip past the creative minds in this room."

Dr. al-Harbi chimed in. "Isn't that what the WHO does?"

JP made a sour face. "During the Ebola outbreak of 2017, I was in Sierra Leone. I was there in the Congo in 2018 as well. Was there a vaccine? No. Was there coordination between governments to create one? No.

"Disease knows no borders. In times of extreme

crisis, politics and governments are roadblocks to success. They are barriers that kill millions of innocent people. Project Deliverance will break through all those unnecessary boundaries. We are scientists. We see the truth in its full glory and we seek knowledge for the betterment of our fellow humans."

"But to create viruses so dangerous . . ." Katie McDonough's accent betrayed her Australian roots. "It seems reckless. What if someone steals them?"

JP nodded. "Now you understand the need for absolute secrecy. Now you understand the security that is so evident here." He picked up his glass of champagne.

"I ask you to stand and join me in a toast." JP waited as everyone got to their feet; then he raised his glass.

"To Deliverance!"

CHAPTER 16

Tysons Corner, Virginia

Don Riley adjusted the tray of pastries on the credenza and lifted the pump handle on the coffeepot. Everything had to be perfect for this visit.

His phone buzzed, an incoming text from the security officer on the front desk. *Mattias is in the building.*

Don wiped his hands on his trousers and smoothed the front of his suit coat. He took a deep, cleansing breath. Emerging Threats was about to give their first major presentation.

For Don, everything was on the line. A private briefing for the CIA's ops and resources director was a rare event. Mattias controlled the finances, equipment, and personnel in the Directorate of Operations.

While not technically part of Don's official chain of command, the head of the Operations and Resources staff carried enormous sway within the CIA power structure. His visit meant Don's group was on someone's radar.

In the never-ending budget battles that went on in the bureaucracy of every government agency, results mattered—and Dylan Mattias was a man who demanded results. If Mattias liked what he heard, Don's stock would rise.

If not, well, there were two sides to every coin.

The door to the conference room snapped open and Mattias entered. His dark hair was swept straight back from his forehead, with just enough hair product to hold it in place, but not enough to make him look smarmy. The flash of gray at his temples hinted that his age was north of forty, even if his youthful face said midthirties.

He was fit and moved with energy, his tailored Italian suit clinging to him like a second skin. Like most case officers, he acted with a quiet confidence that came from a lifetime of persuading people to do things they didn't want to do. He crossed the room to greet Don, hand outstretched, with a wide smile.

"Don," he said, "it's been a long time. How've you been way out here in the sticks?"

Don returned the smile, doing his best to mirror the other man's warmth and confidence—even though he felt neither. "Fine, Dylan. The new digs are great."

Mattias's attention to detail was legendary. Don could see that the man was assessing everything. The quality of the security protocols, the behind-target staffing levels, probably even the quality of the coffee and Don's damp handshake.

"We brought in a couple things for breakfast—"

"Already ate," Mattias cut him off. "Let's get down to it."

Don threw a questioning glance at the door. "Did you bring any staffers?"

Mattias shook his head and sat down, pulling a slim notebook from his jacket pocket and a gold Cross pen. "This is just you and me today, Don. The director asked me to take stock of the situation and make some recommendations."

Recommendations. The word hit home like a punch in the stomach. Emerging Threats had been active for only a few months and now Mattias was here to make "recommendations."

"Right." Don kept the frozen smile in place. "Let me pull in the team."

Mattias pointed at the seat across from him. "I thought maybe you and I could chat for a few moments first."

Don did his best to look nonchalant, but inside his stomach was gushing acid. He drew the chair out, feeling his armpits slicken with new sweat. "Sure thing. What'd you have in mind?"

Mattias made a show of opening his notebook and dating a fresh page. He laid the pen across the open page. "This is a great opportunity for you, Don. For us. We're at a crossroads. Politically speaking, I mean. No one in the administration wants to get involved in another overseas conflict."

Mattias gave a what-can-you-do shrug. "'Emerging threats' means different things to different people, so I want to be clear. Your job is to stop these issues before they emerge into the public awareness. This Mahdi character needs to be contained."

"I've got my best people on it," Don said. "Anything we can do to put this thing to bed quickly, these three are the ones who will get it done."

Mattias tapped his pen on his open notebook. "These are the same three who were involved in the North Korea incident, correct?"

"The very same. If there's something there, they'll find it." Don paused. "That said, we are very early in this process. 'Emerging threats' by definition means that we don't have the full picture, so drawing conclusions from any analysis is not only difficult, but dangerous."

Mattias squinted across the table. "We get paid to make the hard choices, Don. The president is crystal clear on this point: He wants to play offense. If we have anything that smells actionable, we deal with it quickly, and quietly."

Don took a deep breath. This was moving very fast and not in the direction he had anticipated. Everett, Ramirez, and Goodwin needed to be extremely careful with their speculations in front of Mattias.

"Let's see what your superstars have for us, Don," Mattias said.

As the three officers trooped in together, Don couldn't help but feel a swell of pride. The trio looked every inch the smart, young professionals they were—and he'd had a hand in making that transformation happen.

Dre Ramirez had been just what the group needed to reconstitute their previous balance of skills. She wore a business pantsuit that hung on her slim hips and a cream-colored blouse under a dark blue jacket. She was the first to greet Mattias and shook his hand with confidence as she introduced herself. Whatever demons she had been dealing with in Hawaii were behind her as far as Don could see.

Janet wore a stylish royal-blue dress and had pulled her blond hair back into a ponytail. She eyed Mattias warily. As the spokesperson for the group, she was sizing up her audience.

Michael Goodwin had paid a visit to the Men's Wearhouse. His suit was off the rack, but the young man had the physique to make it look good. Don still harbored a special sense of pride in Goodwin. He'd recruited the young man to the Naval Academy and been there as he grew from a kid into a naval officer.

Mattias held on to Goodwin's hand after they shook. "Michael Goodwin," he said. "I read your paper on bioinformatics as it applies to warfare. Impressive."

Don raised his eyebrows. He hadn't known Michael had even authored a paper on bioinformatics.

Michael reddened. "Thank you, sir. It seemed like a natural connection. Predicting the variability of an epidemic seems like a good way to approach the larger issue of bioweapons. We spend so much time on the issue of lethality, but I think the real key is the transmission method."

Mattias was still nodding as he took his seat. He surveyed the three officers. "It's your dime, ladies and gentlemen. Don here tells me you three have been looking at this Nile River basin issue, top, bottom, and sideways. Let's hear what you have to say."

Janet touched the smart screen that was slaved to her desktop back in the Cave, the group nickname for their office. She summarized what they knew about the Mahdi so far.

"So, you think Egypt is behind the attack?" Mattias interrupted. "What about Iran?"

"The Mahdi is a religious figure in Islamic culture; the name roughly translates as 'reborn' or 'messiah.' The term is not in the Quran, but has broad cultural significance. Depending on which sect of Islam you are from, the meaning of the Mahdi can take different forms, but the general arc of the story is the same: the second coming of a unifying religious figure who precedes the Day of Judgment."

Mattias stroked his chin. "Day of Judgment. That sounds ominous. Does the Mahdi give us any indication of how and when this day of judgment will take place?"

Janet shook her head. "The Mahdi and his followers take great care to ensure their message is able to be consumed by a secular audience." She briefly described how the site accommodated language translation automatically. "They are extremely tech-savvy. To date, we've been unable to hack their website. That's very unusual."

"And what conclusions do you draw?" Mattias pressed her.

Don was relieved at Janet's cautious answer. "They're well funded, for starters. And they have access to some serious cryptographic resources."

"But what's their goal? They have a stated desire to remove all foreign direct investment from the region, which leaves what?" Mattias let the question hang in the air.

Goodwin spoke up. "I've examined the foreign investment in the region, sir."

He threw a spreadsheet onto the screen and scrolled through a long list of projects separated by dollar amounts and region. The total was into tens of billions of dollars, with thousands of line items. Don's eyes scanned through construction companies, business parks, medical clinics, schools, new road projects.

"There's nothing here that is out of the ordinary for projects of this scale," Michael continued. "Most of them are run via shell companies, which is par for the course in this region of the world, but all of them are legitimate as far as we can tell."

"So, your conclusion is what?" Mattias continued pressing for an answer.

"I think we don't really have enough—" Don began.

"I'd like to hear what your team has to say, Don," Mattias said.

Janet spoke carefully, weighing her words. "Egypt would have the most to lose as these dams come online."

"Is there any indication that Iran is backing this Mahdi operation?" Mattias asked.

"Nothing conclusive," Janet said.

"There is another possibility," Michael said.

The room went still. Janet, Dre, and Don all stared at the young man, but Michael had a pensive expression on his face. Don knew that look. Michael's brain was working overtime. Don started to interrupt, but Mattias was quicker.

"Go on, Goodwin," Mattias said. "I'd like to hear your thoughts."

Michael scrolled to the top of the list of projects. "There is a massive amount of money being poured into the region. Whoever controls this part of the world essentially controls the fate of a good portion of the Middle East and northern Africa. These are some of the poorest countries on earth being catapulted into the twenty-first century in one giant step. What took a century in Europe or the US will take place in a decade in the Nile River basin. This is an economic realignment of massive proportions."

"I'm listening," Mattias prompted.

Don tried to signal to Michael to slow down, but the young man was too wrapped up in his own ideas to notice.

"This realignment cuts across political, cultural, and religious boundaries and deals with the very thing that defines life for the human race: water. If someone wanted to control this resource, this region, there would be no easy way to do it. No one—not even the US or Russia or the Saudis—could overthrow the governments of that many countries without someone objecting. But what if you took control from the ground up?"

"I'm not following," Mattias said. The man seemed fascinated by Goodwin's analytical ponderings.

"You have to own all of it," Michael said, pointing to the list of investments. "You can't just own one tree, you need to own the whole forest. If you owned enough of these companies, you could influence the region from the ground up. You harvest a tree here and there, but what you're really doing is managing a forest of investments for your own gain."

Don broke in. "Wow, Michael, that's some story. I suggest we—"

"But it fits, Don," Dre said. "And if he's right, then the Mahdi is a distraction. What are the chances that a brand-new terrorist group with no known affiliations and great technical savvy just appears? The Mahdi gives us exactly what we're conditioned to look for: terrorist attacks, the bloodier, the better. While we chase the terrorists, the real crime is being committed at the local level."

"There's one problem with this entire theory," Don snapped. "You can't prove any of it."

"Yet," Janet said.

"Pardon?" Mattias said.

"We can't prove it yet," she replied. "If Michael and Dre say it's there, we'll find it."

"And how do you propose to do that?" Mattias asked.

Don wanted to scream at the three of them to shut up.

Michael, for whom Don's anger had still not registered, squinted at the list of Nile River basin investments as he considered Mattias's question.

"We set a trap," he said.

CHAPTER 17

Berenice Harbor, Egypt

Berenice occupied a narrow strip of land between the mountains and the Red Sea. In antiquity, the port's sheltered anchorage and its location as the end point for the great Coptos Road connecting the Nile to the Red Sea made it famous. Today, Berenice was a backwater, a local port for goods coming into Egypt from the east.

Alyan Sultan al-Qahtamni arrived by private jet, landing at the tiny airstrip on the outskirts of the sleepy town. A car waited for him on the dirt runway to take him to the dock.

It was hard to miss *Al-Buraq* from shore. Anchored a mile away, the sixty-meter sea yacht was resplendent among the tired break-bulk freighters and fishing vessels dotting the harbor. Alyan stepped from a low dock into the small inflatable boat for the trip out to Saleh's yacht.

Alyan was determined to arrive first for this meeting—and not only to make up for the tardiness of his last visit. He wanted to see Saleh privately about the coalition's investment in the biopharma company.

As they drew close to the fantail, he admired his fellow Saudi's magnificent ship. The sleek hull hugged the water, evoking speed even when still.

Saleh waited for him on the upper deck. Alyan gave a mock salute as he stepped from the launch to the low fantail. The ship was stable under his feet as he climbed the steps to embrace his friend.

"*Salaam alaikum,*" he said.

"*Alaikum salaam,* my friend," Saleh replied. "Welcome to my home."

Saleh led him inside, where they could wait for the others in comfort. Tonight, Saleh was planning to serve dinner before the board meeting, so the atmosphere was relaxed. Perfect for what Alyan wanted to discuss.

Saleh indicated a side table where drinks and appetizers were available, but Alyan shook his head. He did his best to be a practicing Muslim. Although he fell off the wagon occasionally, tonight would not be one of those nights.

Saleh freshened his own drink. "I admire a man of faith. I mostly keep the bar open for our Israeli comrades, but I don't mind a drink every now and then."

"How is Zarecki's health these days?" Alyan asked in their mother tongue.

Saleh eyed him. "Why do you ask?"

Just like a former intelligence officer to answer a question with a question, Alyan thought.

"No reason." He picked up a glass of fruit juice and walked to the window facing the shore. "The last time we met, he seemed to have declined some. At some point, we need to discuss our venture with one less partner."

Saleh joined him. "Our friend has accomplished much in his lifetime. But there are still things he wishes to finalize before he passes."

Alyan rolled his eyes. "Iran," he said.

Zarecki's hatred of Iran and his funding of hard-right political groups in the Jewish state, and in America, were well documented in the press.

It had surprised Alyan when Saleh had sponsored Zarecki into the Arab-Israeli Benevolence Coalition. The two men had been on opposite sides of the Middle East political-religious spectrum for their entire careers, so their sudden partnership seemed an odd pairing.

As the primary investment manager, Alyan didn't care. Politics was not part of his investment vocabulary. He was not political, and Zarecki's money was as green as the next person's.

The coalition existed to turn money into lots of money. So far, it had worked out well. It would also lift millions out of poverty, which was in line with his faith.

"You look troubled, my friend," Saleh said. "Talk to me."

"I wanted to ask you about something I saw after the last meeting."

Saleh's smile tightened.

"I saw you and Zarecki taking a private meeting with the biopharma CEO," Alyan said. "It seemed intense."

Alyan blushed. "Forgive me. I forgot my phone and overheard you."

Saleh studied Alyan's reflection in the dark glass. "I knew Manzul many years ago, when he worked for a fellow intelligence agency. We have some mutual acquaintances."

"But why keep it a secret from the rest of the board?" Alyan pressed.

Saleh shrugged. "Zarecki wished to speak with him. He's an old man and I cannot find it in my heart to deny him small favors." He faced Alyan. "He's on oxygen now, you know. Still smokes, of course." The two men shared a laugh.

Alyan detected the buzz of an outboard approaching the yacht.

"I think that will be our friends," Saleh said, moving to the open door.

In the moment of solitude, Alyan mulled over his conversation with Saleh. He was well aware how the older man had changed the subject away from Alyan's original question, but did it matter? Why was he so stuck on this Manzul character anyway? He was one investment of hundreds, but one that kept coming up in his mind over and over again. Years of experience would not let him ignore these subconscious warning signs.

His thoughts were interrupted by the arrival of Haim Zarecki and Itzak Lehrmann. The latter moved straight for the bar. Alyan followed.

"That old bastard complained the entire trip," Lehrmann said in English. "Nonstop bitching. That's the last time we travel together." He tilted a bottle of Jameson in Alyan's direction.

"No, thank you."

"Suit yourself. I'm going to inoculate myself from Zarecki's voice right now." He took a deep drink.

A white-coated waiter approached them and gave a discreet bow. "Dinner is served, gentlemen," he said in a soft voice. He led them into the dining room, where a magnificent glass table set for four waited.

Saleh seated himself at the head of the table. "I have a new chef," he said, settling a linen napkin on his lap. "Bertrand, from France. Let's see if his food matches his reputation."

"You know it's going to be expensive when the chef only has one name," Lehrmann joked.

Bertrand lived up to his single name over six courses and two hours. Alyan watched his colleagues as the dinner progressed and the alcohol flowed freely. Even Saleh seemed to be loosening up. Maybe he could satisfy this nagging question of Jean-Pierre Manzul's connection with Zarecki after all.

Lehrmann told a funny story about when he and his brother stole an IDF Jeep while on leave in Tel Aviv.

Alyan laughed along with the punch line, but the reality was the four men had little in common except money. They were separated by age, religion, and life experience.

Zarecki was an old warhorse from another era. On

paper, he was a shipping magnate, but Alyan knew he'd made his real money as an arms dealer. His politics were hard right and very public. Most people Alyan knew socially would cringe at the thought of being in the same room with the man.

Saleh was just as stalwart in his beliefs from the other side of the spectrum. He had served the Royal House of Saud as a loyal keeper of secrets and disposer of bodies for as long as Alyan had been alive. There was not a thing of note that had happened in the last thirty years in the kingdom that did not have Saleh's tacit approval, if not his fingerprints all over it.

The closest thing to a peer Alyan had in the coalition was Itzak Lehrmann, but even they were separated by nearly a decade and a world of ideology. Lehrmann's extended family had deep roots in the Israeli government.

At his core, Alyan was an idealist. A rich idealist, but no one ever said money and ideals couldn't exist in the same space. His talent was money, making it move and making it grow. But the coalition's investment portfolio in the Nile River basin project was an order of magnitude beyond what he'd ever attempted before—and it was working.

A young man entered and placed a black pouch next to Zarecki's chair. He helped the old man fit a clear plastic tube under his nose. Saleh shared a glance with Alyan.

"The doctor has me on oxygen now," Zarecki said with a wheeze. "I don't have to use it all the time, but it can be helpful when I travel."

Saleh prodded his Jewish counterpart. "Perhaps you should stop smoking, Haim."

"Perhaps you should stop drinking, my good Muslim friend," the old man shot back.

After a dessert of fresh berries, Saleh called his head of security on his radio. "Clear the ship," he said.

The waiters and even Bertrand himself trooped to the back of the yacht and boarded one of the launches. The Arab-Israeli Benevolence Coalition repaired to the boardroom.

Alyan inserted an encrypted thumb drive into the side of the table and unlocked it with his thumbprint. The familiar map of the Nile River basin appeared on the table's surface. Alyan overlaid it with a list of projects in which they had invested.

"I am pleased to say that as of today our investment value has grown to nearly two hundred billion dollars," Alyan began.

Even Zarecki looked impressed.

Alyan highlighted the Merowe High Dam in Sudan and the GERD project in Ethiopia. "In these two projects, we have secured the majority of the bids for the accompanying infrastructure once the electrical-generation capability comes on line. Business parks, roads, bridges, apartments, we have a piece of all of them. In short, gentlemen, the people in this room own the Nile River basin." He paused to let his pronouncement sink in.

The complex web of shell corporations he had set up to support this investment scheme was mind-boggling.

It took over an hour for him to explain how the money flowed from their personal accounts into a series of double-blind real-estate companies managed by Lehrmann, then into the hundreds of shell companies managed by Alyan that owned thousands of local companies providing services and construction for the dams.

"Our investments are virtually untraceable," Alyan concluded. "It would take forensic accounting on a grand scale and access to hundreds of financial institutions around the world to trace any of this back to us. And even then, that would link us to only one company. Multiply that by a hundred different investment routes and that gives you a sense of the effort needed to find us."

"What about the Americans?" Zarecki growled. He had ditched his oxygen and was back to smoking cigarettes.

Alyan cleared the tabletop. "Nothing is foolproof, but the question is why would they bother? Anonymity is not illegal. We're not funding terrorism, we're bringing electricity and modern conveniences to millions of poor people. We get a generous piece of the profit, but the host countries win as well. Is it a monopoly? Yes, but those things don't really matter in this part of the world.

"That's the good news," Alyan said as he extracted the thumb drive. "But there are some current developments that concern me."

Saleh raised an eyebrow. "The Mahdi, that's what you mean?"

Alyan nodded. "On the one hand, it improves our investments in the security services, but the instability . . ."

"It's the filthy Iranians," Zarecki interjected. He paused to light another cigarette. "They can't stand to keep their mitts out of our world. They're agitating the Egyptians who are funding the locals. It's them. I know it."

"The Mahdi message is what concerns me," Alyan said. "He speaks against foreign investment and that could have a long-term impact on us if these attacks continue."

"These terrorists come and go," Saleh said. "The Mahdi is no different. Today he's a messiah, tomorrow he's a pariah. Stay focused on the money, Alyan. Leave the Mahdi to me."

Saleh stood, hoisting his empty glass. "Gentlemen, I propose we adjourn this board meeting and we move on to the next phase of the evening." He raised his eyebrows. "I have arranged for some local talent to join us. I am told the women in this region are delectable."

"I'm afraid I need to beg off tonight, my friend," Alyan said. "I have a meeting in the morning and a jet waiting for me."

Saleh walked him to the fantail, where he radioed for the launch. "The item we talked about earlier. It's nothing. I'll handle Manzul, okay?"

"As you wish." Alyan stepped carefully into the Zodiac, waving as the pilot pulled away from the yacht.

The water in the harbor was like glass and the night still, broken only by the hum of the outboard. A frothy wake trailed behind the small craft.

Alyan breathed a sigh of satisfaction. It was all coming together. The financial web he had built for the coalition was making more money than any of them—including him—had dreamed possible. There was nothing to stand in their way.

A second Zodiac, packed with female passengers, approached them, en route to *Al-Buraq*.

Alyan could hear their excited voices over the drone of the engine. The pilot of Alyan's launch steered close to the incoming vessel, calling to the girls in the local dialect.

Alyan froze as the oncoming Zodiac zipped by. The half dozen women were clustered together in the center of the craft. But in the rear of the boat, next to the pilot, sat a man. Alyan had assumed he was part of Saleh's security team, but as they flashed by he got a look at the man's face.

It was Jean-Pierre Manzul.

CHAPTER 18

Great Bear Lake, Northwest Territories, Canada

Jason Winslow paused at the top of the ladder protruding from a fifteen-foot-diameter hole in the permafrost. He turned up the collar of his coat and tugged his watch cap over his ears against the chill wind roaring down from the Arctic Circle.

A few flakes of snow whipped past his face. They had a week, maybe ten days, before they would have to pack up the camp for the season. They'd already pushed things beyond the point of safety. No matter how good the money was, he would not risk getting snowed in up here.

Clouds the color of lead hugged the horizon. The only relief to the endless brown-green landscape was the piles of dirt they had extracted from the hole and four tiny buildings that constituted his work camp.

Fifteen thousand years ago, this spot had been the shore of an inland sea, a virtual supermarket for native peoples, providing fish, roots, and access to fresh water. Ground-penetrating radar had suggested that this was the site of an ancient camp, but the only sign of human existence in their dig had been a few stone points that might have been spearheads.

Until now.

"Jason! Are you coming down?" The voice of Lydia Guevarra, known as "Che" to her friends—which did not include Jason—blasted out of the hole in the earth, overpowering the buzz of the small gas-powered generator. Jason flinched at the shrillness of her tone.

"I know this kid's been here for fifteen thousand years, but could you get a move on, please? We're freezing our asses off."

Jason muttered to himself as he started down the ladder, his heavy boots ringing on the aluminum rungs. Damned kids. Always complaining, always whining, always bitching about one thing or another.

Since he'd started the dig so late in the season after receiving the cash infusion from Harold Mortimer, Jason had to settle for undergrads, and inexperienced ones at that. He reached the bottom of the ladder, his boots crunching in the frozen soil.

It was still and cold at the bottom of the hole, surrounded by icy frozen earth. A tunnel, tall and wide enough for him to be able to walk upright with arms outstretched, extended into the permafrost. Every ten feet or so a naked lightbulb housed in a plastic shield hung from the ceiling. The walls were hewn smooth by the handheld power tools they used to cut through the ice.

A normal archaeological dig would have dug into

the earth carefully, documenting every inch of soil removed. But with the potential for Mortimer's bonus money, Jason favored speed over care. The undergraduates, once properly calibrated, had gone along with his wishes. He was in this for the money, and the more dirt they moved every day, the more his chances of finding an intact corpse increased.

The peer review board at the university could kiss his ass. Besides, by the time any of the undergraduates returned to civilization to report him, he'd be long gone. Probably living with some little mama-san in a love hotel in Thailand. That thought brought a smile to his lips.

"Jason! Get a move on, man." Che's voice echoed down the tunnel.

Jason stamped his feet, muttering another curse. Only a few more days and he'd either be done for the season or on the road to easy street. Either way, he'd be out of this hellhole.

He walked down the tunnel in mincing steps. When there was active digging going on, the dirt on the floor softened into a muddy glaze. The last thing he wanted to do was fall on his ass in front of Che. He ignored the mammoth humerus bone embedded in the wall. A nice trophy, but worthless next to a human corpse encased in ice.

At the end of the thirty-foot tunnel, the two young women had set up a floodlight to illuminate the back wall. Ramona Garcia stepped back so Jason could get closer to what they'd uncovered.

He gave Ramona a wide berth. In their first few days

in camp, Jason had gotten drunk one night and grabbed her ass. She slapped him and made a huge scene. Ever since then, they made a point of staying out of each other's way.

Yet another reason to get out of this hellhole, he thought to himself. Back to civilization, where women showed a little respect for a real man.

Che pointed to a spot halfway up the wall where a bit of dark fur protruded.

"Looks like hair," she said, her normally brassy voice hushed.

Jason knelt down for a closer look. It did look like hair—human hair. His pulse quickened. This could be it. This could be what they were looking for, what he was waiting for.

"Gimme a chisel," he said to Che, holding out his hand.

He felt the slap of the steel implement in his gloved hand. He chipped at the icy dirt around the shock of black hair.

"Careful," said Ramona.

"Shut the hell up," Jason muttered. He saw the two women exchange a glance and heard the combined hiss of their frustrated breaths.

He ignored them. If this was what he thought it was, they didn't matter anymore. It was all about him now.

Twenty minutes of careful work with the chisel revealed a human ear and the curve of a jawbone. The corpse was in a fetal position on its side, its face pointing away from them.

He stood and used the chisel edge to sketch out a rough square on the wall.

"Cut along these lines with the saw. We'll take it out as a solid block."

The brusque order earned him another passive-aggressive war of glances, but they did as they were told. He stepped back to let them, wishing he had brought earplugs with him as the saw started up.

It took another two hours for them to remove the material around the body. Jason stuck his head into the carved-out area and snapped his fingers for a flashlight.

He shone light on the face of a fifteen-thousand-year-old body.

It was a young man, probably midtwenties. The corpse was well preserved, as if the body had been flash-frozen. So well preserved, in fact, Jason thought he could make out a rash covering one side of the young man's face.

He felt a rush of renewed hope. If Mortimer was interested in ancient viral infections, then this find would surely be worth a bonus.

He wormed his way back out of the hole and struggled to his feet. Neither of the women offered him a hand up.

"All right, let's finish the job. Get in there with hand tools and cut this block of ice free. I'll go back to camp and get the guys so we can haul the whole thing topside."

He marched down the tunnel, ignoring the whispered curses behind him. This was it. This was what he was waiting for. His knees were shaking so badly he could barely climb the ladder. His feet crunched on a new layer of frost and he sucked in a huge lungful of fresh air. The breeze chilled his skin, but he barely felt it now. He was going to be a rich man. All he had to do was make one phone call and he was out of here forever.

He set off on the hundred-yard journey to the camp at a brisk pace. There were three insulated huts that served as living quarters and one structure that doubled as a lab and utility shed for the tools. He made a bee-line for the middle shed and banged on the door.

"What?" said an irritated voice from within.

"Get your asses out here," Jason said. "Get down in the hole with the girls. We found a specimen and we need your help to haul it out."

During the early days of the dig, Jason had put himself into a rotating-shift work schedule. But after a few days, he tired of the hard work of digging and hauling frozen soil and decided his talents were better used as a manager.

He set a new work schedule of four-hour shifts, sixteen hours a day. Basically, the young people were either on shift or in bed. There had been a brief flirtation between Che and one of the young men, but that ended when the shifts divided into genders.

Meanwhile, Jason spent his days playing video games on his laptop, watching porn, and sleeping. He tried to make sure he got into the hole at least once each shift, but even that was a stretch goal for him after a few days.

He stamped his feet on the frozen ground, growling at the bitter wind until the two young men came out of the trailer. Their sleepy faces were covered with scrag-gly beards and they eyed him with undisguised looks of disgust.

"What the fuck, man?" the one named John said. "We're off-shift." His brother Mike glared at Jason in silent resentment.

"Get down in the hole," Jason snapped. "We found what we're looking for and the girls need your help to get it out." The young men stamped off in a blizzard of muttered cursing.

Jason entered his own hut and turned up the electric heat to a balmy seventy-five degrees. He stripped off his gloves and hat and unzipped his coat. The cold skin of his face tingled in the heat.

He found the satellite phone that Mortimer had given him at the bottom of his footlocker between his last two bottles of scotch. The battery was nearly dead, so he rummaged further until he found the power cord and plugged it in. He poured himself a drink and stared at the flashing battery symbol.

Finally, he raised the antenna and thumbed down to the single phone number stored in the device. He pressed SEND.

The phone rang four times before a woman's voice answered. "Hello?"

"This is Dr. Winslow, Jason Winslow," he said, shout-ing in the confines of his trailer. "I am trying to get ahold of Harold Mortimer. I have a message for him."

"Please wait," the voice said. It was a full minute be-fore a new voice came on the line, long enough that Jason worried that he might run out of battery. He squatted down and plugged the phone back into the power cord.

"Dr. Winslow. This is Harold Mortimer. Do you have what we discussed?"

Jason licked his lips. "Yes, I have it. An excellent specimen. But I think the number we discussed is too low. I'm considering looking for another buyer."

Mortimer did not answer right away.

Jason held his breath, cursing to himself. This was a bad idea. Why did he always do this? He had a perfectly good deal and he was trying to get blood from a stone.

"I'll double the original price," Mortimer said.

Jason pumped his fist. That was why he did it. Because he was the Man and no one messed with the Man.

"That would be acceptable," Jason said.

"I'll be there in forty-eight hours, Dr. Winslow."

——————

The sound of an airplane engine woke Jason from his nap. He rushed from his hut in time to see a yellow seaplane pass low over the camp and touch down on Great Bear Lake.

Mortimer. His big payday had arrived.

His head throbbed. In the heat of his newfound wealth, he'd shared one of the bottles from his stash of scotch with the kids as a reward for all their hard work. They didn't drink with him, but it sounded like they had a good time. He felt a flush of generosity. From the look of things, John and Che might have patched up their relationship.

Jason rousted a hungover John out of bed and sent him down to the lake with one of the ATVs to bring Mortimer back to camp. Then he put on his cold-weather gear and headed to the shed.

It had snowed again last night. Only an inch, but the weather promised more to come. He'd scheduled the flight out for the whole team for the day after tomorrow, and it would be not a moment too soon.

He turned on the lights in the shed and squatted down next to the frozen corpse.

Civilization . . . money . . . bars . . . women. Soon they would all be his.

They had chipped away the ice from the head and torso, but left a shell of ice over the rest of the corpse. It was a remarkable specimen, Jason had to admit.

The rash on the young man's face and chest was definite. If Mortimer was looking for ancient pathogens, that would be a good place to start.

Jason smiled to himself. He was quite the dealmaker, if he didn't say so himself.

He heard the approaching ATV and got to his feet.

His payday had arrived.

Mortimer climbed off the back of the ATV, sharing a laugh with John.

Jason felt a flash of jealousy. John barely said two words to him on any given day and here he was yakking it up with this rich asshole after five minutes.

No matter. Mortimer's money was as green as the next guy's. He'd buy a hundred friends with what he was about to get paid. Jason pasted a smile on his face and pulled off his right glove to shake Mortimer's hand.

"Mr. Mortimer," he said. "Welcome to the edge of the world."

Mortimer laughed as if it was the best joke he'd ever heard, and Jason felt himself laughing along and meaning it.

He studied Mortimer's face. He looked different. In the bar in Seattle, he'd seemed like a wuss, but out here he looked more . . . formidable. Maybe it was the mustache. He'd had a mustache in Seattle, but it was gone now.

"Shall we take a look?" Jason spun around, calling over his shoulder, "That'll be all, John. Go finish packing."

"I'll catch you later, Harry," John said. "We'll have that drink."

"Maybe you can show me where the specimen was found," Mortimer said. "I'd like to meet the rest of the team. Take a picture at the dig site."

"Sure thing, Harry—"

"That'll be all, John," Jason said again. Inside the shed, he turned on the overhead light and pulled the tarp away from the frozen corpse.

Mortimer pulled a mask from a jacket pocket, covering his mouth and nose as he squatted next to the specimen.

"Amazing," he said. "Truly amazing. This is excellent work, Dr. Winslow. Really."

Jason swelled with pride. "Well, I did most of the digging myself. Between you and me, the undergrads are good for grunt work, but not much else."

Mortimer extracted a penlight from another pocket

and was inspecting the face of the corpse. "Perfect specimen. You will receive your full reward and then some." He stood. "I'd like to see the dig site."

Jason nodded with enthusiasm. "Of course, I can show you."

"I'll get John to show me. I promised to get a picture with the team. Perhaps you could harvest the samples for me?" He squeezed Jason's arm. "When I get back, we'll settle up."

Mortimer was gone only a few minutes, barely enough time for Jason to harvest muscle, skin, and lung tissue samples. He heard a noise outside the shed and found Mortimer leaning the aluminum ladder against the building. He saw that John had fitted the plow to the front of the ATV.

"John asked me to bring this back," Mortimer said. "He said it would help with the packing effort."

Jason clapped his gloves together. "Sure, whatever. We're all set in here. Except for the payment, I mean."

He reentered the shed and came back out with the sample case. Jason felt the grin slide off his face. Mortimer held a blocky black pistol in his bare hand, pointed at Jason's chest.

"Your payment," Mortimer said. The weapon fired twice and Jason found himself flat on his back, a tremendous weight on his chest.

Mortimer loomed over him. "You were a long shot, but you paid off." He gripped Jason's collar and dragged him to the sled attached to the back of the ATV.

He was dimly aware of the ATV starting up and the sled moving. Gray sky passed overhead. With a rush, his breath returned and pain flooded his body. He heard his own voice half weeping, half begging.

There was no reply. The sled stopped. Jason's free hand scrabbled among the tools in the bottom of the sled. His bare hand closed on the handle of an ice ax.

He heard the crunch of Mortimer's boots. Felt the man's hand grip his collar.

With all his strength, Jason lashed out with the ice ax, feeling it bite into flesh.

Mortimer let go and Jason heard him cursing. He laughed to himself. Mortimer kicked him in the side, but Jason barely felt it. All his senses seemed to run together.

The hand on Jason's collar was back. Dragging . . . falling . . . his body slammed into frozen dirt.

The gray sky was a circle above Jason. Mortimer's face appeared, then went away.

With what little strength remained in his body, Jason rolled over. Che's lifeless eyes met his. He shifted his gaze and there was John with a neat red-black hole in the center of his forehead.

Jason tried to call out, but the only sound he could make was a gurgling noise.

In the distance, he heard the ATV engine revving. Clods of frozen dirt began to rain down.

He was being buried alive.

CHAPTER 19

Tysons Corner, Virginia

Dre Ramirez watched the video screen from the second row in the large briefing room with Michael and Janet flanking her. She could sense the people in the room shifting in their seats as the black-and-white video, shot from an overhead drone, rolled across the screen.

Every Monday morning at 10:00 A.M., Don Riley held an all-hands staff meeting for the twenty-four intelligence analysts, cyberoperations experts, case officers, and support personnel at Emerging Threats. They had already been through a dozen open case files on threats that were being investigated and had finally arrived at what she and her friends were working on.

The Grand Ethiopian Renaissance Dam formed the backdrop for the grisly scene. From the size of the overturned dump truck, she could estimate the radius of the blast zone and the immense breadth of the dam structure. The dam and surrounding riverbanks would have concentrated the explosion, turning the area into a total killing zone. Like setting off a firecracker in a tin can.

The drone camera zoomed in on the blackened chassis of a pickup truck, the origin of the explosion. A star-pattern blast zone radiated from that point. A handful of other vehicles and earthmoving equipment had been scattered and charred by the blast. Thankfully, the bodies had been removed by the time the drone arrived on scene.

There was no sound associated with the drone footage, so Don Riley narrated. "The bomb was placed in a food truck, parked here." He shone a red laser pointer at the center of the blast zone, then continued.

"We don't have people on the ground, but analysts say this pattern is consistent with the use of EFPs, or explosively formed projectiles, a favorite of the Iranians and their proxies."

"The Iranians," one of the other analysts said. "I thought we had a claim on this attack?"

Don punched a button on his remote, and the image on the screen shifted. "We do."

Dre watched the high-definition video for the hundredth time. The room with colorful rugs on the floor. The low, Arab-style sofa backed by a rich tapestry along the back wall. As always, the man who stepped into the frame had his face and hands blurred. His words, even with his voice run through a synthesizer, were fluent English.

She had watched the previous videos so many times, she could almost repeat his message by heart: ". . . the infidels have used their money and their power and their weapons to subjugate the children of Islam. No more. I am the Mahdi, the Redeemer, the Reborn, the Uniter of Islam's children."

Don paced at the front of the room. As Emerging Threats expanded, Don had left the Mahdi in the sole jurisdiction of the three naval officers.

"Do we think this is an Iranian front?" the same analyst asked.

"Unknown," Don replied. "He claims no affiliation with existing groups and supports no religious ideology. Since it was an attack on a dam, the natural culprit would be Egypt, but there's no hard evidence to support that theory either."

Don's eyes found Dre sitting in the second row. "Where are we on cracking the website, Ms. Ramirez?" Next to her, Michael sat up straight.

"No progress since yesterday, sir," Michael said.

Don's gaze shifted from Dre to Michael.

"Unacceptable," he said. "But since you answered, Goodwin, what about the traps on financial transactions?" The way he said "traps" was like a swear word.

Dre couldn't tell if Don's negative attitude about the financial traps was about the quality of the idea or the fact that Michael had proposed it in a meeting with Don's upper management. It was not Michael's finest hour, and both Janet and Dre had explained to him how he had embarrassed Don Riley.

The fact that the implementation had not gone well only added to Don's angst. He regularly reminded the officer team that he had to report progress to Dylan Mattias twice weekly.

It had taken the three of them a solid week to set up monitoring on every shell company doing business in the Nile River basin, and they spent a good portion of every workday chasing down leads that led nowhere.

But there was nothing to be done. The director had approved the plan on the spot and ordered Don to "make it happen." To add insult to injury, it seemed to Dre that Mattias was pretty okay with seeing Don Riley squirm on the end of a bureaucratic hook.

"We haven't gotten any useful leads out of the financial-transaction data, sir," Michael said in an even voice.

Don let his sour expression speak for itself.

"What about the encryption on the website?" Don asked.

"No new progress since last report, sir," Michael said.

Don's complexion reddened further. "I'm disappointed, Mr. Goodwin. You and I both know there is no such thing as unbreakable code. If someone wrote that code, you have to find a way to get us inside. That's why you're here, Michael."

Dre could feel the rest of the room getting restless, undoubtedly experiencing the same discomfort she was feeling at seeing her colleague getting chewed out by the boss. Janet started to speak, but Michael put his hand on her knee to stop her.

"I understand, sir," he said.

Don seemed to realize his criticism had overstepped and he quickly moved on to the next case file.

Michael stayed silent. As soon as the meeting ended, he stood and immediately left the room. When they got back to the Cave, he was already at his desk, all three of his monitors loaded with scrolling code. Michael, hands folded in his lap, stared at the monitors.

Dre and Janet exchanged glances. They had seen this look on Michael before. He was hunting for something, a pattern in the code, the way the coder had arranged the program, something that would give him the clue he needed to get inside.

He might not even know what it was, but it was in there—somewhere—and only he could find it. They knew better than to disturb him.

The morning crawled by as she and Janet researched financial transactions. At lunchtime, Dre stood behind Michael and cleared her throat.

"It's lunchtime, Michael."

"Not hungry. Thanks."

She watched lines of code slowly scroll in tandem down the screen. Michael's breathing was even as his eyes flicked across the monitors.

When they got back from lunch, Michael still had not moved. Dre placed a roast beef sandwich by his keyboard, but it remained untouched for the rest of the afternoon. She and Janet slogged through another round of financial leads to no avail.

It was nearly seven o'clock in the evening when Michael sat up straight in his chair and punched a button on his computer to stop the scrolling text.

"There" was all he said.

Janet and Dre gathered around Michael's computer. He highlighted a single line of code on each screen.

"What do you see?" he asked.

"I see three lines of code, Michael," Janet said. "What am I looking for?"

Michael broke into a grin. "All these lines of code serve the same function in the same program, but they're all different, why?"

Dre looked more closely at the three screens. She recognized the source code for the Mahdi website, but he was looking at three different versions.

"I'll bite, Michael," she said. "Tell me why you've got three different versions of the same source code."

He pointed at the screen on the right. "This is live from the website. These other two are copies we took after the last two Mahdi broadcasts," he said. "After each event, we took a copy of the source code so we could analyze it offline."

"So why are they different?" Janet asked. Her tone suggested she was getting a little frustrated.

"That's just it," Michael said. "They shouldn't be different, but they are."

Dre studied all three lines, all places where they had tried to gain entry into the website. "I don't get it. They updated their code, so what?"

Michael shook his head. "That's not what's happening. When we copied the website, it responded by changing the code. That's why every time we tried something new it failed."

"Now I'm really confused, Michael," Janet said.

"How about you explain to me like I'm a five-year-old, because that's what I feel like right now."

Michael's tone, normally calm, was tense with excitement. "Our intervention forced the code to change. What does that mean?"

Janet shrugged. "I don't know."

But Dre knew now. "It's metamorphic encryption," she said. "If you copy the data, you change the state."

Michael clapped. "Exactly, Dre!"

"I understand what you're saying, but I don't understand what it means," Janet said, looking from Michael to Dre.

"I wrote a paper last year on the future of dynamic encryption, so I know a little bit about it." He turned back to the screens. "But this website is something I've only read about and even that was in a top-secret document. There's only one place in the world even close to implementing this kind of tech."

"Well?" Janet demanded.

"Israel," Michael said. "I think the Israelis built this website."

CHAPTER 20

Project Deliverance, undisclosed location in Sudan

It turned out that if you removed all the financial and personal distractions from a group of scientists at the top of their intellectual game, they turned into children.

Not a single person in the Project Deliverance common room had to apply for a grant for next year or worry about their next review from the university board. No one had to deal with a significant other having a bad day or worry about the latest political crisis in their home country.

All they had to do was work—and they loved it.

There was no such thing as small talk in this group. Everything was shop talk. Over community meals, they swapped stories of horrific symptoms, gruesome patient deaths, and side notes of arcane genetic humor that often caused the entire group to break into uproarious laughter.

On his rare site visits, JP smiled along with them in

these moments. Although he enjoyed the camaraderie, he was intellectually so far out of his depth with this group that he didn't even bother trying to keep up. On the other hand, Talia seemed perfectly at ease with the little community of scientists they had brought together in the desert of Sudan.

At the end of each workday, the team gathered in the common room for a drink before dinner. In their underground bunker, the assignment of night and day was artificial, but this lack of sensory detail only seemed to add to the cocoon-like quality of the sequestered team.

It was all a game to them, a challenge of their intellect against the Blue Team. In this game of genetic chess, they produced weapons that could wipe out the human race, and the Blue Team figured out how to stop them.

All the intellectual freedom of creation and none of the responsibility. The lack of ethical curiosity both stunned and fascinated JP.

Talia circulated among the group, topping off glasses from an open bottle of wine. As she and JP had planned, Talia carefully cultivated a personal relationship with each scientist. She clinked her wineglass with Faraj's fruit juice. Their lone practicing Muslim remained steadfast in his faith even as he produced viruses that could slaughter every human on the planet.

Tonight's meeting was a celebration of sorts. The end of their first new disease minted by the combined efforts of the Deliverance Red Team. JP's eyes strayed to the whiteboard shoved up against the wall.

Faraj's constant sobriety meant he normally served as the group scribe, and the board was covered with his neat block handwriting. During the end-of-day sessions, each scientist provided an update on the team effort to amplify the Ebola virus so it could spread more easily. It had been Talia's idea to try to control the incubation period of the virus so the patient showed no symptoms while still being able to infect those around him. Katie McDonough, the CRISPR expert from Australia, had managed to figure out a way to achieve the time delay by splicing in genetics material from a slow-growing fungus.

The Deliverance team decided to name their first two test subjects Fat Man and Little Boy, a macabre nod to the first two nuclear weapons developed by the Americans as part of the Manhattan Project.

The two rhesus macaques, who were neither fat nor little, were brothers. They were microchipped for positive identification, but JP could tell them apart by sight. Little Boy had a stripe of lighter-colored hair down the center of his forehead, while his brother's crest was darker.

JP had never thought of himself as an animal lover, but he felt for the two monkeys. On the other hand, the scientists seemed to be able to compartmentalize their feelings with startling ease.

Three days ago, Fat Man had been dosed with the new Ebola virus. After a twenty-four-hour period, the monkeys were placed in separate cages.

JP's eyes strayed over to the always-on, closed-circuit TV monitor that showed the two brothers. They lived in adjacent cages in the level-four section of the underground lab. Prior to being separated for the test, the monkeys spent their days playing and grooming each other's tawny fur. To JP's eye, their humanlike faces and pointed ears showed personality and intelligence.

The team was testing both the lethality of the new amplified Ebola virus and their ability to control the timing of the incubation.

Greta Berger, well into her third glass of wine, gushed about the paleoviruses she harvested from the tissue samples JP had supplied. The Swedish scientist had quizzed him closely about where he had obtained the specimen and the conditions of the body, such as burial depth, but had shown little interest in how he had managed to secure the samples. No one was asking her to fill out a grant application and that seemed to be enough for her.

They're like children, JP thought. When it concerned their work, they were all id, no ego.

"Guys, I think something is happening." Lakshmi was standing next to the monitor, her face close to the screen as she studied the images of the rhesus macaques.

Fat Man was lying on his side, facing away from the camera. Little Boy paced at the glass partition between the cages, calling to his brother.

Talia connected her laptop to the large TV screen in the sitting area. With a few keystrokes, she brought up a suite of full-color security cameras that covered every angle within the monkeys' cages. She selected one at floor level showing the face and body of Fat Man and clicked on it. The image enlarged to fill the whole screen.

Fat Man's eyes were closed, his lips parted as he panted. A thin line of blood ran from his nose. Visible in the background, Little Boy let out a scream of frustration.

"Can you zoom in on his face?" Faraj asked. "I'd like to see if we can detect any hemorrhaging yet."

Talia complied. The full-color image showed every detail of Fat Man's face, down to the nap of his hair. Blood welled out from under the monkey's closed eyelids. As JP looked away, the rest of the group crowded closer.

The evening meal was forgotten. For the next three hours, the group sat riveted as they observed the rapid deterioration of Fat Man's physical appearance. The Ebola virus had done its work. The rhesus macaque was clearly dying a swift and very painful death.

Little Boy cried and yowled at the cameras, but he did not look sick yet.

"How much longer until Little Boy starts showing symptoms?" Lu asked.

Talia worked the cameras so they had a good view of the active monkey. "He's in the window now," Talia said. JP could sense the tension in her tone. Controlling the incubation period was a major project milestone.

"There," said Lakshmi in a breathless whisper. She pointed at the screen.

A thin line of bloody drool slipped from Little Boy's lips. The creature wiped it away, then rubbed his fingers together in what JP saw as an eerily human gesture. Slowly, the monkey lay down and curled up.

"We did it!" Talia leaped to her feet and raised both fists in celebration. All around her, the scientists cheered and high-fived each other.

It took another six hours for Fat Man to die, and it was a horrible passing. His features seemed to melt as the hemorrhagic fever took a toll on his body. The talk of the group had already moved to the autopsy phase and everyone agreed they would find massive internal bleeding. JP had long ago set aside his wine and his stomach roiled with acid. He took a seat on the sofa, away from the group.

Talia engaged Greta Berger in her discussion with Lu about paleoviruses, speaking loud enough that JP could overhear snippets of the conversation.

"If we were able to splice in elements of the paleo-virus components into the existing platform, we could increase the Ebola efficacy, right?" Talia was saying.

Greta pinched her lip. "You're talking about making a chimeric," she said. "I've written papers about it and I've designed experiments, but until now, I've never had access to paleogenetic material." Her voice went soft as she considered the concept.

"It will take some time to isolate the new genetic se-quence from the samples and develop the right combi-nation, but it's feasible. The testing protocol would be a little more difficult to develop . . ."

They moved toward the kitchen, out of earshot. Talia saw JP watching them and winked.

JP started as Dr. Lu sat down next to him. The short Chinese man picked at the cuticles of his stubby fingers, a habit JP noticed he often did when deep in thought.

"The other aspect of the project you asked me to look into," Lu said finally. "I have an idea."

Lu loosened a cuticle on his thumbnail and stripped it away, leaving a bloody trail.

"It might be possible to introduce a genetic marker into the virus," he said.

"That would allow the virus to target a specific subgroup of people?" JP asked.

"It's possible. Genetic-specific diseases exist already. Dubin-Johnson syndrome and congenital myasthenia gravis, for example, show up in Persian Jewish populations, but this specificity would be very difficult to replicate on a larger basis."

"But it is possible?"

Lu sighed. "Possible, yes. Probable, no. And if you factor in intermarriage and dilution of the genetic basis, this idea has less applicability, I think. And then there's the biggest question of all."

He peered at JP through his square glasses. "How do you propose to test it?"

JP looked back to the TV. Fat Man's dead body lay still and grotesque. Little Boy's rib cage rose and fell with rapid breaths. He would be dead by morning.

In the kitchen, JP heard the pop of a wine cork and Talia's laughter filtered toward him.

"We'll let the Blue Team handle that problem, Doctor."

CHAPTER 21

Al-Qahtamni Enterprises, Riyadh, Saudi Arabia

Nasir al-Qahtamni stared at the bank balances on his computer screen.

Ethiopian Coffee—$3,000,000.00.

Khartoum Security Services—$9,768.00.

He was going to miss his date with Rania over this bullshit.

Nasir wished he could wave a magic wand and reverse the bank totals. The coffee company had drawn down exactly five hundred dollars in the last month, while this stupid security company had burned through all their extra cash to pay for new hires.

Nasir cursed under his breath at this Mahdi fellow who was behind all the bombings along the upper Nile. Blasted Egyptians. Always stirring up trouble for the rest of the Arab world. Sometimes they were no better than the damned Iranians.

He sighed as he opened a new tab on his computer

screen. Uncle Alyan was very strict about money transfers. He couldn't just take money from one company and move it to the other. These were shell companies, he had explained. Companies used to obscure the ownership of local assets and funding sources. His uncle had a very strict protocol for moving money into one of their shell companies—

Nasir's phone buzzed.

Where are you? Rania texted him. She followed up with a pouty-face emoji.

Rania. He had been seeing her now for nearly a month and she was unlike any girl he'd ever known. In a land where arranged marriages were the norm, she might be the best of all possible worlds: an eligible girl that he was legitimately interested in.

More than interested.

Rania had gone to school in France for three years and she was anxious to show her independence in ways that he hadn't fully explored yet.

His phone buzzed again. A selfie of Rania next to a car with an open driver's-side door. She was dressed in tight jeans and an open-necked blouse. She made sure to include the curve of her ass in the photo.

If you don't come get me right now, I'm outta here, the text read.

As he was pondering that last pic, she sent him a new photo with her winking from a high angle. He could almost see the lace of her bra.

Hurry, lover, she texted.

That did it. It was Friday afternoon and the rest of

the office was away at a conference in Europe. Uncle Alyan was very strict about who he trusted to make wire transfers, so Nasir couldn't just fob off the responsibility on one of the secretaries.

He sighed as he turned back to his computer screen. Uncle Alyan's procedure called for taking the funds from the real-estate holdings in Dubai and routing them through three different banking systems in varying amounts before depositing the funds in one of the shell companies. He would need to wait for the funds to arrive at the new destination before initiating a new routing to the next stop.

It could take hours. He might not even complete the task before the close of business, and then where would the Khartoum Security Services be?

Unless . . .

He looked at the bank balance of the Ethiopian Coffee Company. Would anyone really notice if he took a small sum—say, fifty thousand dollars—from the coffee-company account and sent it to the security company?

His gaze strayed to his phone. Beautiful Rania, whose mind was filled with all that lustful Western television, was waiting.

Fifty thousand dollars would tide the security company over for the weekend. On Monday, he could do a proper transfer.

Nasir licked his lips. Uncle Alyan wouldn't be back until next Wednesday. Nasir would have the whole transaction cleared up by then—

His phone buzzed again. A new selfie of Rania behind the steering wheel, throwing a smoldering look at the camera.

The bank transfer took less than ten minutes to clear. Fifty thousand dollars moved from the Ethiopian Coffee Company to Khartoum Security Services. That would be enough to hold them until Monday.

He slapped his laptop shut. Uncle Alyan rewarded initiative, Nasir reasoned. He was always saying young men should work hard and show initiative.

Nasir snatched up his phone and fired off a text to Rania:

I'm on my way, darling.

Tysons Corner, Virginia

Dre set the carton of chicken lo mein next to her computer keyboard and stretched her arms to the ceiling. All she wanted to do was get out of the office and go for a run, or a walk, or maybe just stand on her head for a few minutes. Anything to break the boredom of sitting on her ass all day.

She did the time-difference calculation between DC and Hawaii. If she were still on the *Murphy,* she'd just be getting to work. Walking the ship like she used to do every morning, saying hello to real people instead of staring at a computer screen all day. . . .

Dre sighed and loaded another screen of financial transactions. Michael's financial-trap program idea had been wildly successful at generating endless lists of all the transactions related to the Nile River basin shell companies. The problem was that someone still had to sort through them. Janet, Michael, and Dre had gotten pretty good at plowing through the financial transactions quickly, but it still took about three hours a day of combined effort from all three of them, something that Don frequently needled Michael about in their staff meetings.

And God help you if you skipped a day and got behind the power curve. . . .

So far, their search had yielded exactly zero connections between any of the shell companies and not even a whiff of anything to do with the Mahdi. Even more worrying, their report to Don Riley about the advanced Israeli encryption on the Mahdi website had disappeared into a black hole of bureaucracy.

Dre focused on the first transaction. The equivalent of five hundred dollars in local currency to a business in Eritrea. She rolled her eyes and clicked for more details. Looked like a payment for office furniture.

With the clarity of hindsight, the digital dragnet that had seemed like such a phenomenal idea in the meeting with Mattias was actually a giant time suck in real life. Most of the transactions were like this one: penny-ante dollar amounts to local businesses or vendors.

Occasionally one of the shell companies received a large incoming financial transaction, hundreds of thousands or even millions of dollars, which the officers tried to track back to the source. Almost always, the source turned out to be a numbered account in a different country and the trail went cold from there. The few times when they got through the first layer of financial routing, they were stopped at the second level. And to further complicate things, the money amounts were completely appropriate for the companies involved— every transaction appeared to be normal business expenses. No anomalies.

Whoever was behind these shell companies knew how to move money around the world. While that spoke of a financial savviness, it did not mean what they were doing was criminal. For that, they needed to see the data.

Dre clicked through three more lines on the screen before she allowed herself another bite of her lunch. Still chewing, she opened the next item, a transfer between the Ethiopian Coffee Company based in Addis Ababa and Khartoum Security Services based in Sudan.

She pursed her lips. Fifty thousand dollars across international borders . . . this had potential. She clicked on the financial routing details and nearly dropped the carton in her lap. She studied the screen, blinked, then reread the whole transaction carefully to ensure she was not missing anything.

Dre set down the chicken lo mein. "Guys."

No reaction from either Michael or Janet.

Dre continued, more emphatic this time, "Guys, I think I have something."

Janet and Michael swiveled their heads in her direction, their faces illuminated only by the glow of their monitors. Red-rimmed eyes showed a distinct lack of enthusiasm.

Dre snapped her fingers. "Get your asses over here. I said I've got something and I mean it."

With matching sighs, Michael and Janet trooped over to Dre's workstation. They'd all been through this drill before. After dozens of false alerts, the sense of excitement about possibly cracking the case had gone stale.

Dre walked through the cross-border transaction and showed them the routing information. Michael's eyes widened. "Who authorized the transaction?"

Dre switched screens to look up the transaction routing. Her voice went up a notch with excitement. "It was authorized by Al-Qahtamni Enterprises in Saudi Arabia."

The lethargy of her friends evaporated as they leaned over her shoulder, alternately moving her mouse and punching buttons before she shooed them away.

"I found this, dammit," Dre said. "Now let me do my job."

But Michael was too excited. He rushed back to his computer and hammered at his keyboard.

"Al-Qahtamni Enterprises is a holding company based in Riyadh, Saudi Arabia." He cranked the computer screen in their direction to show them the picture of a well-dressed Middle Eastern man with carefully parted dark hair and an engaging smile. "Meet Alyan Sultan al-Qahtamni, founder and CEO. It says he's focused primarily in green energy and developing countries."

Michael leaned back and folded his arms. "With the amount of investment opportunity in the Nile River basin, Saudi money is not a surprise. The question is why would he go to so much trouble to hide all of his other transactions yet not this one?"

"We need to show this to Don right away," Janet said.

"This is the first real lead we've gotten with this project." She pointed at Michael's monitor with the picture of the Al-Qahtamni CEO. "Then we'll do a deep dive on that guy."

Dre started to put the screen grabs into an email, then stopped. "Why don't you tell Don what we found, Michael?"

Minutes later, they were in Don's office, where he was just ending a phone call. "Perfect timing," he said. "Your report on the Mahdi website cryptography has ruffled some feathers in high places. We've been invited to a personal briefing."

"NSA?" Janet asked.

Don frowned. "Uh . . . Not exactly. The Israelis. They want to talk to us in person—all of us. Go home and pack. We have a flight out of Dulles tonight."

"They want all three of us to go?" Janet asked. "Isn't that overkill?"

Don shook his head. "They were very specific about the request. They want to see all three of you and they want to know exactly how you figured this out. I told them, but I'm not sure they believe me. I'm leaving a note with my lawyer in case I don't come back." He gave them a weak smile. "I'm kidding, of course."

Dre shot a glance at Janet. No one laughed at the joke.

Don made a shooing motion with his hands. "Go! I'll see you in a few hours at Dulles."

"But wait," Dre said. "We found something from Michael's financial-trap program."

Don's head snapped up. "Tell me."

Dre and Janet let Michael walk Don through the

suspicious financial transaction. Their boss let out a low whistle when he saw the connection to the holding company in Riyadh.

"Looks like somebody finally made a mistake," he said. "And we get the benefit of it. Good work. All of you, I mean it." He held Michael's gaze for a second longer than was necessary.

"Well, do you still want all three of us to go?" Janet asked. "Don't you want someone to stay here and run this lead down?"

Don shook his head. "Pass this off to someone else in the group. Our orders are explicit. I am to bring all three of you to Israel with me. No exceptions."

CHAPTER 22

Project Deliverance, undisclosed location in Sudan

JP slipped out of bed and stood in the chill of the darkened bedroom. His body told him it was dawn even if the underground bunker deprived him of any external clues. Although the scientists didn't seem to mind the lack of natural light, it bothered him.

Talia shifted under the bedcovers. With her hair splayed out across the pillow and her lips parted, she looked young and innocent.

JP padded across the carpeted room and carefully opened the door to the en-suite. He slid it closed before he flipped on the light switch. He blinked in the harsh overhead light reflecting off the white surfaces of the bathroom.

When he designed the Project Deliverance living quarters, he'd made some accommodation for creature comforts in the bedrooms. High-quality mattresses and bedclothes, carpeted floors, and warm colors on the walls. His thinking had not extended to the bathroom design. They were functional spaces: a toilet, a large walk-in shower, a sink and counter, and a large mirror on the wall. All blinding white, and the only source of illumination came from a single overhead light.

He thought back on the years of planning this venture. If all he had to regret when this was done was the bathroom design, he'd consider himself lucky.

JP turned on the shower and let it run, then returned to the sink and splashed cold water on his face. He studied his reflection in the wide mirror.

This job, the lifestyle, and age had all taken their toll on his body. Constant travel between time zones interrupted his sleep patterns, and poor diet had added a few pounds to his midsection. He looked and felt older, slower.

Steam billowed out of the shower. He felt a twinge in his calf and bent down to peel the bandage off his leg. The wound was a nasty two-inch cut from Winslow's ice ax.

Exhibit A, he thought to himself. *You got stabbed by a college professor. You're losing a step, old man.*

But soon, the job would be complete. He and Talia would fade into the kind of obscurity that can only be accessed via fabulous wealth. No more underground bunkers and deadly viruses, just beaches and endless days of leisure.

He heard the door slide open.

"What happened?" Talia's voice was still husky with

sleep. Her tousled hair spilled over her shoulders and she hugged herself against the chill of the air-conditioned room. Gooseflesh prickled the soft skin of her upper body.

"You said you got a little cut when you collected the paleo samples," Talia said. "There's a gouge out of your leg, JP."

"Just a scratch," he said, wrapping his arms around her. She pressed her curves against him. "It doesn't even hurt."

That was a lie. It hurt like hell, and the shower was not going to help the pain, either. But he wasn't about to tell Talia the truth.

Talia slapped him on the backside. "Into the shower," she ordered. "We need to get that cleaned properly."

JP grinned at her. "If you want to play doctor, I have a few ideas . . ."

"Prick," she said, laughing.

"That's exactly what I had in mind."

Talia stepped into the steaming shower, letting the hot water soften her curves and warm her skin. She grabbed JP's hand and pulled him close. "Get in here."

JP gritted his teeth as the hot water touched the cut on his leg. He kissed Talia to distract himself, and she responded by slipping her arms around his waist.

In idle moments, he wondered what he had done to deserve this woman. She'd come into his life at a time when nothing else made sense—and she helped calm the chaos.

At that point in his life, he despaired for the world

and his place in it. His time with the French DGSE left him empty and distrustful.

But Talia had been different, unlike any person he'd ever met before.

She saw the world clearly and without pretense. There were no shades of gray in the mind of Talia Tahir—that's what drew JP to her. Her certainty kept him going.

There would be casualties, and JP regretted that, but it was for a greater good.

Talia took a washcloth and a bar of soap and knelt on the floor of the shower to clean the wound on his calf. She carefully dabbed at the gash. JP tried not to wince, but it really did hurt.

"You should have cleaned this much more carefully," she said. "You know the risks of getting an infection."

JP grumbled, but it was mostly for show. Her ministrations showed how much she cared for him. "You're right, dear."

"Don't be patronizing." She snapped him on the thigh with the wet washcloth.

She finished dressing the wound, then looked up at him, grinning. "As long as we're playing doctor, what else hurts?"

―――――――――――

JP pulled on his dress shirt. He caught Talia's reflection in the mirror as she pulled on a pair of jeans. He watched the blue denim slide up her slender thighs.

Talia caught him looking and smiled. "Haven't you had enough, old man?"

"Never." He finished buttoning the shirt and threw a tie around his collar. Like the rest of the lab staff, Talia dressed casually in jeans and a T-shirt, but JP was leaving today and needed to be in business attire. He started a double Windsor knot.

"I've been thinking about you getting hurt," she said. "I think we should look into security for you."

"We have security," JP began.

Talia's cold stare stopped him. "I'm not talking about the militia types around here," she said. "I'm talking about personal security. Someone who can travel with you, blend in."

JP concentrated on his tie. He knew she was right, but that did not make it easier. The former Sudanese Janjaweed militia at the site were fearsome fighters, hard men. They were ideal for providing security for a place like this, but to bring them to a corporate venue would only invite stares—and questions.

To get personal security would be an acknowledgment that he couldn't handle himself any longer. Had he really reached that point?

"I'll think about it."

Talia came up behind him and slid her arms around his midsection, peeking over his shoulder seductively. "I want you to do more than think about it. I want you to promise me. I mean it, or the next time you show up here, I'm cutting you off. Cold turkey."

JP assumed a look of mock horror in the mirror. "Yes, ma'am," he said. "I'll get right on it."

Talia held his gaze in the mirror.

"There's more?" JP asked.

Talia stepped in front of him and adjusted his tie. He let her fuss over him.

"I think I should do the next test," she said. Talia put her hand on his chest to stop him from protesting. "I know how things are done in Yemen. I can get in and out of the country easily."

"You're dead, remember?" JP said gently, taking her hands in his. "Besides, you're needed here. Only you can make sure the paleoviruses that I brought back are being used to best effect. You know this."

JP tilted her chin up. "You know I'm right. I'll be in and out of Yemen in a day or less. And I promise as soon as I get back, I'll look into personal security."

Talia pressed her lips together, then nodded reluctantly. From her dresser, she picked up a small cylindrical padded bag. She slipped a silver canister about the size of a can of soda out of the bag and unscrewed the top. Underneath was a nozzle and a small black readout.

"This is the latest aerosol device. The sample inside is completely contained. Remove the top, use these buttons to set the timer, and leave it anywhere in a confined space. The virus has been amplified. All you need to do is infect one person in the population. The virus does the rest."

She screwed the cap back on the bottle and slipped it inside the padded pouch.

"And then you hire a bodyguard."

CHAPTER 23

Tel Aviv, Israel

"Don!" The man seated behind the massive wooden desk stood as Don and the three young officers were ushered through the door.

"Binya," Don replied in a much less boisterous tone. Benyamin Albedano's dark eyes, arching eyebrows, and carefully trimmed goatee lent an air of aristocracy to his look, but behind the refined appearance was a sharp mind that Don had come to know well during the years-long international manhunt for the terrorist Rafiq Roshed.

The Mossad director of operations stepped from behind his desk and moved across the room with light, quick steps. He wrapped his arms around Don and kissed him on both cheeks. Don blushed at the show of affection and patted his longtime friend on the back.

"Always good to see you, Binya." Don introduced his three officers one by one.

Binya took Janet's hand in both of his own, looking her in the eyes with his penetrating gaze, and said his name again. He did the same with Dre, but he paused when he came to Michael and cocked his head.

"Michael Goodwin. A pleasure." Binya shot a look back at Don. "This is the one you were telling me about?"

"Michael is the one who figured out what we were dealing with," Don said, choosing his words carefully.

The young man blushed as he shook Binya's hand. "It was a team effort, sir."

Binya stepped back and stroked his goatee. "Hmmm. I don't think so."

He studied Michael for another moment; then his face lit up with a bright smile. "You all have traveled such a long way, and here I am being an uncivilized host."

He ushered them across the room to a small conference table. A quick phone call later and a young man entered with a tray containing coffee, tea, and a plate of sandwiches. When the refreshments arrived, so did a young woman, who took a seat next to Binya at the table.

She had dark hair that she wore in a thick braid down her back. She had high cheekbones, sharp features, and quick, birdlike movements. She said nothing as she studied the Americans, especially Michael.

"This is Shira Fishbein," Binya said. "She works for me."

He introduced Don, Janet, and Dre, but when he came to Michael, he said to Shira, "This is the one."

Shira shook Michael's hand stiffly. Don took a

sandwich and passed the tray while Binya poured coffee and made light conversation. Shira refused a sandwich and a drink. Finally, Binya settled back in his chair and crossed his legs. He balanced a coffee cup on his knee.

"Donald," he said. "Your message about this encryption method was surprising to me—to us." He indicated Shira, who bristled. "Perhaps you could explain how you came to the conclusion that Israel was mixed up in this Mahdi situation?"

Don let Janet take the lead. The two women officers had wanted Michael to lead the discussion, but Michael insisted Janet was the group spokesperson.

Janet cleared her throat. "We have been monitoring the Mahdi website for months now. Despite our best efforts, we have been unable to hack into the website. We found this very unusual and frankly we took it as a challenge. We're pretty good at what we do.

"It was really Michael who made the connection," Janet continued. "We found subtle changes, which led us to the idea that this site could be using a form of metamorphic encryption—"

"And how did you come to that conclusion?" Shira's voice had a sharp, penetrating quality. Two spots of color appeared on her cheekbones and she leaned into the table when she spoke.

We've touched a nerve somewhere, Don thought.

"Michael figured it out," Janet said. She met Shira's aggressive gaze without flinching. If anything, the young woman's reaction seemed to make Don's team even more curious about what was going on.

"*Exactly* what did you do to figure this out?" Shira asked again. She glared at Michael. "I want to know how you decided this was metamorphic encryption."

Michael rested his elbows on the table and responded in a calm voice, as if determined to show he was not intimidated by Shira. "I compared the live coding of the site with two prior copies simultaneously. I looked for differences. I found them."

"And what program did you use to do that?" Shira pressed.

Michael shrugged. "I didn't use any program. I used my eyes. I'm pretty good at pattern recognition."

Shira stared as if daring him to lie to her. "I don't believe it. No one could compare three code bases simultaneously and find these kinds of subtle differences. It's just not possible."

Don decided to step in. "I assure you, Ms. Fishbein, it's not only possible, but it happened. Ensign Goodwin is one of our finest and he has a rare gift for pattern recognition. It's been proven in operational situations before."

Don shot a look at Binya. The Mossad director was one of the few people outside of the United States who knew what had happened in North Korea and Michael's role in that operation.

Don returned his attention to Shira. "We didn't come here to be questioned about our capabilities. In fact, you asked us here because we apparently found something you didn't want us to find. Is that correct?"

Binya put his hand on Shira's arm. "I told you," he said. "We can trust them. If my friend Donald says they found this by visual means then I believe him. And you should, too."

The young woman sat back in her chair as if willing herself to relax.

Don saw the opening he'd been waiting for. They'd obviously passed some kind of test, and it was high time they got some information in return. He leaned his elbows on the table.

"It's time for you to come clean, Binya. You drag the four of us halfway around the world on a moment's notice to tell us something that could not be entrusted to any form of secure communications. We'd like to know what's going on."

To his surprise, Binya deferred to Shira, who stood. "Follow me, please."

The young woman marched out of the room and led them to the elevator. Once inside, she used a security card to access the lowest level of the building. The elevator doors opened onto a rough concrete hallway, which led to an unmarked door. Binya and Shira left their mobile phones in a bin outside the door. For operational security reasons, Don's team had left all of their electronics with their American driver outside the Mossad building.

Inside was a plain conference room table and six chairs. There was nothing else in the room, not even a wastebasket, let alone a telephone or a whiteboard.

When everyone was seated, Shira flipped a switch on the wall, and the light over the door turned from red to green.

"I should introduce myself more formally. I am the

head of cyber operations at Mossad." She gave a wry smile. "We call this room the 'bubble.' It is the most secure room in the entire country of Israel. Electromagnetically sealed and swept continuously with electronic noise to jam any possible listening device within twenty meters. It is not possible for us to be overheard in this room."

She glanced one more time at Binya, who nodded encouragement before she continued. "What I am about to tell you has only been shared with one other person within the Mossad directorate or the political structure of our country. It absolutely must stay within the confines of this room. Do you understand?"

Don nodded along with the rest of his team.

Shira took a deep breath. "The code that you found on the Mahdi website was first created in Israel."

Dre broke in. "So, the Mahdi is an Israeli front?"

"Of course not!" The two spots of color returned to Shira's high cheekbones. "We would never do such a thing."

Binya interrupted, his voice tense. "What Shira is trying to say is that the encryption you discovered was stolen from Mossad."

The Mossad operations chief sat back in his chair, exhaled, and became very serious.

"We have a mole, and we need your help to find him."

CHAPTER 24

Melaba, Yemen

In his two years with Médecins Sans Frontières, Dr. Jacques Legarde had never driven into a Yemeni village and not been greeted by at least one person.

Except for today.

He looked in the rearview mirror at the two young men asleep in the backseat of the Land Rover. They were twin brothers, Yemeni by birth, trained in France as medical techs, who had volunteered to come back to their native land as translators for Doctors Without Borders. Their given names were Lando and Jalal, but they preferred to go by their French nicknames Frick and Frack, which the brothers thought were hilarious.

"Frick, wake up!" Jacques called. "This is the place?"

The young man elbowed his brother awake and compared the map with a handheld GPS unit. "This is it, boss."

Jacques opened the door of the white MSF Land

Rover and stepped into the noonday sun of interior Yemen. The tiny village, no more than two dozen houses arranged around a haphazard town square, was silent and still in the baking heat.

He'd never been this far east in Yemen before. The village of Melaba was forty miles east of the Haraz Wildlife Sanctuary, which served as a natural buffer between the fighting in the west and the interior of Yemen to the east. The village was deep in Houthi territory, but MSF had received a tip that the town had suffered a serious outbreak of some kind.

The political elephants in Sanaa were talking up another humanitarian cease-fire, which was all the brothers needed to talk their way through the Houthi roadblocks.

Jacques relished his role as the Doctors Without Borders vanguard. Even after two years in the field, the job still held allure for him. He liked to think he'd helped make the world a tiny bit better for his efforts.

But he'd seen some horrific sights as well. While the Saudis and the Iranians fought a proxy war, the Yemeni population suffered. Lack of food, clean water, and routine medical care had devastated small communities like this one.

But still, there was always someone there to greet him when he arrived in a new village.

"*Allons-y,*" he said to the brothers. "See if you can find someone in charge."

While the pair split up to search for villagers, Jacques lowered the tailgate of the Land Rover. The interior was packed with the equivalent of a Doctors Without

Borders first-aid kit. He could manage the basics from the Rover, but anything more complicated required a field hospital.

Frick returned to the car at a dead run, his eyes wide. "It's bad in there, boss," he said in rapid-fire French. "The whole village is sick. Started three days ago. Everyone is sick. It's—it's . . ." Frick sputtered out a few unintelligible words in his native tongue.

Jacques automatically pulled out boxes of masks, latex gloves, and safety glasses. Frick had seen some unspeakable conditions, and if he was shaken, it must be bad.

He handed a mask to the young man. "Show me."

They jogged to the nearest building, a squat mud-brick hut with a stone door lintel and a dirt floor. Jacques put on his safety gear and stepped inside, letting his eyes adjust to the gloom after the bright sunshine. His nose didn't need adjustment. The scent of dead bodies in the heat nearly overwhelmed him.

Gradually, the dark interior dissolved into the forms of a young family. A husband and wife with five children ranging from young teens to a toddler. His medical training kicked in as he triaged the situation.

The husband was dead, as were four of the children. The wife, who looked to be midthirties, clasped her youngest child to her chest. The woman was barely conscious, and the child stared at him with dull eyes.

Jacques knelt in the dirt and took the woman's pulse. Her heart was beating like a rabbit's and she was burning up with fever. The child let out a deep hacking cough that made Jacques instinctively back away.

"Bring me two IV kits," he said to Frick. "And I want you and your brother to put on full bio suits, okay?" Frick's eyes widened at the sudden note of command in Jacques's voice, and he raced out of the room, calling for his brother.

The woman's eyes rolled back in her head and she mumbled something in a language he didn't understand. Her hand pawed at the air like she was reaching for something.

"It'll be okay," he whispered. "I'll do what I can."

He gently pulled the child away from her mother. He saw now his guess about the child's age had been wrong, a common mistake in this country where malnutrition was rampant. The young girl was closer to six years old than three, and she had the sunken eyes and pinched features of someone who'd grown up with not enough food.

She was light in his hands as he laid the child on the dirt floor. Jacques had to blink away tears. He didn't understand politics, he didn't understand war, but he did understand the suffering of children—and it broke his heart every time.

Frick returned wearing a white bio suit, with a bag of supplies. Working quickly, Jacques slipped an IV needle into both patients and gave them a shot of broad-spectrum antibiotics. It was a guess at best. He had no idea what was causing the fever and pulmonary distress, but it was better than nothing. He felt a rush of frustration at his impotence.

Frack appeared in the doorway, also clad in full bio gear. "It's like this all over the village, boss. Every house. At least half of them are dead already. What do we do?"

"You do your job," Jacques said. "Triage the patients, get fluids into the survivors, and give everyone a shot of antibiotics. I'm going to call for reinforcements."

Outside, Jacques squinted in the sunlight. He carefully took off the gloves, mask, and glasses, then scrubbed down his exposed skin with sanitary wipes. From the glove box of the Rover, he retrieved a satellite phone. The device seemed to take forever to boot up and get a signal.

Leon's firm professional voice gave Jacques a shot of much-needed confidence. Back in the real world, Leon was a cosmetic surgeon from Chicago, but as the MSF country coordinator, Leon had seen it all.

"It's bad here, Leon. I mean really bad." Jacques's voice broke. "We have a small village, possibly up to one hundred fifty people in the midst of a full-scale epidemic." He consulted the map and read off the GPS coordinates for Melaba. "The patients I've seen so far show symptoms of severe bleeding and respiratory distress. The mortality rate is fifty percent and rising. We need a full field hospital on the ground ASAP."

Leon sounded tired, but that was par for the course. They were all tired. Tired of seeing people dying for no reason, tired of seeing children starving for no reason, tired of patching fighters up only to see them blown up the next day.

"Cease-fire just went through this afternoon," Leon said. "I'll get choppers in the air before these idiots change their minds again and start shooting at each other. We'll be there before nightfall. Hold down the fort, buddy. Reinforcements are on the way."

"What about WHO?" Jacques asked. "If this is an epidemic, they need to be on it right away."

"I'll get one of them on the chopper, if I can," Leon replied. "You just worry about the immediate situation."

"Just hurry, man," Jacques said.

Between Jacques and the brothers, they separated the dying from the dead and did their best to make them comfortable. They were out of saline after the first hour. He dispensed all of the antibiotics he had in the Rover, as well as the morphine. By late afternoon, they were reduced to applying cold gel-pack compresses to the foreheads of the feverish.

Jacques chafed at his impotence. He was treating symptoms, but he had no idea what had struck down an entire village.

Shadows stretched long across the village square when he heard the sound of a helicopter in the distance. Jacques raced out of the makeshift sick ward and quickly stripped off his bio suit. Underneath he was dripping with sweat, and he felt a little light-headed.

Jacques directed the incoming choppers to a field adjacent to the village.

Through the billows of dust kicked up by the rotor blades, he could see that Leon had been as good as his word. The helo was one of the heavy cargo units. The ramp started to lower before the dust even settled, and

MSF staff streamed out of the open doorway. The sight made Jacques want to cry with relief.

By the time the moon rose, a white MSF field-hospital tent had been erected in the village square and bright floodlights lit the entire area. The survivors had been moved inside and were being treated.

Jacques felt his knees soften with exhaustion. He staggered back to the Rover to find the brothers asleep in the backseat. He smiled to himself as he climbed into the passenger seat and closed his eyes.

In his dreams, Jacques saw the panicked look of the young child he had taken from her mother. She tried to say something, but he couldn't understand her. She coughed on him and the skin on his arms turned an angry red. He scratched at his own arms, tearing at his skin. Someone tried to hold back his hands.

"No!" he shouted. "Get away from me."

"Jacques? Jacques Legarde?" The voice spoke in English.

Jacques pried his eyes open to find a man dressed in a biohazard suit standing outside the Rover. Jacques wiped his forehead. He was sweating and it was hard to catch his breath.

"Who are you?" he demanded. Jacques opened the car door and staggered out. His legs felt weak, barely able to hold his weight.

Dawn was starting to light the eastern horizon, and the high desert air was still and cool in the early morning. Glaring floodlights from the field hospital silhouetted the man, making him look like a ghost.

"Are you Jacques Legarde?" the man asked again.

Jacques nodded. His mouth tasted like sand and he had a pounding headache.

"My name is Sven Gunderson. I'm from the World Health Organization, Cairo office."

Jacques sank to the dirt. "I need to sit down. Sorry."

Gunderson handed him a water bottle with a gloved hand. "You are Jacques Legarde and you were first on scene, correct?"

Jacques nodded again. He took a long swallow of water before he answered. "Yes, to both questions. My techs and I were first on scene."

"I know what caused this outbreak," Gunderson said.

Jacques rubbed his eyes. He would give anything for a hot shower right now.

"And?"

The man squatted down next to Jacques, then looked around as if to make sure they were alone. "It's Ebola."

Jacques wasn't sure he heard the man correctly. Ebola in Yemen? "I don't understand."

"I don't understand either," the man said. "That's why I'm here. There's more."

Sleep melted away from Jacques as his brain processed what Gunderson was telling him. "How did the Ebola virus get to a remote Yemeni village?"

Through his goggles, the man's eyes squinted. "That's the problem. This virus is a genetic match for a sample that was in WHO custody only a few months ago, but it's been modified."

"I'm sorry," Jacques said. "You're not making sense. How did it get here?"

Gunderson swallowed hard. "There's only two possibilities. One is we've had a miraculous outbreak of an exactly matched strain of Ebola in the middle of nowhere."

"What's the other option?"

"Someone is testing a biological weapon." Gunderson's shoulders slumped. "And you've been exposed."

CHAPTER 25

Ad-Damazin, Sudan

The old woman settled on her blanket spread out on the pavement beneath her tea cart. The night air was cool, but the heat radiating from the banked coals in the brazier in her tea cart kept her old bones warm.

A few yards away, a loaded truck began its long drive up the grade to the top of the Roseires Dam. The gears ground as the driver downshifted and a belch of thick exhaust blew into the night.

The oily smoke didn't bother the old woman. It was an occupational hazard. If you secured the most profitable spot on the most traveled road in all of Ad-Damazin, you held your ground until you ran out of supplies.

Besides, traffic was thin this time of night and the slight breeze carried the smell away. In the rush of the morning, when cars and trucks and buses wound from the top of the dam down into the city, the air was so thick with exhaust smoke she could barely see across the highway.

Traffic jams were when she made the most money. Lorry drivers, engines idling, would order tea and cakes from their seats. Passengers in luxury cars would roll down their windows, order, and roll the tinted glass up again. People would file off the buses, place an order, and walk a few paces to catch up with the crawling bus.

She heard the crunch of tires and the purr of a well-tuned engine pull into the turnoff where her tea cart was set up. She peered under the cart to see a car door open and a pair of polished boots hit the sidewalk. The old woman struggled to her feet.

"Can I help you?" she said.

The polished boots belonged to a strapping young man dressed in blue jeans and an untucked shirt. He held up four fingers.

"Tea. Four." His accent told her he was from the south.

She busied herself with the brazier, bringing the water to a boil. The car was a late-model black SUV with tinted windows. She heard a mobile phone ring in the vehicle, and the driver answered it.

"We're here. The job will take us an hour or so, then we'll start back." The driver noticed the old woman watching him and rolled up the open car window.

She lined up four teas on the front of her cart and beckoned to the young man. He carried them to the vehicle and she got a look inside as the windows came down. Four men, all well-fed and muscled.

The polished boots, the way these men carried themselves, the peek of a handgun when the young man stretched to hand the tea to the men in the backseat. She knew these were military men.

"What do you have to eat?" the driver asked.

The old woman uncovered a tray of honey-and-almond desserts, a local delicacy.

"Try one," the driver said to the young man. He picked one up and bit off half.

"Good," he said, his mouth full.

The driver beckoned for her to come closer. The old woman carried the tray over to him and collected his empty tea glass. He took two, wolfing them down in just a few bites. The tray was empty when she returned to her cart.

"Pay her, Rocky," the driver said to the young man. "And get the stuff out of the back."

The young man pulled a wad of cash from his pocket and peeled off a handful of Sudanese pounds, far more than the cost of the tea and pastries.

"Thank you, auntie," he said, pressing the money into her hands.

When he smiled, his eyes were cold. The old woman clutched the bills.

He went to the rear of the SUV and raised the lift gate. When he got into the passenger side of the vehicle, he passed out hard hats and safety vests to the rest of the men in the SUV.

The car roared away into the night.

———————

The old woman slept fitfully for the rest of the night.

Traffic started to thicken before dawn. By the time the sun touched the tops of the buildings across the street, the flow of traffic had slowed to a crawl and her tea business was running at full capacity.

One of the competing tea carts set up shop on a corner fifty paces down the hill. At this rate, the old woman would be out of supplies by noon and would be forced to surrender her spot. She smiled and waved to her competition. With the generous tip from the men in the SUV last night, this had been a very profitable week for her.

BOOM!

The sound rolled down into the city of Ad-Damazin, echoing through the buildings.

All around her, everyone held their breath, frozen in space as the detonation rolled over them.

Boom! Boom! Boom!

Three more blasts in quick succession.

The old woman craned her neck to see up above the city, where the road ran across the top of the dam. There were four columns of black smoke rising into the pale blue morning sky.

Then the rain started. Bits of concrete, shards of plastic and metal from blasted cars; a hubcap sailed down and bounced off the roof of a car in front of her.

And mixed in with the material were tiny bits of bloody red flesh.

A woman screamed. Pandemonium reigned as drivers tried to reverse their cars and get as far away from the carnage as possible.

The old woman packed up her tea cart and pushed it down the hill.

CHAPTER 26

The sticky note affixed to the door of Rachel's dorm room was characteristically brusque.

See me. The scribble beneath it represented Noam's signature.

Her heart leaped. A new assignment?

Rachel entered her room and toweled the pool water from her hair. She donned a fresh uniform and a shined pair of shoes, then drew her thick hair back into a bun at the nape of her neck.

She checked her appearance in the mirror, smoothing the green uniform shirt against the flat of her belly. She was fitter than she'd been in a long time, and she looked relaxed and healthy.

Still, she needed to make a good impression. As leader of the *kidon,* the decision to send Rachel into the field was Noam's alone. He would be watching her for weaknesses, for any reason to keep her at Scorpion's Ascent.

Rachel moved swiftly through the halls. The dinner hour was nearing and most of the work for the day was done. She nodded to the few people she socialized with in the center. One of the assessments by the psych team was social interactions, so she made an effort.

The door of Noam's office was closed when she arrived. She rapped her knuckles three times below his nameplate.

"Enter," the rumbly voice from within said.

She threw open the door and took three steps forward and saluted. "Officer Rachel Jaeger reporting as ordered, sir!"

Noam looked up in surprise, then collapsed back into the cushions of his chair, guffaws of laughter filling the office. He waved his hands at her.

"Have a seat, Rachel," he said, still laughing. "When was the last time you saluted me?"

Rachel grinned at him. "I wanted to make a good impression."

Noam's mirth lessened and he wiped his eyes. "A good impression. A good laugh, you mean. I think maybe Psych needs to take another look at you."

Outside, the setting sun outlined the bulk of Scorpion's Ascent, but Rachel's eyes were drawn to the pictures decorating the wall of Noam's office. A much younger, and much thinner, Noam in an IDF uniform. A photograph of a young boy next to an army officer. A picture of that same boy a few years older at a funeral next to a woman dressed in black.

Noam followed her eyes. "My father," he said. "He died in the Yom Kippur War in '73. I had just turned thirteen." He sat back in the chair with a sigh. "Big shoes to fill. Still."

Rachel swallowed. They all had reasons to be here. Patriotism, guilt, duty, or just running away. But motivation was less important than results—and she was good at her job.

"I have your evaluation here," Noam said, paging through a file on his desk. "But what I really want to know is: Have you learned your lesson?"

Rachel nodded smartly. "Absolutely."

Noam raised his bushy eyebrows, planted both elbows on the desk, and posted his chin on his fists. "Tell me."

He was baiting her. Rachel knew it, but she couldn't resist. "Not to wear high heels on a mission," she said. Noam's eyes clenched together in suppressed laughter. She waited for the outburst to subside.

"You're lucky I don't send you to a board for your fitness for duty evaluation," he said. "They'd never let you out of here. No wonder the psych people don't know what to do with you."

Rachel's spirits fell. So that's what this meeting was about. That idiot doctor wanted her to open up about her dead husband and how she was dealing with the pain of loss. Rachel dealt with Levi's death by working as long and as hard as she could. She dealt with his murder by taking as many of the bad guys off the board as was humanly possible and with extreme prejudice when she could get away with it.

Levi had been killed years ago, but she was still angry about losing him. She knew she used his death as a motivator for this work, but so what? She was good at what she did.

Rachel set her jaw, her shoulders tightened. Let them ramble on about feelings and motivations as much as they wanted, but count her out. She wasn't playing that game.

"What did they say this time?" she asked. Rachel did her best to keep the sarcasm out of her voice and failed.

Noam's eyebrows showed he'd heard the tone. "Same as before, mostly. They want you to talk about your motivations as an agent and you don't."

"So, what's different now?"

"What's different now is that I need you in the field."

Rachel tried to suppress the smile that threatened to spread across her face. "You have a new assignment for me."

Noam sighed and tossed a folder over the desk to her. She caught it and eagerly opened it.

Rachel found herself looking at the face of a man in his forties with penetrating dark gray eyes. The shade of his skin and the wave of his hair suggested North African blood in his heritage, but the name on the bottom of the page was French: Jean-Pierre Manzul, CEO of Recodna Genetics.

Noam busied himself with another cigarette. "Our American friends discovered a suspicious money transfer between two shell companies in the Nile River basin. One was a coffee company, the other one was Khartoum Security Services." He paused to suck on his cigarette. "Khartoum Security Services only has one customer: Recodna Genetics."

"What was suspicious about the bank transfer?"

Noam's lips bent into a humorless smile. "It was initiated by a Saudi Arabian holding company. A big one, billions-of-dollars big."

"So why not go after the Saudi connection?"

"It turns out that the CEO of Recodna Genetics is in the market for some high-end personal security. Someone who knows how to handle themselves but looks good doing it."

Rachel flipped the page on the briefing packet. Jean-Pierre's bid request had gone to some of the most exclusive security firms in Europe. This would not be a cakewalk.

"Your new identity is Zula Bekele. Italian-Ethiopian heritage. Clearwater Security in the UK owes us a favor. They have agreed to bid you out for the job. The details of your company history are all in the packet."

"What am I after?" Rachel asked.

Noam didn't answer, which told her all she needed to know.

He didn't know what they were looking for.

Noam smashed out a half-smoked cigarette. "The whole thing stinks. Saudi shell companies funneling money to a security company that only has one customer, which happens to be a bio company. We don't like it. We want you to get close to Jean-Pierre and figure out what he's up to."

Rachel studied Manzul's picture again. Now she knew why the eyes bothered her: They reminded her of Levi. They both had the same piercing quality to their gaze that even in a photograph seemed to look right through her. She flipped the page to hide Manzul's face.

She hadn't thought about her late husband in days, a rarity for her.

"And what do I do when I get close to this guy?" Rachel asked.

"He's your client." Noam shrugged. "You keep him safe."

Rachel smiled sweetly. "I'll leave my high heels at home."

Noam's laughter followed her out of the office.

CHAPTER 27

Camp Lemonnier, Djibouti, Africa

For the second time in the same day, Dre Ramirez found herself on an airplane, the same CIA-owned Gulfstream V that had carried them from the United States. Except on this flight, they had Shira Fishbein with them.

Janet fell asleep before the plane taxied to the runway. Next to her, Don huddled over his laptop, his face locked in a scowl of concentration. Michael and Shira sat together, deep in conversation, which left Dre to her own thoughts.

At the end of the runway, the jet's engines rose in pitch. The acceleration pressed Dre back into her seat, emphasized how tired she was. She closed her eyes as the cabin angled upward in a steep climb.

But sleep would not come. Instead, she tried to piece together in her mind all the facts they had gathered.

A mysterious, messianic figure claims a desire to

unite all Islam, but uses violence to inflame tensions between Egypt and the upstream countries of the Nile River basin. His website uses top-secret cryptography stolen from the Israelis, who claim no knowledge of the terrorist attacks.

Nothing made any sense.

She rested her head against the window and let her mind drift as the plane reached cruising altitude and leveled off. The land beneath them was a carpet of rich browns as they left the Dead Sea behind and headed south over the Negev Desert. From this height, it was not easy to tell where Israel ended and Jordan began. A few minutes passed and Dre could see the Gulf of Aqaba in the distance. Somewhere in that vast expanse of brown, Jordan ended and Saudi Arabia began, another political border.

"It's beautiful, isn't it?" Shira's voice brought Dre's stream of consciousness to a screeching halt. The Israeli woman indicated the empty seat next to Dre. "May I?"

Dre looked past Shira to see Michael's head bowed in sleep. She shrugged.

Shira pointed out the window. "The Red Sea will be coming up soon. The amount of container traffic through the Suez Canal is amazing. You should be able to see US Navy ships on patrol."

Shira was obviously trying to make a connection, but until Dre knew more about her and this mysterious Mossad software program, she would keep her own counsel. It seemed odd that they were taking a Mossad cyber expert into a secure US forward operating base, but that decision was well above her pay grade.

To change the conversation, Dre nodded toward the sleeping Michael and leaned close to Shira. "What do you think of our Michael?"

She watched Shira's expression soften. "I think he's remarkable. I still can't believe that he was able to figure out the website was secured by metamorphic encryption without using some sort of program."

"That's our Michael," Dre said with no small measure of pride. "He's also single, in case you're wondering."

Two spots of color appeared high on Shira's cheekbones, a sure sign that Dre's intuition had been correct.

"Thanks for that." Shira recovered enough of her composure to smile back. "I might be interested."

"You think your software was stolen?" Dre asked, switching topics again. "Or is this some sort of double-blind operation?"

The smile evaporated from Shira's face. "That program represents years of work by some of the best minds in the country of Israel and now . . ." Her voice trailed off and Dre noted Shira's hands clenched in her lap.

"Why not break into the website on your own?" Dre asked. "Why wait for us?"

"In case you're right." Shira's voice was soft, tentative. "If it is an Israeli operation, then it's being run outside of Mossad and that means—"

"It means your boss is compromised," Dre finished for her.

Binya and Don had hatched the idea of hacking the Mahdi website from the confines of Camp Lemonnier, the only wholly owned US military base in the region.

If the Mahdi was an Israeli rogue operation, they would attribute the hack to the Americans. Mossad's role in the hack would remain a secret.

This was the part about the intel business that made Dre's head hurt: the lack of trust. Every major operation was compartmentalized against the possibility that someone in the chain of operations might make a mistake—or worse yet, be working for the other side.

In a move that even surprised herself, Dre reached over and squeezed Shira's forearm. "You'll know soon. It'll be okay."

They spent the rest of the flight in silence, with Dre trying in vain to re-create her former stream-of-consciousness state of mind. Somewhere in the mountains of intel they had consumed, there were threads of information, clues that belonged together. She knew it, and the idea of solving the puzzle kept her going, but the solution was just out of reach.

Dre knew from experience not to try to force the answer.

She watched the shipping traffic from her window seat. Shira was right about the volume of container ships and tankers. The massive vessels steamed north to where the Red Sea narrowed into the Suez Canal. At this height, they looked like toy ships in a bathtub, trailed by feathery white wakes.

Dre spotted a US Navy ship, an Arleigh Burke–class destroyer, amid the commercial traffic and wondered what the crew of the *Michael Murphy* was doing at that exact moment.

As they traveled farther south, the Red Sea began to

narrow again and the coastline of Yemen appeared on the left of the aircraft. In the distance, black smoke drifted up from the ground. In the war-torn country, the smoke could be a Saudi bomb strike or a farmer burning his fields.

When they passed over the Bab el-Mandeb Strait, where the Red Sea entered the Gulf of Aden, the Gulfstream made a wide turn and began to descend.

Janet opened her eyes and yawned, stretching her arms over her head. She smiled at Dre, smacked her lips, then rooted around in her bag for a bottle of water. Don closed his laptop down and slid it into his bag. Michael's head snapped up and he looked around wildly for a moment before he recognized his surroundings. Shira and Dre shared a quiet laugh at the expense of Dre's colleagues.

The Gulfstream touched down in midafternoon. When Dre disembarked she found a hot and humid atmosphere more akin to a summer in Annapolis than a military base in the desert. The Gulf of Aden glimmered in the distance beyond the end of the runway.

They each carried their own bags to the waiting white passenger van where a young army enlisted man welcomed them to "beautiful Camp Lemonnier." After closing the door, he rushed around to the driver's side and put the vehicle in gear.

He shouted names of buildings over the roar of the air-conditioning on max fan. Cold air blasted through the cabin of the van.

"That's the PX."

"Commissary," Michael said to Shira.

"That's the CLU," the driver shouted.

"Barracks," Don translated.

To Dre's eye, Camp Lemonnier seemed to be constructed entirely from shipping containers. People lived in shipping containers stacked on top of one another like LEGO buildings. Shipping containers were smashed together to make bigger rooms like the mess hall and the commissary.

They passed through a second level of base security, where they all had to show their IDs, before the van finally stopped in front of another building made from combined shipping containers.

The enlisted driver rushed to open the door for them. "Welcome to the Combined/Joint Special Operations Task Force for the Horn of Africa," he said in a near shout. He offered a military shorthand for the acronym that made no sense to Dre. "We've set you up in this facility."

A pair of hard-eyed, well-armed soldiers checked their IDs again in the lobby as they signed in. Dre saw one of the soldier's eyebrows tick up at Shira's Mossad ID, but he cleared her after checking the access list.

Finally, they were led to a familiar sight: a tactical operations center, or TOC, filled with dozens of multi-screen workstations. As this was a "combined" joint task force, the flags and uniforms of other nations showed prominently in the room. United Kingdom, France, Canada.

Their enlisted guide led the group to a smaller, enclosed space just off the TOC that held three computer workstations, a wall screen, and secure phones.

"It's a temporary SCIF, sir. Per your orders," he said to Don. He eyed Shira again. "Once the door is engaged, it's isolated from the rest of the facility. You've got a direct, secure connection back to DC. All the accesses you asked for are ready to go."

Dre, Janet, and Michael each dropped their bags and selected a workstation. Shira looked like a fish out of water watching them, but the agreement between Don and Binya was that she was there as an observer—and to give them the key to the Mahdi website encryption.

"Well?" Janet asked Don.

"No time like the present," Don replied. "Let's see who's behind the Mahdi's mask."

Dre found the Mahdi page on the unclassified internet connection and went to the maintenance access login. Her cursor blinked in the empty box. She looked back at Shira. "You're up."

Shira removed a thumb drive from a lanyard around her neck. The block lettering on the side of the thumb drive read CERBERUS.

She smiled faintly. "We named the program after the three-headed dog that guards the gates of Hell." Her voice turned bitter. "Now that someone sold us out, it's more like a yapping lapdog."

The room was silent as Dre inserted the thumb drive into the workstation. The machine recognized the incoming program.

"Here goes nothing." She hit the Enter key.

For a full ten seconds, nothing happened. Dre heard Shira's feet scuff against the floor as she shifted her weight from foot to foot.

"It's a query and response program," said Shira, her voice at a whisper, "based on millions of quantum-state possibilities. The host computer offers the incoming program a problem to solve. If it solves it, they move to the next level. Each level unlocks a new quantum state. If the query fails to achieve a level, it's locked out."

"Like a video game," Michael said. "Brilliant."

"Thank you," Shira whispered back.

Dre's screen cleared. Her cursor blinked in the upper left-hand corner of the blank screen.

"I'm in," she said.

The rest of the crew crowded around her workstation. "Let's see what we've got," Don said.

Dre queried the IP address of the server and got a dotted decimal string in reply.

"They're using a reverse proxy setup from a server based in the Netherlands. That routes to four different servers . . . all of them commercial providers, except for this one." Dre highlighted an IP address.

"Look up that address," Don said to Michael.

"Don't bother." Shira's voice cut through the tension in the room. "I recognize it. It belongs to Iran. That's an IP address for the cyber wing of the Islamic Revolutionary Guard Corps." She extracted the Cerberus thumb drive from Dre's workstation. "This is our worst fear. I need to let Binya know." She left the room.

Don blew out a breath. "If the IRGC has access to Israeli encryption that we can't crack . . . I better let Washington know." Don left the room.

Dre stared at the screen. The Iranians were behind the Mahdi. It made perfect sense. They wanted to stir up trouble in the Sunni world, get faction fighting against faction for the scarce water of the Nile River. But it also felt too . . . predictable.

Why steal the toughest encryption in the world and then point the website right back to your home server?

When Dre looked up, she saw Michael and Janet watching her.

"Are you thinking what I'm thinking?" Janet asked.

"This is too easy?" Dre said.

"I feel like I'm a hammer searching for a nail," Michael chimed in.

"I agree," Janet said. "Let's go to work."

CHAPTER 28

Camp Lemonnier, Djibouti, Africa

"It's a hoax," Michael said. His pronouncement was met with stony silence. The gentle rush of the air-conditioning filled the void.

The smooth skin of Shira's forehead clenched into a frown. Don Riley pressed his lips together.

"Explain," Don said.

Michael took a seat at his workstation and spun the chair around. "This server is an exit node for the Tor network," he said. "They use it to upload new content to the commercial servers. Whoever is behind the Mahdi assumed that any entity with enough resources to break through the encryption would have preconceptions about who was behind the terrorist attacks. The Islamic Revolutionary Guard is the perfect foil."

Shira's frown deepened, and her tone had an accusatory note. "I didn't hear an explanation, Michael."

Michael spun his chair around to face Shira. "This

Iranian server is ancient and the software is way out of date. Someone boosted the hardware and made a Tor exit node. The only time they use it is when they upload a video, so no one would notice."

"We're back to square one?" Don asked.

Janet spoke this time. "Whoever's running this is tech-savvy and well financed. They have access to the highest-quality encryption"—she shot a look at Shira—"*stolen* encryption in the world and they still go to great lengths to hide their identity. We can assume that when the Mahdi broadcasts they will use an IP-hopping program to shield their true identity."

"How do you know that?" Shira challenged.

"Because that's what we'd do," Michael said.

"There has to be a way to track them down," Don said.

"There's only one way," Janet replied.

"You're going to track him when he's broadcasting," Shira said.

Michael nodded. "Exactly. Which is why you need to leave the Cerberus key with us."

Shira shook her head. "That's not going to happen," she said. "You're stuck with me for the duration, Michael."

"I'll deal with it," Michael said, but he was smiling.

"I don't like it." Don was having none of it. "Your plan is to wait for another terrorist attack?"

Janet nodded. "That's the best we've got, boss."

Dre tapped a few keys and threw the contents of her monitor to the wall screen. "I set up a trap program that will let us know as soon as the Mahdi starts the next broadcast. We can immediately log into the Mahdi website and run a trace program to track them to the source, but our window will be incredibly short."

Don scratched at the scruff on his chin. "We'll have what? Two minutes, maybe three minutes?"

"We'll have as long as it takes for the broadcast to upload," Michael said. "They'll probably leave the connection open long enough to make sure the file's not corrupted."

"We could be waiting here for weeks," Don said to Shira. "Will Binya go along with this?"

Shira hesitated, the skin of her forehead again wrinkling into a frown.

"I don't know that we have much of a choice," she said. "We either turn over the Cerberus program to you or I stay here as one of the team until we figure out who's behind this mess."

"In that case," Don said, "you can help with our next assignment."

He used Janet's workstation to call up a new file. A picture of a strikingly beautiful brown-skinned woman in her midthirties showed on the screen.

"This is Dr. Talia Tahir," Don said. "Up until recently, she was a lead researcher at the World Health Organization, Cairo office. In fact, the doctor was in line to become the next head of the Eastern Med region."

"And?" Janet asked.

"Dr. Tahir was killed in a plane crash while transferring virus samples from the Cairo office to the new WHO office in Brazzaville, Congo. One of those samples was a very specific strain of the Ebola virus.

"For those of you not up on your viruses, Ebola is a hemorrhagic disease, highly transmissible and extremely deadly."

He tapped the keyboard again, and the picture changed to a large white tent in the middle of a ring of mud-brick homes. A person in biocontamination gear was exiting the tent.

"This is a Doctors Without Borders site in Melaba, Yemen. Three days ago, there was an Ebola outbreak in this village. There were one hundred and forty-seven people in the village, and as of right now one hundred and forty-five of those people are dead. There were three MSF first responders who have also contracted Ebola."

Don paused. The only sound in the room was the whirr of the computer cooling fans. "The Ebola virus strain found in Melaba is a genetic match to the virus carried by Dr. Tahir, except for one thing. It's a whole lot more lethal than the original."

The team stared at Don.

"The working hypothesis is that we are looking at a bioweapons attack."

CHAPTER 29

Khartoum, Sudan

The Al-Mogran Supercity, a vast glass-and-steel enclave of modernity, rose up next to the confluence of the Blue and White Nile Rivers. Rachel took the glass elevator up to the sixteenth floor and found the room where the interview for the private security job was to take place.

When she opened the door to the office, she found five other interview candidates inside, all men. She scanned her competition. Two of the men were big with heavy Germanic features, both of them well over a hundred kilograms, with expensive, tailored suits that molded to their brawny upper bodies.

They sat together and seemed to know each other. Rachel mentally dubbed them Hans and Frans. These were men who provided private security for people who wanted the world to know they had private security. Intimidation and brute force were their go-to tools.

A third man, equally as large, sat next to Hans and

Frans. He had a shaved head with snow-white skin and chiseled Nordic features. His stunning good looks were spoiled by a smirk when he saw Rachel enter the room. She would call him Thor.

She crossed to where a receptionist in traditional Muslim dress sat behind a desk and waited until the young woman looked up.

"You must be Zula Bekele," the young woman said in a stage whisper. She handed Rachel a single sheet of paper. "You will need to sign this, please."

It was a standard nondisclosure agreement that lasted for the duration of the interview only. Rachel signed it without bothering to read it and handed it back.

Facing the three giants were two other men, with an empty chair between them. One was tall and lean, well over six feet tall, with huge hands. He wore his hair long and ragged, like a schoolkid. He smiled at her, patting the seat next to him. "You can sit here, ma'am," he said. His accent suggested he was an American. She would call him Stretch.

Rachel took the open seat and checked out the final man in the room using her peripheral vision. He was small and wiry, only an inch or two taller than Rachel herself, and they probably weighed in within five kilos of each other.

He held out his hand in greeting. "Name's Danny. You?"

Rachel detected an Irish lilt in his voice. His skin was dark, but not as dark as her own. Another candidate with a mixed heritage. Some other company had read

Manzul's file and was trying to gain an edge. Danny's grip was firm and self-assured.

"Zula," she said. "Nice to meet you."

"Likewise." Danny had an infectious smile that shone even under the glaring gazes of Hans and Frans.

They didn't have long to wait. The secretary's phone buzzed and she answered it. "Yes, Mr. Manzul," she said, and stood. "If you would all follow me, please."

Hans and Frans exchanged glances. They were all going in together?

Rachel saw immediately that the interview was not going to be quite what she had expected. A boardroom that looked out over the city and the Blue Nile had been emptied of furniture, and the floor was covered with sparring mats.

A man in an open-necked blue Oxford shirt and no suit jacket waited by the window, admiring the view. He stood in his bare feet.

When Manzul turned to greet the group, Rachel met those eyes again and for a split second the mission left her mind. His eyes traveled over the group then locked on her.

"One of these things is not like the others, I see," he said with a laugh.

Hans and Frans snickered. Rachel felt herself blush.

"My name is JP Manzul," he said. "Chief executive officer of a high-tech company here in Khartoum. Recently, I was on assignment and someone attacked me. I managed to ward them off—I have some training myself—but my partner would feel safer if I had personal security with me at all times." His eyes seemed to linger on Rachel for a few seconds longer than was necessary. Rachel felt her stomach clench in response.

"You've all been highly recommended by your respective companies. I have no doubt you are all well qualified, so I thought we would make this interview more interesting." He pointed to Hans. "You. You will fight me."

Hans looked at Frans, then back at Jean-Pierre.

"You want me to fight you?" Hans tapped his barrel chest.

JP took a fighting stance. "If you beat me you get the job," he said with a grin.

Hans doffed his suit jacket and slipped out of his shoes, stepping confidently onto the mat. When JP attacked, it was a blur of speed that surprised even Rachel.

Hans took a shot to the throat and ate mat within the first second. JP let Hans get to his feet. The big man wiped the trickle of blood from his lip and raised his hands. "Let's go, old man."

JP attacked again, this time from the other side. An ambidextrous fighter, another wrinkle that Rachel— and Hans—hadn't seen coming. Hans took a shot to the head, but still managed to grasp Manzul's arm. JP only used the grip as leverage. He spun and clocked Hans on the point of his chin with an elbow.

Hans's grip loosened and JP slipped behind him. After a few seconds in a choke hold, Hans tapped out. Manzul helped the big man to his feet.

"You don't need personal security, old man. You need a leash," Hans said as he picked up his jacket and shoes.

JP retrieved a bottle of water from the small table next to the door. He took a sip, then pointed at Frans and Thor. "You two. Show me what you've got."

Instead of watching the fight, Rachel watched JP as he assessed the fighters. His jaw clenched as the two big men clashed. She could tell what he was thinking. Both of them were strong fighters, but they relied on their strength rather than find a winning strategy against a similarly sized opponent. After a few minutes, JP stopped them.

"Thank you very much, gentlemen." He pointed at Frans. "You can go."

He sipped his water, considering the three remaining fighters. Finally, he pointed to Rachel. "You"—he pointed at Stretch—"and you. Go."

Rachel stepped onto the mat flexing the balls of her bare feet on the spongy surface. The American took his time, watching her, assessing.

He had a very long reach. Rachel needed to either stay away from him or drive inside and try to finish him fast. They circled a few times, sparring, getting the sense of each other's style.

He stung her on the cheek with a jab and moved in, but she spun away before he could wrap her up. The circling continued. She was lighter and faster. Rachel could outlast him, but JP struck her as a man impatient for results.

If she wanted to impress him, she needed to do something bold—and quickly.

Rachel allowed Stretch to cut down the mat, working her into the corner next to the windows. She saw a smile tease his lips. He thought he had her. Any second now, Stretch would make his move.

There was a curtain rod over her head used to support the heavy drapes that could be pulled across the glass to block out the bright sunlight. This had to be timed perfectly.

Stretch's shoulders twitched.

Now.

Rachel launched herself up, grabbing the bar with both hands and pulling her knees up as hard as she could. His hands found air where her body had been and her knees slammed into his chin with all the strength she had.

He stood to his full height, then toppled over. Rachel was on his back in a flash, a choke hold in place.

"That's enough," JP's voice cut through the pounding pulse in her ears.

Rachel released Stretch and rolled onto the mat, breathing hard. Stretch's foot lashed out and caught her in the side just below the rib cage.

JP was on Stretch in the space of a breath, putting the younger man into a rear wristlock.

"Get out. You're done," JP barked. He released Stretch, then held out a hand to help Rachel up. His eyes locked with hers and she felt her stomach do a little flip-flop. What the hell was the matter with her?

"I'm sorry about that," JP said, his voice kind. "Very unprofessional of him."

Rachel took her time getting back to the edge of the mat, stretching to relieve the stitch in her side. They were down to three now. She'd get a rest while the other two had it out.

JP beckoned Thor and Danny onto the mat. He pointed at Rachel.

"You two fight her."

Rachel's instincts kicked in immediately. She took two steps onto the mat and delivered a hard kick to the side of Thor's knee. She felt muscle and cartilage give way as the big man went down.

Then Danny was on her, knocking her flat on her back. He slammed a knee into her injured ribs and his fingers went for her neck.

Rachel drove her knee up, but he turned his thigh to protect his groin. She tried the other side and he anticipated her move again. But she added a twist, driving her extended fingers into his eyes when he rolled his body.

Danny flinched and she snaked away, landing a kick in his side as she staggered to her feet.

Thor was back. His bald head was flushed red and his eyes held a murderous gleam. She launched a roundhouse kick, knocking the big man down again.

Danny's arm snaked around her neck. Sleeper hold. She drove her head back, trying to smash his face, but he evaded her.

Rachel's toes scrabbled at the mat as she tried for better leverage against Danny's choke hold.

Thor rose from the mat, his face a mask of red fury. He drew back a massive fist and drove it into Rachel's solar plexus.

The force of the blow knocked her and Danny off their feet. Rachel's vision exploded with light as the pain blasted through her body.

Danny held on, choking her air supply.

"Tap out, goddammit," he whispered in her ear.

Her vision tunneled. All color slipped away from the scene, leaving everything in black-and-white.

"That's enough." JP's voice rang out. Danny released her immediately and she rolled onto her belly, alternately sucking in great lungfuls of air and retching from Thor's punch.

JP helped Danny and Thor to their feet and ushered the two men out of the room before he returned to Rachel.

She got to a sitting position. She could feel a black eye forming, and the kick from Stretch still stabbed at her every time she drew a breath. She would be wearing a high-collared shirt for the next few days to hide the bruising on her neck. Rachel accepted JP's help to get vertical again. She swayed and he caught her arm. His touch on her bare skin was electric.

"You fought well, Ms. Bekele," he said. JP smiled at her. Even with all her aches and pains, the transformation on his face almost took Rachel's breath away again. His gaze was warm, intimate.

He handed her his open bottle of water, a sign of intimacy that somehow seemed perfectly natural. She took a grateful sip. It hurt to swallow. She nodded her thanks.

"I especially liked your reaction time when I put two of them on you," he said. "Not really a fair fight. But when is a fight ever really fair?"

Rachel took another sip of water. It was better to let him talk. She wasn't sure she trusted her voice right now.

"You have an impressive file, but I suspect, based on what I've seen, there's a lot more to you than what's on paper."

Rachel's reply was a hoarse whisper. "The color of my skin and my lack of testicles means everyone underestimates me in this business. I use that to my advantage whenever possible."

JP threw his head back and let out a great bellow of a laugh. "I appreciate your honesty, Ms. Bekele."

"Zula, please," Rachel rasped.

"A beautiful name. I like it." He touched her arm again and she felt the same jolt of energy. "My friends call me JP."

"Then I will call you JP."

JP drew close, closer than he needed to be. She felt the heat of his breath when he spoke.

"Tell me, my warrior princess, have you ever killed a man before?"

"Yes," Rachel replied without hesitation.

"I thought so. I can tell."

"When can I start?" Rachel asked.

JP smiled. "You already have."

CHAPTER 30

Larnaca, Cyprus

As the Learjet broke through the low clouds, JP kept one eye on the window and the other eye on Zula. The woman wore a short skirt with an open leather jacket cut to allow for the sidearm holster under her left arm. Her long slender legs were crossed and she angled her body so she could watch their approach to Larnaca Airport out the window.

He found himself fascinated with this woman. In the week since he'd hired her, they had done nothing but travel from home to work, where she sat in the lobby and read a book.

He noticed that Zula no longer winced when she turned to the right, a sign that the bruise on her side had healed. This was the first day she'd worn a low-collared shirt since the job interview. The smooth dark skin of her upper body rippled with muscle, and he sometimes found himself staring at the hollow of her throat. If he looked closely enough, he could see the marks of still-healing bruises.

JP still chuckled to himself at the thought of her fighting skill. She was a lioness, that one.

Last night he had nearly invited her into his apartment, but at the last moment thought better of the idea. There was an old American saying about dipping your pen in the company inkwell. And then there was Talia. He'd told her he had hired personal security, but had not mentioned that Zula was a woman—and an attractive one.

As if reading his thoughts, she turned her head and met his gaze. He saw a flare of emotion in her eyes that seemed intimate and calculating at the same time. And then it was gone.

Once again, they were employer and employee.

The call that had set him on a course to Cyprus had come from Talia before the sun had risen over Khartoum earlier in the day. In the Project Deliverance compound, she was the only one who had unrestricted access to the internet, from a secure room adjacent to their bedroom.

The encrypted satellite phone was only supposed to be used for emergencies.

"Have you seen the news?" Talia's voice was tight with anger and a tinge of fear.

JP rolled over in bed and sat up, pressing the mobile phone to his ear. "I don't know what you're talking about, dear."

"The site," she hissed. "They didn't destroy the test site. It's on the news."

JP padded across the bedroom to his desk and opened the lid of his laptop. The machine sprang to life. He logged on to the Al Jazeera website and did a quick search on "Yemen." There was a new story, a mysterious disease outbreak in Houthi-held territory.

"Are you still there?" Talia's voice had softened. She sounded more afraid now than angry.

"Yes, I'm looking at it now." He gritted his teeth. The World Health Organization had been called in. There was even a picture of Sven Gunderson, Talia's former supervisor, consulting with a group of doctors from MSF.

There was no mention of the type of virus, but if the WHO was involved, it was just a matter of time before they figured it out.

"The article says Cairo is involved," Talia said. "How long will it take them to trace it back to me?"

JP focused on the picture of Gunderson. He chose his words carefully, even though the call was encrypted. "The article I'm looking at has your boyfriend in it," he said. "It looks like he's joined the party already."

Talia made a noise like a wounded animal. "What happened to your contact? This never should have happened. I told you I should handle it."

She was blaming him? JP started to snap back but held his tongue. "How close are we to the next version?"

Talia was silent for a long time. "I'm sorry I said that. It was unfair, my love." Her voice broke. "I've waited for so long, and now . . ."

JP closed his eyes. He wanted to hold her, comfort

her. "Focus on the end goal. How long until the next version is ready?"

"A few days, a week maybe. These things are not predictable."

"I'll go to see you-know-who immediately," JP said. "Today."

"This could ruin everything," Talia said. "You need to fix this."

She hung up.

JP thumbed his phone to Zula's number. The voice that answered was husky with sleep, which he found strangely appealing.

"We'll be traveling today," he said. "Pack for one night. Bring whatever you need for an international trip."

"Where are we going?"

JP considered his answer for a moment. Where were they going? Nothing he had to say to Saleh could be said over the phone. He would have to track down the old man on that stupid yacht of his.

"I don't know yet. Just be ready."

He sent an encrypted email to Saleh and padded to the window. Nothing to do now but wait.

Predawn stillness cloaked the city of Khartoum. There was no more sleeping for him this night. In a few moments the Muslim call to prayer would ring out and the metropolis would come to life. He redialed Zula's number. When she answered her voice told him she had given up sleep as well.

"I'm going for a run," he said. "Be downstairs in ten minutes."

Zula was there when he arrived, dressed in a pair of tight shorts and a matching tank top, her hair pushed back by a headband.

He eyed her as they did some light stretching. Her frame was even more slender than he had imagined, and tight with muscle. In this Muslim country where women lived under layers, he rarely saw a true female form except for Talia's.

They started off slow, with Zula ignoring the stares from traditional Muslim women they passed. JP was acutely aware that he was older than her and slower and she was deliberately taming her pace. By the time they made the turn onto the promenade above the Nile, his muscles were loose and he picked up the pace.

The river flowed dark and smooth beside them as they ran from one pool of streetlight to the next. Zula's breathing sounded even and measured next to his harsh panting. The eastern sky lightened enough for him to make out the distant shape of Victory Bridge, his normal turnaround point.

When they passed the fruit seller's donkey cart, JP kicked his pace up a notch. Zula matched him. The woman ran like a gazelle, with long strides that ate up the sidewalk. Next to her, JP felt like a thundering rhinoceros.

At one hundred meters from the bridge, JP said, "Race me to the bridge." He switched to an all-out sprint without waiting for an answer. Head up, arms pumping, for a few seconds, he thought she hadn't heard him.

Then Zula flashed by in a blaze of red-and-white running gear, beating him by an easy five meters. The sun crested the horizon, creating a halo around her head when she turned to face him.

JP put his hands on his knees to catch his breath. "You're supposed to let the boss win."

Zula pressed her hands against the bridge abutment to stretch out her calves, ignoring the stares of the passersby. "I never let a man beat me. Ever."

She was facing away from him, so JP couldn't see if she was smiling.

He suddenly missed Talia very much.

===================

He let Zula leave the jet first to check out the Mercedes-Benz limousine waiting on the tarmac of the Larnaca Airport.

When she was satisfied, she beckoned to him and he got into the car.

"To the harbor," he told the driver. The man behind the wheel was good at his job, making short work of the heavy Cyprus evening traffic. Zula sat in the front passenger seat, hands on both knees, her eyes constantly surveying the external environment for potential threats.

"You're good at your job," JP said.

"In my line of work, one mistake is too many," she replied. A smile traced her lips, but she did not look back at him.

JP forced himself to watch the traffic instead of the woman. He needed to be sharp for this meeting.

Saleh and Zarecki. The Saudi spymaster and the Jewish arms dealer. Two old men with more money than time and a burning desire to change the world before they left it. In rare moments like this, when he was being honest with himself, they disgusted him.

But rich men with unfinished business and a ticking clock were useful to JP's cause. Their burning desire to destroy the Iranian regime required money and lots of it.

Money JP was only too happy to take.

The Church of St. Lazarus flashed by, the ancient stone building already lit for evening services.

At the dock, he and Zula left the limo and made their way to a waiting Zodiac boat. The air was still and heavy with moisture. The low cloud cover had turned dusk to darkness early. Lightning flashed on the horizon. A storm was coming.

The water in the harbor was flat as glass; the only vessel in motion was their own.

He watched Zula's face as they approached Saleh's magnificent yacht. She scanned the long vessel, but seemed unimpressed by the display of wealth. On the other hand, their pilot was part of the yacht crew and obviously proud of his charge. He said something to Zula, who nodded and smiled.

They approached the fantail at speed and the pilot flared to a stop, reaching out to grab a cleat with his bare hands to pull the craft close. JP stood, taking the offered hand of the security man on deck.

He turned back to the boat. "Stay here, Zula. I won't be long."

When she started to protest, he snapped, "Just do it."

Saleh's security man, still wearing the semiautomatic strapped to his chest, stepped into the RHIB and the pilot roared off to take station a hundred meters away.

Saleh waited for JP at the top of the stairs. The old man had a stormy look on his face. "You brought a woman with you?"

"She's not a woman. She's my personal security. And we have much more important things to talk about than whether or not I'm traveling with a woman." He brushed past Saleh and stepped inside.

Zarecki was already there, looking even closer to death than when he'd last seen him. His skin had the consistency of candle wax, and he was hooked up to his oxygen tank. A half-empty pack of cigarettes lay on the table. He was dozing when JP entered the room, and when he raised his eyes, JP could see they were yellow and rheumy.

The brief assessment confirmed what JP already knew: This man had months to live, and that was if he took care of himself, an unlikely prospect given the cigarettes. When he shook the old man's hand, his fingers were like slimy, bony sausages. It was all JP could do not to wipe his own hand on his pant leg.

Whatever the outcome of this meeting, he knew one thing. His and Talia's plan to change the world was on the same timetable as Zarecki's health.

Saleh closed the door. He took his seat and slapped his hand on the table. "You insist on this sudden meeting, you bring a woman to my home, and you treat me with disrespect in front of my employees. I hope there is some explanation for this behavior."

"You failed me, Saleh," JP said in as even a voice as he could manage. "You said you had the Saudi Air Force under your control. You said you could destroy the test site. What happened?"

Saleh scowled, shifting in his chair. He looked at Zarecki first, then finally met JP's gaze.

"The cease-fire," he said with disgust in his voice. "There was nothing I could do. The jets were grounded and a Doctors Without Borders rabble-rouser found the village before we could stop him." He smirked at JP. "Does it really matter? I'm told everyone in the village died."

JP wanted to slap his palm against his forehead. "Viruses are genetic organisms, living things. They have DNA, which makes them traceable. It's only a matter of time before they track the virus back to the source.

"If they can track the virus, it will eventually lead to me," JP said. "And I lead to you."

That silenced the two men. In the stillness, JP felt a rumble of distant thunder.

"We can't use Yemen for testing anymore," he said. "It's too risky. The new virus will be ready soon and I'll need a new test site."

Saleh snorted. "How can you wipe out an entire village and not have anyone notice? At least in a war zone we can clean up the mess with a bomb or two."

JP heard fat drops of rain spatter against the deck of the boat above him. He briefly thought about Zula getting soaked in the rain, and the image of her running form flashing by him in the Khartoum sunrise came to him.

"I have an idea," JP said. "But I will need to create a distraction. A major distraction."

CHAPTER 31

Project Deliverance, undisclosed location in Sudan

JP climbed out of the Land Rover in the underground parking lot of the Project Deliverance compound. He was tired and anxious to see Talia.

Zula exited the vehicle from the other side. Despite the fact that she had sat for three hours in a downpour in the Larnaca harbor and they had flown overnight, she looked fresh and alert. She took in the underground garage at a glance, her eyes sucking in details.

"Where are we?" she said.

JP gave her a tight smile. He had taken her electronics before they took off from Cyprus. "Sorry. Some things have to stay secret—even from you, Zula. This is a secure research lab for Recodna. You won't find it on any company registers or even any maps."

"Funded by the owner of the yacht?" she replied.

A heavy door behind JP opened with a crack of steel. Kasim, his head of security, entered the garage.

"What do we have here, boss?" Kasim said in his booming voice. "You bring me a gift?"

The big man moved into JP's line of sight, his hand resting on the submachine gun strapped across his body armor. His gaze traveled up Zula's body, his face a leer.

"Ms. Bekele is my guest here, Kasim," JP said sharply. Too sharply, he realized. Zula could take care of herself. "Find her a place to sleep in the security quarters. We'll be leaving in the morning."

"She can share my bed, boss."

JP laughed as he moved toward the elevator. "I'd like to see you try, Kasim. I think she likes to be on top."

"Where are you going?" Zula said.

"The laboratory below is off-limits to security. The only person who's not a member of the research team that has access is Kasim, and that's only under my specific authorization." He smiled at her sour expression. "Don't worry, Zula. It's safe."

When JP exited the elevator into the upper-level living quarters, he expected to find everyone at breakfast, but the common room was deserted. He checked the security monitors, cycling through the screens until he found them. It looked like the entire team was in the viewing area for the level-four biosafety room. Most of the basic work was done in less secure labs. The BSL-4 lab, which required positive-pressure biohazard suits, was only used when they handled live viruses.

JP's pulse raced as he hurried to the stairs. Talia had said they were close to a breakthrough on the next version of the virus. Maybe this was it.

He clattered down the steps to the lowest level of the compound, and strode toward the knot of people crowded at the end of the hall. He heard Talia's voice, her tone excited, and a reply came through the intercom.

"It's JP," one of the women said to Talia.

When Talia turned toward him, her face was flushed with excitement.

"We've done it, JP!" She pumped a fist in the air. "We've done it." She threw herself at him and planted a kiss on his lips. Her body pressed against him, her energy contagious.

The rest of the scientists crowded around them. They were like children, with their expressions of rapturous glee and the way they awkwardly high-fived each other.

"Okay, I take it the news is good," JP said, with a smile. "How about you share your new toy with an outsider?"

Talia motioned for Greta to do the explanation. "She did most of the modifications, so I'll let her explain."

Greta beamed. "This is so exciting." She took a deep breath. "Our first test proved we could control the latency of the Ebola virus, remember?"

JP nodded, recalling the test with the rhesus macaques.

"The follow-on work showed we could amplify a known strain of virus."

JP nodded again. He felt Talia's hand tighten on his arm as she reacted to the reminder of the discovered test in Yemen.

Greta continued. "Now we have successfully com-

bined Ebola with the paleo-flu virus. We have aerosolized Ebola paired with a completely unknown flu-virus
template. Let's see the Blue Team figure this one out!"
She high-fived Lakshmi again.

Talia touched the intercom button so she could be
heard inside the lab where Dr. Lu and Faraj waited in
bulky positive pressure suits. "Xianshan, can you show
the microscope pictures again, please?"

She positioned JP in front of the high-definition
displays. He saw the familiar tangled string image of
the Ebola virus next to a cluster of spherical flu virus
samples.

"This is what we started with," Talia said. "The high-
latency Ebola and the paleo-flu virus." She tapped the
keyboard, and the screen showed a sphere twice the size
of the original flu virus, with large glycoprotein protru-
sions from the Ebola virus studding the exterior.

"And this is the finished product. A virus within a
virus." Talia's eyes shone and she seemed close to tears
as she gripped her lover's hand. "A true chimera.

"This is it, JP," she whispered. "I can feel it. This is it."

"What about delivery?" JP asked. "How confident
are you that it can be aerosolized?"

Dr. Lu's precise voice took on a robotlike quality
through the intercom. "With the flu virus as the carrier, this has the characteristics of an airborne virus
with the theoretical lethality of Ebola. We don't know
for sure if we've retained the effectiveness of the Ebola
virus until we test it on live specimens, but I see no reason why that can't be achieved."

"How long will that take?" JP asked.

"The latency in this version is three days," Lu replied.

JP was already planning in his head. Three days for an internal test, but they would need a real-world test. Yemen was no longer viable, so he needed another test site. . . .

"JP," Talia's voice interrupted his thoughts. "You're not listening to me."

He realized the entire group of scientists was watching him. "I'm sorry. It's just so overwhelming, such good news."

"I think we all agree with that, but what about a name?"

"A name?"

"Yes." Talia looked back at all the scientists, who nodded in unison. "We all feel like we've given birth in a way. Our creation deserves a name and since you're the proud papa, we think you should be the one to do the honors."

A thousand ideas flooded JP's mind. Chaos . . . Shiva . . . the list went on and on.

"I think of this as our child," Talia whispered. "Something we created together from the seeds of humanity. It's beautiful."

JP absorbed the inquiring looks of the team.

"You're right," he said, looking at the screen. "I think we should call her . . . Pandora."

"Pandora," Talia said, as if savoring the taste of the word on her tongue. "I think it's a marvelous name."

"We should get a sample to the Blue Team as soon as possible," JP said. "Prepare a sample and I'll take it with me in the morning."

CHAPTER 32

Project Deliverance, undisclosed location in Sudan

Where in the holy hell was this place? Rachel wondered.

She followed Kasim's broad back up a flight of stairs, taking her away from JP and whatever was behind that elevator door. Kasim waved a badge in front of a pad and she heard a magnetic lock disengage. She also saw the glint of a camera lens above the door.

The interior room had the look and feel of an army barracks. Neatly made-up cots lined both walls all the way to an open kitchen area. Rachel automatically counted the beds. Thirty. To her left stood a double-wide opening, and a smell told her the latrine was through there. Adjacent to the rows of beds was a carpeted lounge area with four flat-screen TVs and a small fleet of sofas. Two huge black men occupied a sofa, playing a first-person-shooter game. They didn't look up when Kasim and Rachel stepped into the room.

Kasim strode down the center of the barracks with Rachel in tow.

"Why so many guards?" Rachel asked in Arabic. "You expecting an invasion?"

Kasim shrugged. "I get paid. I don't ask questions."

They reached the open kitchen area at the far end of the room, where two men were preparing food. They eyed Rachel.

"We don't get many women here," Kasim said with a snide smile. "Actually, you're the first. The men will be expecting to be entertained."

The two men at the kitchen counter broke into laughter.

"The only entertainment I'll be providing is when I kick your ass," Rachel said to the nearest one.

He froze, his dark skin reddening. "You dare to speak to me like—"

"Shut it, Rocky," Kasim barked. "Zula is a guest of the boss, and she will be treated that way. She's here for one night, let's not be animals."

"One night, huh?" Rocky sneered at her. "We could make it a good one."

"In your dreams, asshole," she shot back. Rocky's skin took on a shade of deeper red.

"I see you make friends everywhere you go, Zula," Kasim said. "Think on it, woman. There are many of us and only one of you. The boss is busy with his own woman and it's a long night."

Rachel considered her odds and decided to take the high road. "How about you just show me a place where I can take a nap and we'll call it even?"

Kasim passed through the kitchen into a short hallway. He pointed to an open door on the right. "You can stay there. That's Rocky's room." He jerked his thumb at the one on the left. "That's my room—in case you get lonely."

Rachel surveyed Rocky's room from the doorway. Despite his rough talk, Rocky appeared to be a fastidious man. The room consisted of a single bed with a nightstand and lamp, a footlocker, a small closet, and a sink. The bed was neatly made with crisp hospital corners and the floor swept. The only decoration in the room was a tattered poster of Sylvester Stallone as a boxer in the movie *Rocky.*

Rachel closed the door and opened the footlocker. Socks, underwear, workout gear, and two pairs of shoes. The closet held hanging clothes. The same olive-green paramilitary uniform Kasim and the rest wore, plus a few civilian shirts and pants. Rachel checked the collar of the civilian shirt. The tag had been removed. She checked the pants and found the same thing.

She heard a noise in the hallway and quickly closed the closet. Rocky pushed the door open.

"Don't you know how to knock?" Rachel said. "Or didn't they teach you that in the Janjaweed?"

"My room, my rules." He threw a blanket at her. "Don't touch my stuff." He slammed the door closed on his way out.

Rachel noticed he didn't deny the Janjaweed comment. This entire operation, from Kasim's bearing down to the way the beds were made, had military overtones.

Janjaweed had been a shot in the dark, but that still didn't tell her what was going on here.

Rachel took off her shoes and sat on the edge of the bed. She looked at the blanket longingly. She was bone-tired. She'd stayed awake all night on the flight from Cyprus trying to figure out where they were going.

As soon as they had gotten back on the Learjet, JP went on a full security lockdown. He took her mobile phone and weapon and locked both in the cockpit with the flight crew. The windows on the premier jet were self-tinting and JP turned them as dark as they would go.

"Security precautions" was all he would say.

JP had retrieved her from the Zodiac well after midnight, reeking of alcohol and in a foul mood after his meeting on the yacht. They went straight to the airport and boarded the jet. She thought they headed west after takeoff from Larnaca, but in the blacked-out cabin and deprived of her mobile phone, she was only guessing. Hours later, they landed in this desert hideaway.

Her best guess, based on the atmosphere and the makeup of the security team, was that they were somewhere in Sudan. Kasim and his men were ex-Janjaweed militia, but this was not a Janjaweed operation.

The physical conditioning and discipline of the men, the quality of the facility, and the attention to details such as the cut-off tags on the civilian clothes told her this was a professional, well-run security operation. Kasim knew what he was doing.

By the time she had pieced together this much, it was lunchtime. She waited, but no one came to invite her to eat. After the noise in the kitchen died down, she put her shoes back on and left her room.

Kasim was sitting at the table alone, drinking coffee and finishing the rest of his lunch. Everyone else had eaten and the dishes were washed and stacked neatly in a drying rack. Another sign of unit discipline.

Rachel motioned to an empty seat next to Kasim. "May I?"

The big black man took a deliberate sip of coffee. "Sit."

Rachel pulled out her chair. "What do they do down there?"

"What do I care? I get paid." He raised his eyebrows. "They're doctors. Scientists. They stay down there and they look at test tubes. We stay up here and we stand guard over nothing, but I get paid. A lot."

"How many scientists are there?"

Kasim's eyes narrowed. "You ask a lot of questions."

Rachel took his empty lunch plate and carried it to the sink, where she proceeded to wash it and put it in the drying rack. She turned and crossed her arms, resting her hips against the counter. "I'm bored. I'm in the middle of Sudan without a phone, what am I supposed to do?"

Kasim grinned. "No phones here." He pointed to the video games and TVs in the corner. "We get all the best DVDs, all the best video games, but no phones. No internet. Not allowed." His smile morphed into a leer. "I can think of something we could do."

Rachel briefly considered the cost-benefit of attempting to seduce Kasim and dismissed it. "I'll pass. I'm not that desperate yet."

She went back to Rocky's room and sat on the bed again. Kasim confirmed what she already suspected. They were cut off from the outside world—no internet, no satellite, no mobile phones, nothing that could be traced back to this compound.

But JP had a phone. There would be crumbs of information—maybe more than that—on his device. If she could get her own phone back, she had cloning software installed, but the process was painfully cumbersome. His device needed to be unlocked and her phone practically on top of his. The cloning process might take fifteen minutes.

But the potential for useful intel was staggering.

Rachel fell asleep in the afternoon, waking just before the evening meal as the sun was setting outside. She splashed water on her face and poked her head out of the room.

The men were gathering around the table, but there was no invitation to join them, despite the fact that at least three of them saw her.

Screw it. She was famished. Rachel stepped into the kitchen and took a place at the end of the table. The conversation instantly died down and there were awkward, angry looks among the men.

"Don't mind me, gentlemen," she said. "I'm just here to eat."

Kasim watched her from his perch at the head of the table but said nothing. The rest of the meal passed in silence.

When she went back to her room, Rachel did not turn on a light. The sounds in the kitchen died away as the men settled in for the night. She stretched out on the bed in her clothes and thought through the problem again.

What was JP hiding out here in the middle of the desert? That was a question worth answering.

She dozed, then was awoken by the trill of a telephone ringing in Kasim's room, across the hall.

Rachel moved to the door and pressed her ear against it. She heard the slap of Kasim's feet on the wooden floor. Then the ringing stopped and she heard the sound of a phone being picked up from its cradle.

"Yes, boss." Kasim's voice, clogged with sleep. A long pause as he listened.

"Two teams, tomorrow morning. Got it. How many men?" Another pause.

"Understood." He hung up the phone and she heard the creak of his bed as he lay back down.

Rachel went back to the bed. JP needed two teams to do what?

Rachel was up before the sun. She took a brief sponge bath in Rocky's sink and dressed.

Kasim's door stood open and his room was empty. Rocky waited for her in the kitchen.

"Wait here for Kasim."

Rachel ate a quick breakfast of a red millet porridge and yogurt, washed down with hot tea. Kasim arrived just as she was finishing.

"Boss wants you," he said.

Four black SUVs were parked inside the underground garage. Eight of Kasim's men, all armed but dressed in civilian clothes, waited near two cars. The other two vehicles had armed and uniformed drivers standing by.

Kasim pointed to one of the empty SUVs. "Get in."

Just as she reached the vehicle, the elevator door opened and she caught a glimpse of JP deep in conversation with a woman. She was dressed in traditional Muslim garb with a heavy head scarf and carried a padded tube under her arm about the size and shape of a small thermos.

The woman looked up as the door opened and Rachel caught a glimpse of her face. High cheekbones, a wisp of auburn hair escaping the confines of her head scarf, and brilliant, flashing blue eyes.

"In!" Kasim said from behind her.

Rachel got in the passenger seat and closed the door. She watched in the side mirror as JP helped the woman into the back of the SUV behind them and leaned in. Rachel cracked open her car door.

". . . three days" was all she heard before Kasim pushed the door closed again.

As JP climbed into the backseat of the SUV, the garage door of the compound opened. All four cars accelerated up the ramp into the bright sunshine. The two cars on Rachel's right peeled away, headed north.

Rachel looked into the rearview mirror. JP was watching her.

"Who was that woman?" Rachel asked.

JP pursed his lips, then drew a pair of sunglasses out of his jacket pocket. He looked out the window.

"Nobody."

CHAPTER 33

Lake Nasser, Egypt

The atmosphere in the vehicle had been tense and silent since they crossed the Egyptian border, over two hours ago. The headlights from the lead SUV carved a dual cone of illumination into the darkness. The second, identical black SUV stayed right on their tail, its headlights two pools of light on the tinted back window.

Rocky shifted in the passenger seat, wanting to crack a joke or do something to ease the tension. Instead, he retightened the straps on his body armor, the sound of ripping Velcro unnaturally loud in the quiet cabin.

They had crossed the Egyptian border with Sudan in the desert to avoid detection. Before they linked up with the highway again, Nasri, who was driving, stopped the caravan and told them to gear up. During the stop, he also divided the explosives between the two vehicles.

Rocky had been on countless ops with this crew and

knew what to expect. They were professionals, ready to do whatever was required, which usually came down to whatever Kasim told them to do.

Like Rocky, most of this crew had worked for Kasim for the last decade. They'd come a long way from their early days in the Janjaweed. From there, they'd been absorbed into the Sudanese Defense Forces as a paramilitary wing of the regular army.

Working outside the system was something Kasim was good at. He always found a way to get them paid.

Nasri slowed the car as a large painted sign loomed out of the darkness: MUBAREK PUMPING STATION, in Arabic and English lettering.

Nasri keyed his radio. "This is it. Just like we planned it. Fast and furious." He grinned at his own joke. Nasri was a big fan of the American movies of the same name.

The road was crushed gravel, but it was fast and flat. Nasri switched off the air-conditioning and rolled down the window. Chill desert air rolled in.

Rocky could smell the water, a humid, rotten smell left when fresh water receded from the banks of the lake. He squinted into the darkness, looking for a gleam of Lake Nasser.

Rocky could feel his nervous energy building in anticipation of the raid. He could hear the two guys in the backseat checking their weapons again. The Uzi submachine guns harnessed to their chests, the handguns. There was a *zwick* sound as one of the guys slipped out his blade and then reseated it into the sheath.

This raid was different. For months, Kasim had emphasized covert action. Nasri and Rocky had bribed the food truck guy to take a bomb into the Ethiopian dam work site. Another time, they impersonated a road crew and set IEDs on the highway at Ad-Damazin.

But tonight was different. They were there to make a show.

Those were Kasim's words: *Make a great show.* He finished off with that deep rolling belly laugh of his.

Nasri took a curve in the road at high speed and nodded to the windshield. "That's it," he said.

Rocky craned his neck to get a look. The destination was a concrete block structure set in the middle of the lake, like an island. A bridge connected the island and the mainland.

According to Nasri, the building pumped water from Lake Nasser into a canal where it flowed a hundred miles into the desert. The Egyptians were trying to build a new Nile River Valley. Sounded like bullshit to Rocky.

There was a guardhouse with a steel bar that blocked the road. Two guards, according to the mission brief.

It was nearly three in the morning, the perfect time for a raid. A man in a blue uniform appeared in the glass door of the guardhouse. He rubbed his face like they'd woken him up.

Nasri started to slow down, then hit the accelerator and the SUV surged forward. The steel bar twanged back like a paper clip.

Rocky twisted in his seat. The second SUV had stopped at the guardhouse to finish the job. He counted two sparks of handgun fire, then two more.

The pumping station building was huge, at least

thirty meters high, and washed in harsh floodlights that showed the imperfections in the concrete as rough shadows.

Nasri took the quarter-mile-long bridge at speed, grinning. Rocky gripped the armrest. Dark water flashed beneath them.

The bridge opened onto a wide courtyard in front of the pumping station. Nasri spun the wheel and skidded the SUV to a halt twenty meters from a pair of massive steel loading doors.

All four of the vehicle occupants bailed out. Nasri and the two guys in the backseat moved to the lift gate. Rocky walked to the front of the SUV, flipping off the plastic end covers on an RPG-22 antitank rocket launcher as he moved. He extended the weapon with a snap and manually cocked it by raising the rear sight. He checked to make sure the backblast area was clear and shouldered the weapon. He sighted on the center of the doors that led into the pumping station.

"Fire in the hole!"

A tremendous whoosh, a gout of flame erupted behind him, and the rocket corkscrewed into the doors. The resulting explosion nearly knocked Rocky off his feet.

When the smoke cleared, one of the blasted doors was on the ground, the other hung at a crazy angle.

Nasri whooped as the second SUV roared past Rocky, driving straight into the blown-open doorway.

Rocky dropped the spent RPG-22 and moved to the open lift gate of the SUV. He hoisted a rucksack loaded with explosives onto his shoulder and hustled after his team into the pumping station.

The inside of the concrete building was open, like a stadium. A deafening whining noise filled the space. Enormous mechanical structures, each the size of a small house, were linked by a series of meter-wide pipes. The scale was such that it took Rocky a second to realize they were pumps.

Over the din, Rocky could make out the *pop-pop* of small arms fire. That would be the second car taking out anyone in the control room.

Nasri slapped him on the shoulder. "Stop gawking! This way." He pointed to a set of double doors labeled POWER DISTRIBUTION and a red HIGH VOLTAGE sign.

The four of them crashed through the door together. After the deafening hum of the pump room, the power distribution room was almost silent. The room was full of gray-painted steel cabinets, each as tall as a man, arranged in four rows.

The team raced to their assigned places in the room. Two in the far corners, one in the center, and one by the door. Rocky dropped his rucksack and ripped open the zipper.

Inside each rucksack was a demolition charge of ten C-4 blocks wired together and attached to a timer. A bright red lanyard was attached to a silver pin—the arming mechanism.

"Everybody ready?" Nasri yelled. Even without the radio, Rocky could hear him in the quiet room.

Three positive responses.

"Arm your charges on my mark. Three, two, one, mark!"

Rocky pulled the pin.

They had ten minutes to get clear.

Back in the noisy pump room, Nasri paused to gawk at the pumps.

"Damn," he said. "Those are big fuckers."

Rocky tugged on his arm. "C'mon, man, we're on the clock."

Nasri did not budge. "Gimme the RPG."

"Why?"

"Just give it to me—and get back."

Rocky handed him the spare weapon and jogged with him to the blasted exit doors. "What are you gonna do?"

Nasri grinned. "Boss said put on a show."

He extended the RPG casing, cocked it, and aimed at the nearest pump.

"Fire in the fucking hole."

CHAPTER 34

Camp Lemonnier, Djibouti, Africa

The worst part was the waiting, Dre thought.

After they hatched the plan to trace the Mahdi after his next attack, Don divided the team into six-hour rotating watch sections.

For Dre, a day defined into six-hour segments felt strangely comforting, like she was back in a watch rotation on the *Murphy*. She and Janet took the evening watch and the morning watch, while Shira and Michael took the graveyard shift and the afternoon shift.

On the evening watch of the sixth day, Don Riley burst through the door of their SCIF. "It's happening," he said. "Turn on Al Jazeera. There's been another attack."

The news anchor on Al Jazeera was a trim, middle-aged man in a dove-gray jacket, matching tie, and carefully coiffed hair. He stared at the camera and said in a modulated English accent, "There has been an attack near Toshka in southern Egypt, on the border with Sudan. Initial reports are that upwards of two dozen people have been killed, and the Sheikh Zayed Canal system required to irrigate the new desert city has been heavily damaged."

Janet was already checking out unclassified internet news sites as well as the classified networks. Already mobile-phone video clips were showing up of smoke pouring out of a large concrete building set in the middle of a body of water.

They switched back to Al Jazeera, which now had a guest on to discuss the economics of the new desert city and the impact of the bombing on the region.

The expert was a professor from Cairo University who spoke in very precise English. "The Sheikh Zayed Canal complex is a system of pumping stations, locks, and canals that deliver water from Lake Nasser to an ever-expanding Egyptian domestic agricultural sector," he said. The screen changed to show a close-up of the region. "The Toshka Lakes shown on this map represent what the Egyptian government likes to call a 'new desert city.' Using water from the Nile, we have transformed hundreds of thousands of acres of desert into productive farmland. Literally millions of people rely on the Toshka project for their daily sustenance. This is not an attack on infrastructure. This is an attack on the people of Egypt."

"But what about the possibility that this act was done in retaliation for some of the attacks on upstream dam projects in the Nile River basin?" the announcer asked.

"This attack is the work of those who want to control the Nile River," the professor said emphatically. "Our neighbors to the south. Sudan and Ethiopia, to be exact."

"And what about the terrorist known as the Mahdi?" the news anchor pressed. "How does he fit into all this?"

The professor's careful accent began to break down as he became more agitated. "He is a fraud. This so-called messiah who claims to want to unite Islam does nothing but tear us apart. The real perpetrators of this attack are those who seek to take the lifeblood of the Nile away from Egypt."

Don muted the television. "Any activity from the Mahdi website?" he asked.

Dre shook her head. "Not yet. In prior attacks, it took hours before there was a claim."

Finally, Michael and Shira arrived together. Shira's eyes flitted from Dre to Janet, and two spots of color formed high on her cheeks. Michael took his place at his workstation.

"All right, people, let's be ready," Don said. "When this goes down, we'll only have a few minutes and we need to make them count."

Time dragged on with no sign of activity from the Mahdi website. Don switched back on the TV sound.

The tenor of the conversation had definitely shifted to a more aggressive tone. The Egyptian Defense Ministry released a statement saying that they would vigorously defend Egypt's natural resources and issued mobilization orders to move troops south to the border with Sudan. There was an implicit rebuke of Sudan and Ethiopia in the statement, and both countries responded with angry denials of any wrongdoing.

"He's broadcasting," Janet announced, her voice pitched with excitement.

After the verbal fireworks on TV, the claim of responsibility by the Mahdi felt almost tame in comparison. The Mahdi began his broadcast with the same background music and the well-appointed sitting room.

The atmosphere in the room went electric with anticipation. Dre called up the IP trace program.

"Initiating the tracker program now," she said, hitting the return key on her workstation.

"Put it on the big board, please," Don said.

Dre threw her feed to the wall screen in the tactical operations center. A map of the world showed with a blinking dot on Iran. Their starting point was the Islamic Revolutionary Guard Corps's server.

The blinking dot shifted to Geneva.

"It's taking too long," Don said. "That was at least ten seconds."

"We don't know how many hops he'll make, Don," Janet said, but her voice sounded worried. Normally, the Mahdi's broadcasts only lasted about a minute and a half.

Dre checked her screen. "The next hop is being resolved . . . looks like—"

The blinking dot moved to Brazil.

"We've burned more than forty-five seconds," Don said.

"The program is working as fast as it can, Don," Janet said calmly.

Vancouver, Canada.

On the video, the blurred form of the Mahdi was wrapping up with his now-familiar "children of Islam" line.

Tokyo, Japan.

"Come on," Don said under his breath. "Come on."

Cape Town, South Africa. The blinking light turned solid.

"We've got him," Dre said. "Shit, he's gone to a satellite."

The background music on the video faded. The Mahdi's broadcast ended on a black screen.

"Well?" Don said.

Dre pulled up the satellite data. It was a GEOStar-3, a common communications satellite that carried traffic for thousands of commercial customers.

"Run down every bit of traffic on that satellite over the last hour," Don said. "See if we can get any matches with anything we have in the database."

"Don, that's not going to give us a location," Janet said.

Don cursed, a sharp biting sound that stilled the activity in the room.

"I'm sorry," Don said after a few minutes. "That's that, I guess."

"I have an idea, Don," Michael said. "I've been discussing it with Shira, and she thinks I should bring it up to the group."

Dre and Janet exchanged another glance. He was discussing it with Shira? Since when did Shira rate a discussion before the rest of his team?

"Let's hear it, Michael," Don said.

"What if all this is a smoke screen?" Michael said. "What if the Mahdi is just trying to control the news cycle by feeding us what we're expecting to find?"

"Are we really back to this fake terrorist theory again, Michael?" Don said. "If you've got something solid, then let's hear it."

Michael shot a glance at Shira, who nodded. "Okay, we have the Ebola virus attack in Yemen. At virtually the same time, the Mahdi launches an attack on the Roseires Dam in Sudan. That's only one instance, a co-incidence, right?"

Don nodded, but his expression was anything but neutral.

Michael continued. "We had another incident in Yemen a few months ago." He called up a file and threw it to the big screen. Dre scanned the document. A garbled mobile-phone call followed by a Saudi air strike.

"The woman on the call described the bodies as 'melting,' and said the entire village was dead. What does that sound like to you?"

Don's features pinched into a frown. "Single-sourced intel. No backup. That's weak stuff, Michael."

Michael touched his keyboard and split the screen. The first Mahdi attack had happened the same day.

"The only difference between the first attack in Yemen and the second was the cease-fire that grounded all the Saudi warplanes. What if the plan had been to destroy the town of Melaba to hide the evidence?"

"That means there would be a connection between the Saudis and the bioweapons test," Janet said.

"A very senior connection," Shira added. "Someone who had the ability to call in an air strike on a target."

Janet jumped in. "Which brings us back to the Saudi bank transfer, which is linked—"

Don held up his hands. "The last time we went down this rabbit hole, Michael, we ended up spending weeks poring through financial transactions instead of doing our day jobs."

"That idea netted us a good lead, Don," Janet said, her tone sharp.

Don clenched his hands into fists. His face was red. "If you want me to believe there's a connection between the Mahdi and bioweapons attacks in Yemen and the Saudis, then we need a whole lot more to support that argument." He stabbed a finger at Michael.

"Two points make a straight line. If this Mahdi attack is a third point, can you fit the curve? If Michael's theory is correct, then there's already been another bioweapons attack. Correct?"

Michael shot a nervous glance at Dre and Janet. "If I'm right, then yes."

Don pointed at Michael's workstation. "Then go find it."

CHAPTER 35

Project Deliverance, undisclosed location in Sudan

For Rachel Jaeger, the state of Israel had given—and taken away—the best things in her life.

If it were not for Mossad, she would never have met Levi. If it were not for Mossad, she would not have lost her young husband.

It was hard to remember the exact contours of Levi's face after all these years, but she never forgot the way he looked at her. The eyes of an angel, she used to say.

No, that was wrong, too. It wasn't how he looked at her, it was the way he made her feel.

And now, she was feeling it again. From Jean-Pierre Manzul.

"Penny for your thoughts," JP said. "Isn't that the expression?"

"It is, and they're not for sale." Rachel buckled her seat belt in the Learjet and looked out the window at the packed-earth runway of the secret research site.

"You're angry with me." A statement, not a question.

Rachel continued her study of the desert landscape. The door of the jet slammed shut and the engines began to spin. JP darkened the windows until they were opaque black, forcing her attention back to him.

"When do I get my phone and my weapon back?" she asked. Rachel didn't care a whit about the weapon, but she hoped to hell the phone had been left on and was trackable.

"We have security protocols at this site," he said. "Everyone follows them. Even me."

"So, I can have them back now?"

The engines on the jet roared and she felt the craft turning.

"Soon," JP said.

"I feel naked without my phone and gun."

JP didn't take the bait. "I don't need protecting here."

"Why did you bring me here? Obviously, physical security is not an issue."

"You intrigue me, Zula Bekele."

"Who was the woman back in the garage?" Rachel asked. "The one in the hijab."

JP stared at her evenly. "She's my lover. Does it matter?" He said it like a challenge, but he smiled as he said the words.

She met his gaze. "Not to me."

When they landed in Khartoum, Rachel got her belongings back and powered up her phone to check the time. Two in the afternoon. They'd been in the air between four and five hours.

The Mercedes limo was waiting for them. She

inspected the vehicle and held the door for JP before she slipped into the front passenger seat. Rachel assumed the role of professional hawk, her eyes roving over the crowds, looking for someone who was watching too carefully, whose hands stayed out of sight.

Throughout the hour-long drive to his apartment, she could feel the heat of JP's gaze on her.

She ignored him, hearing Noam's gruff voice in her head. *A rushed operation is a botched operation.*

"You're smiling," JP said.

Rachel snapped a glance over her shoulder and met his eyes for a second. "I love my work."

The driver pulled to the curb outside JP's apartment building. She exited the car, her eyes scanning the street. Rachel pulled his door open, her hand on the top of the doorframe.

When JP stood, he put his hand on hers. "Have dinner with me tonight." It was not a question.

"Yes," she answered without thinking.

When Rachel got back to her own apartment, she checked the calculator app on her mobile phone. The register on the calculator read "22," the code from Noam to check in. She sent a text to JP that she was going shopping.

The late-afternoon sun broiled the pedestrians on the westward-facing side of the apartment building. Rachel lost herself in the crowd, heading toward the shopping district, but tacking down side streets whenever she saw an opportunity to assess if she was being followed.

When she was confident she was alone, she stepped

into a café and ordered a coffee. She dialed Noam's number from memory.

He answered on the first ring. "Where have you been?" His voice held the tiniest tinge of concern that made her smile.

"Doing my job. Where have you been?"

"Don't get smart with me. Your phone was off for over twenty-four hours."

Rachel briefly relayed the events of the last two days. The visit to Cyprus, the mysterious yacht, the meeting that had so upset JP, the flight to the secret location.

"The security forces are former Janjaweed and I'm convinced they are behind the Mahdi attacks," she concluded, "but what is going on underneath the warehouse is unknown."

"What's your next move?" Noam asked.

"If I can get close enough, I'm going to clone his phone and insert a tracker program. Maybe we can figure out where the site is located."

"Bold move." Noam didn't bother with pretenses about her safety. He trusted her.

"It's only a bold move if it works. I'll be in touch." Rachel hung up and resumed walking.

She turned down the first side street, a lane full of luxury stores, and pretended to window-shop. A few pedestrians wandered through the shade of the cobbled lane. The street felt a million miles from the heat and dust of the crowded thoroughfares only a hundred meters away.

Dinner with JP called for a new dress, she decided,

something spectacular to distract the man from his phone for a good half hour. A bloodred Christian Dior dress appeared in the very next window.

Rachel let the grin spread across her face.

Noam was about to buy her a new outfit.

═══════════

Rachel surveyed her image in the full-length mirror and liked what she saw. The straps of the red silk dress fastened behind her neck, the fiery color a perfect complement to her dark skin. The plunging neckline and open back showed the perfect amount of skin.

It was a daring choice. Sexy, classy, and she looked gorgeous in it. She unboxed the black Manolo Blahnik sling-backs, giggling to herself at the sight of the slender stilettos. After the Mozambique job, she would never look at high heels the same way again.

She wore her hair up off her neck, which made the occasion feel exotic to her. She replaced her typical silver stud earrings with dangling gold pendants.

Rachel took one last turn in the mirror. Noam never realized he had such good taste in fashion.

Perfume? Her instinct said no.

Her stomach fluttered, as it did before every operation like this. She would be on JP's home turf. If her true purpose for being there was discovered, he would have the advantage on her. Weapons or no, he was a dangerous man.

Finally, she checked her phone again. The cloning program was hidden in the clock function of the device. If she touched three apps on the home screen in quick succession, it would synchronize with any discoverable device within six inches. Fifteen to twenty minutes later, she would have a complete clone of his phone and a tracker program installed. The only catch was that his phone would be unusable during that period.

She used the elevator ride to JP's apartment to calm her breathing. Zula's performance needed to be flawless tonight. In this setting, she would not have the security job to give her emotional cover. She would need to be herself—or rather Zula—and it would require ultimate concentration.

When she stepped out of the elevator, the lights in the apartment were turned low.

"I'll be out in a minute," JP called from the kitchen.

The tall, colonial-style windows in the apartment stood open. Gauzy white curtains stirred in the breeze. Rachel pressed her hips against the windowsill and stared into the night.

The lights of Khartoum lay before her like jewels spread across a velvet carpet. A few blocks away she could see the Nile gleaming between gaps in the buildings as the river made its slow way north. The darkness sanded the rough edges from the squalor of the city, softened decay into quaintness. The freshened breeze took the edge off the heat and carried the sounds of the city to her as a murmured cacophony. On the horizon, a quarter-moon hung in the clear sky.

JP appeared by her side and handed her a glass of chilled white wine. The taste of apples and citrus exploded on her tongue, followed by a subtle melon aftertaste.

"This is exquisite," she said.

"I was just thinking the same thing," he replied. His eyes drank her in, and she felt a heat rise up her neck. "You look beautiful."

"I was talking about the wine."

"Pinot blanc, from the Alsace region of France." He took another sip, studying her from over the rim of the glass. "My mother grew up there. And I still think you look beautiful."

"That was the effect I was going for."

JP laughed. "There's no pretense with you, is there?"

Rachel turned her back on the city. "What's for dinner?"

"Omelets. I only make one thing, but I do it well. Something else I learned from my mother."

Rachel followed him to the kitchen. "Tell me about her." His phone was in his hip pocket.

JP set his wineglass on the stone counter and turned on the stove. He put a well-used omelet pan over the bright blue flame and tossed in a chunk of butter. He watched it melt.

"My French mother fell in love with a mysterious man from Sudan and that's how I came to be. What about you, Zula Bekele? I've seen your résumé and watched you work. Tell me the rest of the story."

Rachel pretended the wine had gone to her head. The story she spun for JP hewed as closely to the truth as she dared. Born in Ethiopia, pursued a degree in African languages and literature, then found the martial arts. Security work paid better than college professor and she enjoyed the finer things in life. She laughed when she said the last bit and plucked at her dress.

As she spoke, JP cooked. He cracked two eggs and whipped them in a bowl while vegetables sautéed in the pan. The beaten eggs covered the vegetables, and he prodded the mixture until almost firm, then flipped the contents, added a handful of cheese, and expertly rolled it onto her plate.

He presented it to her with a bow. "For you, mademoiselle. We'll be eating by the pool." He pointed through a doorway at the back of the kitchen.

Rachel carried her glass of wine and her omelet down the narrow hallway to find a hidden garden area at the back of the apartment.

The pool was lined with sky-blue tiles and lighted from underwater. A small fire burned in a ceramic fire pit on the far side of the pool, and a waist-high stone wall shielded the garden area from the outside world.

Nestled between two palm trees was a table for two and a second bottle of wine chilling in ice. Rachel lit the candles on the table and took a seat, sipping her wine. The deep pool was square, maybe five meters on a side. Soft underwater light rippled in waves across the secluded scene.

JP appeared in the doorway carrying his own plate and wine. He sat down across from her. "*Bon appétit.*" He laid his phone facedown on the table next to his plate.

The omelet practically melted in her mouth, with the cheese and vegetables grilled to perfection.

"Delicious," she said.

"Try it with the wine."

Rachel sipped her wine. The melon overtones in the

wine amplified the egg dish. "Amazing. Your mother taught you well."

After the last bite, Rachel opened her purse and slipped out her phone. She touched the sequence to start the cloning process.

"Thought I felt a text," she said. She dropped the phone back into the clutch and snapped it closed. She placed her handbag on the table.

JP stood and collected her plate.

"You should see what I have for dessert." When he left, his phone remained facedown on the table.

Pulse hammering, Rachel pushed her clutch across the table until it rested next to JP's phone. Now all she needed was to keep JP away from his phone for twenty minutes.

As if on cue, he appeared in the doorway. "Let's go back inside and . . ."

His voice trailed away as his eyes locked with Rachel.

She stood, tugging at the clasp of the dress behind her neck. The silk slid down her skin like a whisper. She heard JP suck in a breath.

Rachel stepped out of her shoes, the stone of the patio rough under her feet. Her heartbeat roared in her ears, blocking out the distant sounds of the street far below them. A strange, quaking emptiness formed in her belly and when she spoke her mouth was dry.

"I think we should have dessert later."

CHAPTER 36

Akwar, west of Marial Bai, South Sudan

Father Alfred peddled his bike through the desert.

On these early-morning rides, he felt very close to God indeed. He left Marial Bai before the sun was up and made his way into the vast desert, following the barely discernible thread of a road using equal parts instinct and eyesight.

His flock was scattered across the land. On the first Sunday of the month he traveled south, the next Sunday north, then east. But on the fourth Sunday of every month, he traveled west. It was twenty miles to the village of Akwar, but he could make it in a little under two hours if he stayed steady on the pedals.

As the packed-earth path rolled beneath his tires, Father Alfred liked to sing. There was no one around and he bellowed all his favorite tunes in as many languages as he could remember. Most were hymns, like the ones he had learned from the missionaries when he was a boy. The songs of the Mother Church made the miles fly by.

He just finished the last verse of "Rock of Ages" when Akwar came into view.

It was a tiny speck of human existence in the midst of a vast desert, barely earning even the title of "village." It rarely appeared on maps, and no roads other than the one he was on passed through it.

The whole of Akwar was ten mud-brick dwellings and one open pavilion with a thatched roof where he conducted Sunday services. The cross atop the pavilion was etched against the morning sky, a sight that always filled him with pride.

Father Alfred stopped pedaling and let the bicycle coast to a stop. The breath of life sang in his ears like music. He was doing God's work, spreading His Word among the war-weary people of South Sudan. Moments of stillness like this one made it all worthwhile.

Normally, four or five boys from the village would have spied him by now and trotted out to meet him, but this morning the road was empty. Even Simon wasn't there.

Simon was a bright eight-year-old with a gap-toothed smile and the voice of an angel. At services, he sat in the front row with his beautiful mother by his side, her hand staying the inexhaustible energy of his active young frame.

Alfred pedaled into town trailing a thin rooster tail of dust behind him. The doors of the village homes were all closed tightly, and he did not see any movement behind the open windows.

He struck up another verse of "Rock of Ages" as he rode to his open-air church. The sun was up, but it was still cool as he unpacked his kit from the back of the bicycle. He spread a clean white linen across the rough altar and unpacked a single candle, holy water, a chalice, and a small package of communion wafers. He kissed the embroidered stole, said a blessing, and placed the narrow strip of cloth around his neck.

He was ready for his parishioners, whenever they deigned to join him.

Father Alfred walked through the church straightening the rough pews, picking up a bit of trash, and shooing out the chickens that liked to wander through his service. He sat on the last bench and waited as the sun climbed higher in the sky.

Still, no one showed up. He walked to the top of the street and cupped his hands around his mouth. "Simon," he called. "Simon, Father Alfred is here."

Still no answer.

With a sigh of frustration, he walked to the nearest house and rapped his knuckles on the door. The silence was starting to unnerve him and he hummed a hymn under his breath.

There was no answer, so he went to the next house, Simon's home.

He knocked loudly. "Hello?"

Nothing, but just as he was about to walk away, he heard something move inside the building. He pushed the door open a few inches. "It's Father Alfred. Is someone in there?"

He definitely heard a groan this time. Alfred pushed

the door all the way open. The stench from within stopped him like a slap in the face.

Gagging, he retreated a few paces and searched in his pocket for a handkerchief. He approached the open door again with the cloth pressed against his face.

"Hello?" he called into the dark interior. "Is someone in there?"

A groan, fingers scrabbling on hard ground—these sounds made him move closer. Someone was alive in there. Someone who needed his help.

Breathing a silent prayer, he stepped inside the door. His eyes took precious seconds to adjust, and when they did, he wished they hadn't.

It was Simon's family—or it had been, at least. The adults were dead, their bodies bloated and deformed. Alfred stepped closer, the handkerchief clamped over his nose and mouth.

The corpses had melted, their skin like black candle wax. Streams of thick black blood flowed from their noses, mouths, and eyes. The white of the eyes were dark with blood. The smell of rotten death clung to Alfred's skin like a soggy blanket.

To his right, on the dirt floor, Alfred saw movement. A scrawny arm rose, fingers splayed.

Father Alfred knelt over Simon's body and took his pulse. The boy was barely alive. His eyes were nearly swollen shut and a thick line of bloodied mucus ran from his nose.

"Simon, can you hear me?"

The arm rose again. He took the tiny hand in his. "I'm here, Simon."

He carried the child close to the door, where he could get some fresh air but stay out of the sun. A fresh flow of blood ran from the boy's nose. When he placed the tiny body on the ground, something rolled out of Simon's blanket.

Alfred picked up a small cylinder. It was machined metal, heavy like steel, with a small black plastic square that read "00" in red numbers and a raised metal nipple covered with white residue. He twisted the top off and inside was a single empty test tube with the same white powder inside.

"Where did you get this, Simon?" he asked. But the boy was unconscious.

He left the open canister on the ground and raced through the village, kicking open the doors of each house, knowing already what he would find.

By the time he had made a complete circuit of the village, Simon was dead.

Father Alfred was the only living human being in Akwar. He staggered back to the church and collapsed onto a pew. This was an epidemic of some kind, some horrible disease. He needed to tell someone. He needed to get to a hospital.

Alfred dug into his pocket for his mobile. His fingers shook as he tried to scroll through his contacts. Then, in the distance, he heard the hum of a car engine and the bite of tires on a dirt road. He squinted into the sun and saw a plume of golden dust.

Someone was coming. Someone who could help. He slipped his phone back into his pocket and raced into the center of the road, waving his arms wildly.

"Stop! Stop, please!" he shouted. The black SUV halted ten meters away, the dust slowly rolling past the vehicle toward Alfred. A woman got out of the car from the passenger side and stood behind the door. She was dressed in traditional Muslim garb, but he could see that under her hijab she had bright blue eyes.

"What are you doing here?" the woman called to him.

"I'm the priest," he said. "It's Sunday. I say Mass here on Sundays—well, not every Sunday, but the fourth Sunday of every month and . . ." His voice trailed off when the woman ducked her head back into the car and spoke to the driver.

The driver was a hulk of a man with brawny shoulders and a muscled belly that pressed against his shirt. He was dressed in green like a soldier. Alfred had seen enough death in South Sudan to recognize Janjaweed. He eyed his bicycle.

The man walked toward him. He pulled a handgun from a holster and pointed it at the priest. "You should not be here, priest," he said in Arabic.

Alfred clenched his eyes shut. *If it is your will, Father—*

The gun went off and Father Alfred was knocked to the ground. His chest went numb as if his whole torso were being squeezed, and he couldn't breathe. Then his breath returned and with it a searing bolt of pain. He tried to scream but all he managed was a wheezy gurgle.

Alfred knew that sound. The bullet had entered his lungs. He would drown in his own blood.

The man and woman passed him, both dressed in white bodysuits with masks and goggles.

"Find it," the woman said. "We're not leaving here without the dispersal unit." The man moved from house to house with plodding steps like a ghostly giant. When the man got to Simon's house, he bent down. He came back to the woman holding the disassembled steel container in his hands.

"Found it," he said.

The woman held out an open plastic bag. The man dropped the disassembled pieces into the opening. She sealed it and set it aside.

"Get the incendiaries," she ordered the man. She approached Father Albert and squatted down next to him. She held up the sealed plastic bag, and said, "Did you take this apart, Father?" Her voice was muffled through the face mask.

Alfred nodded his head feebly. The sun was so bright. All he wanted was a drink of water. He tried to say "Water," but the word wouldn't come out.

She patted him on the shoulder. "I'm really sorry about this, Father. You were not supposed to be here."

The man returned carrying a box. He dropped it into the dirt next to the woman. Father Albert squinted through a wave of dust at the label: AN-M14 TH3 INCENDIARY HAND GRENADE.

"What are you waiting for?" she said in an impatient voice. "Get started."

The man gathered an armful of red canisters and began jogging through the village. At each house, he pulled out the grenade pin and lobbed a canister through the open door. A few seconds later, a flash of blinding white seared Alfred's eyeballs. The houses began to burn.

The last house was Simon's house.

"I'll do this one," she said. "You carry the priest in."

The sun was blocked out by the bulk of the man standing over him. He seized Alfred's collar and dragged him through the dust. Alfred tried to pray but the words were just out of reach.

His legs bumped over the doorsill and he was inside, out of the sun. Simon's tiny body lay next to the door like some macabre melted wax figurine.

Alfred's body dropped to the dirt floor. He rolled on one side. The wound in his chest didn't hurt anymore . . . that was probably a bad sign.

Alfred heard the man grunt and he raised his eyes. The woman stood in the doorway, a gun in her hand.

She shot once, twice, three times, a tremendous noise in the enclosed space. The big man's knees buckled. He collapsed next to Alfred.

He could see her bright blue eyes sparkle as she pulled the pin from the last grenade and tossed it into the house. This woman was enjoying herself.

"You picked the wrong week to say Mass, Father."

Alfred closed his eyes as she walked away. In his mind, he was in the desert on his bicycle. It was early morning and he was singing a hymn at the top of his voice.

He looked at the sun and it grew brighter and brighter . . .

CHAPTER 37

Camp Lemonnier, Djibouti, Africa

The secure briefing room at the Camp Lemonnier tactical operations center was set up like a virtual boardroom. Janet and Don sat together behind a broad desk facing a wall full of screens large enough that the people they were briefing appeared life-sized. The clarity of the video connection was perfect, but there was a half-second delay in the uplink, which left Janet with the unsettling feeling that the meeting was operating in slow motion.

Only two of the screens were live. Janet recognized Dylan Mattias from the CIA's Operations and Resources Management branch, from their meeting in DC when Michael had committed them to man-weeks of work on financial transactions. The other participant was new to her.

Janet studied Judy Simonsen, the assistant to the director for foreign intelligence relations. With a broad, open face and a ready smile, she looked more like a middle-aged housewife than a powerful CIA insider, but Don had been clear: She was the one to convince in this briefing. Her thick brown hair was cut in a curled bob and she wore a bright pumpkin-colored scarf and matching earrings.

"How are you finding Camp Lemonnier, Lieutenant Everett?" Simonsen said.

"It's fine, ma'am," Janet replied.

The woman laughed, a hearty guffaw. "I spent a year there one week. I did not think it was fine."

"Are we ready yet, Don?" Mattias cut in. "I have a hard stop in thirty minutes."

"Patience, young Jedi," Simonsen chided Mattias. "Let the techies do their job."

In the full-sized, high-def picture, Janet saw Mattias's jaw muscle bunch up. The light on the wall above the screens shifted from red to green.

"I have us secure," Don said. He nodded to Janet to put up the first slide on the shared screen.

"Finally," Mattias muttered. "Show us what you've got, Don."

The picture on the screen showed a single timeline aligning three suspected bioweapons tests with the Mahdi terrorist attacks.

"What you're seeing here are three instances of attacks on small villages, two in Yemen and a new one in South Sudan, overlaid with terrorist attacks on installations in the Nile River basin by the terrorist known as the Mahdi." Don was sweating, but his voice was steady.

"I thought we were here to discuss the Mahdi and Iranian connections, Don," Mattias said. "Why are we looking at small village attacks in Yemen?"

"Maybe if you give Mr. Riley more than thirty seconds to speak, he could connect the two, Dylan," Simonsen said.

Mattias glowered as Don continued: "We believe that all three of these attacks were possible bioweapons tests. In the first case, we have a mobile-phone call that described the entire village as dead and the bodies as 'melted.'"

"We have a very garbled mobile-phone call, Don," Mattias said. "I speak Arabic and the translation is suspect. Let's not overstate the case."

"Why can't we confirm it?" Simonsen asked.

"The village was destroyed in a Saudi air strike, ma'am," Don said.

"Hmm. Convenient."

Don plowed forward. "The second attack is now considered a confirmed use of a bioweapon. An outbreak of Ebola was found in a small village in Yemen by a Doctors Without Borders advance team. The date of this incident coincided with an unexpected cease-fire in Yemen. It is possible that this cease-fire interfered with the Saudi efforts to destroy the site."

"Your conclusion is that the Saudis are behind a bioweapons attack?" Mattias's voice was incredulous. "That's a very serious charge to level against a US ally."

"You're calling this a confirmed bioweapons attack, Don?" Simonsen asked.

"Correct, ma'am. The virus was traced to a sample

taken from the World Health Organization office in Cairo."

Janet changed the screen to show a picture of an attractive woman with dark brown skin and blazing blue eyes. Auburn hair cascaded down her shoulders in loose waves. "This is Dr. Talia Tahir from the WHO. She was transporting samples from the Cairo office to the Brazzaville office in Africa when she died in a plane crash. One of the samples she was carrying was the same strain of the Ebola virus which was used in the attack on Melaba. In the course of her duties, Dr. Tahir has been in Yemen at least ten times in the past five years."

"And the third instance?" Mattias said.

Don cleared his throat as Janet put up a satellite photo of a burned-out village, two rows of blackened pits where structures used to be, separated by a narrow dirt track.

"This is the village of Akwar in South Sudan. We discovered this incident a few days ago. The devastation of the site suggests extreme prejudice was used to obliterate this village, probably using incendiaries."

"And were there any indications of a bioweapons attack here?" Mattias asked.

"Unknown." Don swallowed hard. "Even if we could get an asset there, the possibility of anything surviving a fire that intense is minuscule. These are brick houses. Whoever did this turned them into cremation ovens."

"Do we even know if there were bodies in these structures?" Simonsen asked.

"We do not, ma'am."

Simonsen looked stern. "Then why does this have relevance, Mr. Riley?"

"Our theory is the Mahdi terrorist attacks are being used as a distraction for the bioweapons events. Following the latest Mahdi attack in Egypt, we went looking for evidence of a bioweapons test. We found this. The size and scale of the destruction fits a pattern."

"And your assumption is that the Mahdi was unable to use Yemen for this test because of the cease-fire," Simonsen said.

"Yes, ma'am."

"What would it take for us to confirm this was an actual bioweapons test site?" Simonsen pressed.

Mattias entered the conversation. "If we went through diplomatic channels it would be weeks of negotiation and some very probing questions that we do not want to answer. If we sent in a covert team, it's a week of planning and risk of discovery. At the moment, all our assets are tied up with the Egypt situation."

Since the Mahdi attack on the Toshka desert project, the Egyptian army had been massing along the border with Sudan. Special forces cross-border raids were reported and the international news cycle was rife with rumors of a full-scale military assault into Sudan. Even the Ethiopians were preparing for war. All of the United States' diplomats, military commanders, and intel officers were focused on stemming the conflict within the region.

"But that's the point we're trying to make," Don

said. "If the Mahdi is planning something big, he needs a major distraction to shift attention away from his real purpose. What could be more distracting than a war over the Nile River?"

Don leaned forward, his voice earnest. "What we do is not an exact science. We had a theory. We tested the theory and came up with a viable answer. That alone suggests that we're on to something."

Mattias made no attempt to dampen his sarcasm. "And what exactly are you on to, Mr. Riley? I don't see any evidence here. I see some circumstantial bits that might fit together if we look at them a certain way. This whole thing is flimsy."

Simonsen plucked at her scarf. "Tell us more about the Mahdi, Mr. Riley."

Janet showed a screenshot of the Mahdi website. "The Mahdi website has extensive cryptographic capabilities, very uncharacteristic of these types of terrorist organizations."

"I've heard enough," Mattias interrupted. "We have three *possible* bioweapons attacks, *possibly* linked to three terrorist attacks by a *possible* terrorist organization led by a leader of whom we know nothing. Do I have that right, Don?"

Don stared straight ahead, his mouth set in a firm line. Every word of Mattias's assessment was landing like a hammer on Don's skull.

"With regard to the terrorist," Mattias continued, "we have been unable to ascertain a physical location for him and we have no clue what his next target might be."

"The name of my group is Emerging Threats, Dylan,"

Don snapped. "My team has provided an analysis that holds up to a first level of scrutiny. I realize it's not actionable yet, but based on experience I think we're on to something."

"I appreciate your candor, Don," Mattias said. The smile was thin, just short of a sneer. "But we have professionals in these regions who are looking at the same information and coming to a very different conclusion."

"What do you propose as a next step, Mr. Riley?" Simonsen's voice was measured.

"I'd like to bring the Israelis in on this," Don said. "All of it."

Mattias threw up his hands in frustration. "The Israelis? Are you out of your fucking mind?"

"I think that request deserves an explanation, Don," Simonsen said. "After the Stuxnet incident, that's going to be a hard sell."

The Israelis and the Americans had worked together on a years-long, staged computer virus attack to stop the Iranian uranium enrichment project. While the project itself was successful overall, the Israelis got impatient. Without consulting the Americans, they released a modified Stuxnet virus, allowing the covert attack to be exposed in the media. Even after more than a decade, there were still people in the CIA who held a grudge.

"The cryptography used on the Mahdi website came from Israel," Don said. "Mossad is unable to find their mole. I suggest a new plan: Instead of trying to find the mole, why not use him?"

"A sting operation, that's what you're suggesting?" Simonsen said.

"Exactly, ma'am."

"What's the price of admission?" Mattias said.

"We tell the Israelis everything we know," Don said. "Hold nothing back. We make the Mahdi think we're about to come through his front door. Then we see if he blinks."

CHAPTER 38

Mossad headquarters, Tel Aviv, Israel

Dre and the rest of the ET crew followed Shira down the narrow concrete hallway underneath Mossad headquarters. There would be no tea and sandwiches for this meeting with Binya Albedano.

The Mossad director of ops was waiting in the "bubble," along with another man, who did not introduce himself.

Dre shivered. It was more than just the damp chill of the rough concrete walls. The harsh fluorescent lighting, the cheap table around which they gathered on mismatched folding chairs, the whole aura of the place gave her the creeps.

Shira locked the doors of the "bubble" and engaged the knife switch on the circuit box next to the door. The light above the door shifted from red to green.

Binya forced a smile. "Welcome back. I see you returned Shira in good working order." It seemed to Dre that the worry lines at the corners of his mouth had deepened since she'd last seen the man.

Don got right to the point. "I've been authorized to brief you on everything we have on the Mahdi and the attacks."

Dre studied the mysterious meeting participant. He was a heavyset man with thinning gray hair in a ragged crew cut. He had a way of hunching his shoulders forward and sinking his heavy face into the jowls of his neck that left the impression he was half asleep. But when she looked closer, she could see his eyes darting back and forth, hidden by his half-closed eyelids, like a frog waiting to catch a fly. The man locked eyes with her and she immediately looked away.

"Please continue, Don," Binya said. He shot a nervous side glance at the silent stranger. Clearly, the stranger was an influential man.

Don quickly laid out the theory that the Mahdi attacks were being used to cover up for bioweapons tests, first in Yemen and now in South Sudan. When he reached the end of the briefing, he placed his folded hands on the table. In the ensuing silence, Dre imagined she could hear the hum of the jamming equipment protecting the room from electronic eavesdroppers.

The big man at the end of the table stirred. "You were the one who passed on the lead about the Saudi financial transaction," he said to Don.

Don tilted his head toward Dre and her colleagues. "This is the team that hatched the idea and found the connection. It was a lot of work." He threw a look at Michael. "I had my doubts at first."

When the big man nodded, his whole body moved back and forth. "That was good work."

Seconds passed until finally he said, "Because of your information, I was able to place an asset close to Jean-Pierre Manzul."

"The CEO of Recodna Genetics?" Janet blurted out. "What did you find out?"

To Dre's surprise, the big man smiled at Janet. "My name is Noam," he said. "Do you know the term '*kidon*'?"

"No, sir."

"'*Kidon*' is Hebrew for 'tip of the spear.' On paper, we don't exist. We do all the jobs no one else wants to do." Dre caught Janet's eye. Her look confirmed what Dre was thinking: This guy was talking about assassinations.

"My asset," Noam continued. "She is one of the best. She has managed to clone Manzul's phone."

"She cloned his phone?" Dre gasped. "Then we have him, right?"

Noam shook his head. "Not exactly. Manzul is a professional. He uses face-to-face meetings, cutouts, burner phones, encrypted communications. The dump from the phone is not conclusive for anything we have discussed. However"—he raised his eyebrows, which was the biggest show of emotion he had made so far in the meeting—"we can track his phone now. On or off, doesn't matter. If we can get him to return to the research lab, we have the location."

"I think I have a way," Don said. "We use your mole."

Binya sagged in his chair. "We don't know who it is yet, Don. Finding him—or her—will take more time."

"For what I have in mind, we can do it right now," Don said. "Today."

"I'm listening," Noam rumbled from the end of the table.

"I want you to tell everyone the Americans cracked your software," Don said. "You're scrapping Cerberus because it's not secure. The Americans can hack right through it."

Binya's brows crunched together in a frown. "I don't understand. How does that help us find the mole?"

"It doesn't," Noam said. "But your mole is sure to report it and that will force Manzul's hand. He will default to face-to-face meetings as the most secure method of communication. We can track him now. It's a good plan, Don."

"The existence of Cerberus is highly classified, even inside our own government," Binya said. "How do we destroy a program that doesn't officially exist?"

"Gossip is the most powerful weapon in the world," Noam said. "This afternoon, you announce your resignation, no reason given. Shira drops a word here and there about a failed top-secret program."

He pointed a stubby finger at Dre and her colleagues. "You parade these three around the cafeteria, strutting like a bunch of peacocks at how their superior American technology bested the Israelis once again." He laced his fingers over his belly and leaned back in his chair. "Then we let nature take its course."

Binya's face had gone ashen. "But . . . what about—"

"Binya, we're dealing with bioweapons here," Don

said. "We can't stop the Mahdi if we can't find him. Using the mole is our best option."

Dre watched the emotions play out across Binya's face. If he resigned, he would never get his job back—or any other job in Mossad. No matter the outcome, there would never be a way to clear his name.

"You will do it, Binya," Noam said. "For the good of Israel. You will be taken care of, my friend. You have my word."

"Where will you be, Don?" Binya asked.

"After they finish a victory lap around Mossad, Mr. Riley and his team will be back in Camp Lemonnier—with me," Noam said. "When we find the Mahdi, we will need to move quickly."

CHAPTER 39

Khartoum, Sudan

In her dream, Rachel heard a phone ring. Her mobile. She recognized the ringtone. It was the one she used for Levi.

The café around her was packed with tourists. Across the street, St. Peter's Square thronged with bodies under the blazing Roman sun.

She knew this place. This was where he—

Her phone rang again and she snatched it up and cupped her hand over the mouthpiece.

"Hello?" Her voice sounded breathy, scared.

"Rachel, why are you there?" His voice.

This is a dream.

But the scene was so real. She remembered the lady in a bright red floppy hat walking by like it was yesterday. But her name wasn't Rachel on the op, and Levi was supposed to be with her, not calling her on the phone.

"Where are you?" she whispered into the phone.

He hung up.

"Wait."

But he was gone.

The dead phone felt heavy in her hand. Outside the open window, the tourists laughed, holding hands, calling to children.

It was the height of summer, she remembered, a hot summer. The smell of hot pavement and melted ice cream, the wail of a child, the lady in the red hat—

The phone rang again. She stabbed at the screen to silence it.

Rachel startled awake in a dark room, heart racing, throat dry, chest heaving.

Was she really awake now? She pinched the tender skin on the inside of her arm.

The other side of the bed shifted with the weight of a body, and she remembered where she was.

JP's bed, for the third night in a row.

A wave of conflicting emotions washed over her. The deep ache of muscles unused to lovemaking, the guilt surfacing in her brain, the survival instinct of being deep undercover where forgetting who you were for even a second might be the difference between living and dying.

But JP didn't seem to notice her outburst. It was his phone she'd heard. He was sitting on the edge of the bed, his head in his hands, a mobile phone pressed to his ear.

"Now?" he said, his voice still groggy. "We just met a few days ago. What's happened?"

There was a long pause as he listened. Rachel closed

her eyes and strained her hearing, but all she could make out was the sound of a man's voice on the other end. Rough, agitated, throaty.

"Where?" A pause. "I'll be there in the morning."

He ended the call and threw the phone across the room. He leaped out of bed and paced in the darkness, cursing to himself in one long continuous stream.

"Is everything okay?" Rachel asked.

JP stopped suddenly, as if he had forgotten she was there. He came back to bed and sat close to her.

"It's okay. Just a setback, nothing more."

He grazed his fingers over her naked breast, and she felt her skin prickle with anticipation. She hated herself and reveled in the feeling, like wanting to giggle and weep at the same time. He nuzzled her neck, licking the spot behind her ear. Rachel let out a little sigh.

JP pulled back. "We need to go. Right now. Get the car and call the pilot. Tell him I want to be wheels up as soon as we can get there."

"Where are we going?"

JP switched on the bathroom light; his form was silhouetted in the brightness, forcing Rachel to squint her eyes.

"Alexandria first, then . . . I'm not sure yet."

He started to shut the bathroom door, then turned back. "You called out in your sleep. A man's name, I think."

Rachel used the bright light to squint her eyes closed, covering the shock she felt. JP walked back to the bed. Rachel forced herself to appear calm while at the same time scanning the room for potential weapons.

At the edge of the bed, he reached for her. She did not flinch. He cupped her cheek with his hand. "A lover?"

Rachel lowered her gaze. The lamp on the nightstand had a sturdy cast-iron base, a good weapon. "A real lady doesn't talk about her past."

"Is it over?"

"A long time ago. For good."

JP turned back to the light. "I'm glad to hear it."

CHAPTER 40

Camp Lemonnier, Djibouti, Africa

They were back to waiting.

Dre huddled deeper into the extra-large sweater she had purchased at the PX and wished they sold earmuffs to guard against the bone-chilling blast of the air-conditioning in the tactical ops center. The muted TV monitor was tuned to Al Jazeera, where the nonstop coverage alternated between Egyptian army units gathering on the border with Sudan and Sudanese forces mobilizing north of Khartoum. There were reports of Egyptian commandos spotted near the Ethiopian border as well. Every hour or so, they switched to an update on the increasingly frantic negotiations in Geneva as the UN tried to head off a ground war.

She yawned, her jaw cracking as her mouth stretched open. She'd been woken up at 4:00 A.M. Sheba was on the move.

The only thing they knew about the Israeli asset

traveling with Jean-Pierre Manzul was that she was a woman and her code name was Sheba.

To Dre's imagination, the name sounded dark and mysterious, but she guessed reality was a lot different. Being an undercover operative was probably a lot like being a coder. It sounded sexy, but the day-to-day was just hard work, sometimes exciting, mostly mundane.

She rubbed at her eyes and stared at the wall screen along with everyone else. The door to the secure room constantly opened and closed, the magnetic lock clacking as someone came in to give Don an update or he left to call Washington. In addition to Shira, their number now included Noam, who sat on a chair at the back of the room, staring at a spot on the floor. They were all waiting with bated breath for something—anything— to happen. The dot circled the Alexandria airport, lining up for a landing.

"Definitely Alexandria," Janet said. She was seated at the next workstation and looked as tired as Dre felt.

Tension went out of the room like a deflated balloon. Their tiny SCIF enclosure smelled like coffee breath and sweat—and now disappointment. Someone bumped the back of her chair and Dre resisted the urge to snap at them. She hiked the loose material of her sweater up to her ears.

"Probably just a business meeting," Shira muttered. "False alarm."

"All right, people, we're going to stand down until we see new movement," Don said. "Dre and Janet, you can go off shift. Get some sleep, something to eat, and come back in four hours."

The humid heat of the morning sun was a welcome relief to Dre. She uncrossed her arms and turned her face to the sky.

"It's so bright," Janet said with a grin. "But not for long. I'm hitting the rack."

Dre followed her friend back to the shipping-container bedroom they shared. The housing at Camp Lemonnier reminded her of a giant LEGO set. Three rows of two dozen shipping containers each had been stacked on top of each other to form an apartment building. At one end of each room a door opened onto a walkway that stretched the length of the structure. They climbed the steps together, their boots ringing on the metal tread.

The single door to their shared housing unit had a two-foot-square pane of glass, but like most occupants, they'd taped a piece of cardboard over it to block out the blazing African sun. Once the door shut behind them their room was like a cave, the only illumination coming from a few light leaks around the cardboard.

Dre stripped off her clothes and slipped under the covers, but sleep eluded her. Almost immediately, Janet's breathing evened out into a long, slow rhythm.

After two hours of sleeplessness, Dre slipped out of bed, gathered fresh clothes, and went back to work.

Michael was alone in the TOC, his face gray with exhaustion, head bowed over his workstation.

"What are you doing here?" he asked.

"Couldn't sleep." She forced a smile and set her coffee down next to her workstation. "Thought I'd give my little brother a break."

Michael hugged her. The simple act of gentleness sparked tears for Dre. Yet another sign that she was walking near an emotional edge.

"You okay?" Michael said.

Dre rolled her eyes and punched him on the shoulder. "Dude, I'm here two hours early. Don't look a gift horse in the mouth."

He grinned at her. "Don said to text him if the target moves, but don't call the whole team unless they stop at a new location."

"Got it," Dre replied. "Go get some sleep. And 'Shira' is not the Hebrew word for sleep. Preserve your strength, cowboy."

"The Hebrew word for sleep is '*yashan*,'" Michael said. The door closed before she could think of a snappy retort.

Dre pulled the cuffs of her sweater over her fingers and tucked her hands under her arms. She paced the room. There was literally nothing for her to do except watch a dot on the wall screen.

Noam from Mossad had given them the identifying information for Manzul's mobile phone. Don's request to the NSA on the target's phone yielded nothing useful. His communications—apart from a few calls to burner phones—were typical for his business, and he kept the GPS function on his phone turned off.

But the cloning process from the Israeli asset had overridden the GPS switch. They could track him even if the phone was switched off. Now all they had to do was hope Manzul led them to his secret bioweapons lab. . . . Correction, she reminded herself. The secret bioweapons lab they suspected he had built. The evidence certainly pointed toward Manzul.

Dre wondered about Sheba. What did she look like? How did she become a spy?

An alert interrupted Dre's thoughts. Manzul was on the move again, back to the Alexandria airport. She texted an update to Don and got an immediate acknowledgment.

It took the better part of an hour before Manzul's jet took off and began to head west.

The aircraft crossed into Libyan airspace. Another meeting?

Manzul's jet took a new heading, southeast. Another hour slipped by and Janet joined her, but still Dre stayed. The infinitesimal progress of the dot on the large-scale map was hypnotic.

The plane headed due east.

"Back to Khartoum?" Janet said.

"Seems like the long way home," Dre replied. Forty-five minutes later the plane passed south of Khartoum and made a sudden tight turn north. Dre and Janet automatically checked the map. Open desert. The aircraft was still fifty miles from Khartoum.

"I'll let Don know," Janet said.

The plane made a series of turns that brought it closer to Khartoum, but still well into the desert. Finally, the aircraft stopped moving at a spot twelve miles south of the nearest small town.

"This has to be it," Janet said, excitement evident in her tone. She threw an unclassified Google Earth image onto the wall screen. "Let's see what's there."

The overlaid images were poor quality, representing years of compiled unclassified data. She used a laser pointer to highlight a strip of lighter-colored earth on the image. "That could be a landing strip," she said. She moved the image to show a dark block on the map about a half mile away. "Maybe a warehouse?" She zoomed out. On some of the images, she could see cultivated land, on others just brown desert about five miles west of the warehouse.

"Let's get to work," Janet said. She pulled her chair close to her workstation. "I'll focus in on NGA's higher-resolution images, see what we can find. You see if you can figure out who owns that land."

Dre felt the lack of sleep wash away as she accessed property records in Sudan. She called up the in-house translator function on her workstation and prepared for the worst. To her surprise, she was able to enter in a latitude and longitude and gain access to a land title within minutes.

The magnetic lock on the door clacked and Don entered, followed by Michael, Shira, and Noam.

"What have we got, Janet?" Don said.

Janet threw an NGA map onto the wall screen. The National Geospatial-Intelligence Agency map was much more detailed than Google Earth, showing the airfield and accompanying hangar in crisp relief and the warehouse nearby. While the warehouse and airfield were clearly surrounded by desert, less than five miles away the dark green of irrigated land began. Khartoum was less than fifty miles away by car.

"The aircraft stopped at this small airfield. The

presumed destination is this building here." She used her laser pointer to highlight the detail on the image. "It appears to be a warehouse. Dre is looking up property records now."

The attention in the room turned to Dre. She passed the just-discovered land deed to the wall screen. "The property was gifted to a Saudi national over ten years ago. Total land grant was just over half a million hectares along with water rights for cultivation. This structure is on the eastern edge of the property. Maybe the start of a business park?"

She turned in her chair to find Don, Shira, and Noam staring at the wall screen.

"What?" Dre said.

"The name," Don said. "The name on the deed is Saleh bin Ghannam. He was the head of Saudi intelligence for almost a decade. Retired about ten years ago." He looked at Noam. "I think we found it."

"Shira?" Noam said.

"Yes, sir."

"This matches with what Sheba told me. Find out everything you can about that building."

An hour later, the mystery deepened.

"The warehouse and the private airfield sit on a piece of land which was leased to a different company," Shira said. "Long-term lease to a shell company called ZH Agriculture. Headquartered in Panama."

Dre clocked a glance at Janet, who shrugged back. "Give it a shot," she whispered.

Using her secure JWICS connection, Dre logged into

the CIA database and searched for "Panama Papers." A few years ago, a trove of thousands of shell companies set up by a law firm in Panama had been released to the public. A few shell companies related to international political figures made sensational headlines, but there were thousands more that remained shrouded in anonymity.

"I've got it," Dre said. "ZH Agriculture is a shell company with two properties. One in Sudan and one in Switzerland. Business purpose is listed as agricultural research. One shareholder, named Haim Zarecki."

She heard Noam make a choking sound, and then the big man was hunched over her shoulder, staring at the screen. He reeked of cigarettes and breathed in her ear like a bull. His eyes were wide. "I don't believe it."

"Who is Haim Zarecki?" Don asked.

"Ultraright Israeli nationalist," Shira said. "Owns a shipping line, but his real money came as an arms dealer."

"So, a hard-right Israeli nationalist is leasing land from the former head of Saudi intelligence?" Janet said. "What am I missing?"

Noam pointed his thick finger at Dre's screen. "Find out everything you can about this company."

"Let's give these four time to work," Don said with a meaningful look at Noam. "I think we should talk outside."

With input from Shira, Dre, Janet, and Michael worked as a team, accessing databases at CIA and Treasury to piece together a picture of ZH Agriculture.

When Don and Noam returned an hour later, Michael delivered the brief.

"ZH Agriculture has—or more accurately, had—two sites, one in Switzerland, one in Sudan." He flashed a newspaper article on the screen with a picture of a smoking warehouse. "Three years ago, the site in Switzerland burned to the ground. The site was declared a total loss and a hundred-and-forty-seven-million-dollar insurance payout went to ZH Agriculture. The policy was with a company called SAICO."

"Acronym for Saudi Arabian Insurance Company," Janet added.

Noam grunted. "The Swiss site. What did they do there?"

"According to Swiss interviews in local newspapers, the site was a state-of-the-art bioresearch facility, the best in Europe at the time. There's a whole article about how it was built in modules and trucked in to be assembled like an erector set. We've got a complete list of the modules purchased from the original contractor."

"Good work," Noam said. "What was the highest level of biocontainment the facility was able to handle?"

"According to the records, the building was capable of being upgraded to biosafety level four," Michael said, "but that's not the most interesting thing we found."

Michael threw a purchase order up on the wall screen. "Ignore the fact that it's in German. Look at the quantity."

"They bought two of everything," Don said.

"Exactly. From their website, the Swiss site was only large enough to accommodate one facility."

"So, this one was a replacement after the fire?" Don asked.

"No," Noam said. "The second set of modules went to Khartoum."

CHAPTER 41

Project Deliverance, undisclosed location in Sudan

"We'll be landing in ten minutes, Mr. Manzul." The pilot's voice was crisp and professional over the loud-speaker.

The plane began a slow turn. JP touched the control console and undimmed the windows. In the light of the setting sun, Rachel saw open desert reaching to the horizon.

"So, you trust me now?" she said. Rachel made her tone playful.

JP was seated in a leather captain's chair directly across from her. Their knees almost touched underneath the fold-down wooden table between them.

"Can I trust you, Zula?" JP said. He followed her gaze out the window toward the reddened landscape. "I think I'm going to need your help."

Rachel covered his hand with her own. "It's the woman, isn't it?"

For a long time, JP just stared out the window. When he finally met her gaze, his eyes had a haunted look.

"She—we—had a plan," he said. "A vision for a new world. I'm not sure how she will react when I tell her we're not going to get there."

"What's going on in that lab, JP?"

"It's best if you don't know." The plane started to descend. In the last light of the day, Rachel could make out the outline of the airstrip in the desert.

"What you need me to do?"

JP's lips bent at the corners. "Just be ready. For anything."

The jet touched down softly, reversed engines, and drew to a halt. When Rachel got up to lower the steps, she saw Kasim through the window, leaning against a black SUV.

As she came down the steps, the big black man grinned widely, as if he was glad to see her. "Zula is back!" He clapped his hands together. "I can't wait to tell Rocky that he has to give up his room again."

JP appeared in the doorway. "Enough, Kasim," he snapped. "Just drive."

It was full dark by the time they pulled up to the underground garage and the door rattled open. Kasim drove in and shut off the engine. The dome light came on as he opened the driver's-side door.

"Zula will be joining us downstairs, Kasim."

Kasim shrugged. "Whatever you say, boss."

"We're not staying long, Kasim. I'll need you to be ready to travel with two men you can trust."

As she followed JP into the elevator, Rachel hoped

to hell that Noam had this location by now and had a team on the way.

When the elevator door opened again, Rachel stepped into a room that looked like a common room at a college dormitory. Comfortable chairs and sofas, a big-screen TV with a stack of DVDs and a few video-game controllers piled to one side.

On the far side of the room was a kitchen area with five people seated around a dining table. Rachel scanned the faces. Two men, three women. One of the men was Chinese and older, the other a younger, bearded Arab. Two of the women were white and the third was a pretty Indian woman with long dark hair.

The conversation around the table ceased abruptly. The diners all stared at the visitors with intense curiosity. JP led the way and Kasim hustled Rachel past the table in a way that made it clear she was not to interact with the staff.

At the end of a long hallway, JP knocked on a closed door.

The door was opened by the woman Rachel had seen in the garage on her last visit. She remembered the woman's bright blue eyes, but the head scarf had hidden the rest of her features. Long auburn hair framed the delicate lines of her face. Her skin was a warm, creamy brown made even more exotic by her arresting eyes.

She threw herself into JP's arms. "It worked! Pandora worked!" She kissed him with a frantic passion that caused a little surge of jealousy to bloom in Rachel's gut.

JP broke the embrace and turned to Rachel. "Zula, this is Dr. Talia Tahir."

His face was completely open, trusting. If she hadn't been in bed with him twelve hours earlier she would never have suspected anything.

Talia held out her hand. "I'm glad JP has you to rely on for his safety." Her voice was low and husky, matching the sexual aura that she exuded.

She took JP's arm. "Now, perhaps you can fill me in on what is so urgent."

JP ushered everyone into the bedroom and closed the door. "We need to shut it down, Talia."

"Shut what down?"

"Everything," JP said. "All of this. I met with Saleh and Zarecki in Alexandria this morning. The Americans know about us. We've been compromised."

Talia's face hardened. "Compromised? How?" She turned on Zula with a force that made Rachel take an involuntary step back. "By her?"

JP inserted himself between the two women. "No, the website. They broke the code. They can track us here."

Talia paced the room. "That's impossible. Zarecki said the code was unbreakable."

JP moved to intercept her. "I'm sorry, my love, but we don't have much time. We need to leave tonight."

"What about them?" Talia wriggled out of his arms, gestured toward the kitchen.

"We let them go. They don't know anything. They can't hurt us—"

"But Pandora! It works, it works so well, just like we planned it. It was beautiful." Talia bit her lip.

JP captured her hands. She tried to pull away but he held her fast. "The genetic component doesn't work yet. It's not ready, Talia. We need to get you away from here."

"You promised me, JP." Talia wrested her hands free and backed away. She hugged herself. "You promised me."

"We have to go," he said softly. "Now."

Talia took a shaky breath. "If that's what you think is best, dear." She went to the door and called into the hall. "Lakshmi, can you come here, please?"

Rachel used Talia's movement to sneak a look at Kasim. The security guard leaned against the wall, arms folded. He smiled at Rachel when he caught her looking, and she felt a shiver race up her spine.

The Indian woman showed up at the door. Talia placed her hand on the woman's arm. "Can you finish entering the data set from today's research? I need to go over it with JP later."

Lakshmi seemed surprised by the request. Her bright smile dimmed, but she nodded. "Yes, of course. I'll do it right away."

Talia turned to Kasim. "We'll deal with her later. Get everyone downstairs to Lab One, please, Kasim."

The security man marched into the common room where the scientists were finishing dinner. "We're having a security drill. I need everyone downstairs immediately." He clapped his huge hands together. "Now!"

The people in the room sighed as if they were used

to this sort of thing. They trooped to the far side of the room and down a stairwell. Kasim looked at Rachel. "You, too."

Rachel shot a look at JP, who nodded. He had his arm around Talia as he guided her to the stairs.

The stairwell connecting the upper living quarters to the lower labs showed markings that indicated the building had been prefabricated as modules. The name of a European construction company was stenciled on the wall.

At the bottom of the steps, a heavy steel door stood open. Inside was an open foyer area and a thick glass wall labeled LAB ONE in block letters. Through the glass Rachel could see an impressive open lab space, with workstations and microscopes surrounding the perimeter. The scientists were all inside except for the Chinese man, who waited by the door. His arms were folded, his jaw thrust out.

"Inside, Xianshan," Talia said. "You know the drill."

"Are you coming in, too?"

Talia's smile was brittle. "It's not that kind of drill."

"What is going on?" the Chinese man demanded. "There's something going on."

JP stepped forward. "Get inside, Xianshan. Please."

The man relented. JP shut the door and locked it. The readout next to the door glowed green with the message: POSITIVE SEAL.

The Chinese man pushed a button on the wall. "What is going on, JP?" he said through the intercom.

"Unfortunately, we have to terminate Project Deliverance early. Your services are no longer required." The faces of the people on the other side of the glass went slack with shock. "This is only a temporary inconvenience. Kasim will let you out in the morning."

At the back of the lab, Rachel saw a thin line of what looked like steam rising toward the ceiling. She touched JP's arm and pointed to it. He stopped speaking and turned toward Talia.

"What have you done?" His voice was hoarse.

Talia did not flinch. Her tone was light, businesslike. "I'm doing what needs to be done, dear. Did you think I didn't see this coming? We cannot afford to have witnesses."

The implications of Talia's words hit Rachel just before Kasim's fist did. Her reflexes saved her. She ducked her head just enough for the punch to be a glancing blow, but even that was enough for her to see stars.

She dropped her body to the floor, kicking out as she fell. Her toe connected with Kasim's kneecap and she felt a satisfying pop. The big man let out a suppressed scream, but the injury did not stop him from drawing his weapon.

The muzzle of his Beretta looked huge as it swung toward her head. Rachel twisted and kicked at the gun, knocking off his aim. The muzzle flash blinded her, the floor next to her cheek shattered under the impact of the bullet, and the room went silent in her deadened hearing.

She lashed out again with her foot, sweeping his feet out from under him. Kasim went down with a feral howl.

The gun spun away. No matter. He was going to kill Rachel with his bare hands.

Rachel scrambled to her feet. She reached behind her back for the thin blade she had hidden in her belt. It flashed silver in the fluorescent lights.

Kasim got to his feet favoring his right leg, his face flushed with fury.

Rachel attacked. Kasim was a huge man with a long reach. She needed to get close and make the blade count. She feinted right, then drove in from the left, forcing him to put weight on his injured knee. She drove the blade up, toward his midsection. He blocked it with his forearm, the razor-sharp blade leaving a huge gash from his wrist to his elbow.

His fist came from the right, connecting with the side of her head. The force of the blow drove her back into the wall, delivering a second wave of pain. She lashed out with the knife, but it was too late. One of Kasim's meaty paws wrapped around her wrist. Two blows against the wall and the blade fell from her numb fingers.

He gripped the front of her blouse and slammed her body into the wall. Breath left her lungs in a rush. She scratched at his eyes with her free hand and he roared back like a wild animal, but he did not let go.

She drove her knee into his crotch, felt the connection with soft flesh, and saw a fresh wave of pain cross Kasim's face.

But his hands were on her neck now, crushing her airway. Her vision tunneled. Strength fled her limbs.

It was over.

In her dimming vision, light flashed over Kasim's shoulder and a knife appeared in his neck. Her knife. Blood fountained out of the wound.

She stared at it. Had she done that?

Kasim's fingers loosened. Air flowed into her lungs again and Kasim collapsed. Only the cold slick metal of the wall kept Rachel upright.

JP stood in front of her, blood on his hand where he had plunged her knife into Kasim's neck. He caught her when she started to fall forward.

A banging sound made Rachel look up. The scientists were using a stool to try to break through the thick glass.

"Fools." Talia stood with her arms folded, watching the scene. "That's one-inch Plexiglas. They're wasting their time—and they don't have much of it."

As she laughed at her own joke, Talia turned. Her brilliant blue eyes blazed like glass, and her face might have been cut from stone.

"No more waiting, JP. This is our moment. Pandora is ready. I need you with me."

"It's not ready," JP pleaded. "We need the genetic component in place. If you release it, we won't be able to stop it. We could kill millions of people."

"I need you with me, JP. Kill the woman and we leave together. Right now."

JP put himself between Rachel and Talia. "Don't do this, Talia."

A gun appeared in Talia's hand. Kasim's gun.

"We had a plan," JP said.

The weapon was steady, her voice dead calm. "I will not be stopped."

Part of JP's skull disappeared in a bloody spray.

Rachel reacted. As JP's body fell back toward her, she gripped his jacket and drove him forward using the man's flesh like a shield, slamming Talia back into the Plexiglas wall. On the other side of the glass, the Chinese man yelled at her soundlessly.

The gun went off again. A lance of burning pain stabbed her in the side. Rachel seized Talia's gun hand and sank her teeth into her wrist.

Blood rushed into her mouth, the gun went off again, but Talia released the weapon.

Rachel got her finger around the trigger and rolled over. The heavy steel door clanged shut.

She was alone.

Minutes passed. Rachel got to her hands and knees.

"Are you okay?" The voice was coming from the intercom.

Her hand left a bloody print on the Plexiglas wall as she got to her feet. She stabbed at the intercom button.

"I'll live, I think." She attempted a smile and failed. "How do I open this door?" She tapped the muzzle of the handgun on the airtight door of Lab One.

"Don't," said the blond woman on the other side of the glass. "We don't know what's in here. If you open that door the whole facility could be contaminated."

Rachel winced, pressing her hand against her side. "How about a first-aid kit?"

The woman pointed to a wall cabinet on the other

side of the room. Inside Rachel found a well-stocked kit. She put wads of gauze on the entry and exit wounds and wrapped another roll of gauze around her waist to hold them in place. She felt herself swaying. She took two bottles of water and went back to the intercom.

"Help is on the way," she said to the blond woman. "Someone will be here by morning."

"You need to tell them to contact the Blue Team," the woman replied.

"Blue Team?"

"It's the other half of the project. We're the Red Team, we make the viruses. The Blue Team makes vaccines." Behind her the Chinese man began to cough.

Rachel nodded. "Blue Team. I'll tell them. I need to sit down now."

"I'm Greta," the woman said. "What's your name?"

"Rachel." It was an effort to move her mouth, and her speech sounded slurred. "My name is Rachel."

She sank to the floor. JP's body lay next to her, half his face missing, blood and brain matter pooled next to the open wound. She set the gun on the ground.

Her eyelids drooped. She'd lost a lot of blood. She hoped Noam would hurry.

Levi's face swam in her vision. For the first time in a long time, she felt very close to her dead husband.

CHAPTER 42

Red Sea, twelve miles off the coast of Sudan

Lieutenant Colonel Bill West stormed out of the back of the MV-22B Osprey and paced the deserted flight deck of the USS *Makin Island*. He held a satellite phone tightly, as if the strength of his grip would force the phone to ring.

Two hours ago, when he had been given the order to load his raid force onto the ten Ospreys and four CH-53E Super Stallion helicopters, the flight deck had been alive with feverish activity.

The Ospreys, their spinning tilt rotors in the vertical position, had been ready to rise into the humid night sky over the Red Sea. The F-35 fighter escort was already airborne, circling the massive Wasp-class amphibious assault ship, accompanied by a pair of KC-130J refueling tankers launched out of Lemonnier to support the raid.

The moonless night was perfect for an assault. It was all going so well.

But that was two hours ago, before word came down from Colonel O'Malley of the hold.

Now, all around him was silent.

West dialed the phone and pressed it against his ear. It was answered on the second ring.

"Colonel, what's the holdup, sir?" West said. "I've got a hundred fifty Marines sitting on their thumbs. If we delay much longer, we might as well start serving breakfast."

"Keep your pants on, Bill," O'Malley's measured voice boomed in West's ear. "The whole damn Egyptian army is crossing the border into Sudan. As you might imagine, that complicates the picture. If we launch a raid force, someone's liable to get the wrong idea and start shooting at you. The State Department is on it, they just need a few more minutes."

West tried to picture in his mind exactly how a diplomat explained to a foreign government that the United States had determined that a site manufacturing weapons of mass destruction existed on their sovereign soil and the US military was about to launch a full-scale assault on the facility to address that deficiency. Stay clear or suffer the consequences.

"I understand, sir," West said. "But the longer we delay, the harder it will be to contain the site."

West had been briefed on the HUMINT source, a Mossad agent, who had managed to send the site location through undisclosed means. But the agent had gone silent, a possible sign the raid had been compromised.

Their intel on the site was skimpy as well. A warehouse in the middle of the desert east of Khartoum, Sudan, heavily defended by up to three dozen armed soldiers guarding an underground research lab, possibly manufacturing biological weapons.

Bioweapons. The thought made his stomach queasy. Of all the possible scenarios, that was the one that worried him the most. With nukes, if shit went sideways, it would be over so fast you'd never even know it happened. Chemical weapons were bad, but his men carried chem suits to deal with that threat.

But bio, that was something else entirely. If just one man got infected . . .

Thankfully, someone in his chain of command had the good sense to split the mission: His Marines would secure the topside area. There was a team of specially trained spec ops SEALs to penetrate the research lab.

"I hear you, Bill," O'Malley was saying. "AFRICOM is on the phone with Washington right now. As soon as I know, you'll know."

"Aye, sir." West hung up and stalked back to the open ramp of the idle Osprey. The gentle hum of conversation among the Marines facing each other in jump seats ceased.

"As you were," West said, as he passed down the aisle between twenty-four combat-loaded men.

The waiting was not good for morale. Marines were a kinetic weapon—aim and fire. Whether it was one Marine or a whole battalion, they were not trained to reflect on their lot in life.

These were men trained to take action. Patience was not a virtue in their line of work.

Second Battalion, Fourth Marines—better known as the Magnificent Bastards—had a proud lineage that dated back to World War I. Tonight, Bill West planned to add another chapter to their storied history—and history was not written by sitting on your ass in an idle aircraft floating in the middle of the goddamn ocean on the deck of a navy amphibious assault ship.

"Sir," said his enlisted man handling comms for the command element. "It's Colonel O'Malley."

West took the handset. "Yes, sir?"

"Bill, the operation is a go. Release the Bastards."

It took just under half an hour to get their entire assault team airborne. Ten Ospreys and four Super Stallions loaded with twenty-four Marines each, six F-35s as fighter escort and ground assault, and two KC-130J tankers for in-flight refueling. There was also a squadron of Marine Corps F/A-18s out of Djibouti that would arrive as the raid force entered Sudanese airspace to fly high cover just in case Sudan or Egypt decided they wanted to intervene.

"Feet dry," the pilot reported as they entered Eritrean airspace.

West acknowledged the pilot and used the ruggedized tablet to call up the drone feed from the overwatch Reaper.

"Plane landed at sunset, sir." His S-2, a very young-looking captain in charge of his intel team, pointed at the airstrip on the tablet image. "Two pilots, still on board. Two people disembarked and drove to the warehouse. About an hour later, a single SUV with one occupant left the warehouse and drove south to the main highway. Vehicle is in Khartoum traffic now."

West cursed under his breath. They'd let one get away already. "Everyone else is still inside?"

"Yes, sir."

West settled back in his seat, glad for the dimness of the cargo hold for time to think. He was bringing a hundred fifty Marines to assault a terrorist base with a security force of three dozen, according to their best intel. Not a fair fight, and never intended to be one, but right now his biggest issue was time.

The Ospreys had twice the cruising speed and range of the Super Stallions. If he took eight Ospreys and went balls-out to the fight, he could get there twice as fast. The Stallions and remaining Ospreys would serve as reinforcements.

He signaled to his comms man. "Get me Homebase," he said into the mic.

A few seconds later, O'Malley's voice filled the headset. "This is Homebase actual."

"Sir, I recommend we go to plan Bravo. We've seen one vehicle depart the scene and I'd hate to lose any more fish out of the net."

Fifteen minutes later, the decision was made and the vanguard assault force was roaring over the deserts of Sudan. An all-hands call with his assault-team leaders passed on the new orders, which had been part of the initial briefing. Three Ospreys would land to the east and three to the south, forming an L-shaped envelope on the warehouse. The remaining two Ospreys would secure the landing strip. The F-35s would remain overhead for close air support as needed.

He could hear the disappointment in the voices of the team leaders aboard the Super Stallions who were assigned as reinforcements.

Just before 4:00 A.M. local, eight Ospreys flared to a stop in the sand three hundred meters from the warehouse. Marines poured down the back ramps, with four-man fire teams taking up preassigned locations along the front. Less than a minute later, the now-empty Ospreys took off again. Aircraft on the ground were targets. The MV-22Bs would stay on station, breaking off in pairs to refuel.

West hit the sand along with the rest of his men. His pulse hammered in his ears, the smell of disturbed dust heavy in the air. In the green of his night-vision goggles, the warehouse stood dark and silent.

West touched his throat mic. "All units, this is raid leader, advance."

All around him, men got to their feet and started a slow jog toward the building. He stole a glance at the overwatch display, seeing his men advancing along two fronts. Textbook perfect.

They covered a hundred meters, then two hundred, with no reaction from their target.

"Sir," his S-2 said over his headset, "overwatch shows movement on the southeast corner of the building."

As if on cue, a blaze of heavy-machine-gun tracer fire shot out of the second-story windows of the southeast corner of the warehouse. Seconds later, the northeast corner joined in.

The advance stopped as his men took cover and released a deafening volley of M27 IAR return fire. The tracer fire screamed over their heads, and the Marines' return fire sparked like a million fireflies in the night.

From his right, West heard one of the fire-team leaders calling for grenades. Seconds later, he heard the rapid *punk-punk* of an M32 launching grenades in quick succession. Explosions erupted on both corners of the building, and both machine-gun nests went silent.

"Sir, we have two vehicles exiting the garage on the opposite side of the building!" West snatched the tablet from the S-2's hands as he touched his throat mic. "Fighter escort, this is raid leader. We have two runners. You are weapons free to engage."

"Acknowledge weapons free on fleeing ground targets," said the voice of the lead F-35 pilot.

West heard the roar of the jet engines overhead and saw their fiery exhausts disappear over the top of the warehouse.

The first fire teams had reached the warehouse now and were breaching points of entry, streaming into the building. West stayed outside. His presence was no good in close quarters. Two explosions in quick succession told him the F-35s had made short work of their targets. He listened as the platoon leaders reported progress. In the background, he could hear doors being broken down and the occasional pop of small arms fire.

His intel officer provided a running progress report

of the assault team inside the warehouse. "First floor is cleared . . . second floor is cleared . . . six hostiles down in the machine-gun nests. They found a berthing area . . . six hostiles dead, ten surrenders. Looks like there were four hostiles in each vehicle, sir. All KIA." He paused. "Building is secure, sir. Captain Rodgers is in what looks like an underground garage area. He requests permission to breach the elevator."

"Tell him permission denied," West said. "Set up a command post in the garage and collect the dead hostiles in one location for biometrics."

"Aye, sir," the S-2 replied.

West checked his watch. It had been eleven minutes since the Ospreys touched down. He touched his throat mic. "Homebase, this is raid commander, target topside is secure."

CHAPTER 43

Sudanese airspace

Janet felt the nose of the C-130 tilt down and craned her neck to see out the window.

The horizon was a pale pink. Sunrise was coming, but it would still be dark when they landed.

Janet and Don were seated together in the very forward area of the packed cargo hold facing Dre, Michael, Shira, and Noam on the other side of the aircraft. The rest of the cargo area was a full platoon of Navy SEALs in jump seats lining the fuselage. A line of what looked to Janet like modified dune buggies occupied the center of the cargo hold. LT-ATVs, Michael had informed her when they boarded, lightweight tactical all-terrain vehicles. The ATVs were packed with bright yellow cases labeled BIOHAZARD SUITS.

The SEAL team officer-in-charge, Lieutenant Peter "Harmony" Harmon, was seated next to Don. He spoke into his headset to his men, then leaned across Don so Janet could hear him.

"When we get on the ground, I want you guys to stick with me. The Marines have the topside area cleared, but you never know. They left the underground stuff for us." He gave Janet a tight smile.

"We've been on a SEAL team raid before," Janet shouted back. "We won't cause you any trouble."

Harmony's eyebrows hitched up. He was cute, with shaggy red hair, freckles, and a ready smile. "That sounds like a great story. I'll buy you a beer when we get back."

Janet smiled sweetly. "You can buy me all the beer you want, but I'm not gonna tell you anything."

"I'll take that challenge." Harmony winked.

The aircraft crew chief stood and raised his hand in the air, fingers splayed. "Five minutes!" he shouted.

Harmony spoke into the open circuit. "Gentlemen"—he looked at Janet—"and ladies. That's our cue to saddle up."

He climbed aboard the nearest LT-ATV, as did the rest of the SEALs.

The operators were heavily armed. Each of them carried an FN SCAR combat assault rifle as well as a sidearm—most of them opted for the SIG Sauer P226 nine-millimeter—at least one wicked-looking blade, grenades of various types, and breaching charges to penetrate the underground facility.

Under Harmony's supervision, Janet and the rest of Don's team strapped into jump seats on the back of the ATVs.

The C-130 Hercules rumbled as it touched down

on the desert airstrip. Before the aircraft had even slowed, the crew chief removed tie-downs from the ATVs, and the rear ramp began to lower. As soon as it was near the ground, the first ATV driver gunned the engine and launched into the night. By the time the Hercules had come to a complete stop, the cargo hold was empty.

They blasted across the desert sand, whipping past a pair of MV-22B Ospreys, their tilt rotors in the upward, vertical-lift position.

The sun was just cresting the horizon when they arrived at the warehouse. Outside the open garage door, they passed a neat line of corpses and a pair of Marines adding another dead body to the queue. The dead men were all dressed identically, in paramilitary olive-green uniforms and black body armor. Janet guessed there were at least two dozen dead men. The ATV rolled belowground into a large, well-lit garage area.

A Marine lieutenant colonel in full battle gear strode up and shook hands with Harmony. "Bill West, raid force commander. Topside is secure. Twenty-two bad guys taken off the boards and a handful of prisoners." He pointed at a set of closed elevator doors. "I assume you guys are here for that part of the operation. I hear it's a biothreat?"

Harmony nodded. Around him, the rest of the SEAL team was pulling on biohazard suits and checking compressed-air tanks.

"Good luck. Let us know if you need anything. We'll set a perimeter and secure the airfield. The facility is yours."

Harmony called Janet and her colleagues together. He pointed at the elevator, where a pair of his men were erecting a clear plastic enclosure. "We'll set up a temporary airlock around the elevator. I'll lead an assault team in full bio gear to clear the lab. Then we'll let you in. Everyone goes in full bio gear until we're certain what we're dealing with." He slapped a lieutenant junior grade on the shoulder. "This is Dogbone. He'll be topside with you the whole time and you'll be able to see everything on our helmet cameras."

Within a few minutes, the containment area was set up around the elevator doors and ten armed SEALs dressed in full yellow bio suits were inside the clear plastic structure. Ten more SEALs kitted out in biohazard suits waited in reserve.

Everyone's eyes were locked on Harmony's visual feed showing on a small laptop screen. "Dogbone, this is Harmony, how do you read me?"

"Five by five."

"Copy that. Entering the facility."

One of the SEALs used a crowbar to force the elevator doors open. Two more already in rope harnesses stepped up and rappelled off the edge. The picture inside was a grainy infrared image.

"We're on top of the elevator car. Nobody inside, doors closed. We're proceeding."

"Acknowledged." Dogbone muted his microphone. "They're packing low-velocity rounds to minimize damage if there's any shooting. We don't want to break anything we don't have to in this kind of situation."

The interior of the well-lit elevator car looked like

it belonged in an office building. The car was packed with six SEALs, rifles at the ready.

"We're gonna crack this open and see what's inside. Stand by."

Harmony pushed the elevator open-doors button, and the doors parted. The picture rushed forward, and Janet heard cries of "Clear!" She caught glimpses of a table with the remnants of a meal still on it, a sitting area, then a hallway, and bedrooms.

"I've got one!"

The picture shifted to a woman with long dark hair lying on a bed. "Woman, midthirties, no visible wounds, strong vitals. Looks like she's asleep, maybe sedated. We've got a locked steel door in the last bedroom. We're going to breach it. Minimal charge."

Dogbone muted his microphone. "We don't like to use explosives inside a biofacility for obvious reasons."

A SEAL slapped a series of shaped charges on the door's edges and retreated.

"Breach, breach, breach!"

Boom!

The image passed through a smoking door-sized hole and onto the set of the Mahdi.

"We were right!" Don said, a flood of relief in his voice.

"Dogbone, upper level is cleared. Looks like a movie studio in here."

"Understood," Dogbone said. "Based on the reaction I'm getting up here, that's a good thing. Proceed to level two."

The image returned to the two SEALs who had been

left guarding the stairwell. The full team entered the empty stairwell and crept down two flights of steps to a heavy steel door. They crashed through the door in stacked formation.

"We've got bodies," Harmony said. The camera showed an open space hemmed in by a solid glass wall. "One very dead guy dressed like the terrorists upstairs, one guy with his head blown off—"

"That's Manzul," Don said.

"We've got a live one," Harmony continued, "but she's in bad shape."

The image swung to a dark-skinned woman dressed in a business suit. Her face was swollen and she had a wad of bloody gauze strapped to her belly. A handgun lay on the floor next to her.

"That's Rachel," Noam said.

"I'll send a corpsman down—"

"Dogbone!" Harmony interrupted. "We have positive evidence of a biothreat."

The picture shifted to the lab behind the Plexiglas. Janet counted five bodies on the floor. A blond woman was near the glass, her face swollen beyond recognition. Bloody mucus leaked from her nose. Janet couldn't tell if she was breathing.

"We're transporting the survivor upstairs," Harmony said. "Then we'll seal the stairwell."

═══════════

It was midafternoon before the area was deemed safe enough to allow Janet and the rest of the team inside. When Harmony came topside to brief them, his face was flushed and sweaty.

"The door seal on the lab where the bodies are located is intact," Harmony said, "but we sealed off the lower levels anyway. The CDC guys can handle that. We've done swabs all over the living quarters on the upper level. They all come back clean."

"What about Rachel?" Noam asked. "When can I see her?"

"Right away, but I warn you, she's in bad shape. The corpsman can't believe she's still alive after all the blood she lost."

"She's tough," Noam said, but the lines on his face deepened.

Harmony addressed Don. "I'm supposed to let you guys in to access the computer systems. Once you're done, we'll tear it all out and send it back to Lemonnier."

Janet sidled next to Harmony as they made their way to the elevator. "How bad was it?"

The young SEAL shook his head. "You can't unsee that shit. It was like their bodies were melting. What kind of sick mind would do that to another human being?"

The first level of the research compound resembled a cross between a war zone and a college dorm. Next to the pile of discarded bio suits, a dining room table had been turned into a makeshift hospital bed for the injured Mossad agent. She was still unconscious, and her dark skin had an ashen undertone.

"How is she?" Noam asked the SEAL platoon's corpsman.

"She is one tough lady," the corpsman replied. "If you'd asked me two hours ago, I'd have said it was touch and go, but I think she's gonna be okay."

"What about the other one?" Harmony asked.

"The Indian gal?" The corpsman shook his head. "Not good. She was sedated when we got here. Roofied, I'm guessing. When she woke up and saw what had happened, she lost it. I knocked her out again. There's a whole lot of therapy in that woman's future."

Don pointed to the computer workstation in the sitting area. "Dre and Michael, you guys work on that system. We're looking for what these guys were working on, names of the scientists, anything that will help us wrap this thing up."

Janet and Don continued with Harmony to the living quarters. They entered the last bedroom and passed through a breached door into the Mahdi studio.

Don gave a low whistle. "This guy was not fooling around."

Janet had looked at the Mahdi videos so many times that the scene felt familiar. She touched the tapestry hanging behind the couch, tested the plush of the carpet with her toe.

Janet sat behind a computer workstation and logged on to the computer. There was no password. "I guess only one person used this computer and he was pretty confident of the lock on the door."

"Let's see what he was up to," Don said.

Janet scanned the contents of the hard drive, clicking quickly through the folders. She found information for dam projects in Ethiopia, Sudan, and Egypt.

"This looks like our guy, Don."

"Check the search history."

Janet opened the browser. "Search history's been wiped. I'll recover it from the server." After a few moments of work, Janet found that that had been deleted as well.

"Seems like a lot of work for someone who doesn't bother to put a password on their computer."

Michael appeared in the doorway. "We got something."

Dre was working the computer when Janet and Don joined them.

"Using some old security footage and facial rec, we've identified the staff in this picture." She flashed up an image of five people sitting at the same dining room table where the injured Mossad agent now lay. They seemed to be enjoying each other's company.

"They're all top researchers in the fields of various biology specialties and gene-editing work. They are all on sabbatical from their current jobs. We're making educated guesses that these four and the sleeping woman are the ones in the picture. But notice there's a sixth place at dinner."

Dre flashed another still image showing an attractive woman with brown skin and blue eyes. "That's the WHO researcher who was killed in the plane crash," Don said.

"Correct, Dr. Talia Tahir, and very much alive. Yesterday evening, all the security cameras in the facility were shut off except for the one in the garage. This is the last bit of footage we have."

She showed a grainy image of the underground

garage above them. The elevator doors opened, and Dr. Tahir exited with a small bag slung over her shoulder. She got in a black SUV and drove off.

"Okay," Don said. "Tahir is in the wind, our Mossad agent is out of commission for now, and everyone else is dead except for the one woman. Who wants to wake Sleeping Beauty?"

"I'll do it," Dre said.

CHAPTER 44

Project Deliverance, 50 miles east of Khartoum, Sudan

Dre cracked open the door to the darkened bedroom. A small lamp on the bedside table was on, and a veil covered the light, which cast a reddish glow over the room.

"Can I come in?" Dre said in a soft voice.

"Okay."

The woman who answered sat at the head of the bed, her back against the wall, her knees drawn up to her chin and her arms wrapped tightly around her legs as if she was trying to make herself as small as possible. She had long dark hair plaited into a rough braid and wrapped around her neck like a comforter. Under other circumstances, Dre would have thought her very pretty.

But now, her large, dark eyes were red-rimmed and watery, and her round face was a blotchy mess.

Dre sat on the edge of the bed. "How are you feeling?"

The woman started to cry again. "I'm sorry," she said

between sobs. "I just can't stop. I can't believe they're all dead."

"It's okay. I'm Andrea Ramirez. My friends call me Dre."

"Lakshmi." She took a deep breath and held it, then dragged her forearm across her eyes. "I will stop crying now. I promise."

"If you're feeling up to it, maybe you could tell me what happened?"

Lakshmi nodded and swallowed hard. "Last night, Talia called me to her room. She said when JP got back he was going to be very angry and she wanted me to be safe. She was so scared. I've never seen her that scared."

She bit her lip. "I've known Talia for a long time—we were at undergrad together. She's had a lot of tragedy in her life. Her parents were killed when she was very young and she's always been a bit of a loner. We were really close, like sisters." Lakshmi scooted closer to Dre and sought out her hand.

"Everyone went downstairs and when Talia came back up, she was alone." Lakshmi let out a shaky breath. "When I asked her what was going on she got very upset. She asked me to make us both a cup of tea. The next thing I knew, I was waking up and there were men in bio suits with guns and—"

Lakshmi's voice broke. Dre squeezed her hand. "I think we were here for that part."

"I knew JP was a hard man," Lakshmi said, "but I never thought he would . . ."

"It's okay, Lakshmi. There was nothing you could do."

Lakshmi closed her eyes. "That's just it. I knew there was something wrong and I didn't do anything. I was too afraid. I let my friends down."

Dre felt the words like the ache of an old wound in her own chest. The feeling of helplessness. The feeling of knowing you should do something, wanting to take action with every muscle in your body—and still being frozen with fear.

"I know what you mean," Dre said. "I had . . . I had something happen to me. My friend was hurt and I didn't do anything to help her. I was too afraid." Dre felt her own tears starting to well up. "I still think about it. I'm still ashamed, but I honestly couldn't do anything. I don't know why . . . and I hate myself for it."

Lakshmi scooted across the bed and hugged Dre. "That's exactly how I feel," she said, her words muffled in Dre's shoulder. "I was afraid to say anything. Now all my friends are dead."

Dre wrapped her arms around the woman and let her weep. Her own pain felt sharp and raw, as if the scar tissue formed by time had been ripped away.

The racking sobs slowed, Lakshmi's breathing evened, and she pulled her face away from Dre's neck. The wet material on Dre's shoulder chilled in the air-conditioning.

Lakshmi used the edge of her shirt to dry her eyes. "Thank you," she said. "You made me feel a lot better. I want to do my part to help."

Dre smiled, feeling a little buzz of pride at being able to help her.

"What exactly was going on here?" Dre asked.

"Project Deliverance," Lakshmi said as if that explained everything. "Our mission is to rid the world of the worst possible bioweapons. We are—were—the Red Team."

"Red Team?"

"There are two parts to Project Deliverance. We make the viruses and the Blue Team creates vaccines for them. You know, like in a war game." Lakshmi's eyes were starting to clear, and her face had a look of bright innocence.

"I want to make sure I have this right," Dre said. "There are *two* parts to Project Deliverance? There's another site? Do you know where the other site is?"

Lakshmi shook her head. "That would defeat the purpose of the war game if we knew anything about the other site. JP was the only person who knew where the other site was. As soon as we developed a new virus, he would deliver a sample to the Blue Team. The first two were variations on the Ebola virus, and the third was Pandora."

"What is Pandora?"

Lakshmi brightened. "Pandora was the culmination of all the work we had done so far on Deliverance," she said. "It was a true chimera virus: an Ebola strain combined with a paleo-flu virus to make it airborne and far more survivable. It's magnificent."

"Paleovirus?"

"That's the best part," Lakshmi said. "A paleovirus is something that comes from an ancient sample, like a mummy, for instance. JP found a dig site near the Arctic Circle and got us samples. The benefits of using a paleo variant is that it's not in anyone's database yet, they have to start from square one. And, modern humans don't have immunity from such ancient pathogens."

Dre fought back a feeling of nausea at the way Lakshmi reeled off deadly viruses like she was trading baseball cards.

"When you say 'check out a sample,'" Dre said. "What does that mean exactly?"

"We deal with some of the worst viruses in the world here, Dre, so we have an elaborate inventory-control system," Lakshmi said. "The only person allowed to check out samples is Dr. Lu." She stopped, bit her lip. "I did it again. The only person allowed to check out a sample *was* Dr. Lu. He set up the sample-handling system and only he could access it."

"And what happened to the samples?"

"We sent one to the Blue Team and kept the others here." Lakshmi met Dre's gaze and her expression grew thoughtful. "There was no Project Deliverance, was there? No Blue Team."

Dre shook her head. "Those samples you mentioned. They were used in Yemen on innocent people."

The other woman clenched her eyes shut. Her chin trembled with the effort of containing her emotions. "That's why Talia was so afraid. JP was a monster."

Dre licked her lips. "He used them . . . on small villages. Then destroyed the evidence."

"Oh my God." Lakshmi covered her face with her hands. "How could I have been so stupid? All of us—we wanted to believe him, so we did, and now . . ."

Dre put her arms around Lakshmi. The woman's

body quivered with suppressed emotion. "I'll talk to the corpsman and get you something to help you sleep."

"No." Lakshmi sat up straight. "I want to help. The CDC will need someone who knows the systems, knows how this place works. That's me."

She scooted off the bed and stood. "I only want one thing."

Dre got up. "What?"

"These people were my friends. When they cremate the bodies, I want to take their ashes home to their families. I owe them that much."

CHAPTER 45

Camp Lemonnier, Djibouti, Africa

When she was in primary school, her parents would take Rachel and her brother to the local pool on weekends. Rachel was six, two years younger than her brother, and wanted nothing more than to be as grown-up as an eight-year-old.

And to be better than her brother at something. Anything.

She couldn't remember whose idea it was to have a breath-holding contest. All she remembered was that this was going to be her moment, her chance to win.

The rules of the game were simple. Both children jumped into the pool on the count of three and swam to the bottom of the deep end. There was a drain there with a grate they could hold on to so they didn't float back to the surface too soon.

She jumped in and swam to the bottom, feeling the

pressure on her ears eight feet below the surface. The other children were playing in the shallow end and she could dimly hear their splashing in the water. She and her brother, each with fingers hooked into the drain grate, stared at each other. As the seconds ticked by, her lungs began to hurt, her heart beat faster, but she would not let go.

Her brother's eyes grew wider and he started to make frantic motions, but Rachel just held on tighter. Finally, he let go and pushed off the bottom. She watched him go up toward the sun. She had won! The sense of exultation that filled her little body made all the discomfort worthwhile. She tried to let go of the grate, but her fingers were stuck.

She pulled again, and a trickle of blood seeped out of the grate. Her lungs hurt, her vision went all sparkly. She opened her mouth to scream, and a big bubble of air—her air—floated away.

The next thing Rachel remembered was lying on the concrete pool deck, her face up to the sun, trying to breathe and coughing up water. There was a ring of people around her, and her mother's face loomed over hers. Red, angry, crying, happy—all at the same time.

Rachel's throat was raw, but she sat up and said, "I won."

That same feeling of swimming into consciousness came to Rachel now. But instead of just a pain in her throat, she had pain everywhere. Her ribs, her head, her side . . .

She cracked open her eyes and immediately shut them again at the brightness of the room.

A hospital room. She was safe.

She heard heavy, labored breathing nearby, like a bull moose.

"Noam?" Her own voice was a croak like something out of a horror movie.

An enormous warm hand covered hers. "I'm here."

Rachel took another ragged breath and forced her eyes open. The room was bright and airy, with a window that looked out onto desert brown.

"Where am I?"

"Camp Lemonnier, Djibouti. The American base. It's a long story."

Rachel studied her boss. His face was deeply lined and gray with lack of sleep.

"How long?"

"Three days."

Three days.

"The lab," Rachel said. "The people in the lab. Are they . . ." She let her voice trail off when she saw Noam shake his head.

"All dead. Some kind of virus. . . . Bad."

Rachel had seen Noam absorb a lot of ugliness in his career at Mossad, but this event seemed to make a dent in his normally implacable exterior. She could only imagine what kind of impact it took to do that.

"The Americans secured the research lab?"

Instead of answering, Noam looked past her to the

door. Rachel turned her head slowly to see a man in his forties, with reddish hair and a fair complexion.

"We did," he said. "Don Riley, US intel. The research lab is secure. Dr. Tahir is on the run, but we'll find her."

Rachel tried to sit up, and her head exploded with pain. Noam put a hand on her shoulder. "You have a concussion, three broken ribs, and a barely functional windpipe. I think you need to stay where you are right now."

Rachel closed her eyes until the room stopped spinning. "You need to find her. She is planning something, something big and very personal. She and JP were in on this thing together, but he tried to talk her out of it at the end."

"JP?" Riley said.

"Jean-Pierre Manzul. Tahir . . . this is personal with her."

Noam exchanged a look with Riley. "What else can you tell us?"

Rachel tried to recall the exact words. "She said it was time for them to pay, that she had waited her whole life for this moment, and Pandora was the answer. If Tahir got away, she's not running from you, she's running toward something. An attack."

Her head throbbed. Rachel covered her eyes with her hand.

"I'll let you rest, Rachel," Riley said. She heard the door close behind him.

Noam held her hand. It seemed like her hand was the only part of her body that wasn't in pain.

"You were close to Manzul," Noam said.

JP's face flashed in her mind. Then she imagined she felt the spray of his blood on her face and the weight of his body as she used his corpse as a shield.

"He was a target. An asset. I did my job. Now he's dead."

Noam held her hand as she drifted off to sleep.

CHAPTER 46

Camp Lemonnier, Djibouti, Africa

When Don got back to the TOC, the officers were watching the wall screen, where one of the CDC scientists was holding up a plastic bag. Inside two layers of plastic was a steel object about the size and shape of a soda can.

"We found this in the back of Lab One," he said. "It's the device used to disperse the virus." He pointed the end at the camera, showing them a pinhole nozzle and a small black square of plastic that read "00" in red LED numbers.

"Basically, it's an aerosolizer. It's got a timer mechanism and a built-in propellant. When the timer goes off, it disperses the contents through this nozzle. It's also insulated. If you put a cryogenic sample in here, it'll stay viable for days, maybe weeks."

"Did you determine what killed the people in the lab?" Don asked.

The CDC scientist nodded. "Ebola, without a doubt. It's a particularly virulent strain and it looks like someone messed with it genetically. We'll need to do more testing, but I know one thing: This was no accident." He held the bagged aerosolizer close to the camera. "This was murder."

The news settled on Don. They had all known this at some level, but the scientist's words lent a finality to the room.

He studied the bagged object. "Is there any special handling for the aerosolizer once it's loaded?" he asked.

The doctor shrugged. "Probably not. There are threads here, so I assume there's a lid that goes on top to protect the nozzle. I guess if I was transporting it, I'd want a carrying case of some kind. Probably insulated if the original sample was frozen."

"Thank you, Doctor," Don said. He indicated to Janet to kill the connection.

A carrying case . . .

Don's mind raced. "Dre," he said, "pull up the security footage of Dr. Tahir leaving the site."

Within a few minutes, Dre had the grainy video on the wall screen. Don watched Tahir exit the elevator and hurry to a black SUV. As she opened the door, she turned her body.

"Stop," Don said. He used a laser pointer to draw a circle around the doctor's arm on the screen. "She's carrying something."

Dre zoomed in. The case was a small, padded cylinder with a strap like a carrier for a water bottle.

"What does that look like?" Don asked.

"I thought it was a purse," Dre said, "but now . . . I'm thinking it could be a carrying case for one of these little devices."

Don nodded. "That's exactly what I was thinking. I visited our friend from Mossad in the infirmary. She was very clear that Tahir was on a mission, something big, something that involves Pandora."

"But the Pandora sample is intact," Janet said. "The CDC verified the inventory."

"We're missing something," he said. "Dre, let's look at the handling system again."

Dre put the automated sample-handling system specs on the screen. "State-of-the-art, off-the-shelf storage system for cryogenic samples. According to Dr. Chandrasekaran, Dr. Lu handled all the samples himself. The system uses facial rec, or a passcode, or both. Because the site only had a few people, they turned off facial rec."

She pulled up the logs from the system. "The last time the system was accessed was the day before the raid. Dr. Lu accessed two samples, Ebola and Pandora—"

"So, Dr. Lu checked out the sample that eventually killed him?" Janet said.

Dre studied the logs further. "According to this, he accessed the Pandora sample but immediately put it back."

Michael spoke up. "You said the system has facial rec?"

"Yeah," Dre replied, "but it was turned off."

"I know, but was the camera turned off? Usually the image collection and image verification are two different settings."

Dre quickly found the program files and searched for the system database. "Michael, you are a flipping genius! The images are all there. The camera takes a picture as soon as the system is activated. . . ."

She found the image corresponding to the date-time group of the last day and pushed it to the wall screen.

It was Dr. Tahir.

"Get the CDC lead scientist back on the line," Don said, his voice hoarse.

"Back so soon, Mr. Riley?" The scientist's smile faded when he saw the look on Don's face.

"Doctor, we need to verify something. When you did an inventory of the virus samples onsite, how did you do that?"

"We verified it was physically there and matched the bar code. Why?"

"Was there any test done to verify that the contents of the sample are what the bar code says they are?"

The scientist shook his head. "These are deadly viruses stored cryogenically. To do that, we'd need to thaw them and look at each one under a scanning electron microscope—"

"We need you to verify the Pandora sample. Immediately."

"It will take a few hours, Mr. Riley."

"Please, time is of the essence."

Janet killed the wall-screen video. It reverted back to

Dre's screen, which still held the image of Dr. Talia Tahir. "What now?"

Don pinched his lip, staring at the doctor's picture.

"Find out everything you can about her. Get the NSA on the horn and find the search history for the Mahdi's computer. This isn't over yet."

CHAPTER 47

Camp Lemonnier, Djibouti, Africa

Everyone in the Situation Room at the White House stood when the president entered. Don and Janet, taking the call from the secure VTC in Camp Lemonnier, stood also. It seemed like the right thing to do.

"Be seated, everyone. Please." The president was dressed in a tuxedo. He had just come from a state dinner with the president of France. He shot a glance at the secretary of state.

"What's the status of Egypt and Sudan?"

Although the secretary was dressed for the state dinner, she had been in the Situation Room for the entire meeting prep.

"Stable for the moment, sir. The Sudanese have agreed to keep their distance from the site of the raid. Once we briefed them on the true identity of the Mahdi, the Egyptians agreed to stay on their side of the border. For now." She shot a glance at the screen and said in a wry tone, "Mr. Riley is about to add a layer of complexity to the issue."

The president engaged Don on the screen. "It seems our investment in the new Emerging Threats group is about to pay off." His practiced smile seemed a little brittle.

Judith Hellman, the director of national intelligence, answered for Don. "The situation with the Mahdi terrorist organization has taken a turn, sir."

The most powerful people in Washington shifted in their seats. Hellman was flanked by the secretary of state and Roger Trask, the director of the CIA. On the other side of the table, the vice president sat at the president's right hand, reading glasses low on her nose. Next to her were the secretary of defense and the chairman of the Joint Chiefs, all attired for the state dinner.

"Proceed, Don," Hellman said.

Don could see her watching the room, assessing the mood of the other attendees. This was the worst kind of intelligence briefing to use as the foundation for action. They had a large amount of circumstantial evidence that fit a narrative, but almost zero hard proof. Intelligence work was about connecting the dots, but there was always someone out there who could make a different picture from the same information.

Careers were made—and lost—over these kinds of decisions.

Don cleared his throat and motioned for Janet to show the clips of the captured bioweapons research lab. "Four days ago, United States forces secured the headquarters of the Mahdi, the terrorist who has been operating in the Nile River basin for the past six months. We discovered a biosafety-level-four research facility, which was being used to manufacture biological weapons."

The president squinted at the screen. "That looks like a pretty sophisticated operation. You said this was in the middle of the desert?"

"Yes, sir," Don said. "In Sudan, about a hundred kilometers from Khartoum. The lab is a modular design. It was purchased via a front company in Switzerland and shipped piece by piece to Sudan, where it was assembled by this man." Janet flashed up a picture of the CEO of Recodna Genetics. "Jean-Pierre Manzul was a former French DGSE operative. Based on intel recovered from the raid, we know he was the person in the Mahdi videos."

"So, we caught him then?" the president asked.

"Manzul is dead, sir, but the threat is still very active."

"How was it funded?" the vice president asked. Her dress for the state dinner was a black evening gown and a stunning diamond necklace that glittered when she moved.

"We're still getting to the bottom of that, ma'am," Don said. "But the headline is that at least part of the funding came through an Israeli hard-right nationalist known as Haim Zarecki."

"This is going to be about Iran, isn't it?" the secretary of state said. "Goddamn Zarecki. The Israelis should have muzzled him years ago."

"I'm afraid so," Don said.

Don nodded to Janet to put up a picture of Talia Tahir. "All of the scientists at the facility were either killed or detained, except for this woman, Dr. Talia Tahir, formerly a field researcher with the World Health Organization. Dr. Tahir's past suggests a deep personal hatred of Iran. We believe she and Manzul conspired to use the Mahdi's attacks to conceal a much larger plan to attack the country of Iran."

"You're telling me that the Mahdi was a cover?" the president said.

Don nodded. "We believe the Mahdi attacks were designed to distract the intelligence community from small-scale testing of biological weapons."

The president directed a sharp look at Judith Hellman, whose face had gone still. "Explanation, Director?"

Hellman's face reddened, but she kept her chin high. "It appears that the Mahdi was giving us what we were looking for, sir. A rogue terrorist network with just enough connections to Iran to seem plausible. The discovery of the bioweapons lab leads us to believe that the only purpose of the Mahdi was to distract intelligence agencies such as our own from the real goal."

"In other words, we got taken." The president's lips pressed into a firm line. "Tell me more about this Dr. Tahir."

"Her parents were killed in Lebanon by a Hezbollah bomb when she was twelve years old," Don said. "We believe this is the primary motivator for her actions. Our narrative suggests this plan has been years, perhaps decades in the making. She formed a relationship with Manzul and together they conceived of a secret bioweapons research lab in the Sudan. They secured funding from entities in the region who would like to see the balance of power shifted away from Iran. They convinced a group of leading scientists that they were actually preventing the proliferation of bioweapons by using a Red Team–Blue Team approach."

"Let me guess," the president said. "There was no Blue Team?"

"There was no Blue Team, sir."

"How much weapons-grade biomaterial does she have?" the chairman of the Joint Chiefs asked.

"That's the good news, sir," Don said. "In our estimate, she has only one sample. In airborne form, it could contaminate the room you're in, but not much more. The real damage would be done by person-to-person contact, after the initial infection. From what we've been told, this Pandora virus has near-perfect lethality."

"Do we know where she plans to use this weapon?" the vice president asked.

Don took a deep breath and nodded to Janet to put up the next series of images.

"This is the city of Qom in Iran. Considered the holiest city to Shiite Muslims, Qom is located approximately a hundred and fifty kilometers south of Tehran and has a population of about one point two million people. In four days, it will be the site of a conclave of all the senior leaders of the Iranian government."

The president put his face in his hands. "I see where this is going."

"Yes, sir," Don said. "Our best estimate is that Dr. Tahir plans to deploy the Pandora virus during this event."

The secretary of defense interrupted. "How serious a threat do you think this is, Mr. Riley? This woman barely escaped with her life from that Marine raid. She knows half the free world is looking for her. Why would she risk going to Iran of all places?"

Instead of answering, Don signaled Janet to put up the image of the murdered scientists from the research lab. The room was silent.

"Are those people?" the secretary of state asked.

"These four people were Tahir's coworkers at the lab," Don said. "People she lived and worked with for months. She infected them with a dangerous strain of the Ebola virus and left them to die. I can assure you, ladies and gentlemen, Dr. Tahir is a committed terrorist."

"And that was the Pandora virus?" the secretary of defense said.

"No, sir," Don replied. "Pandora is worse. Pandora is a chimera virus. Through gene editing, the Ebola virus has been amplified and merged with a paleo-flu virus harvested from a corpse thousands of years old. That means we have nothing like it in our inventory. It might take scientists months, maybe years, to come up with a vaccine. By then, Pandora could be all over the planet."

Don had hit his stride now, signaling to Janet to show the picture of the aerosol device. The stainless-steel container was shown next to a soda can for size comparison.

"The sample taken from the lab fits into a device such as this one. By our best estimate, this container will keep the virus viable for as much as two weeks once it is sealed inside. The device also serves as a deployment mechanism with an integrated timer and aerosolizer. In the case of the murdered scientists, a similar device was hidden in the room and deployed using the timer."

"Jesus Christ," the chairman said. "You could hide that in a water bottle in a meeting room."

"Exactly, sir," Don said.

"Okay, Mr. Riley," the president said. "You've successfully scared the crap out of us. Tell us what happens if Dr. Tahir manages to get close to the Iranian leadership."

"According to the one remaining scientist, the Pandora virus has a fourteen-day incubation period," Don said. "During that time the infected individual will show no symptoms but will be highly contagious. If even one infected person got onto a plane, this could become a worldwide epidemic in a matter of weeks."

"Doing nothing and letting the Iranians figure it out for themselves is not an option then," the vice president said.

"State," the president said, "what if we tell the Iranians everything? Tell them there's a crazy woman out there with a biological weapon and a massive grudge? How does that play out?"

The secretary of state stared at the table for a few seconds. "I think there's two possibilities, Mr. President. One, the Iranians consider this an act of aggression—it would not be hard to concoct a story to blame us—and launch an attack. The second possibility is even worse."

"And what is that?"

"The Iranians believe us and they capture Dr. Tahir and the Pandora virus. Iran with a biological weapon is not in the United States' best interest, sir."

The president chewed on the edge of his lip.

"We have a plan, sir," DNI Hellman said.

"Let's hear it."

"We recommend a two-person team," Don said. "One will come from my group, a computer specialist with the ability to access video surveillance in the area. The other would be a field agent to secure the virus and deal with Dr. Tahir."

The president addressed Hellman. "Do we have those assets in place in Iran?"

"We don't plan to use existing assets, sir," Don said. "These are clean skins. We're concerned about Mossad."

"I don't follow."

"The Israelis were instrumental in helping us track down the Mahdi headquarters," Don said. "They know almost as much as we do about what's going on. Our concern is that the Israelis might try to steal Pandora for themselves."

"Remember Stuxnet, sir," Hellman said. "The Israelis might see this as an opportunity to gain the upper hand in the region."

"If we try to use one of our in-place assets in Iran to pursue Dr. Tahir," Don said, "we could be tipping off the Israelis to her location."

"You have someone in mind for this mission?" the president asked.

"I do, sir," Don said. "Active FBI agent with the right security clearances and speaks Farsi like a native."

The president looked at Hellman. "Read her in. The last thing we need is the Israelis pissing in our pool. Our interests may not be in lockstep on this issue. We need the best possible chance of success."

"Yes, sir," Hellman said.

The president shut his briefing book. "Thank you, Mr. Riley, you may proceed with the planning for this covert action. Now on to the next order of business."

"Next order of business, sir?" Don said. "That's all I have."

The president leaned onto his elbows. "Your plan assumes success. What happens if you fail?"

The secretary of defense spoke up. "Sir, in the event of a biological-weapons release within the city of Qom, our recommendation will be a full-scale tactical strike."

"Mr. President," the secretary of state began, "you can't seriously be considering—"

The defense secretary interrupted. "If this weapon is released, make no mistake about it, we will be at war with Iran. According to Riley, if we wait even a day, thousands of people could be infected. Within a few weeks, it's possible the entire leadership of the Islamic Republic of Iran could look like those bodies we just saw. Who will we even talk to at that point? Worse still, the virus would be spreading around the world." He crossed his arms. "If the CIA's covert action plan fails, our only option is a first strike on Iran. Period."

"I agree." The president held up his hand to stop the secretary of state from further discussion. He shot a look at the chairman. "Admiral, move the Teddy Roosevelt Carrier Strike Group as far north in the Persian Gulf as you can without being too obvious. Prepare a first-strike package for Qom and let's hope to God we don't have to use it."

The president jumped to his feet with a wide smile. "Thank you all, but I need to be going. My French counterpart will be wondering where I've been."

The room stood as one. On the other side of the world, in a secure VTC room, Don and Janet stood also. The president's gaze leaped across the distance to Don.

"Mr. Riley—Don," the president said. "Put up that picture again. The one with the bodies."

Janet searched the images and sent it to the viewscreen. The corpse closest to the camera had long blond hair and fair skin that looked more like bloody clay now.

"I want everyone in this room to imprint this picture in your brain. If we fail, this is what could happen to the people you love. These are the stakes."

The only sound was the faint hiss of the phone line.

The president's smile returned like a light switching on.

"But we won't fail, will we, Don?"

CHAPTER 48

Athens, Greece

Don Riley waited at the bottom of the stairs of the Gulf-stream V jet. He was wearing a dark blue blazer over a pair of khakis and a polo shirt and he chewed on his thumbnail. A black SUV with diplomatic plates idled on the tarmac behind him.

"Welcome to Athens, ma'am," Don said to Liz Soroush with a mock salute.

Liz hugged him as hard as she could. "Don, I knew it was you behind all this."

"We're short on time, Lizzie," he said into her ear.

"Of course." She released him and they walked to the SUV together. "You lost some weight, I see."

"I'd like to say it was because of my workout routine," Don said, "but it's mostly stress."

When they were in the car, Liz reached over and held his hand. "It's good to see you, Don. Really good."

Since her move to Minneapolis with the kids, Liz felt

as if she'd lost touch with the anchors of her former life. She missed the reminders of Brendan. He squeezed her fingers.

"Ditto. How are the kids?" He shot a look at the driver. She knew he wouldn't talk about why she was here until they were in a secure location.

"Ahmad is trying to fit into the Minnesota culture by playing ice hockey. Not going so great, I have to say. I was told by one mother that if your kid isn't on skates by the time they're four, you're considered a lost cause." She laughed. "Beth, on the other hand, is doing fabulously well in volleyball. It's a huge sport up there."

She looked out the window. The SUV made excellent time through the sun-drenched streets of Athens. In the distance, she caught a glimpse of the Parthenon. She'd never been to Greece before. She and Brendan had always said they'd go when things calmed down. Liz drew her attention back to Don.

"Brendan's parents are great. We bought a house only a few blocks from them so the kids can go over whenever they want. We got a dog, too. . . ." She sighed. "It's great, really it is."

She studied Don's profile. "You know, I still miss him? It sorta pisses me off, really. If I was the one who was gone, I'm sure he would've moved on by now, right? But I can't seem to get there."

Don focused on something outside the window. "You know that's not true, Lizzie. He was a mess without you."

The car pulled up to the gates of the embassy and stopped while a security guard scanned the undercarriage of the vehicle. Like all United States embassies, the building looked like a fortress.

Once the car had parked, Don hurried her through a back entrance and down into the basement. "We've got a SCIF set up down here." He paused to scan his ID badge at a door, then pushed it open for her. "I brought some friends with me, too. They want to say hello."

The small room held only four workstations facing a large wall screen. Behind the stations were the three people she still thought of as midshipmen, even though they were all now commissioned officers.

"Liz!" Janet got up first and hugged her. Dre and Michael waited for their turn.

Liz felt a rush of nostalgia at their greeting. The last time she had seen them all together was shortly after Brendan's funeral service at the Naval Academy. Intense emotions of that day echoed in her mind.

Don cleared his throat.

Liz wiped her eyes. "It's time for the great unveiling. The only clue I have about why I'm here is that someone handed me a tablet with a language program to refresh my Farsi on the trip over."

The mention of the Iranian language shifted the mood in the room.

"Liz, you're about to be briefed into Operation Pinpoint," Don said, his voice calm and professional. "As you've correctly guessed, it involves Iran and is extremely time-sensitive."

Janet had the wall screen running and ran slides for Don as he explained the background of the operation. Liz's mind reeled as she saw pictures of the underground research lab and the murdered scientists. He finished the brief with the picture of Dr. Talia Tahir. She was a striking woman with exquisite blue eyes and a confident air. Liz found it hard to believe she was a mass murderer.

"You're sure she's going to be in Qom in three days?"

Don nodded. "This is her best chance before the virus expires. The search history we uncovered from the Mahdi's computer tells us this is her target."

"You need a more experienced agent for this, Don."

"We can't risk it, Lizzie. Mossad is on to us. If we tip our hand and the Israelis get access to this weapon . . ."

"I see," Liz said with more confidence than she felt. "Tell me how this goes down."

"Dre has volunteered to go with you as your tech support," Don said. "The most likely target is the conference center adjacent to the Jamkaran Mosque." Liz studied an aerial picture of a stunning mosque with a huge open plaza and an adjoining modern conference center. "The president of Iran will be giving a speech at the conference center following a visit to the mosque. Dre will be able to get us access to video surveillance of the entire area."

Liz looked at Dre, seeing the mix of emotions on the young woman's face. "You're up for this?"

"Yes, ma'am." Like Liz, Dre sounded more certain than she looked.

Michael continued the brief. "You'll be traveling as a Canadian-Iranian businesswoman and her daughter/assistant, looking for a site to hold a venture-capital conference in the city of Qom in one year's time. As part of your cover, you will need to see all the facilities, including security, which is where Dre comes in. She will plant a shell program in the security system which gives us access.

"We'll be running the operation from Al-Udeid Air Base in Qatar. Your comms will go through satellite phones with an AWACS over Iraq for redundancy. Once we have access to the video system, we'll be running a facial-rec program. If Tahir shows up anywhere close to the complex, we'll see her."

"What about hardware?" Liz asked.

"You'll fly into Isfahan Airport, south of Qom, on the red-eye tomorrow night," Janet said. "Smaller facility, less security. When you rent a car, an asset on the ground will deliver a package to you with the vehicle. Inside you will find one nine-millimeter handgun and suppressor. Also, two knives and two earbuds for comms. As your assistant, Dre will carry a laptop equipped with everything she needs for her job."

"The Iranian president and his entourage arrive the next morning," Don said, pointing to a map. "We've arranged for you to stay at a hotel . . . right . . . here." The map showed the location of the hotel, about a quarter mile from the complex. "The next morning Liz will go back to the compound using a pass identifying her as an attendee at the president's speech. If Tahir is going to make her move, we expect it will be that day. We find the target and give you a location. From there it's up to you. The highest priority is to retrieve this device."

Janet flashed a picture of a silver cylinder sitting next to a soda can.

"We believe Dr. Tahir will be carrying the virus in this container," Don said. "This device can aerosolize the virus to make it airborne. It has a timer, which means she can set it and hide it. She's done it before." Don's face was grim.

"What will I be doing while Liz is at the site?" Dre asked.

"You stay at the hotel," Don said. "It's too risky for you to go in during the day of the Iranian president's visit. Security will be much tighter and the chances of you having to speak to someone are too high."

Don focused back on Liz. "You do whatever you need to do to secure the biological sample, including deadly force. If the timer has been activated, we're not sure if it's able to be turned off. The best thing you can do is submerge it in water and get the hell out of there."

———

The situation room at the White House looked a lot like it did on television, Liz thought.

She stood along with Don when the president entered. His eyes searched the room and found the video screen. They stopped on her for a second, then swept away.

"Seats, please," the president said.

Director of National Intelligence Hellman got right to the point. "Mr. President, we're here for mission approval of Operation Pinpoint. With your permission, Mr. Riley will brief you on the particulars of the operation."

The president opened his briefing book and nodded without looking up. Don spoke for ten minutes straight.

His voice was firm and precise, and he relayed the exact details they had gone over earlier that afternoon.

At the end of Don's briefing, the president steepled his hands together and touched the tips of his index fingers to his lips. Liz had seen this gesture many times in pictures in the media. Critics called it his "thoughtful pose," but it seemed genuine to her.

A few seconds went by before the president spoke.

"The mission is approved," he said. "It's a pleasure to meet you, Special Agent Soroush. I don't often get to meet the agents who do this kind of work."

"Thank you, sir." Liz didn't know what else to say.

"Don't thank me yet," the president said. "I want you to hear the rest of the story." He nodded at the chairman of the Joint Chiefs of Staff.

The presentation screen changed to a map of the city of Qom. The complex where the operation was to take place was contained in a bright red box. The chairman's voice was deep and he had a methodical cadence to his words.

"In the event we are unable to prevent deployment of the biological weapon, Mr. President, we recommend a first strike on the target designed to contain the risk of infection. A layered attack strategy will ensure complete and total destruction of the target.

"Layer one will be delivered by a pair of B-2 stealth bombers—a primary and a backup, code-named Cyclone One and Two—each carrying two GBU-57A/B Massive Ordnance Penetrators. This ordnance is packed with fifty-three hundred pounds of high explosives and has been modified to detonate on surface contact. The result will be a massive fireball designed to vaporize everything within half a kilometer. We'll ensure this Pandora virus is destroyed."

When he paused, Liz heard the secretary of state whisper, "Jesus Christ."

"With your approval, sir, the Cyclone strike force will depart Whiteman Air Force Base tonight to be on station in time."

The president pursed his lips. "There's a second layer to this plan?"

The chairman smiled thinly. "We believe in belt and suspenders, sir. In the event the Cyclone option fails or is not successful in any way, we recommend a conventional strike of sixty-four Tomahawk missiles launched from the Teddy Roosevelt Carrier Strike Group currently deployed in the Persian Gulf. They'll hit the target area a minute ahead of an alpha strike by the entire air wing embarked aboard the carrier. This sounds like overkill, but we'll only get one shot at containing the virus. We need to make it count."

The chairman paused, waiting for the president to acknowledge that he understood. Liz could see a sheen of sweat on the chairman's bald pate. The president nodded.

"Immediately upon missile deployment, Mr. President, the strike group will draw back from the northern end of the Persian Gulf and assume a defensive posture. We believe the Iranians will consider this an act of war, sir."

The president cocked an eyebrow. "I should think so."

The secretary of state cleared her throat and picked up the conversation. "We will have diplomats pre-positioned at all of the major countries in the region as well as the UN to meet with heads of state and explain the situation. We also recommend a nationwide broadcast from you, sir, in the event that we have to resort to the military option. The draft text of your speech has been included in your package."

At some level, Liz knew a military backup plan was inevitable, but it was difficult to listen to all the same. If she failed, she would likely be in the blast zone. If she was contaminated during the struggle to obtain the biological weapon, she would have to remain inside the blast zone.

She was thankful Don had the foresight to keep Dre away from the conference center on the day of the Iranian president's visit.

"Special Agent Soroush?"

Liz looked up to find everyone staring at her. The president spoke again. "You understand why I wanted you to hear this briefing?"

Even through the flat video screen, the president's gaze was soft. He knew the stakes and he was asking for her permission to sign her death warrant.

"Yes, sir, I understand."

CHAPTER 49

Isfahan International Airport, Iran

Instead of feeling self-conscious about wearing traditional Muslim dress, Dre felt oddly comforted. At the embassy in Athens, Dre had been given a new identity—and a new wardrobe.

She was now Chantal Homayouni, a twenty-four-year-old Canadian, born and raised in Vancouver. She was traveling in the company of her mother, Lili, but this was her first trip to the country of her ancestors. She was unfamiliar with the language or the traditional Muslim dress.

The women in Athens dressed her in layers. A dress, called an abaya, followed by a hijab, or head scarf, followed by a chador, an overgarment similar to a cloak that had a hood and she could hold closed with her hands. In the end, the only things that showed were her face and her hands.

The layers gave her a feeling of anonymity that she so desperately wanted.

The customs line moved at a crawl, and the air in the customs area was stifling. Dre kept her eyes on the floor, her senses racing for any sign of danger. Although she had not slept a wink on the overnight flight from Athens to Istanbul to Isfahan, she was wide awake, her nerves on edge.

The line moved forward a few paces. Liz, perhaps sensing Dre felt overwhelmed, reached back for Dre's hand, giving her a comforting squeeze before releasing her fingers. Dre wanted to hold on to her for dear life, but she just moved their roller bags forward. Their luggage was filled with typical clothes and personal effects that a mother and daughter from Vancouver, Canada, would travel with. There was a story with each item—where she'd bought it, how much it cost, who was in each picture in her wallet—that would stand up to at least first-level scrutiny.

Finally, they were called together by a mustachioed customs agent, a swarthy man with beady black eyes and a gruff manner. Liz spoke to him in a pleasant tone as she handed him both passports. Dre kept her eyes on the floor during the rapid-fire exchange in Farsi. The man said something directed to her and Dre choked down a wave of panic.

"Lift up your head, dear. Look into the camera," Liz said to her softly in English.

Dre did as she was told. When she saw the flicker of the camera lens, she braced herself for the inevitable rush of armed guards to take her off to prison.

Nothing happened.

Liz said something to the customs agent that was

clearly about Dre, and he laughed loudly as he handed back their stamped passports.

"What did you say to him?" she whispered to Liz as they walked through the crowded baggage-claim area.

"I told him you were a stupid girl here to see the land of her forefathers for the first time."

The rental-car agency was called EuropCar. The brightly lighted, Kelly-green banner with English lettering seemed to Dre like a beacon of familiarity in a land of swirling Farsi script.

Liz's pleasant demeanor was on display again as she spoke to the rental agent. He was a helpful man in his midthirties with a neatly trimmed beard and quick dark eyes.

"Do you require a GPS with your vehicle?" the man asked Liz.

"Yes, I am unfamiliar with this part of Iran," Liz replied. Dre knew this was the coded phrase to establish bona fides.

"The mountains are beautiful this time of year," the man said.

"Unfortunately, our time is short," Liz said with a smile. "Maybe on our next trip."

The agent nodded as he tapped away at his computer, barely acknowledging Liz's response. He collected a set of keys and small black attaché case and escorted Liz and Dre to the far end of the parking lot. He opened the trunk of a late-model black Toyota sedan and stowed their luggage, then handed the case to Liz. Dre caught the word "GPS" in the chatter.

Liz navigated through the midmorning traffic on the

highways on the outskirts of Isfahan. They were heading north, into the desert. After the first thirty minutes, the traffic thinned and they were on an open highway.

Liz checked the rearview mirror. "You can open the case now."

Dre settled the case on her lap and snapped it open. Underneath the foam cover was a SIG Sauer P226 nine-millimeter handgun with a suppressor and two magazines, two knives in sheaths, and two earpieces. She found the tiny dip switches on the earpieces, turned them on, and paired them with the commercial satellite phones she and Liz carried. Their signals were bounced from their phone to the satellite to Al-Udeid Air Base in Qatar. She handed one to Liz and slipped the other in her ear.

"Michael, can you hear me?" Dre said.

There was a long pause, making Dre think maybe she'd done something wrong; then Michael's low voice sounded in her ear. "I got you five by five, Dre. Good to hear you again."

A feeling of relief flooded through her at the familiar voice. She hadn't realized how on edge she'd been for the last twelve hours, but this visceral reaction to Michael's voice told her that she had not been fooling anyone—least of all herself.

"What's the status, Liz?" Don's voice.

"We're on schedule. No issues." Liz shot a glance at Dre and winked. "We're just a couple of Muslim chicks headed to the holiest site in Iran for a working holiday."

Dre laughed. The release felt good. Liz reached over and patted her knee.

"We've got another hour and a half, Dre," Liz said. "Why don't you take a nap."

Dre eased her seat back a few notches. She turned her head toward the window and watched the countryside fly by. It was high desert here, undulating hills of dry brown soil broken only by the occasional shrub or tree or roadside stand. It reminded her of Sudan and the land around the Project Deliverance site.

She closed her eyes. She knew sleep would not come, but she needed to try.

When the dream came again, it was different. Dre wasn't watching Janet. This time, she had taken Janet's place. She could feel the hard, cold floor of the North Korean bunker under her body.

And she could not move.

Footfalls behind her. A shadow slipped over her body, but she was paralyzed. The muzzle of a gun appeared above her and slowly descended until it touched her forehead.

Dre startled awake.

"We're here," Liz said. "You okay?"

Dre straightened her seat. They were back in heavy city traffic. The scenery around her was filled with people and cars and buildings. Women, mostly dressed in black, but with a few splashes of color in the crowd, hurried along the streets, clutching bags in one hand, small children by the other. People in Western clothes mixed in with the pedestrians.

Liz made a turn and pointed through the windshield. "That's the mosque."

Dre tried not to gawk, but the building was magnificent. Two towering minarets flanked an elaborate tiled archway overlooking a vast marble plaza. Rising behind the entrance like a beautiful hot-air balloon, an enormous blue dome gleamed in the sun. On either side of the main mosque were two smaller golden domes with their own entrances.

"It's beautiful," she said.

"It's reputed to be the mosque of the twelfth imam, the Mahdi, the one who would unite all Muslims under one true faith. That's where the president will come tomorrow morning. Once he visits the mosque for noon prayers, he will cross the street"—Liz pointed to a brick building across the street—"to go to the conference center for lunch and deliver a speech."

Liz found a parking lot. Under the cover of her chador, she secreted the handgun and the knife in pockets already sewn into her undergarments. She stowed the empty GPS case in the trunk.

"Bring your computer," Liz said. "This is where you shine, daughter."

Dre nodded, feeling the knots of tension ripple up her back as she shouldered her slim computer bag.

As they walked toward the glass-fronted entrance of the conference center, Liz seemed to transform before Dre's eyes. The pleasant, agreeable Liz became haughty and imperious, a foreigner with a sense of entitlement. She strode through the front doors, making a direct line to the information desk. She rapped out an order to the young woman sitting behind the desk.

The young woman's eyes widened. She snatched up a phone and spoke without taking her eyes off Liz. Dre hung back, watching her "mother" tap her foot impatiently. The girl at the desk handed them each a clip-on visitor badge with the seal of the conference center on it.

Moments later, another woman came rushing out. She was tall and thin and wearing a chador with a fashionable floral print. Liz eyed the woman's garb with obvious distaste.

Liz switched to English. "I would like to include my daughter in the conversation. Do you speak English?"

The woman nodded.

"Good, that is important for my clients." Liz lowered her voice. "Bill Gates might be attending this conference, so it needs to be perfect. Do you understand?"

"Please, this way." Their guide showed them into a ballroom that was being set up with dozens of round tables. "The space is being set for the president's visit tomorrow."

Liz sniffed. "A little small, but this will do. Show me the kitchens."

The guide took them into a service hall that ran along the length of the ballroom, ending in a set of double doors that opened into the kitchens. "Employees and staff all enter from the rear of the building. There is security screening in the back."

"What about the facilities?" Liz demanded. "Air and water services."

The woman pointed back toward the ballroom. "Those are on the other side of the building, along with security."

"Show me."

The woman marched them back through the ball-room and through a set of doors into an open area piled high with stacked chairs, tables, and carts full of linens. She pointed to a set of stairs leading up to a door in the high wall.

"All of the HVAC systems are up there in the mez-zanine. The rest of the facilities are in the basement."

Their guide walked with quick steps, constantly turn-ing to watch Liz for signs that she was meeting her expectations. "The event tomorrow will have more than one thousand attendees," she said. "Dignitaries from all over Iran."

"Your security can handle that?" Liz walked slowly through the storage area, her eyes taking in every de-tail.

"We will have all staff members on duty, plus lo-cal police." The guide pushed through a set of double doors back into the foyer. They had made a complete circuit of the facility.

The door to the security office was just off the foyer. A pair of uniformed men looked up when they entered. One was watching security monitors. The other one looked like a dispatch officer.

Their guide engaged in a long discussion with the dis-patch officer, but her manner was timid. He shook his head. Liz stepped forward and took over, unleashing a furious diatribe at the man.

Finally, the guard got up from his desk and unlocked the door behind him using a ring of keys.

Dre squeezed past Liz into the room, and her heart

dropped. Instead of the ancient Russian monitoring system she expected to find, there was a brand-new Chinese model. The server racks blinked at her as she pretended to inspect the system.

While Liz continued to harangue the guard, Dre slid her hand in her bag and extracted a wireless connection disguised as a dummy ethernet plug. She ducked behind the server rack, found an open ethernet connection, and slammed the plug in.

When she reappeared, the guard saw her and angrily spoke back to Liz.

"Tell him I was checking to make sure his hardware was up to date. Their hardware is excellent. We're all good to go."

Back in the foyer, Dre said to Liz, "I need to use the restroom, Mom."

The restroom was empty. Dre locked the last stall and pulled out her laptop.

"Michael, are you there?" she whispered.

"I'm here, Dre." His voice sounded so close.

"Change in plans, buddy. They have a state-of-the-art BingCheng model. I went to plan B."

"You know what that means, right?"

"Yup." Dre found the boot-up sequence for the video cameras and inserted a short program.

"Are you sure about this?"

"There's only one way to find out."

Dre found the server software code base and added two lines of code. She hit the Enter key.

"I gave it five minutes," she said.

"Dre, what if it doesn't come back on?"

"Then we go to plan C."

She walked out of the bathroom holding her belly. "I think I'd like to go to the hotel now, Mother."

When they got back to the car, Liz eyed her. "Well?"

"Give it a minute. I had to force a restart of their system to gain access for Michael."

Liz frowned. "Was that the plan?"

"Nope, but it was necessary."

Minutes ticked by.

"Michael?"

"Still nothing, Dre."

It was ten more minutes before he spoke again. Relief flooded his tone.

"We're in."

CHAPTER 50

Qom, Iran

In the gray light of predawn, Liz drew the bedcovers up to her chin and thought of lives that might have been.

She was here to kill another human being, Liz knew that. There was talk of recovering the bioweapon and taking Tahir into custody, but that was a remote possibility at best.

I could have—should have—refused.

But in the quiet of their hotel room, with Dre's breath sighing in the background, Liz faced the truth about herself.

She wanted to be here.

Her children had no father and she was on the other side of the world engaged in an operation that risked her life.

And somehow, she was okay with that.

Maybe it was an overdeveloped sense of duty, maybe

it was just pure selfishness, but the truth was when the call came, she didn't hesitate.

She went to the window, looking down on the streets below. Even this early, the city was electric with anticipation of the Iranian president's visit. There were security blockades on the street and people already filling the space behind them.

She watched the women dressed in black, only their faces and hands visible. If her parents had not emigrated to America when she was a child, she might be among their number.

The morning sun caught the blue dome of the mosque and Liz drew in a deep breath.

Her moment of self-reflection was behind her. She was here, in this place, to perform a duty for her country. She would take a life, if that life needed to be taken. She would get home safely. She would get Andrea Ramirez home safely.

It was time to go to work.

Liz washed and dressed quickly. She checked her weapons and stowed them in the pockets under her chador. She went through the sequence of drawing them multiple times, laying hands on each item until they were part of muscle memory.

She woke Dre gently. "Chantal," she said. She had cautioned Dre to ensure they used their cover names while in the hotel room just in case anyone was listening.

"Chantal. Wake up, sweetie."

Dre opened her eyes, saw Liz already dressed, and sat up in bed. Her eyes darted around the room as she realized where she was.

"It's okay," Liz said, taking Dre's hand. "I'm leaving now. I'll be back in a few hours. If anything happens, you know what to do."

The young woman nodded, still wiping the sleep from her eyes. As Liz started to get up, Dre wrapped her arms around Liz, whispering in her ear, "Be safe."

"Always."

Liz closed the door behind her and slipped the earpiece into her ear.

"Morning, Liz." Don's voice was confident. "We're looking excellent on this end. Solid coverage for blocks around the conference center. If she's there, we'll find her."

Liz took her time on the street, letting the flow of the crowd move her along. All around her, people chattered excitedly about the president's visit. Children rode on their fathers' shoulders, vendors sold trinkets and snacks. There was an air of a carnival about the day. Even international press vans were prominently evident.

If Tahir wanted a place to make a global statement, this was it.

Liz found a place where she could see the Jamkaran Mosque and the conference center and settled down to wait.

An hour passed. Word swept through the crowd that the president's plane had landed and his motorcade was on its way from the airport. People pressed against the security barriers. After another thirty minutes, a line of black cars roared down the street, headed for the mosque. The crowd cheered.

"We've got her," Don's voice said in her ear. "Tahir is entering the convention center now. Main entrance."

"I'm on my way." Liz pushed against the flow of the crowd. At the security checkpoint for the conference center, she showed her fake entry pass and said she had an appointment with the facility director. After a moment, the security guard let her pass.

When she entered the foyer, she ducked her head. "I'm inside. Where is she?"

"South side."

Liz recalled the layout of the conference center. Tahir was in the storage area with access to the air systems.

"Copy." Liz averted her face as she passed by the security office and pushed through the double doors into the long storage hall. She drew her weapon but kept it under her chador.

"She's on the mezzanine level, Liz. She's going for the HVAC system."

"Copy." Liz strode to the steps and took them two at a time. She could hear the hum of machinery through the heavy steel door.

"There are no cameras inside the mezzanine," Don said. "We're blind."

"I'm going in." Liz opened the door and slipped in quickly, letting her eyes adjust to the dimness. The roar of the air handlers was deafening.

Don's voice sounded distant. "Be careful, Lizzie."

The room was located over the main ballroom. HVAC units, each the size of a large truck, populated the perimeter of the space. Shoulder-high air ducts ran out from the air handlers to vents in the ceiling. Amid the din of the operating air systems, Liz stood on her tiptoes looking for Tahir's head poking above the ducts.

Nothing.

A narrow catwalk ran around the perimeter of the room, with branches running in the alleys formed between the massive ducts. With her weapon out, Liz advanced quickly past the first air-conditioning unit. The first catwalk was clear.

So was the second.

The third alley showed a woman trying to remove a maintenance access panel from the side of the air duct. Her back was to Liz.

She advanced down the catwalk, the sound of rushing air all around her.

When she was less than ten feet away, she called out in English, "Freeze."

The woman's back stiffened.

"Show me your hands."

The woman's fingers were long and elegant, with painted nails.

"Stand up. Turn around. Slowly."

Liz looked into the brilliant blue eyes of Dr. Talia Tahir.

"Don, I've got her."

25,000 feet over Hatra, Iraq

Of all the sensations in the universe, for Captain Darrin "Witcher" Hammet everything was a distant second to flying.

Everything.

Of course, that feeling waned some when you were sixteen hours into a projected thirty-eight-hour combat mission on a B-2 bomber.

The *Spirit of Kitty Hawk,* operational call sign Cyclone One, was just completing their third in-flight refueling since they had departed Whiteman Air Force Base, Missouri, late last night.

To Witcher's right, mission commander Lieutenant Colonel Randy "Thunder" Peebles handled the in-air refueling logistics with the massive KC-46 tanker that flew above and slightly ahead of the B-2. The refueling boom ran down to them from the rear of the tanker to the refueling port in the top of the B-2.

Thunder keyed his radio. "Exxon One-One, Cyclone One. That's a hundred K and we are topped off. Request disconnect."

"Stand by to disconnect," came the crisp reply.

The V-shaped wing that marked the end of the fueling boom connecting the *Spirit of Kitty Hawk* to the tanker appeared over them.

"Confirm disconnect," Thunder said. "Descending to the bottom of the box. Thanks, gents."

"Cyclone, Exxon, good luck."

As Witcher moved them away from the tanker and ascended, the mission commander closed out the refueling checklist.

"Post air-refueling checklist complete," Thunder reported.

Witcher verified that the refueling port on top of the aircraft had rotated back into the fuselage, restoring the plane's trademark smooth appearance. "Doors closed."

Witcher leveled out at forty thousand feet and put them into a racetrack holding pattern the size of Delaware. "Autopilot engaged," he said.

"Copy," Thunder replied. He sighed as he pulled off his helmet and raked his fingers through a thick mop of jet-black hair. "No updates on the tasking?"

Witcher knew the answer was no, but checked the laptop screen anyway. "Nothing yet."

"I'm gonna get some shut-eye, partner, okay?"

Witcher grinned. "Roger that, boss."

"Wake me if we get any tasking updates."

Thunder hoisted his six-foot frame out of his seat and stepped to the rear of the cockpit. Although the B-2 was a massive aircraft—170-foot wingspan and 70 feet long—the space allotted for the crew was tiny. A four-by-six-foot open floor area behind the pilot's and mission commander's chairs was all they had for a rest area. Although the Air Force provided a folding cot for sleeping comfort, Thunder did what most B-2 pilots did: He rolled his sleeping bag out on the floor. When Witcher glanced over his shoulder a few minutes later, he saw the mission commander's chest rise and fall in an even rhythm.

Witcher settled into his chair and established his solo routine. *Instrument scan, horizon scan, four deep breaths, repeat.*

Life as a B-2 pilot on a mission was a marathon, not a sprint. Self-discipline was the key to success. You needed to plan ahead and think smart. Flying out of the continental US to hot spots all over the world meant missions were grueling events, typically lasting more than twenty-four hours.

Through marathon training sessions in the simulator, pilots learned to plan what and when to eat, when to sleep, and how to fall asleep quickly so as not to waste precious downtime.

With only twenty B-2 bombers in the US Air Force's arsenal, the cadre of pilots was small and highly trained. The Air Force mined the ranks of the best fighter and bomber squadrons all over the world to cross-train as B-2 pilots.

Instrument scan, horizon scan, four deep breaths.

He hadn't been on as many missions as Thunder, but this one felt different, and from the way Thunder was acting, his mission commander felt it, too.

The sudden nature of the call-up with only a few hours' notice was not typical, but not unusual either. On the other hand, their payload was a different matter altogether.

The B-2 could handle a payload of sixty thousand pounds, an astonishing amount of ordnance when he saw it laid out on a hangar floor. Today, they carried only two bombs.

The GBU-57A/B, better known as the Massive Ordnance Penetrator, or MOP, was the most powerful non-nuclear weapon in the United States military's arsenal. At nearly thirty thousand pounds, each unit measured twenty feet long and thirty-one inches in diameter. The satellite-guided weapon was designed as a "bunker buster," used to obliterate a hardened target. For this mission, the ordnance had been modified to trigger on contact.

No reason was given for the last-minute modification. Another unusual aspect of this mission.

Instrument scan, horizon scan, four deep breaths.

Somewhere out there was Cyclone Two, their mission backup, outfitted with an identical set of ordnance in their bomb bay.

Witcher checked the laptop and immediately saw the new message header: CYCLONE ONE—NEW TASKING. He opened the message and scanned the contents. He forced himself to slow down and read the message again.

Instrument scan, horizon scan, four deep breaths.

"Thunder?" Witcher reached behind his seat to tap his partner on the shoulder.

"Yeah." The mission commander snapped out of sleep instantly. His voice was clear and sharp.

"New tasking is here."

Thunder rose without a word, stowed his sleeping bag, slid into his chair, and donned his helmet. He reviewed the tasking message, but the only outward sign of emotion was a bunching of his jaw muscles.

"So," he said finally. "Iran, huh?"

Witcher nodded. The orders were to prep for a bombing run on a city called Qom, Iran, and wait for a voice release.

Thunder clipped a checklist to the writing surface on his right thigh.

"Stand by for stealth mode checklist."

CHAPTER 51

Qom, Iran

Dre lay in bed for a long time after Liz left the hotel room.

There was nothing for her to do. Her part in this operation was done.

Except for the waiting.

She got up, made some coffee, and sat back in bed. Finally, she pulled out her laptop and logged into the connection she had installed yesterday.

There were nearly a hundred cameras associated with the security zone. Dre cycled through screen after screen, looking idly for Liz amid the crowds of people. She pulled up a screen, scanned it, then moved on to the next one.

Dre had just shifted screens when her mind froze.

She had recognized a face in the crowd—but it wasn't Liz.

A face that should not be there.

She toggled back to the previous screen and carefully studied the faces as the camera slowly panned.

Nothing. Her mind was playing tricks on her. She had just about given up when she saw the face again.

In her mind's eye, Dre stripped away the head coverings and added long dark hair in a braid.

Dr. Lakshmi Chandrasekaran. She froze the image, staring at it.

It couldn't be her. But it was her.

Dre took the laptop to the bathroom and turned on the water in the tub, creating a racket. She inserted her earpiece.

"Janet, are you there?"

"I'm here, Dre." Janet's voice was tight with tension. "We found Tahir on the—"

"I need you to check something for me," Dre interrupted. "I need you to check if Lakshmi Chandrasekaran is at the bioweapons site."

"What?"

Dre repeated it. "I know it sounds crazy, but I think I just saw her on one of the cameras."

"I'm on it."

While she waited, Dre dressed quickly. Less than five minutes passed before Janet was back with her.

"She's not at the site. The CDC let her take the ashes of one of the doctors back to Saudi Arabia. Don's loading her image into the facial-recognition system. We'll run a scan."

"Copy that. I'm going in."

======

"Where is it?" Liz demanded.

Talia Tahir's brilliant blue eyes blazed with hatred. Her mouth was set in a firm line and she said nothing.

Liz moved closer. "On your knees."

Still silent, Tahir complied.

Liz ran her hands over the doctor's body. She didn't even have a purse with her.

Liz peered inside the open access panel. The duct was empty. Liz looked under the duct. Nothing.

She had gotten here within a few minutes of Tahir; it would take her at least that long to remove the screws for the access panel.

"Where is it?" Liz said again.

Tahir's face twisted into a cruel smile. "You're too late."

Liz stepped back. This whole thing felt wrong. Talia Tahir had waited her entire life to destroy Iran and she knelt calmly in front of Liz?

She cupped her hand over her ear. "Don, I have Tahir, but the device is not here."

"We're looking at the footage again, Liz," Don said. "She wasn't carrying anything when she went into the building." He hesitated. "I think we've been had."

"What do you mean?" Liz watched Tahir's face closely.

"There was another doctor, the one who survived from the research-lab assault." Don was talking so fast his words started to jumble together. "She may be—could be—a double agent. Dre thought she saw her on video. We're running facial rec right now."

"What's the other woman's name?" Liz asked, watching Tahir's reaction.

Tahir's face shifted. Her eyes grew wide and she bared her teeth. With a scream, she threw herself at Liz.

Liz pulled the trigger. The suppressed nine-millimeter barely sounded above the background roar of the air systems. Tahir stopped like she'd been punched. Liz shot her again, center mass. Tahir went down.

"Where is she?" Liz pressed the muzzle of the weapon against the woman's forehead. "Your accomplice, where is she?"

Tahir hissed at her. "You're too late. You won't stop her."

"We have her!" Don said in Liz's ear. "Dre's on the way to intercept her."

"Andrea? No, tell her to stay away. I can handle this."

Liz pulled the trigger again. A neat round hole appeared in Tahir's forehead, just below the line of her hijab.

"I'm on my way."

———————

Dre fought her way through the crowd to the employee entrance on the south side of the Jamkaran conference center. The security guard at the blockade was barely older than her. He was standing on his toes, trying to see over the heads of the crowd for a glimpse of the president.

Dre tried to walk past him, but he grabbed her arm and launched a torrent of unintelligible Farsi at her.

She fought down the growing sense of panic. Lakshmi had passed this way less than three minutes before. There was no time to lose. She scanned the people around them to see who was paying attention as she reached for her knife.

Her hand brushed a thin plastic card in her pocket.

She thrust the visitor badge from the tour the previous day into his face and dredged up the only Farsi phrase she could remember.

"*Bayad dastshouie beram!*" she said. *I need to use the bathroom!*

With a disgusted look, the security guard waved her on.

Dre ducked her head as she walked. "Where is she, Janet?"

"Lakshmi went into a service hall on this side of the building that leads to the kitchens. Liz is on the way."

Dre fast walked through the back entrance. The long hallway was empty.

"Where is she?" Dre whispered.

"There's a room at the end of the hall, on your right, outside the kitchens."

At the end of the hall was a women's bathroom. "It's a restroom. I'm going in."

"Wait for Liz!"

Dre eased the door open to find a long line of wooden stalls facing a row of white sinks. The room was empty, but in the very last stall, a pair of hands was pushing up a ceiling tile.

The plan was obvious to Dre: Lakshmi was going to crawl into the ceiling over the kitchen and dispense the virus through the air vents, contaminating the staff and the food.

"Dre! Report!" Don's voice was like a shout in her ear.

She didn't dare even whisper a reply in the echoing bathroom.

Knife drawn, Dre moved silently across the tiled floor until she was in front of the last stall. Just as she reached for the handle, the door burst open. Lakshmi plowed into Dre full force.

As she went down, Dre's head cracked against the edge of the sink. Her vision exploded in a burst of color. Her body slammed into the ground, Lakshmi's knees on her chest.

Dre stabbed up with the knife. Lakshmi screamed and fell off her.

Dre rolled to her side, unable to catch her breath from the force of the impact. She lashed out as hard as she could with a foot. The kick connected with some soft part of the other woman.

Then Dre saw it: a silver canister, about the size of a can of soda, sitting on the floor beside the commode. She shot a look at Lakshmi as she struggled onto her hands and feet. The woman had both hands on the knife sticking out of her thigh. As Dre watched, she ripped the blade out of her flesh.

Dre lunged toward the steel canister, but not before Lakshmi reacted. The other woman jumped onto Dre's back, driving her face into the tile floor.

Lakshmi crawled over Dre and grabbed the canister. Dre rolled over in time to see Lakshmi standing over her, knife in hand.

Lakshmi's body stuttered. The white wall tiles behind her shattered into a spray of ceramic and blood.

Even with the suppressor on Liz's weapon, the sound of the gunshots in the small space was deafening.

Liz advanced across the tiled floor, weapon never moving from Lakshmi's body. Dre ripped the silver canister from Lakshmi's death grip.

"Hurry!" Liz reached a hand down to Dre. "We need to get out of here!"

"No . . ." Dre showed the top of the canister to Liz. The red LED lights were counting down.

30 . . . 29 . . . 28 . . .

Dre struggled to her knees in front of the toilet. She jammed the silver canister as far into the commode as she could. Then she flushed the toilet. The bowl filled up but the canister was too large to get swallowed by the pipe. The water line in the bowl stopped just below the rim, then started to recede.

Another gunshot. Liz ran back to the stall with white plastic bottles in each hand.

"I shot the lock off the janitor's closet." She tossed Dre a plastic bottle. "Bleach. Cover it in bleach."

Dre dumped in an entire bottle, then ripped off her head coverings, stuffed them into the bowl, and dumped the second bottle on top. The chemical stung the open cuts on her hands.

She got up and backed away from the stall.

"Don," Liz said from behind her. "The package is secure. Call off the air strike."

"Roger that," Don replied. "Can you make it to the extraction point?"

"That's not going to happen," Liz replied. "We're going off comms now."

She took out her earpiece and handed it to Dre. Her fingers gripped Dre's for a long moment. "Flush these. Lock the door behind me and don't open it unless I tell you to."

Dre nodded woodenly, staring at the earpiece in her palm. "What are you going to do?"

Liz pulled the door open. She gave Dre a faint smile. "I'm going to tell them the truth."

———————

There were security guards at the far end of the hall, running full tilt at Liz. Staff stood in the kitchen doorway, staring at her.

"Go inside," Liz said to them in Farsi. "Lock the doors. Now." The staff disappeared.

She faced the advancing security guard and got on her knees. She placed her handgun and knife on the ground in front of her. She took off her chador and head scarf and pulled up her sleeves.

Liz spread her arms wide.

"My name is Elizabeth Soroush," she shouted in Farsi. "I am a United States FBI agent. There has been a biological-weapons attack on this facility . . ."

CHAPTER 52

An undisclosed location in Iran

It was a week before Dre saw Liz again. At least it felt like a week; she wasn't really sure how much time had passed.

The day of the attack, it took nearly six hours before the door to the women's restroom at the Jamkaran conference center opened again. She'd heard Liz shouting in Farsi outside the door, heard the heavy tread of men's boots, the rattle of weapons—but no gunshots—then hours of silence.

For a long time, Dre huddled on the tile floor next to the body of Lakshmi and the toilet that reeked of bleach.

Her brain refused to work. She was a spy. All this had been explained to her before she agreed to come to Iran. If she was caught, the United States would not acknowledge her existence. She was on her own.

Finally, Dre got to her feet and ran water in the sink.

She washed her face and hands and dressed her injuries as best she could. She had a raging headache, a huge black eye, and bruises all over from the fight with Lakshmi. . . .

And possible exposure to a bioweapon.

She stared at her reflection. Other than that, she was in decent shape.

Dre took a seat on the floor as far away from the contaminated toilet and Lakshmi's body as she could get. And waited.

She heard someone working on the door lock. When the door finally opened, the two men who entered were dressed in biohazard suits. One of them had a gun. He spoke English.

"Get up," he said, his voice muffled through the suit. He motioned with the muzzle of the weapon for emphasis.

"Strip," he said when she was on her feet.

"Pardon?"

"Take off your clothes." He held up a hospital gown. "Put this on."

Dre took off her clothes until she was in her bra and panties.

"Everything."

She shut off the part of her mind that felt embarrassment and stripped naked. She had signed up for this. She was on her own.

Clad in the paper-thin hospital gown, she stepped into booties outside the restroom with the two men's help. They escorted her outside, where they had a shower set up in the parking lot.

"Strip," said the one with the gun.

Dre shed the gown and booties and stepped into the ice-cold spray of water. Under their direction, she soaped and washed every square inch of her flesh with a harsh disinfectant. Her teeth chattered. They gave her a blanket and bundled her into the back of an ambulance.

At the hospital, Dre was placed in a room with no windows, white walls, a glass door, and a camera high in the corner. She had a bed and a toilet and the lights were on twenty-four hours a day. All the twenty-first-century means of spending time—TV, books, phone, internet—were absent.

The only interruption in her solitude was two meals and two blood draws each day. She found she longed for someone to walk through the door and stick a needle in her arm just to break the boredom.

Dre slept when she was tired, ate when food arrived, and stuck out her arm when the doctor came in for blood. In between those fleeting moments, she sat cross-legged on the bed and stared at the opposite wall.

Fourteen meal–blood draw cycles passed before a doctor pushed through the glass door. He was not wearing a face mask. "You were not infected," he said in halting English.

Dre felt like a great weight had been lifted from her chest. She had suspected as much, but confirmation was still a relief she had not known she was seeking.

"What happens to me now?"

The doctor shrugged and left.

She got her answer an hour later when two armed

policemen in bulletproof vests walked through the door. They shackled her hands and feet to a chain around her waist, and she followed them, still wearing hospital pajamas and sandals. It was cold outside and she shivered, but neither of the men cared. She was put in the back of a police van without windows.

The vehicle moved through stop-and-go traffic, and then there was a long stretch of highway during which she fell asleep. Dre woke up when the van began to jounce along a bumpy road. When the doors opened, she saw a flash of snow through an open doorway. The men hustled her down a gray-painted damp hallway and into a cell.

Liz was there.

Liz had a bruise healing on her face and she held her arm close to her body in a protective way. She hugged Dre with her good arm.

"You're okay?" Liz said.

"I was in a hospital for a few days. They said I was not infected, then they brought me here." Dre looked around the cell. A bunk bed, a toilet, a sink. "Where is here?"

"I don't know. They took me west—I think. It's been ten days—I think. If they kept us alive this long, they must have plans for us."

"Like what?"

Liz put her hand behind Dre's neck and pulled her close until they touched foreheads. "It could get bad. They could use us against each other. Just . . . you know your training. Just do your best. That's all anyone can ask for."

Despite the cloud of doubt over her situation, it was a relief to have someone to talk to. They huddled together on the bottom bunk and spoke in whispers. Dre talked about her mother and the farm where she grew up. Liz told her funny stories about her kids and how she let Brendan know she was pregnant the first time.

In those moments, Dre never felt closer to another human being.

They marked time by the appearance of meals twice a day, two plates of rice and a stale flatbread to share. No matter the meal, the menu was unchanged. If they were lucky there was some meat or other sauce on the rice, but that was rare.

Every few days, the door would open, and a new set of guards would move them to a new location.

"My guess is they're moving us so that anyone who's looking for us can't find us," Liz said with a tinge of hope in her voice. "That might mean somebody in the US is trying to locate us, but . . . who knows."

Liz got thinner. The circles under her eyes deepened and darkened as the days passed. After their fifth move, she developed a hacking cough.

Neither woman was surprised when the door to their cell opened and a new set of guards strode in. Dre noticed immediately that these were military men and they wore a different type of uniform.

"Revolutionary Guard," Liz whispered.

The bigger guard slapped Liz across the face, yelling something that Dre took to mean shut up. They were hustled outside, their thin shoes slapping against the frozen ground. It was nighttime.

The transport vehicle was different, too: an army transport with the insignia of the Islamic Revolutionary Guard emblazoned on the side. They were placed in the rear seat and hoods were drawn over their heads.

The big diesel engine roared to life and the transport shot away.

Liz leaned her head next to Dre. "I don't like this," Liz whispered. "All the other changes were done by police. The Revolutionary Guard . . . this is . . . not ideal, Dre."

The men in the front spoke in low tones and smoked constantly. The vehicle left the paved road, bounced along for what felt like an hour, then began to climb.

When they stopped, the men left them in the back for a long time. She could hear one of them on the phone outside talking and walking, his voice fading in and out.

"What's he saying?" Dre asked.

"He's waiting for some kind of authorization, I think." Liz's voice was tight with emotion.

The doors to the vehicle opened on both sides and chill night air rushed into the cab. One guard grabbed Liz, the other Dre. Dre was force-marched across rocky, uneven ground, a hand clamped on her elbow.

They stopped. Dre felt the wind whip past her bare legs.

The guard ripped the cover off her head.

Liz was next to her, her head uncovered, blinking. A half-moon hung in the sky, illuminating a mountain vista all around them. Dre looked down. They stood on the edge of a precipice, the depths below them lost in shadow.

The breeze raised gooseflesh across Dre's skin.

The lead guard barked out an order. Liz whispered, her voice shaking. "He says to get on your knees."

Dre felt the rocky ground bite into the skin of her knees. The dirt scuffed under the thin soles of her prison sandals. The second guard unlocked their shackles, dragging the chains away. He said something to the first one and they both laughed.

She heard the rack of a slide on a handgun and closed her eyes. Liz reached across the space between them and laced her fingers into Dre's. Her hand was ice cold.

"Remember what I told you: Don't cry and don't beg."

Dre took a deep breath of the clean, thin air and closed her eyes. She tried to think of a prayer, but nothing came to mind.

She took another breath, feeling as if time had somehow stopped. Would this be the last breath? Or would there be one more?

The slam of the car door made her jump, her hand convulsively clenching Liz's.

The vehicle roared to life and spun out in a cloud of dust.

Seconds passed. They knelt on the edge of the precipice. Fingers together, hearts beating. Breath being drawn.

Liz sagged back on her heels. "I—I think they're gone."

The words had no sooner left her mouth than headlights stabbed the darkness.

Dre lunged to her feet, pulling Liz up with her.

Together, they got their first clear look around. They were on top of a mountain. There was nowhere to go.

The vehicle raced into the open space, skidding to a halt. Billows of dust floated toward them.

The door slammed shut. A flashlight beam cut through the darkness, pinning them in place.

"Dre? Liz?" Don Riley's voice.

Dre felt herself falling. Strong arms caught her.

"I got you, Dre," Michael said. "You're safe now."

Janet's face appeared in the moonlight. She swooped in for a hug, leaving fresh tears on Dre's cheek.

Don had Liz wrapped in a bear hug, weeping on her shoulder. "We've been back-channeling for weeks with no response and then today, they just called and gave us these coordinates on the Iran-Iraq border. No trade, no demands, just a place and time."

In the shadows beyond the headlights of the Humvee, Dre saw the shapes of soldiers moving. An army captain stepped into the light. "We need to move, Mr. Riley. We're exposed here."

Don, his arm still around Liz, reached for Dre's hand.

"Let's get you home."

CHAPTER 53

Tel Aviv, Israel

Noam sat alone at a café table that looked comically small next to his bulky body. An umbrella shielded him from the hot noonday sun, but he also wore a floppy sun hat and a pair of cheap sunglasses. The combination made him look like a European businessman unhappily on holiday.

Rachel hiked her sunglasses up into her hair. "Is this seat taken?"

Noam made a who-cares gesture with his hands.

Rachel drew out the chair, feeling the muscles twinge in her core. She no longer had to wear a sling on her arm, and the headaches were mostly gone, but her side still bothered her.

"You're looking well," Noam said. "Not fit for duty, but well."

"You look like a snowman in disguise," Rachel shot back.

The deep rumble of Noam's laugh shook the small table between them. "I missed you."

"It's only been a month, for God's sake. I'm not your wife, after all."

Noam lit a cigarette as Rachel ordered coffee and a scone.

"What happened to Pandora?"

"The Americans took care of it," Noam said.

"They found the doctor?"

"You were right. She was crazy and she had a crazy plan. Crazy enough to . . ." As his voice trailed off, he jerked his head to the east.

Rachel gasped. She lowered her voice: "Iran?"

Noam's nod was barely perceptible.

Rachel sat back as it all clicked into place. She could picture Talia's rage at JP, the passion in her voice. That kind of anger always ended badly.

"We weren't part of the takedown?"

"We tried," Noam said. "We had all the known US assets under surveillance, but they sent in clean skins. Two of them, complete unknowns. From what we hear, they stopped the attack, but they didn't get out." Noam's face had a sour expression, but whether from the fate of the American agents or the lack of Israeli success she couldn't tell.

Rachel's coffee arrived and she sipped it. She shivered despite the warm sun. She knew what Iran did to spies. Some brave son of a bitch had done a very stupid, very noble thing. The world would go on, unknowing, uncaring, and those two agents would end up in a shallow grave in the desert—if they were lucky.

"It was a close-run thing," Noam continued. "They ran the op from their new Emerging Threats group. Took us completely by surprise. That won't happen again."

"What about the funding?" Rachel asked. "The Saudi connection?"

Noam watched the plaza, crowded with tourists. Rachel knew his mood. He would tell her when he was ready.

She bit into the scone. It was buttery and flaky, just the way she liked it.

"It was a good lead from the Americans," Noam said finally. "We picked up Alyan al-Qahtamni and he sang like a canary. Told us everything we wanted to know. Four rich guys trying to get even richer." His lips puckered like he wanted to spit something sour on the sidewalk.

"Two Saudis and two Jews formed the Arab-Israeli Benevolence Coalition, a massive network of shell companies all over the Nile River basin worth close to two hundred billion dollars."

"And you shut them down? Permanently?"

"Itzak Lehrmann will be going to jail for tax fraud. We turned al-Qahtamni over to the Saudis. They let him go. The rumor is he's friends with the crown prince. I guess it's all about who you know."

"The yacht owner?"

Noam tapped out another cigarette. He allowed a ghost of a smile. "That one turned out a little better. Saleh bin Ghannam was the Saudi mastermind behind the plot. We dropped a word into the right royal ear and it seems the *Al-Buraq* suffered an accident at sea. The ship sank without a trace. Terrible tragedy."

Noam lit a celebratory cigarette.

"That leaves one more," Rachel said.

"Haim Zarecki." Noam said the name like a curse. "His nephew was the mole who stole Mossad's cryptography. The nephew will stand trial for treason. Zarecki was the one who helped Manzul build the lab. He was the one who hatched the whole plan—him and bin Ghannam. A couple of old bastards who wanted to screw the world over before they left it."

"And?"

Half of Noam's cigarette disappeared in one drag. "We can't get to him. We have a hands-off order, right from the very top." He stabbed the cigarette into an ashtray. "Last I heard he was living out his days in Europe somewhere. Geneva, I think."

Rachel pushed the scone away, suddenly nauseous. News like this shouldn't sting her, but it did. Politics was part and parcel of their business. Decisions about operations were swayed by relationships all the time. Facts were twisted and bent to the needs of the moment. It was just how the world worked.

Zarecki was not a well man, she told herself. He would die soon. Problem solved.

But Zarecki was also a traitor to his country. His actions had placed the lives of millions at risk. Rachel had a hole in her side that she could trace back to Zarecki as the proximate cause.

That problem deserved a solution.

Noam stood. "I just wanted to check in," he said,

handing her a slip of paper. "I thought you might like to take a vacation during your convalescent leave."

He lumbered away, his broad back disappearing into the crowds of people around them.

Rachel unfolded the slip of paper. It was an address in Geneva.

Geneva, Switzerland

Haim Zarecki's new home overlooked the Rhône River where it flowed out of Lake Geneva.

From his third-floor apartment, he could look down on the marina, the park, and on a clear day, possibly even see Mont Blanc in the distance. In the weeks before Christmas, the fall colors had disappeared, leaving only bare branches and damp cold on the cobbled streets of the well-heeled neighborhood.

Rachel used Airbnb to rent a small sailboat at the marina on the Quai du Mont-Blanc. The cabin was tiny, consisting only of a fold-down table, a narrow bunk, an ice chest that served as a refrigerator, and a single burner.

But it offered an uninterrupted view into the panoramic windows of Haim Zarecki's third-floor bedroom.

For five days, she did nothing but eat prepackaged ramen noodles, drink coffee, and watch the comings and goings of the Zarecki household through a spotting scope.

The old man was a shut-in. He never left the third-floor bedroom and never closed the curtains. All his meals were brought to him by round-the-clock skilled nursing care, and he wore oxygen all the time. The day nurse was a heavyset Germanic woman with a mole on her right cheek. She arrived promptly at seven and stayed until three. The evening nurse was a college-aged blonde who wore her hair in a ponytail and expertly fended off Zarecki's gropings for most of her shift. At 11:00 P.M. every night, a black woman came on duty. She was fortyish and walked with a limp. She took frequent smoke breaks.

Zarecki's security staff consisted of an armed man behind a desk inside the first-floor street entrance. He buzzed people in, flirted with the blond nurse, and watched TV. Two men lived onsite, taking alternating twelve-hour shifts behind the desk.

By the end of the week, Rachel had the outline of a plan. She followed the night nurse home for the next three days.

The woman's name was Angelique. She lived in a third-floor walk-up in an immigrant community on the outskirts of Annemasse, France. She had two children, a boy and a girl, aged fourteen and twelve, and no husband.

It took two more days to secure the necessary items for the operation. At a medical supply store, she found a set of nursing scrubs similar to the ones Angelique wore, and she found a similar jacket at a secondhand store. A visit to a veterinarian and a wad of cash yielded the rest of the needed supplies.

It was snowing the night Rachel followed Angelique

from her bus stop a quarter mile from Zarecki's apartment. Fat flakes of snow coated the empty streets, muffling all sounds.

Angelique passed under pools of light cast by the streetlamps, her hood up, shoulders hunched against the weather.

Rachel approached the woman from behind. "*Excusez-moi?*"

When Angelique turned around, Rachel hammered a fist into her face. She was careful not to break any bones, but she wanted the woman to have a healthy bruise. Angelique fell to her knees, crying, and Rachel pinned her to the ground. She uncapped a loaded syringe with her teeth and stabbed a small dose of ketamine into the woman's arm.

Angelique's body went limp.

Rachel checked her breathing and pulse, then rifled through her purse, taking her cash, but leaving her ID. Then she called the local police.

"There's a woman who has been assaulted." She gave the street address. "Please hurry. She's unconscious."

Rachel waited at the corner until she heard the police sirens, then continued on her way. Angelique wouldn't wake up for a few hours with the sedative Rachel had given her. Her presence in the police station at the time of Zarecki's death would be an airtight alibi.

She climbed the steps of Zarecki's house and waited to be buzzed into the main hallway. She stamped the snow from her boots on the mat inside the door.

The young blonde was waiting for her. "Where have you been?"

When Rachel peeled off her hat, the blonde stepped back. "Who are you? Where is Angelique?"

"She called in sick." Rachel kept her head angled away from the camera over her right shoulder. "The agency sent me. I'm new."

"Whatever." The blonde threw on her coat. "Just don't be late again. He's in his room. Hopefully, for your sake, he's asleep. He likes to grab your ass, so be careful." She called in to the security man in the front room. "Henri, I'm going. She's here."

Henri grunted a reply, the door slammed shut behind the departing nurse, and Rachel was alone.

She climbed the steps to the third floor of the house. Zarecki's room smelled like old man's feet overlaid with the sharp tang of menthol. The room lights were dimmed to a dull yellow, just enough to illuminate the fat flakes of snow sifting past the panorama window.

Rachel looked out into the dark, trying to see the tiny sailboat where she had spent the last ten days, but the snow was too thick. She studied Zarecki's reflection in the darkened window.

He lay in a hospital bed, his head elevated to a forty-five-degree angle. There was a full medical crash cart in the corner, ready to extend his miserable life, if needed. He wore an oxygen tube under his nose. His face looked like it was carved out of pale clay, and his skin had a clammy sheen of sweat.

His eyes opened. "Angelique?"

Rachel walked to his bedside. "No."

She snatched the call button away before he could reach it.

"Angelique's not here."

His yellowed eyes searched her face. "Do I know you?"

Rachel nodded. "You saw me in Cairo," she said, "if you were looking. Or maybe in Cyprus. I was with JP Manzul."

Zarecki's eyes widened in fear. The oxygen tube fell away as he struggled to sit up in bed.

"Who sent you?" he said.

Rachel picked up a pillow from the foot of his bed and fluffed it in her hands, taking her time.

"Who are you?" Zarecki demanded.

Rachel smiled at him, and said in Hebrew, "My name is Death."

She pinned his face with the pillow. The old man thrashed wildly, but not for long.

His body went still.

Rachel lifted the pillow away, studied his face. His bared teeth were yellow and jagged, his rheumy eyes wide open, the pale skin blotchy and age-spotted.

She felt nothing. No satisfaction, no remorse, no more emotion than if she'd stepped on a cockroach.

Rachel stripped the pillowcase off the pillow and stuffed it into her pocket. She tidied up the corpse, replacing his oxygen tube and sitting Zarecki upright in bed. She wiped down anything she might have touched during her short stay, then donned her jacket and hat and hurried down the steps.

"I'm going out for a smoke," she said to Henri, who waved without looking up.

Rachel rode the early bus to Annemasse. The snow stopped as she made her way to Angelique's apartment.

She knocked on the door and waited. "Who is it?" said a boy's voice.

"I'm a friend of your mother's. She asked me to stop by." Slowly, the boy unbolted the door and opened it a crack.

Rachel smiled at him. "It's okay. I don't want to come in. I just came by to drop something off." She took a sealed envelope out of her inner pocket containing €10,000 in cash. She passed it through the door to the boy.

"Give this to your mother when she gets home," Rachel said. "And tell her I'm sorry. Okay?"

The boy nodded and closed the door.

Rachel turned on her heel and walked away.

CHAPTER 54

Washington, DC

SIX WEEKS LATER

The dinner took place in a small French restaurant, located a few blocks outside of the Georgetown limits. The restaurant itself, sandwiched between a Mexican grill and a bakery, was not much to look at, but it had a reputation for excellent food.

It also had a private dining room, easily accessed by an alley that ran behind the building.

Dre waited in the dining room with Liz Soroush. It was the first time she had seen the older woman since they had been debriefed following their return from Iranian custody. Then, Liz had been in rough shape, with a case of severe bronchitis and a separated shoulder courtesy of her Iranian handlers.

But they had stayed alive. That was all that mattered.

Tonight, Liz was the picture of health. Her dark eyes flashed with laughter when she told Dre how her son,

Ahmad, had responded to seeing his mother after her internment.

"He's so much like his father, it just kills me, Dre," Liz said. "I don't know what I was thinking when I said yes to Don."

"Well, you weren't thinking about yourself, that's for sure, Lizzie," Don said from the doorway. "And Brendan would have kicked my ass for calling you in the first place."

"Don." Liz crossed the room and hugged him hard.

Dre gave him a wave. They saw each other every day at work.

In the intervening six weeks since their return from Iran, the world had returned to some semblance of normality. The bioweapons lab had been stripped of all useful intel, destroyed in place, and all US military personnel withdrawn. The State Department worked overtime to calm tensions in the Nile River basin and get the water-management talks between Egypt and the other countries in the basin back on track.

Lastly, tensions with Iran had eased for the moment. There were rumors about restarting nuclear talks, but Dre had her doubts.

Liz poured Don a glass of wine. "Well, can you tell us what's behind this mysterious meeting now, Don?" she teased.

Don looked at a text that popped up on his phone and smiled. "Yes, I can." He strode to the dining room door.

A trim man with gray hair and a neatly groomed goatee waited in the hallway. He wore a charcoal-gray suit and carried a slim attaché case.

"May I present Davoud Rashemi, the foreign minister of the Islamic Republic of Iran," Don said.

Dre saw Liz's posture stiffen. Rashemi approached Liz and bowed to her before extending his hand. Liz shook his hand reluctantly, the good humor from a few moments ago drained from her expression.

As Rashemi moved to Dre, Liz shot a glance of undisguised fury at Don.

"Miss Ramirez, it is a great honor to make your acquaintance." His voice was low, and he spoke perfect English with a slight British accent.

Rashemi placed the attaché case on the table and opened it. Inside were two medals, a teardrop-shaped golden flame suspended by a blue-and-red ribbon. He plucked one from the case and held it in his palm for them to see it more closely.

"This is the Iranian Order of Courage. It has been awarded only twenty times in our nation's history. It is our nation's highest honor, equivalent to your Medal of Honor, and is only awarded to Iranian citizens." He looked directly at Liz.

"Until tonight. By direction of the president of the Islamic Republic of Iran, it is my honor to award you both the Iranian Order of Courage for your bravery and for saving the lives of countless Iranian citizens."

He handed a medal to Dre. The insignia was the size of her palm, and heavy. Rashemi placed the second medal in Liz's hand and pressed his palm over hers. He leaned in and spoke softly to her. Liz nodded in response.

Rashemi stepped back and bowed again. He offered

a wry smile. "As you Americans like to say in the movies: I was never here."

He turned on his heel and left the room.

Don cleared his throat. "I'm sure you two have already figured this out, but you can't keep the medals. They'll go into storage at the CIA. Someday, when this whole affair is declassified, you'll get them."

"Well, we can enjoy them during dinner, right?" Liz said. "Let's eat."

"What did Rashemi say to you?" Dre asked, as Liz leaned over to refill her wineglass.

Liz touched the golden insignia. "He said Qom is where he grew up. His family still lives there. Even though the world may never know the story of what happened, he is eternally grateful we were there."

"We made a difference," Dre said, raising her wineglass for a toast. "That's what matters."

A NOTE FROM
THE AUTHORS

We ended *The Pandora Deception* on a happy note.

In a world where tensions between Iran and the US are as high as they've been in our lifetimes, we thought having an FBI agent save the world on Iranian soil might be just the ticket. For the record, the ending to *The Pandora Deception* was written a year before the killing of Islamic Revolutionary Guard Corps general Qassem Soleimani by a US drone strike or the COVID-19 outbreak in Qom.

David Bruns and J. R. Olson make up the Two Navy Guys writing team. We're both US Naval Academy grads and former naval officers. David was a submarine officer and J. R. was a career naval intelligence officer.

Our brand of thriller is the kind of books we grew up reading, but adapted for our modern era. We call our novels "national security thrillers" because today's threats are no longer just military in nature. If that thought keeps you up at night, then welcome to our world.

We populate our work with characters from the CIA, NSA, FBI, and any of the other alphabet soup of agencies and allies that work together to protect our world and our values from harm.

Many of our readers have been with us since *Weapons of Mass Deception,* our first novel, in 2015. If that describes you, then know that your support has meant everything to us.

On the other hand, if *The Pandora Deception* is your first contact with the Two Navy Guys, then visit us at twonavyguys.com and start reading from the beginning.

Thanks for being a reader—

David and J. R., aka the Two Navy Guys

ACKNOWLEDGMENTS

Bringing a book to life is not a solo endeavor—or even a duo endeavor, in our case.

We could not have done this without the help of Keith Kahla and the entire team at St. Martin's Press. This was definitely easier the second time around.

Although *The Pandora Deception* is a work of fiction, we drew on many resources to try to get the descriptions right, including Richard Preston's *The Hot Zone,* and *Epidemic* by Reid Wilson. Both of these books provide detailed (and terrifying) insights into the Ebola virus and how epidemics are contained.

A big measure of gratitude goes out to our early readers and technical advisers, including Jennifer Schumacher, Joe Chihade, Doug Baden, Shemi Hart, Rick Campbell, Paul "Nuke" Tibbets, Tom Cappelletti, and Alex Bruns.

To our USNA alumni supporters who have been there

since the very beginning, especially Chip Sharratt '74, Alex Plechash '75, and Chris Bentley '79, we thank you. You have been with us as readers and friends since before the first book.

To our wives, Christine and Melissa, thanks for putting up with this third career dream we've cobbled together.

Lastly, we need to thank the United States Navy. We are privileged to have attended the greatest service academy in the world and to have served our country in the finest navy on the planet. It is no exaggeration to say that without the Naval Academy, this book would not exist.